Behind her she could hear Morgan's laughter and the thud of Tempete's hooves as the stallion followed her. Her breath was coming in gasps but still she ran on, the long golden legs flashing in the rays of sunlight that permeated the thickness of the forest.

Morgan suddenly kicked Tempete into a gallop and swiftly bore down on the slim, racing figure. With one effortless swoop, he captured her in his arm and swung her up in front of him. Leonie still fought, twisting in his hold, her soft body like a sweet intoxicating flame wherever they touched.

Whatever control Morgan may have had over his emotions, vanished the instant his mouth touched hers, and with a groan of sheer sensual pleasure, his lips and tongue slowly, caressingly explored the warm honey of her mouth. He held her firmly against him reveling in the exciting twistings of her soft body as she fought to escape, and half-blindly, half-knowingly he guided Tempete deeper into the forest.

Also by Shirlee Busbee
WHILE PASSION SLEEPS
and published by Corgi/Avon

Deceive Not My Heart

Shirlee Busbee

 CORGI   AVON

DECEIVE NOT MY HEART

A CORGI/AVON BOOK 0 552 12520 2

First publication in Great Britain

Published by arrangement with Avon Books, 959 Eighth Avenue, New York 10019

PRINTING HISTORY
Corgi/Avon edition published 1984

This book is set in 9/10½pt Century

Corgi Books are published by Transworld Publishers Ltd.,
Century House, 61-63 Uxbridge Road,
Ealing, London W5 5SA.
Made and printed in Great Britain by
Hunt Barnard Printing Ltd., Aylesbury, Bucks.

DEDICATION

This one is for my favorites.

MRS. GALENA TERRY, my favorite "modiste," who cheerfully and cleverly sews wonderful creations from my haphazard, confusing directions.

MR. L. DEAN KASTENS, my favorite boss, who encouraged and took such sincere delight in my success and that of his other secretary, Rosemary Rogers.

MRS. CHARLOTTE BUSBEE WHITNEY, my favorite mother-in-law, who laughs when she hears of my latest klutsy experience and then takes pity on me and comes to cook dinner.

And of course, as always, Howard.

PART ONE

THE DOUBLE-DEALERS

> Song's but solace for a day;
> Wine's a traitor not to trust;
> Love's a kiss and then away;
> Time's a peddler deals in dust.
>
> *Hearth-Song*
> Robert Underwood Johnson

1

The house resembled a gracious elderly lady that had fallen upon evil times, but it was still a lovely old building. It sat with timeless elegance near a bend in the Mississippi River some miles below New Orleans. Once it had been lavishly, lovingly, and meticulously kept, but since the death of Monsieur Claude Saint-André's only child, Damien, some fourteen years before, the old man had lost all interest in the plantation and had let Château Saint-André fall into its present faded, crumbling state.

Even in its prime it had not been an overwhelming house, but even now it possessed an elegant charm that was instantly recognizable, despite its faded exterior. The main house, with its matching pair of colonnaded *garçonnières,* had been built in 1760 when Louisiana had been a French possession, and it was typical of the houses of that period. The first floor was cement-covered brick; it served as a basement, office, and storage place, while the upper level with its wide galleries and slender wooden colonnettes was where the family lived.

In the front of the house there was a graceful horseshoe-shaped staircase, which led to the second level of the house, and at the rear, underneath the overhanging galleries, was a carriage entrance. Several tall double doors with glass casements served as both window and door; the painted cypress shutters hanging on either side of the doors provided additional protection during the short winter or when a howling hurricane struck.

The signs of neglect were everywhere. The sun-bleached blue of the house and the blistered white paint of the columns told the story, as did the missing shutter here and there. The broken step in the staircase and the gaps in the

3

wooden railing that enclosed the galleries completed the tale. But to sixteen-year-old Leonie Saint-André, the heiress to all this faded elegance, it mattered little. She loved the house even with all its faults; it was where she had been born and lived all her life. The Château Saint-André was home and she couldn't have imagined ever living anywhere else, and being Leonie, she would have objected rather heatedly if anyone had ever attempted to remove her from it.

But in this summer of 1799, all was not well with her beloved home and none knew it better than she—she had kept the account books since she was thirteen and the plantation manager had been let go because her grandfather's gaming debts ate up any profit the plantation earned. The field slaves had gone next, and without the field hands there was no one to work the indigo fields, and without indigo there was no money, and without money there was no—

Ah, bah! Leonie thought disgustedly as she slammed shut the leather account books she had been perusing intently. One slim, tanned hand toyed absently with an intricate, gold crucifix that hung from a slender chain about her neck. If only *grand-père* would cease gaming, she thought angrily, they might be able to redeem the vouchers he had scattered all over New Orleans and have some money for their own use. Sighing impatiently she stared through the trunks of the moss-hung oaks towards the swirling Mississippi River. Her sea-green eyes narrowed against the glare of the bright sunlight. *Mon Dieu, but I shall have to think of something soon,* she decided grimly.

Leonie was not a beautiful girl, at least not in the accepted sense of the word. Sultry, exotic, and striking more accurately described her, and yet even those words could not precisely convey the vivid impact of golden skin, ruby lips, laughing and slightly slanted green eyes, and a tawny mane of hair that cascaded in tousled curls about her slender shoulders. Her mouth was full, almost too full, but the lips were delicately carved, and it was a mouth that smiled often; the cheekbones were high, the nose straight and finely molded, and with those almond-shaped green eyes between the thick, curling lashes and the slashing golden-brown brows, she had the look of some half-wild swamp cat that had been magically transformed into human shape.

She was a small girl, but she appeared far more fragile than she actually was. Though wearing an outgrown cotton gown, the outline of the firm young bosom could be clearly seen, and while the high waist of the gown hid the slenderness of her hips and waist it was apparent from the neat ankles and bare feet, which showed beneath the too-short hem, and from the slender arms, revealed by the puff sleeves, that she was delicately built.

As her bare feet and faded yellow gown attested, Leonie cared little for the trappings of fashion—the one piece of jewelry she wore, the uniquely fashioned crucifix, had belonged to her mother and Leonie treasured it. Clothes were merely to cover her nakedness; she had little use for them. Which was probably just as well, considering the state of the family's finances, she reminded herself angrily as she stood up from the desk and stepped outside.

Ordinarily she wouldn't have been angry, but *grand-père* had returned home late the night before from another of his extended visits to New Orleans and had casually informed his anxious granddaughter that the money she had thought would be used to buy the barest of necessities to keep them going for a few months longer had been gambled away . . . again. Worse, he had admitted to signing more vowels for the money he had lost above what had been with him.

It had not always been so, but Leonie herself could never remember a time that her grandfather hadn't gambled away every bit of money they had. The house slaves— Mammy in the kitchen, Abraham, the head groom to a nonexistent staff and stables, and her own personal servant, Mercy—had told her often enough of the days when Claude Saint-André had properly run his plantation, of the happy times, of the gold that he had made and spent lavishly on the Château, of the grand parties he had given with only the *very* best people of New Orleans attending, and of the blooded stock that had filled his huge stables. But all that had changed in the terrible flood of 1785 when the rampaging Mississippi had ripped away the carefully erected levees, and had swept over the land destroying

5

everything in its awesome path. The house had miraculously survived, but one of the galleries had been torn away, tragically sweeping Leonie's parents and her grandmother into the churning waters. Rescue had been impossible and all three had drowned. After that Claude Saint-André had lost interest in everything, even his small two-year-old granddaughter, and he had begun to drink heavily and gamble with a reckless disregard for the future.

Leonie hadn't minded as a child. In fact she had reveled in it. Not for her the restraints that usually surrounded a young girl of her station. She grew up like a wild thing, more at home in the nearby swamps and bayous than in the elegant homes she should have graced. Claude had paid her little heed beyond seeing that she was fed and clothed and that she had some sort of education—not an extensive one; what would she need it for? At the proper time he would see to it that a respectable husband was found, and what gentleman in his right mind wanted a woman with her head stuffed full of book learning?

But Leonie, for all her wildness, possessed a thirsting, inquiring mind, and she had consumed everything the impoverished English governess could teach her, and then demanded more. For Madame Whitfield it had been a pleasure; she had happily sought to impart to this volatile, enchanting, half-wild creature every scrap of knowledge in her possession. But Madame Whitfield's resources were limited and sadly there came a time when she felt that she had nothing more to give Leonie. Unfortunately Claude would not even consider hiring someone who could have given Leonie the knowledge she craved.

Madame Whitfield had gone not long after the plantation manager departed and Leonie had been miserable for weeks. Not only had she lost her preceptress, but also a very dear friend—something *grand-père* did not understand at all!

There existed between Leonie and her grandfather a curious relationship. At sixty-seven Claude Saint-André was set in his ways and made no effort to conceal it. Arrogance was obvious in his every movement and although his dark, aquiline features were lined and creased from years of self-indulgence, he was still an attractive man. He had a full head of silvery hair and dark eyes that cynically viewed the world from under slender, arching gray brows. A slim man, barely average in height, he had lived all of his life certain that his slightest whim would be instantly gratified. He had expected his granddaughter to be docile and well-behaved, and he was always unpleasantly surprised by Leonie's unpredictable actions. When she had taken over the account books he had been scandalized, but Leonie had merely given him a long, thoughtful look and murmured sweetly, "And if I don't do them, who will, *grand-père? Vous?*" That had ended the discussion, for Claude was appalled at the idea of doing anything so *common* as pottering about with ink and ledgers. Fortunately Leonie didn't think quite so highly of herself. Although she had plenty of the Saint-André arrogance, she was far more practical about things than her grandfather.

The little tussle over the ledgers had not been the first test of wills between them, nor would it be last. When Claude had made the decision to sell the field hands a year later, Leonie had been heartsick and furious. The sea-green eyes blazing with golden flecks of rage, she had stormed, *"Non!* You cannot sell them! They've lived here all of their lives. They're our people, they belong with us! How can you disrupt them this way and just *sell* them?"

Appealing to Claude's finer senses didn't seem to work, so desperately Leonie tried another tact. "And when they are gone," she asked with deceptive calm, "how are we to work the fields, *grand-père?*"

Claude was unmoved by that argument too, and finally, Leonie was reduced to pleading. *"Pour l'amour de Dieu,* I beg of you . . . don't sell them! They are as much a part of Château Saint-André as we are!" Claude had sniffed disdainfully, but grasping at straws Leonie had begged, "I know the indigo is not selling as well, but we can wait one more year. Just one?" Almost hopefully she added, "Let us try the sugar cane this year. Please, Monsieur de Bore says that cane will soon be a most profitable crop. Let us *try* it!"

Claude had been most affronted that a fourteen-year-old girl would dare to tell *him* how to run his affairs! All the slaves except for the house servants had been sold within the week and Leonie had watched them being led away, her eyes filled with angry, painful tears.

Thinking of that incident now, Leonie's full mouth thinned and for a moment she looked exceedingly fierce, like a small, infuriated kitten. But then catching sight of a slight figure, much like her own, walking beneath one of the old oaks near the house, her face was transfixed with a sunny smile.

"*Holà!* Yvette, *bonjour!*" she called out, waving one hand above her head.

Yvette, born just three months before Leonie, stopped on her journey to the hen house for fresh eggs and waved a hand back. "*Bonjour*, Leonie! Where have you been? Your *grand-père* is asking for you."

Leonie's smile faded and with a determined set to the firm, little chin she walked over to where Yvette had stopped. Approaching the other girl, Leonie demanded almost angrily, "Why do you always refer to him as *my grand-père*? He is *yours*, too!"

Yvette's sweet smile vanished and the great dark eyes wouldn't meet Leonie's. In a soft voice Yvette murmured, "Leonie, *mon ami*, let it be. He will never acknowledge me—and you shouldn't have either. How can you overlook the fact that I am his son's daughter by an octoroon mistress? And how can you expect *him* to do it?"

Leonie scowled. "Ah, bah! You are my sister and it doesn't matter who your mother was—she is dead just like our papa, but you and I are alive and here, together!" Peering intently into Yvette's lovely face, Leonie said earnestly, "You must stand up to him, Yvette! He will never acknowledge you, I know, but you must not let him frighten you! I know he is gruff and shouts a great deal, but it is all thunder and lightning. As long as you scurry about and shrink into walls whenever he is near, he will bully you unmercifully." A sudden mischievous grin flashed across Leonie's expressive features. "Call him *grand-père* once and watch his face turn purple! He'll not be so quick to shout at you the next time, I promise!"

Yvette smiled her slow, sweet smile but shook her head resignedly, "I am not you, Leonie. I could not do it."

"Peuh!" Leonie muttered with displeasure, but then

with all the good will in the world she accompanied her half-sister to the hen house.

They made a pretty pair, Leonie with her lion's mane of unruly, tawny curls and Yvette with her shining black hair caught in a tidy coronet of braids on the small head. Both were of the same size, and each had a slender, finely boned figure, but while Leonie would never be a conventional beauty, Yvette was breathtakingly lovely with her soft creamy skin and dark liquid eyes. As a matter of fact everything about Yvette was perfect—a perfectly chiseled mouth and a sweetness of disposition that would be hard to match.

Looking at the two of them, one might be forgiven for thinking that Yvette was the true daughter of the house, for while her blue muslin gown was just as old and faded as Leonie's, Yvette's fine needlework had seen to it that the dress fit properly and the black slippers she wore had been polished just this morning. Leonie, with her tumbling curls, too-small gown and bare feet, could just as easily been mistaken for the daughter of some backwoods farmer—something that wouldn't have bothered her at all. *She* knew who she was!

The eggs having been gathered into a small straw basket that Yvette carried over her arm, the two girls walked back to the house, the sunlight turning Leonie's mane of tawny hair the color of warm, golden honey.

Just as they reached the house, the sea-green eyes sparkling with anticipated pleasure, Leonie asked, "Will you come with me this afternoon, Yvette? I'm taking the pirogue to *le petit bayou* to hunt for crawfish." And as Yvette's nose wrinkled in distaste, Leonie added, "You don't have to touch them . . . not even the bait. Do say you'll come!"

Yvette hesitated, willing to do just about anything Leonie wished, but she hated the swamps and particularly she hated skimming over the dark, mysterious waters of the bayous in the lightweight pirogue that Leonie propelled so effortlessly with a long pole.

"Leonie . . . I really don't want to," she said finally.

Leonie shrugged good-naturedly, not the least put out. The easy amiability between the two girls might have indicated they had known each other all of their lives. Precisely the opposite was true—in fact they had only met for the first time one stormy, wet day in February the previous year.

It had all started with the letter Yvette's mother Monique had written when she knew she was dying. In all the years since Damien Saint-André's death she had never asked for anything from his father, and Claude, paving his own path to hell, certainly had not given his dead son's octoroon mistress and her child any thought. But now she was dying of consumption, and knowing her time was running out she had finally swallowed her pride and had written to Monsieur Saint-André pleading for his protection for his son's child, Yvette.

If Claude had been at the Château when the letter had arrived the tale might have ended then and there. Fortunately he had just left for another of his frequent and too-long sojourns in New Orleans and the letter was delivered to Leonie.

Ordinarily Leonie would not have opened her grandfather's correspondence—she would have sent it along with one of the servants to the decaying townhouse in New Orleans. But there was something about this particular letter that drew her attention, something that pulled at her, as she stared at the fine, flowing script on the envelope. She hesitated, started to put it with the other items to be sent along to New Orleans, and then, not understanding why, she snatched the letter back and, taking a deep breath, opened it.

Upon learning that she had a half-sister who was soon to be orphaned and turned penniless upon the world, Leonie had not waited a moment. Consulting no one and taking no time to think of the consequences, which was typical of Leonie, she had commandeered two of the servants and within the hour she was riding along the river road that led to New Orleans.

New Orleans was only half a day's journey from the Château Saint-André, and by late afternoon Leonie was knocking impetuously on the door of the small, white cottage on the ramparts below the city where Yvette and her mother lived. Instinctively Leonie had not sought out her

10

grandfather, having a fairly good idea of what he would do if he learned of her interference and rash actions.

Monique had waited until the very last moment of her life to appeal for help and she had died two days previously, the letter having left her hands barely an hour before she breathed her last. Consequently when Leonie arrived she was greeted by a bewildered, grief-stricken Yvette, unable to comprehend or believe that her mother was dead.

Before Yvette had realized it, she had found herself efficiently bundled up, all her meager belongings stuffed in one old leather valise, and on her way down river with a small, tawny-haired whirlwind—who forthrightly declared that she was *her* sister!

Yvette had been aware that her father had been Damien Saint-André, but she'd had no idea that her mother had written to the family asking for help. If she had known she certainly wouldn't have expected the daughter of the house to descend without warning and whisk her away in this breathtaking fashion, but from that moment on an unbreakable bond had been formed between the girls.

The two family servants who had accompanied their young, unpredictable mistress had been most disapproving of this new "companion" and back at the Château Saint-André, Mammy, the nearest thing that Leonie had to adult supervision, had been most suspicious. But Leonie determinedly brushed away every objection and question. Hands on her slender hips, a warning gleam in the golden-flecked green eyes, Leonie had faced the mountainous black woman and announced firmly, "Yvette is to be my companion. I chose her myself, and where she comes from is none of your business. I will tell you this . . . she is an orphan of good family and has lived in Louisiana all of her life—even you will admit that she is far more ladylike than I am!"

Mammy had rolled her big black eyes skyward and had snorted and muttered, "How's could she *not* be? You is a hell-born babe if I ever seen one!"

Leonie had flashed a limpid smile and murmured dulcetly, *"Enfin!* There you are! That's why I need an example to teach me proper manners. Yvette will be perfect."

11

Mammy had been forced to allow Leonie to have her own way, and beyond grumbling dire prophecies of Claude's reaction to this unexpected addition to the household, she had wandered off.

The confrontation with Monsieur Claude some two months later had not gone as smoothly, but by then Leonie was so filled with the sheer joy of having a friend her own age that nothing short of murder would have separated the two girls.

At first Claude had been pleasantly surprised, almost pleased that Leonie had found herself a young girl of obviously impeccable breeding to act as a companion—he should have thought of it himself! It had only been when he had inquired after Yvette's family, and wondered aloud about parents who would allow their daughter to leave their roof at such a tender age, that the truth came out.

Leonie had considered lying. Only she and Yvette knew the true circumstances and both had agreed that there was no reason to reveal them—it would have been most uncomfortable for Yvette, they had both decided, but only after Yvette had gently pointed out that fact to Leonie. But lying was not in Leonie's nature and she told her grandfather the truth.

He had been astounded and then positively horrified. *"Ma petite,* how could you? A bastard with the blood of slaves in her veins! Have you no modesty? No shame? You should not even know of such things, much less associate with such a creature!"

Leonie's young features had frozen. With glacial Saint-André arrogance she had asked, "I am to deny my own sister? You would have me do this? Bah! I think, *grand-père,* that you are a fool!"

Claude's dark face had flushed with fury and the brown eyes had been glittering with anger under the gray, bristling brows. *"Sacre bleu!* You dare to speak to me like this? I should beat you!"

Leonie had lifted her chin defiantly and in a soft, dangerous voice had warned, "I would not, *grand-père,* if I were you."

Claude had eyed the stiff, angry young figure speculatively. That Leonie! And because Claude was basically a

12

weak man, one who preferred peace at any price, he had shrugged and said, "Do as you will. But do not ask me to acknowledge the creature. I shall tolerate her presence and that is all, do you understand?"

A brief smile had flitted across Leonie's face. *"Oui, grand-père!"* Then surprising them both she had flown into his arms and pressed a rare warm kiss on his lined cheek. *"Merci beaucoup, grand-père,"* she had said softly, and Claude felt something catch painfully at his heart. Aware that he was a poor excuse for a mentor and guardian and awash with a sudden feeling of regret, one blue-veined hand had reached out and gently tweaked a tawny curl. "You are a minx, *ma petite,* and I am a reprobate—perhaps we are a good pair, *oui?"*

Leonie had grinned and nodded vigorously. During the remainder of that visit there were no clashes between them. Leonie was pleased that *grand-père* had proved reasonable for once, and Claude was conscious for the first time that he must begin to think of Leonie's future. But then the old lure of the gaming tables and drink had called to him, and once again he had put aside his responsibilities and disappeared down the river to New Orleans, leaving Leonie to run the plantation.

On this morning the outlook for the future was very black, Leonie decided as she sought out her grandfather in his bedchamber. There was, she thought glumly, nothing to do but sell off some of their land—and that, she felt unhappily, would be the death of the Château Saint-André.

Claude himself, sitting in regal splendor in the middle of a huge bed hung with faded crimson, brocaded night curtains, was thinking much the same. With a pile of snowy white pillows at his back, he was tranquilly sipping a cup of very strong, very black coffee as he contemplated the future—or rather Leonie's future—but his thoughts were anything but tranquil.

His days were numbered, the sands of time had run out for him; the doctor had told him so this last trip to New Orleans. With death facing him from a heart that no longer beat as it should, Claude realized that the tomorrows when

13

he would assure himself of Leonie's future were suddenly upon him.

He had returned to the Château the previous night, and after feeling his carriage shake and rattle from the ruts and dips in the long drive that led to the house, he had admitted to himself that his own selfish foolishness had brought his estate to ruin. The tattered elegance of the furnishings of the house had made it even more evident, and this morning, while staring at the worn Turkish carpet on the floor, and the old satin curtains at the French doors, he wondered how he could salvage something for Leonie.

Marriage was the only answer. Having come to that decision, Claude wasted little time in brooding over the past and what he should have done, or would do if he had a chance to live it all again. Instead he turned his mind to the selection of a suitable husband for Leonie. None of the sons of their immediate neighbors would do. Not that he wouldn't have welcomed such a match, but everyone knew that the Saint-Andrés were ruined. No, it would have to be a stranger, a wealthy stranger—and yet one with a sense of honor who would not mistreat or abuse Leonie once he discovered the true state of affairs concerning her wealth, or rather *lack* of wealth.

Claude didn't mean to cheat a prospective husband. As a matter of fact, without Leonie's knowledge, he had managed to retain a very large sum in Spanish gold which had always been intended to be part of her dowry. He had hoped it would be larger and that a profitable, productive Château Saint-André would go with it, but that had not occurred and he accepted the blame. Yet, on that hot morning in June, he decided the money could be used as bait. Once the marriage had taken place . . . well, Leonie should be able to convince the bridegroom that it wasn't such a bad bargain.

It might work, he mused slowly, as he set down his cup and saucer and picked up a warm, flaky croissant. Leonie was sixteen and it was time she married. She came of good blood and did not require a great deal. For a moment a frown crossed the dissipated dark face and a look of sadness entered the brown eyes—ah, if only he had done things differently. But then he shrugged his slight shoul-

14

ders for there was no undoing the past, and Claude wasn't so certain he would live his life in a different manner if he had it to do over again.

In his fashion Claude loved Leonie and in his way he was planning to do the only thing he could to insure her some sort of security once he had left this earth. He rather conveniently pushed aside the disagreeable thought that if he had taken more of an interest in her life sooner, he might not find himself in his current state of affairs.

Marriage, of course, was the answer, but it would be difficult to find the right man. Five thousand Spanish doubloons would attract many men, but Claude's Gallic pride balked at buying just *any* husband. One must remember that noble blood ran in their veins. Claude's father, who had emigrated to New Orleans when it had been a swampy huddle of huts on the banks of the Mississippi River, had been the youngest son of the Comte Saint-André. Even more to the point, after the revolution had swept France and the Comte Saint-André met his death on the guillotine, Claude became the Comte Saint-André. He was now the only living male member of a once proud and illustrious family.

There was no question of his returning to France, where that upstart Corsican General Napoleon ruled the army and might soon rule France herself; he was too old and too tired. But if Leonie had been a boy . . .

The object of his thoughts walked into the room and Claude smiled to himself. Leonie might be a mere girl, but in just about any contest of wills, he would put his money on his young lioness of a granddaughter.

They greeted each other warily, Claude conscious of the money he had wasted at cards at Governor Gayoso's and Leonie suspicious of her grandfather's reasons for wanting to see her. Neither one spoke of the lost money; they never did. Instead they acted out a pitiful and familiar charade. With no hint of recrimination in her voice Leonie asked politely, "Did you enjoy yourself, *grand-père?* You were not gone as long this time."

He nodded, making some light reply, and watched with mixed emotions as she sat at the foot of his bed like an Indian with her legs folded underneath her. It was on the tip of his tongue to mention the bare feet and to inquire acidly if she ever intended to control that mane of tawny hair, but he held back the criticism. If she didn't mention the money, he wouldn't comment on her deplorable dress. . . .

For a few moments they talked of this and that, but as Leonie seldom wasted time in drawing-room conversation, even with her grandfather, she asked bluntly, "Yvette said you wished to see me. Why?"

A pained expression crossed his aquiline features at the mention of Yvette. But then, being just as blunt as his granddaughter—to their mutual horror they shared many of the same traits—he stated baldly, "I have decided upon your future. I shall arrange a marriage for you."

Leonie stiffened and the green eyes narrowed. "To whom?" she demanded in a tone of voice that made Claude distinctly uneasy.

Airily waving one hand, Claude replied, with more confidence than he felt, "I have not yet decided, you understand. It is merely that I thought I should tell you first . . . that is, before I looked about for a suitable husband for you."

Leonie settled back on her haunches and gave her grandfather a long, assessing look. With studied indifference she replied, "I do not wish to marry, *grand-père.*" When Claude started to protest, she added flatly, "I will not marry. You cannot force me."

Claude was instantly infuriated. His lips thinned with rage and his voice shook with anger as he threatened, "You will either marry the gentleman of my choice, or that precious bastard of an octoroon whore you secretly dare to call *sister,* will find herself in the meanest brothel in New Orleans!"

Her great sea-green eyes glittered with golden flecks of sheer temper; the expression of mingled fear and fury that flickered across the triangular-shaped face caused Claude to wince. It had to be done, he reminded himself sadly; Leonie's future *must* be made secure whether *she* wanted it or not.

Leonie, leaping up in one furious bound and springing catlike to the floor, approached her grandfather and spat, "You would *dare?*"

16

Stonily he returned, "I would."

Her small bosom heaving with the force of the furious emotions that tore through her, she stared disbelievingly at him for a moment. She knew her grandfather well, they fought and made truces and then fought again, but this was one battle she was terrified he would win. She was wise enough to know that she could not protect Yvette at all times, as her grandfather was incredibly crafty when he chose to be. If he said Yvette would find herself in a brothel he wasn't making idle conversation. Realizing that for the present there was no escape, she stared at his fixed features and said in a tight, little voice, *"Eh bien.* I will do it."

Claude nodded and said coolly, *"Bon!* We will return to New Orleans shortly to find you a husband."

Leonie looked at him and with a surprisingly docile expression on her small face, she picked up the china coffee pot and asked sweetly, "More coffee, *grand-père?"* Before Claude guessed her intent or could react, she swiftly proceeded to pour the entire pot of hot liquid right over her grandfather's very elegant, white linen nightshirt.

Spluttering with rage, Claude called down a string of curses on her head, but Leonie was gone, a mocking smile curving her mouth as she ran from the room.

2

Even to the most casual observer it would be obvious
that Bonheur, situated some distance from Natchez in the
Mississippi Territory, was the estate of a wealthy gentleman. The tree-lined drive that led to the residence was indeed impressive. The branches of the old oaks nearly
touched as they soared towards the brilliant blue sky; the
red dirt road was smooth and unrutted, revealing that
time and money had been spent to make it so. In between
the trunks of the massive oaks with their gray-green
beards of Spanish moss, neatly manicured stretches of
green lawns could be glimpsed, the vast open expanses
broken only by majestic oak and magnolia trees.

The drive ended in a sweeping circular carriageway; beyond the drive and the spreading magnolia trees rose the
mansion itself. The house towered three stories in the air;
tall stuccoed columns, topped by wooden colonnettes surrounded it on all four sides, and the extended roof line created wide, cool verandas. Soft green outer walls contrasted
pleasingly with the dark green shutters that hung at the
many long windows, and from the upper story, huge purple
masses of wisteria cascaded to the ground near one corner
of the house. Bonheur was all grace and elegance from
the steeply pitched roof to the broad, white steps that
stretched entirely across the front of the building.

Inside it was much the same; each room evidenced
wealth and good taste. Axminster and Oriental carpets covered the floors; giltwood furniture upholstered in Gobelin's
tapestry graced the main salon; an exceedingly fine mahogany set of dining room furniture dominated the spacious chamber. Yet Morgan Slade, the heir to all this
wealth, paid it little heed—after all, he had been born at

18

Bonheur and had lived here off and on for his entire twenty-seven years.

While finishing a last cup of coffee he was reading, on this particular sunny morning in June of 1799, a letter from his uncle in England. The beginning of a frown marred his otherwise smooth forehead. Seated across from him, his younger brother Dominic noted the frown and inquired, "Trouble, Morgan? Is the war against France going badly for England?"

Morgan's lean face cleared, and sending Dominic a slight smile, he murmured, "No worse than can be expected. Admiral Nelson is beating them on the sea, but the land war is not going well. Napoleon certainly knows how to surprise the English! Uncle seems to hope, though, that it will not go too badly for England, and he writes that they no longer fear an immediate invasion from France."

"Then why are you frowning?"

Morgan sighed, knowing that until Dominic was entirely satisfied the questions wouldn't abate. Flicking aside the letter he said carelessly, "It seems our esteemed cousin Ashley is, as usual, causing his father a bit of trouble."

Robert, the brother some two years younger than Morgan, looked up quickly. He, as well as Morgan, had been educated at Harrow in England and knew from close experience exactly what kind of trouble Ashley naturally gravitated toward. In his quiet manner he asked, "Women, drink, money . . . or all three?"

Morgan laughed, his even white teeth flashing in a dark face and the vivid blue eyes dancing under heavy, black brows. "All three! And what is worse, it appears that dear cousin Ashley is not only *not* in England but upon our own fair shores."

"Good Lord! He's not coming *here?*" Robert asked with a startled expression, remembering uncomfortably the scandals and unpleasantness that followed Ashley wherever he went. His face disapproving, he said slowly, "I would have thought that the trouncing you gave him—after he forged your signature to his gambling vowels and impersonated you to seduce a tavern wench—would have given him the good sense to keep an ocean between you. I seem to recall

19

that you threatened to blow his brains out if he crossed your path again. A prudent man would have heeded your warning."

Morgan shrugged. "Prudence is the last thing that Ashley possesses! But don't worry, Rob—Ashley is going to find himself on the first ship back to England. I'll see to it, rest assured!" His features taking on a wry expression he added, "Which is precisely what our uncle has written asking me to do. It seems they argued over Ashley's debts and rakehell living, as usual, and uncle disowned him . . . again. Cooler thought has now prevailed, and he wants me to find Ashley and convince him to return home."

The trio of young men exchanged a knowing glance, all three thinking with a certain amount of sympathy of their uncle, the Baron of Trevelyan, whose heir was their abominable cousin Ashley. Looking at the trio as they sat at the round oak table, it was obvious they were brothers. All three had the same dark hair, black as a raven's wing, which they had inherited from their Creole mother; each had the Trevelyan chin, determined and very masculine, that had come to them from their father, as well as Matthew Slade's rather lowering black eyebrows and deep-set eyes. The two older brothers had the same piercing blue eyes as did their father, but Dominic's eyes were a cool beautiful gray.

Morgan was by far the most striking: his eyes seemed brighter, more vivid than his younger brothers'; his skin darker; his cheekbones higher and more pronounced; his nose stronger; and his mouth fuller. Robert was the truly handsome one, his features so symetrical that one adoring young lady had likened him to a Greek god—much to his intense embarrassment, for Robert was somewhat shy and retiring despite his stunning handsomeness. Dominic was every bit as good looking as his older brothers, but his face still showed a youthful prettiness, and he would never be quite as handsome as Robert. Yet, there was a mischievous curve to Dominic's mouth and a teasing sparkle in the gray eyes that made him particularly appealing to the opposite sex.

The Slade family was a large one. In addition to the three brothers there were still at home the lively, rambunctious ten-year-old twins, Alexandre and Cassandre. A married sister, Alicia, lived in Tennessee with her planter husband and growing family.

It would seem on the surface that the Slade family had been untouched by tragedy of any kind, but that would be untrue. Nineteen-year-old André had been killed three years ago in a senseless duel, and there had been an even younger sister, Maria, who had died of malaria at the age of twelve, only the past year. And then there had been Morgan's tragic, ill-fated marriage. . . .

Noelle, their petite, pretty mother entered the room and the three gentlemen all rose and greeted her as she was seated by the white-garbed Negro butler. At forty-five years of age, Noelle Slade was still a beautiful woman, a bit plump it was true, but then eight children were bound to have left their mark upon her. Her face was that of a true Creole beauty from New Orleans—smooth, magnolia skin and dark, sparkling eyes with an abundance of shining black hair arranged in soft curls about her smiling face. And like most Creole women, her family was everything; she would have cheerfully slaughtered *anyone* who caused her husband or one of her children a moment's pain. Fortunately or unfortunately, it was a trait that had been passed on to her children. The Slades were intensely protective and loyal to one another—the man who had shot André had discovered this trait, to his regret, when he found himself face to face with a narrowed-eyed Morgan on the same dueling field where young André had died not twenty-four hours before. The man, a braggart and a bully who had forced the duel with André, had not left the field alive.

Noelle had just been served her coffee and toast by a servant when the head of the family wandered in. Matthew Slade, his rich chestnut hair liberally sprinkled with gray, was still an imposing figure of a man despite having turned fifty-four some months ago. He was tall, and it was from him that his sons, Morgan in particular, got their long, lithe bodies.

Greetings were once again exchanged and then the conversation became general for several moments, as Matthew decided on breakfast and busied himself with

21

pouring cream into his coffee. It was Dominic, ever eager to be the first with any news, who brought up the subject of Ashley.

"Ashley's in America, father! And Morgan is going to put him on a ship for England after he blows his brains out—uncle wrote and asked him to do it!" Dominic stopped abruptly, looking a bit sheepish, and then added, "I mean uncle wants him put on a ship for England. It's Morgan who wants to blow out his brains!"

At the mention of Ashley's name, Noelle's dark eyes flashed and with surprising violence she said, "That swine! I almost wish Ashley *would* get his brains blown out . . . at least then his brother could inherit!"

Morgan smiled grimly. "If you wish it done, I am at your service."

Uncertainly Noelle looked at him. *"Mon fils,* let it be," she said at last, her own volatile temper evaporating as quickly as it had surfaced.

Morgan sent her a cool, mocking smile. "Of course, if it is what you wish." His reply was polite enough but there was a note in his voice that caused her to glance at him sharply. Morgan had always tended to be headstrong; even as a child he had been aloof, going his own way, but there was a difference these days. Once she had known his every thought, had shared his youthful dreams, and despite his iron-willed personality, there had been a sweetness in him—especially with women . . . but no longer. Not since the terrible end of his marriage barely two years ago. . . .

The conversation switched to other subjects and the meal continued in leisurely harmony, but an hour later, as she sat in a small room which looked out towards the cotton field behind Bonheur, Noelle's troubled thoughts were on her eldest son.

He is so wary and hard, so far away from us, she mused unhappily. *It is almost as if he has erected a barrier to protect himself from women, even from me.* Her small face tightened and for a moment she looked quite ferocious. *That Stephanie! I could kill her, if she were not dead already! To treat my good Morgan so, to break his heart, to shame him, to take away his child, and to destroy his trust*

22

in women! Mon Dieu! I would like to cut her heart in little ribbons!

Staring blindly out the window, oblivious to the soothing view before her, she recalled vividly the day Morgan had come to her, his face alight with joy and pleasure, and nearly stammering with excitement he had burst out with the news that Stephanie Du Boise had consented to marry him. Noelle had been full of reservations from the beginning—he was too young; Stephanie, hardly eighteen, was also too young. Noelle was very much afraid that Stephanie had been as attracted to Morgan's wealth as much as his person. The Du Boises, while of good blood, were poor, and it was known all about Natchez that the girls *had* to marry money. Stephanie was a lovely girl, that Noelle couldn't have denied, and at first she *did* seem sweet and charming.

Certainly Morgan, just twenty, had been plainly besotted by her blonde beauty and great green eyes—there was nothing he wouldn't have done for her. And Noelle had stilled her doubts and had smiled to herself at the sight of her usually determined son ready to do anything that his adored bride had wanted.

It was a marriage that should have brought them happiness, and if Stephanie had truly loved Morgan, it might have, Noelle reflected sadly. They had been young, Morgan deeply in love with his wife, and within a year there had been a healthy, handsome son. Thinking of her first grandchild, of Phillippe's first tottering steps and his happy gurgle as he had played in this very room, her brown eyes misted with tears and her throat closed with a tight ache of pain. *Mon Dieu, does the pain ever go away?* she wondered. Did Morgan, behind that cool, uncaring exterior of his, grieve too? Noelle knew he did—sometimes when he thought he was unobserved, an expression of unutterable misery would cross his chiseled features—and she guessed that he must be remembering his little son. If he had been besotted with Stephanie, he had adored his son. How many times had she seen him put aside his growing air of maturity and like a child gambol on the floor with Phillippe? Too many times to think about, she decided tiredly.

When had it all gone wrong? Noelle wondered. There had

23

been no blight on the horizon in the beginning. Stephanie had appeared happy and contented and Morgan's feet never seemed to touch the ground.

So when? When Morgan first began to talk of moving away from Bonheur? Of setting up his own residence, of building a fine home away from Natchez for his young family? Had it been then that Stephanie had shown the first signs of discontent? Or had it been because in that last year Morgan had left her alone with his family at Bonheur, not wanting to subject her to the rigors of carving out a new home in almost virgin territory, far away from any major city and the elegance and amusement she was used to.

Thousand Oaks, as Morgan had proudly named the five thousand acres Matthew had given him as a wedding present, was not far from the Mississippi River and was situated midway between Natchez to the north and Baton Rouge to the south. Morgan had planned to make it as elegant and handsome as Bonheur for his young wife. Had it begun then? Or had it simply been that Morgan had been away and Steven Malincourt had been here in Natchez?

Her small hand clenching into a fist, Noelle cursed again the day she had introduced Steven to her daughter-in-law. But how could she have known? She closed her eyes in anguish. To think that Stephanie could have deserted Morgan, who adored her, for a fortune hunter like Steven Malincourt! A man of a good family, it was true, but to take him over *Morgan!* To leave Morgan—completely unsuspecting when he arrived home full of joy at the thought of seeing his wife and son after a three-month absence— nothing but a hastily written note. The note had been brief and unnecessarily cruel, telling him of her sudden love for Steven and the galling, painful information that Phillippe would be returned to him as soon as he agreed to the divorce—and gave her a generous settlement.

Never will I forget his face, Noelle thought with a shudder. *Never!* How the light died from his eyes, leaving them cold and empty, and how his face slowly hardened as if under the warm flesh and bone there existed only cold, icy steel. He had gone after them, naturally—not for Stepha-

24

nie, for she had chosen her path, but for his son—and then fate had played its cruelest trick.

When the fleeing lovers had left Bonheur, they had started their journey north by taking the notorious Natchez Trace. The Trace was often called the Devil's Backbone, and a treacherous deadly trail it was, with robbers, thieves, and all manner of wicked men lurking near every bend of the wilderness trail. The legends of robberies and murders and of vanished people were well known, but it was the way north. And Stephanie with her son and lover had taken it and met their violent deaths in the shady glen where Morgan had found them.

For his sanity, Noelle was forever grateful that someone else had been with him, that he had not been alone when he had come across the mutilated bodies of his wife and son. He never spoke of it—it had been from Robert and Morgan's childhood companion, Brett Dangermond, that the family learned of Stephanie and Phillippe's tragic fate. They had been robbed, then carelessly murdered and left like so much refuse to be found by the next traveler on the Trace.

Morgan had been so different after that. Oh, not that he had shut out his family entirely, but Noelle, watching him with a mother's concerned eye, saw the changes: the coolness that hadn't been there before; the way he could seldom bear to stay for more than a few weeks at Bonheur, as if it held too many painful memories; the hardness that crossed his face whenever a woman would attempt to flirt with him; and the cynical expression that appeared far too often in the sapphire blue eyes whenever marriage or eligible young ladies were mentioned.

Noelle guessed that there were still women of a sort in his life—he was, after all, a virile, handsome young man—but it wouldn't have shocked or surprised her to discover that the females he now sought out were not precisely respectable. Certainly she was positive that there was no woman at present who could win his anguished, wary heart. *Ah, Morgan,* she thought despondently, *will you ever love again? Or trust another woman?*

Morgan would have answered that question with a snort and a blunt, emphatic, *No!* But at the moment women

25

were the last thing on his mind—he was too busy trying to explain tactfully to Dominic why he didn't need that young man's company when he sailed down the Mississippi River next Monday on his way to New Orleans.

The two of them were in Morgan's bedchamber, *not* the same room he had shared with Stephanie, and Morgan was in the process of changing from his elegant, gray morning coat to the well-cut, brown frock coat and buckskin breeches that he frequently wore for riding.

"Dom," he said patiently, "I do not need your very generous offer of help with Ashley. I appreciate it, but Ashley has very little to do with my current trip to New Orleans, and you know it. It's just a coincidence that he happens to be there at the same time I will be." Morgan suddenly grinned. "It is damned convenient, though. I would have disliked coming back from there to find uncle's letter, waiting for me, with the news of Ashley's presence in New Orleans and of his plea that I convince Ashley to return home to England."

"But you *do* intend to darken his daylights before putting him on the ship for England, don't you?" Dominic persisted as he lounged casually on Morgan's bed.

Morgan sent him a look. "More than likely, but I still don't need you along to make certain that I do it to your satisfaction."

"I know that!" Dominic replied hotly. "But I want to watch you do it!"

Morgan snorted. "What a bloody little savage you've turned out to be!"

"No different than you, from what *maman* says!" Dominic shot back. "Oh, Morgan, *please* let me come! I promise I won't do anything to embarrass you. You know that I am very grown up for my age—even papa says my manners are very nice. Do let me come!"

Morgan hesitated. Dominic was extremely difficult to resist when he made up his mind he wanted something, but thinking of the dangers that a wicked city like New Orleans could offer to a high-spirited, ripe-for-mischief young man like Dominic, he shook his head. "Next time." And when Dominic opened his mouth to protest further, Morgan added, "I promise. This trip has been planned for months and you know that I am not going to New Orleans for pleasure. Half the time I'll be closeted with estate agents, and there will be quite a few evenings when I meet with Spanish officials to discuss trade agreements. Dom, you'd find yourself at a standstill and bored in the bargain. Besides," Morgan finished lightly, "my dealings with Ashley will be a mere trifle, over in a few minutes, and *then* what would you do for the rest of the time, hmm?"

Dominic hunched a shoulder. "I'd find something to do!"

"Which is precisely *why* I'd rather you remain here!" Morgan murmured dryly as he pulled on a polished top boot. "Come along now and show me that prime bit of blood and bones our neighbor has for sale. A dapple gray stallion, I believe you said, with Arabian blood?"

As horses were at the moment Dominic's premier passion, he eagerly followed his older brother's lead, and the trip to New Orleans vanished from his mind. They spent an agreeable morning together; much to Dominic's delight Morgan decided to buy the stallion.

"I told you he'd make an excellent stud for your stables!" Dominic crowed when the deal had been struck and they rode back to Bonheur.

"So you did, bratling," Morgan replied with a quick grin. The remainder of the day passed pleasantly and Morgan's trip to New Orleans was not mentioned again until that evening.

It was late evening and everyone else in the family had retired. Morgan and his father were seated in cane-backed chairs on the veranda at the side of the house, enjoying one last cigar before retiring. The conversation was desultory between father and son until Matthew asked casually, "I know you intend to work out some sort of trading agreement with the Spaniards; does that mean you'll be seeing our ex-governor, Gayoso?"

Morgan nodded. "It seems as good a place as any to start, don't you think? He knows our family and he knows that I am nominally a subject of Spain as long as I hold Thousand Oaks. We entertained him here at Bonheur while he was governor of Natchez, so it wouldn't be as if I were meeting the man for the first time."

Matthew grunted and took a puff of his cigar. "Now that

he's governor of New Orleans, do you think he'll try to bribe you to spy for Spain?"

"Probably, if I hint that I'm agreeable to it . . . which, I might add, I'm not! A General James Wilkinson I am not!"

"For God's sake, don't say things like that!" Matthew rumbled. "I'll admit there's rumor aplenty about Wilkinson's dealings with the Spaniards, but no one can prove anything. You'd best watch that tongue of yours or the general might feel compelled to defend the honor he's always trumpeting about."

Morgan smiled in the encroaching darkness. "I don't fear Wilkinson, papa. Nor do I think he is man enough to challenge me to a duel—he knows I would accept *and* win! Besides, I'm certain that if I took the time, or the interest, I could prove that our general really is a spy for Spain. You forget that Phillip Nolan and I are friends of a sort."

"I don't like that young man—never did!" Matthew said slowly. "It's not only his association with Wilkinson, but the way he makes a living. Catching wild horses in Spanish territory—what kind of life is that?"

"It's a damn sight more honest than the way Wilkinson earns his!" Morgan shot back tartly.

"Mmm, you're probably right. At least Gayoso is a somewhat honorable man; be thankful it is he you will be dealing with in New Orleans and *not* Wilkinson."

"True, but it might be easier with Wilkinson—all I would have to do would be to offer a big enough bribe! With Gayoso it doesn't always work that way," Morgan murmured thoughtfully.

"You don't think you'll have any trouble do you? Morgan, we need those wharves and warehouses in New Orleans—without them, it's going to be damned difficult!" Matthew said earnestly.

Morgan sighed, aware of the problem as was everyone up and down the Mississippi River. New Orleans was the only feasible port for the dispersal of their goods, and without Spanish permission to use the port, their goods—cotton, indigo, and even furs—would be worthless. The Treaty of San Lorenzo, signed in 1796 between Spain and the fledgling United States of America, guaranteed the right of deposit for the Americans and their uncontested use of the Mississippi River for three years, but time was running out.

The thought of the Spanish revoking the American rights at any time was uppermost in everyone's mind, and dealing with Spanish officials in New Orleans was a nightmare. It seemed there was always one more hand to be crossed with gold before the necessary permissions and documents were granted.

Staring out into the darkness, Morgan said slowly, "If only we could acquire New Orleans. Then this continual haggle with the Spaniards would cease."

"Ha! Might as well ask for the moon! Spain isn't about to give up one more inch of territory. Look how long it took the Dons to evacuate the territory they ceded to us by the treaty . . . it was years!"

Morgan took one last drag on his cigar and then tossed it in a nearby brass spittoon. "You're probably right, papa, but it would certainly solve a lot of problems for all of us this side of the Appalachian Mountains." Standing up he added, "Well, I am for bed, what about you?"

"In a moment." Matthew hesitated, then brought up a subject near to his heart. "Morgan, when you're in New Orleans, there isn't any particuliar young lady you're going to see, is there?"

A derisive expression flitted across the lean, dark face. "If you mean a *marriageable* young lady, the answer is *no,* papa! You'll have to be content to have your other offspring breeding your grandchildren."

"Now, Morgan—" Matthew protested.

But Morgan held up one hand and said in a voice laced with steel, "Don't! I will not talk about it, and if you want us to part on unpleasant terms, just continue the subject."

Wisely Matthew abandoned what he had been going to say. Morgan could be so implacable, he decided half-angrily, half-admiringly, as he puffed on his cigar and followed his son into the house.

Sleep came hard for Morgan that night, his father's words bringing back memories that he had thought were behind him. Apparently not, though, he admitted bitterly, as Stephanie's lovely face floated in his mind's eye. An-

29

grily he got up out of bed and stood at the tall windows that overlooked the carriageway and drive.

Moonlight gilded the magnolia trees in the center of the circular drive, making each leathery green leaf seem edged in silver, but Morgan was blind to the beauty of the night. He slammed his fist against the wall. *How could I have been so misled by a beautiful face? . . . Why didn't I realize that she had only been after money all along?* he wondered bleakly. But while he could think of his dead, deserting wife, his grief was too deep to touch on Phillippe's death. Stephanie had been a woman grown, following her own destiny, but his little son had merely been a pawn. He had adored both his wife and his son, but his love for Stephanie had died the instant he had read her cruel note. Love had died and left in its place an icy anger against her, which little Phillippe's death had only intensified. *Faithless bitch!* he cursed furiously, filled with hate for what she had done to him. Bitterly he laughed in the darkness—*and papa wonders if there is any special woman waiting in New Orleans for me! I'll burn in hell before I ever believe a pair of lying eyes again,* he promised himself fiercely. *Never will I fall in love again. Never!*

3

Morgan woke with a start, the nightmare still very real; for a moment he didn't recognize his surroundings. With a blank, uncomprehending stare he gazed around the handsome, spacious room, trying vainly to identify his whereabouts. From the elegant, expensive furnishings it was obviously a place of wealth; his eyes lingered on the crimson silk hangings of the bed before wandering to an intricately carved mahogany chest against one wall. It looked to be of Spanish origin, and with that thought memory came flooding back—he was in New Orleans, at the governor's residence.

Arriving the previous day in the city, Morgan had wasted little time and had gone immediately to call upon Governor Gayoso in his offices. Gayoso had greeted him warmly, and upon learning that Morgan intended to be in New Orleans for some weeks he had, instantly and almost insistently, pressed an invitation upon Morgan to stay at his home. Morgan had sought politely to refuse, preferring not to be so completely under Gayoso's observation, but Gayoso had been determined, and as it would be foolish to insult one of the most powerful men in Louisiana, Morgan had eventually agreed. After all, he told himself, he did have business with the governor and what did it matter where he stayed?

Aware of the wisdom of not instantly broaching all of his reasons for being in New Orleans, Morgan had followed Gayoso's genial lead and had settled down to enjoy a few days of the older man's company and openhanded hospitality, grimly aware that business would be discussed only when the governor was ready. Gayoso never rushed matters, believing firmly in the concept of *mañana*.

31

Manuel Gayoso de Lemos was a slim man of perhaps fifty; his dark hair, black eyes, and swarthy complexion made his Spanish blood very apparent. He was an oddity amongst the Spanish officials in that he seldom used his power and office for gain. That is not to say all of his dealings would survive scrutiny in the bright light of day, only that he had an honor of sorts. A hard drinker, his love of liquor was legendary, and it had been his ability to drink any Natchezian under the table, as well as his lack of blatant fortune hunting, that had made him so agreeable to the people of Natchez when he had been their governor a few years before. A charming, debonair, extravagant man, Gayoso made friends effortlessly and was an excellent host.

The evening had passed pleasantly, the food, the wines, and the company of the finest quality. After they had dined, Gayoso and Morgan had excused themselves from the ladies of the family and had spent the remainder of the evening, doing as gentlemen do so often, drinking and gambling in a handsome room the governor had set aside for that purpose.

A few more gentlemen had joined them, all strangers to Morgan, but they had proved to be agreeable company, particularly an aristocratic old gentleman by the name of Saint-André. The Frenchman had a witty tongue and a pleasing manner, and Morgan had found himself enjoying Saint-André's company immensely . . . at first. He had *not* enjoyed watching Saint-André become drunker and drunker, nor had he been comfortable watching Gayoso accept vowel after vowel from a man obviously unable to realize what he was doing.

But Gayoso's actions didn't come as a surprise to Morgan. The governor was a curious blend of avarice and generosity, and some of his methods of gaining money—and Gayoso *always* had need of money—were neither nice nor proper. Unable to stand by and watch the old man openly robbed, Morgan had put an end to Gayoso's unfair practice simply by calling it an evening. He adroitly convinced the completely inebriated Saint-André that he too should retire for the night. Morgan even found himself offering to escort the old man to his home.

Saint-André had been flattered, but he had declined, explaining somewhat incoherently that his own servants were waiting and that they would see him to his townhouse as they usually did. Feeling there was nothing more he could do, Morgan had bowed, made his adieus and retired for the night, Saint-André vanishing from his mind.

Morgan had slept soundly at first, but then just as dawn had been breaking on the horizon, the nightmare began again. It was always the same dream and it had haunted him from the moment he had seen his little son's lifeless body lying in that shady glen on the Natchez Trace. In his dream Morgan knew Phillippe was in terrible, mortal danger, and urgently, fear shrieking throughout his body, he rode desperately to rescue him. To his horror, he always arrived just in time to see a dark stranger slit his son's young throat and then disappear into the green jungle of the Trace, leaving Phillippe to strangle in his own blood. And, as happened this morning, Morgan would come awake with his heart pounding uncontrollably, his body bathed in sweat, his brain silently screaming out an anguished, furious denial.

If Morgan woke from the night's sleep with a nightmare, for Claude Saint-André the waking was an entirely different matter. It was true that his head was pounding like an African drum and that his mouth felt as if the entire Spanish Army had trampled through it, but he was full of confidence and excitement. He had found *Leonie's husband!* Monsieur Morgan Slade was *everything* a man could wish for in a granddaughter's husband! He was handsome, wealthy, and honorable—Claude had not been so drunk that he had not realized the motives behind Morgan's abrupt ending of the evening. Morgan Slade had given the definite impression of being a strong, determined young man who would brook no nonsense from a willful, headstrong little minx like Leonie. Claude was elated.

There would be difficulties, to be sure, but Claude, with his usual disregard of unpleasant facts, waved them aside. He would contrive. *Naturellement!*

As could be expected, that afternoon when Claude informed Leonie that he had found her a husband she was less than pleased. She had been furious at being compelled to leave Château Saint-André to come to their shabby townhouse for the express purpose of being married off to the first convenient man her grandfather found. It had been bad enough being forced to agree to grandfather's infamous bargain, but to have a prospective husband shoved down her throat on their fourth day in New Orleans was more than she could swallow.

The sea-green eyes flashing with helpless anger, Leonie had asked bitterly, "And this Monsieur Slade, he has agreed to the marriage?"

Claude had hesitated, not wanting Leonie to guess he had not yet even broached the matter to the young man in question. Deciding that the sooner Leonie realized that her fate was sealed, the better off they all would be, he replied easily, *"Mais oui!* We did not finalize everything last night, you understand, but he is most agreeable. I will meet with him tonight to discuss your dowry and the date of the marriage."

Her eyes narrowed and Leonie queried sharply, "What dowry?"

Aware that she would find out about the money eventually, Claude said with deceptive innocence, "A handsome dowry of five thousand doubloons in gold that your father and I set aside the day of your birth." Smiling almost proudly he added, "You see, *ma petite,* despite all my faults I managed to save that for you."

He would have gone on, but Leonie's eyes went round with astonishment. Then, as the impact of what all that money would mean to her beloved Château Saint-André, an exuberant grin crossed her face and she burst out happily, *"Grand-père! Mon Dieu,* but you had me worried! We are saved! With that much gold we can buy so many things for the Château—new livestock, new tools, and perhaps even hire people to work the fields! *C'est merveilleux!"* Throwing herself against her grandfather's chest, she hugged him impulsively and laughed gaily, "Oh, how afraid I was that you really meant to marry me off!"

Aghast at her attitude, gently Claude disengaged himself from Leonie's embrace. Almost tiredly he answered, "But I do intend to marry you off, *ma chèrie.* The money is for your dowry, and I will not squander it on land that will

34

take it and then demand more. *Non!* You will marry, and the money will buy you a wealthy, respectable husband who will take care of you."

Unable to believe him, Leonie stared openmouthed, the happiness dying from her face. *He is mad,* she thought wildly. *He must be mad! Hard, cold gold could do so much for the Château . . . and he wants to throw it away on something as useless as a husband!* She swallowed with difficulty, fighting back a nearly irresistible urge to throw a flaming tantrum the likes of which Claude had never seen. With an effort she attempted to control herself, but unable to completely suppress her emotions, she stamped one small foot with unladylike temper and demanded fiercely, "Why do you insist that I marry? You are forcing me to do something that will make me hate you for the rest of my life! Why do you do this to me?"

"It is for your own good!" Claude shot back. "You need a husband to control you! I am too old and tired for the task and it is time you were married."

Leonie flashed her grandfather a withering look and muttered, "Ah, bah! I do not understand you in this mood. You are an imbecile!"

Claude merely smiled at her anger and, walking toward the door, said with chilling finality, "Perhaps so, *ma petite,* but you *will* marry, and tonight I will attend to the final details with Monsieur Slade."

Knowing that for the moment further argument would gain her little, except the satisfaction of releasing some of the helpless rage which surged through her slender body, Leonie dropped the subject and, instead, brought up another, equally explosive one. A set look on the young face, she asked tightly, "How many more vowels did you sign last night? Is that how you met this man—over cards and drink? Did he take your vouchers too?" Scornfully she finished, "Is he a man so without honor that he takes money from a drunkard?"

Claude's features froze and his dark eyes suddenly very hard, he snapped, "Shut your mouth, you little she-devil and hear me out—I will not be questioned or dictated to by my own grandchild! Understand?"

"Zut!" Leonie replied inelegantly, her chin tilted at a re-

bellious angle. "You are throwing my life away . . . *my future* . . . and I am to say *nothing!* Bah! It is *my* life, *grand-père,* and *I* am fighting for it! *You* would do the same in my position, you must admit."

Some of his anger fading, Claude acknowledged the justice of her remarks, even if he disagreed with the idea of a woman having any control of her future. Unwillingly he confessed, "It is true that I met Monsieur Slade at Governor Gayoso's last night, but he is an honorable man. When he saw that I was—when he noticed that I was in no condition to continue gambling he very properly brought the evening to an end." And thinking to make Leonie view the genteman more kindly, Claude added, "I was losing rather badly, and because of his intervention, Gayoso holds fewer of my vowels than he would have. You should be grateful to Monsieur Slade."

One of Leonie's slashing eyebrows shot up and she murmured disgustedly, "I doubt it! He is probably just more clever than Gayoso and means to have you think he is a good man . . . especially if you mentioned the amount of my dowry. It would tempt many men." Her expressive little face suddenly changing, the rebellion fleeing, and only anxiety and affection in the cat-shaped eyes, she begged, "Please, *please, grand-père,* forget this nonsense! Let us take the money and spend it on the Château." Almost desperately she pleaded, "Don't go back to the governor's tonight—you will only drink and lose more money." Her voice growing urgent, she asked, "How much longer can you expect your voucher to be respected? Sooner or later, they must be paid." Unable to look at her grandfather's proud features, in a low tone she rushed on, "You know it is only kindness that allows your friends to take your vouchers now—they all know you cannot pay them. What if Gayoso calls them in? And he may . . . if not this week, then the next or the next." Her eyes suddenly meeting his, she finished painfully, *"Grand-père,* you simply cannot ignore the disastrous state of our finances and continue to gamble as if we had an unending source of money."

Leonie was very lovely as she stood before her grandfather, her eyes soft and luminious from the intensity of her emotions, the full mouth an enchanting curve of rose. For once the tawny hair was neatly confined in two shining coils about her small head and the apricot shade of the gown she wore gave her skin an even more golden tone than usual, but despite the charming picture she made, her words went deep, cutting into Claude's heart and pride like razors.

Shamed, outraged, his pride more damaged than it had ever been in his life, Claude reacted with arrogant fury. His mouth thinned with anger, he snarled, "If you were a man, I'd kill you for that! *Mon Dieu,* but I would! How dare you speak of things that you know nothing of!" In a voice shaking with rage, he said, "My vowels are accepted everywhere—no one would *dare* refuse Saint-André!" Throwing her a glance, almost of hatred, he snapped, "I *will* go as I damn well please! No one tells me what to do . . . and certainly not a female of sixteen!"

Her heart was filled with compassion and yet Leonie was furious with her grandfather as she watched him stalk from the room. She let out her breath in a long, gusty sigh and almost absently flung herself down in a nearby high-back chair. Once the chair had been covered in a glorious, burgundy velvet; now the nap of the material was worn and the color faded, but Leonie enjoyed the softness of the old velvet as she idly ran her hands over the arms of the chair, her thoughts churning distractedly.

The room showed the same signs of lack of money as did the Château Saint-André—the carpets, drapes, and furniture, all obviously elegant, expensive items, had been allowed to wear with age. There were only a few rooms of the townhouse that were actually still furnished—Claude having sold off the contents of the others long ago—but this room had always been one of Leonie's favorites. The places on the walls where exquisite paintings had once hung were very apparent from the difference in color, but overall it was still a pleasant room, the carpet a warm shade of cream, almost yellow, the chairs of burgundy velvet, and the drapes at the windows in the same color and material giving it a striking appearance.

Zut! But this was a nasty coil, Leonie mused unhappily as she sat staring blankly into space. *Grand-père* was *so* stubborn at times! *I must think of something soon,* she

37

decided grimly, after several minutes of furious concentration. *And the first thing is those damnable vowels grandpère has signed to Monsieur Gayoso!*

Her little face somber with determination, she reviewed the situation and found it just as daunting as ever. Surprisingly, the proposed marriage was the least of Leonie's concerns—at the moment the most important things in her mind were saving Château Saint-André and, somehow, miraculously retrieving her grandfather's gaming vowels—which would be nearly impossible. But if she could prevent *grand-père* from signing *more* vowels . . . or, and she sat up alertly, if there were some way of getting her hands on any *new* vowels he might sign!

Mon Dieu! If only I could! she thought fiercely. If only there was some way of snatching those little pieces of paper that would ultimately spell final ruin for them all. She frowned, unconsciously tapping her lips with one finger. *What if I were to follow grand-père to the governor's tonight? Bah! And do what, you stupid creature—beg the governor not to accept your grandfather's vowels?*

Leonie shuddered. No, she couldn't do that, not only would her grandfather *never* forgive her, but she wasn't so certain she could forgive herself for shaming Claude so. *But I must do something!* she cried silently.

If only grand-père would forget about this silly idea of marriage . . . the money he was determined to throw away on a husband could be put to so much better use, if he would only listen. And not continue to gamble, she added glumly. If he would just stay at the Château and oversee his lands, or let her do so, they could manage. . . . They could sell the townhouse, for despite its faded air the house and land it sat upon were valuable, and from its sale, not even touching the dowry, they could gain time . . . and who knows what would happen in a year or two? A few years of judicious economy and good crops, and they would be safe for a while. Not wealthy, not even well-to-do, but at least they would have their lands and their situation would be much better. *Anything* would be better than the current state of affairs, Leonie told herself cynically.

For just a moment she thought about the marriage that Claude was so set on. *What would* that *accomplish,* she wondered scornfully. *Absolutely nothing but to waste more good money!* Mon Dieu, *but I could shake* grand-père! *If he thinks I will tamely submit to his dictates . . . ha!* Briefly she imagined herself and the unknown Monsieur Slade standing before the priest as he read them their vows. *Grand-père* would be there, Yvette, Monsieur Slade's family, and perhaps a few of the good sisters from the Ursuline convent would also be witnesses. But witness to what? Leonie giggled, picturing the expression on everyone's face when she suddenly threw herself on the mercy of the startled priest and begged dramatically for sanctuary for her herself and Yvette! She smiled to herself, the green eyes dancing with amusement. *And I'd do it,* she vowed passionately. *If* grand-père *forces me to, I shall do it!*

The problem of the destestable marriage solved for the moment, Leonie once again turned her thought to her most pressing problem. Knowing, in view of their exchange this afternoon, that her grandfather was going to gamble with a reckless abandon tonight, if for no other reason than to prove to her that *no one* told Claude Saint-André what to do, she must think of a way either to stop him or to find a method of redeeming the vowels he would sign.

There must be a way, she thought stubbornly, unwilling to admit to defeat. A timid knock on the door interrupted her thoughts and scowling blackly she snapped, "Who is it?"

The door opened slightly and Yvette peeked her dark head around the edge, "It is only me. Has your *grand-père* gone?"

Leonie made a face and muttered, *"Oui!* And a good thing too—he is impossible today!"

Yvette sent her a gentle smile. "I think he is *always* impossible! What did he do this time?"

Leonie made some reply, but she did not tell Yvette the real reason, just as she had not told Yvette of her grandfather's ultimatum. She had not held back the information from any attempt to deceive Yvette, but rather to protect the girl. Yvette was such a sweet, unassuming soul that if she had the slightest idea that Claude was using her as a weapon against Leonie, she would promptly remove herself from Claude's area of influence. *And to do what?* Leo-

39

nie had thought affectionately, *find herself in practically the same situation that I am trying to keep her from.* Non! *Yvette must not know. I will think of something!*

Yvette's presence in New Orleans had been tacitly and mutually agreed upon between Leonie and her grandfather. Neither one trusted the other not to take advantage of Yvette's unprotected state while the two principals were away from the plantation. At the moment, Yvette represented a treasure to Leonie and Claude, and neither one was about to leave it lying carelessly about for the other to snatch away. At least with Yvette here where she could see her at any time, Leonie felt a little safer. If Claude did try anything underhanded she would know immediately, but if Yvette had been left at Château Saint-André, it might be days before Leonie would learn that her grandfather had spirited the girl away—something Leonie wasn't about to let happen.

She thought for a moment of warning Yvette, but afraid Yvette would do something noble and completely unnecessary, Leonie stilled the words and continued to hide the true state of affairs from her half-sister. Besides, there was the fact that she didn't want to alarm Yvette and have Yvette spend the following days fearing the outcome of the latest battle between Leonie and her grandfather. *If only Yvette were more like me,* Leonie decided regretfully, *we could give* grand-père *a fight he would remember for a long time.*

Yvette took a chair opposite Leonie's and said earnestly, "Leonie, what is it? I know you are hiding something from me. What did you two argue about this time?"

"Money, as usual. I cannot seem to make *grand-père* understand that he is driving us deeper into debt. That if only he would stop gaming, we would not be in such straightened circumstances," Leonie answered glibly, glad that she could tell part of the truth.

"And did he listen?"

Leonie shrugged her slim shoulders. "He listened and then stalked out in a black fury! He still thinks that one of these days he will begin to win." Cynically she added, "When one needs to win, one never does. And when one has all the money they could wish for . . . *then* one wins!"

A depressing silence fell between them, but as Leonie's spirits were never dampened for more than a few minutes, she suddenly jumped up from her chair and said briskly, "Bah! What silly little fools we are to sit around looking so gloomy! Come, let us go out into the courtyard—the sun is shining, and I'm certain I can wheedle some lemonade and pralines out of Berthe in the kitchen."

A few minutes later the two of them were seated under the huge, old pecan tree that shaded the bricked courtyard, and sipping the cool, refreshing lemonade and nibbling at the rich, sugary pieces of praline candy, Leonie instantly felt more confident than she had in days. Startling Yvette, who was staring dreamily off into space, she said suddenly, "I shall follow him tonight!"

"Your *grand-père?*" Yvette offered hesitently. And at Leonie's vigorous nod, she asked with bewilderment, "But why? What can you do?"

Leonie slowly bit into the brown sugar confection. "I don't know," she answered honestly, "but I simply cannot sit here and let him continue to do as he pleases. I must find a way to stop him from throwing away what little money we have left."

"But, Leonie, you can't go about following your *grand-père* like a shadow! Something could happen to you—he goes places that you should not even know about, much less see. He is gone all night—you cannot mean to roam the streets of New Orleans by yourself after dark! It is dangerous!" Seeing that her very proper and common-sense words were having no affect on her volatile half-sister, Yvette asked desperately, "What do you think you can accomplish? What good can come of your rash actions? What do you think you can do?"

Leonie's face was set in stubborn lines and grimly she replied, "I'll think of something—I *have* to!"

4

Despite Yvette's pleas and arguments to the contrary, Leonie remained adamant in her determination to follow her grandfather that night. Nothing Yvette could say dissuaded Leonie and finally in exasperation Yvette had cried angrily, "You are very like your *grand-père!* You are just as stubborn and selfish as he is!"

Leonie had considered the remark seriously for a few moments and then returned thoughtfully, *"Non!* Stubborn, yes! But selfish, no!"

Her temper roused as it seldom was, Yvette had glared at Leonie and with a very good imitation of Leonie's own expression of disgust, she had muttered, "Ah, bah! Do it then, see if I care." And with her head held high she had marched out of the room.

Yvette's unexpected fit of temper did not distress Leonie—she was as aware as her half-sister of the danger involved in what she planned to do, and she didn't blame Yvette for being furious. *But it has to be done,* Leonie told herself resolutely. *We can afford no further debts!*

She had changed her gown for one of dark brown cotton, deciding that if she was to be lurking in the shadows at the governor's residence she would be better off in darker clothes. Unfortunately, like so many of Leonie's gowns, this one too had been outgrown. Her firm young bosom rose above what had once been a demure neckline; it seemed if she took a deep breath her breasts would burst from the material. Her hair was still neatly coiled and pinned to the top of her head, but she had removed her slippers in anticipation of following her grandfather when he left the house.

It was a common practice for the ladies of New Orleans

to walk barefooted through the muddy or dusty streets until they reached their destination. Once there, servants would wash and dry their feet, and then the ladies would put on their silken stockings and delicate satin slippers to dance the night away. Leonie had no intention of dancing, but she was definitely aware of the wisdom of going barefoot—there had been a thundershower earlier and the black loam of the streets would be like a thick grease.

Leonie's estimation of her grandfather's reaction to their conversation earlier in the day had been entirely correct, and he had spent the remaining hours until he left for the governor's residence at Toulouse and Levee Streets, drinking and brooding in a small, shabbily furnished room at the rear of the house.

By the time Claude, nattily attired, as always left the house a few hours after sunset, he was in a dangerous frame of mind and full of the bravado found so easily in a bottle of fine French brandy. He owed money all over New Orleans—the tradesmen were beginning to object to more credit and even his devoted tailor had suggested recently that some payment be made on his bill. But Claude was confident tonight—soon their trials would be over! Leonie watched him go from her window on the second story of the house, the expression on her young face grim and determined.

Aware that his destination was the governor's residence just a short distance from their own house on Toulouse Street, Leonie did not immediately follow her grandfather but let several hours pass before she snatched up her old reticule and slipped out of the house. It was a little unnerving, even she would admit, to walk alone down the streets of New Orleans after dark; the only light, and frail light it was, came from an occasional oil lamp that had been hung from wooden posts at the order of Gayoso's predecessor, the Baron de Carondelet. Fortunately this was an area of fine houses and respectable people and she arrived at the Gayoso residence without incident.

Unlike Claude having reached her destination Leonie did not enter Gayoso's house from the front; instead, moving like a small shadow in the darkness of the warm, muggy night, she prowled around the back alley searching for an entrance to the rear of the building. She eventually found one through the governor's stables. Creeping silently and breathlessly between the rows of restive horses, and cautiously pushing open a door at one side of the stables, she found herself, to her immense satisfaction, in a small courtyard at the side of the house.

Having come this far without any unpleasantness and unchallenged, Leonie sighed with relief and leaned back gratefully against one of the cool walls of the courtyard, her heart thumping just a little at her brazen actions, one slim hand unconsciously clasping her mother's gold crucifix. If she were caught lurking like a criminal in Governor Gayoso's courtyard . . . *Mon Dieu,* it didn't bear thinking about! Impatiently Leonie pushed aside any thought of failure, and keeping herself in the shadows, she inched her way nearer to the house.

The governor's courtyard was not large, compared to the rambling courtyard at the Saint-André townhouse, but the house itself was easily three times the size of the Saint-André residence; and looking at its sheer size and the lights that streamed out into the darkness from the various windows, Leonie felt her heart sink. The one-story structure resembled a commodious inn more than a dwelling, and the narrow courtyard where Leonie stood ran along one side; against the other was a low gallery screened by latticework. How was she to find out in which room her grandfather was gaming—and what good would it do her?

Slightly daunted by these uncertainties, Leonie hesitated, actually considering going no farther. Should she continue . . . or go back to the townhouse and accept defeat? *Non!* she thought vehemently. She would not give up without having at least attempted to do *something! What* she was going to do was the problem.

Edging closer to the house, her dark brown gown blending easily into the shadows of the narrow courtyard, Leonie stopped when she reached the corner of the house, her eyes giving the silent courtyard a quick, uneasy assessment. *Bon!* All was well . . . so far.

Having come this far, there was nothing else to do *but* continue, she told herself sternly and warily approached

44

the first window. Carefully she peered around the edge of it and was uncertain whether she was disappointed or cheered to see two women seated comfortably on a sofa busily plying their needles.

It was the third window that brought her at last to the room where the gentleman of the house and his guests were enjoying their cigarillos, whiskey, and cards. Leonie felt her heart leap in her breast when she peeked in and saw her grandfather facing her direction, as he sat at a round, mahogany table concentrating on the cards he held in his hand. Even though this was the room she had been looking for, it was a shock, and a small exclamation of surprise escaped her lips.

The window was open, and a tall, black-haired gentleman with his back to Leonie suddenly lifted his head and asked in a deep voice, "Did you hear something?"

All three of the other men, including Leonie's grandfather, glanced up from their cards, and after a long, agonizing moment for Leonie, Gayoso said lightly, "You are hearing things, *amigo*. Or do you think to distract us from our cards, *sí?*"

The tall man laughed, "Hardly! You are too clever for that ploy, I can assure you."

The gentlemen then went back to the game, and with a silent sigh of relief Leonie sank down to the ground outside the window. Now that she had found her grandfather, what was she to do—burst in and demand that Gayoso and his friends not continue to accept his company? she thought half-hysterically.

Still, Leonie was feeling just a little pleased with herself at having succeeded so effortlessly in discovering her grandfather's whereabouts in the governor's residence. And now all that remained was for her to come up with some plan to accomplish—what? She bit her lip, and then squirmed around and took another peek, just as her grandfather pushed across a slip of paper to a smiling Gayoso.

Her sense of pleasure evaporated and she felt a spurt of rage dart through her, as she noticed the pile of vowels in front of the governor and the unpalatable fact that her grandfather was very drunk indeed. The Governor's face was in profile to her, but Leonie decided there was something exceedingly sinister about his smile and had a sudden urge to throw something at him.

She sank back down again, trembling with anger. It was robbery! All three of those men at the table with her grandfather knew he was in no condition to play cards for money and yet they allowed him to do so. It was criminal! She looked again and was further infuriated to see another vowel from her grandfather join the previous one. Covertly she eyed the pile of papers and money in front of the governor. How much of it was her grandfather's? And more importantly, how was she going to get it back?

Frowning fiercely she glared around the shadowy courtyard, as if an answer to her question were out there taunting her in the darkness. After several minutes of wild schemes and improbable plans she came to one desperate decision—*I shall steal the vouchers from the governor! He is stealing from* grand-père *and it is only fair that I steal them back! I shall do it!*

Having come to a decision, she settled back against the wall of the house, aware that the party must disperse before she could even attempt her reckless plan. She would have to discover where the governor put the vowels and then at the first opportunity, nip into the house, steal them and depart—all undetected, she admitted glumly; not an easy task. But Leonie was determined and so she sat like a still little shadow and waited impatiently for the gentlemen to end their evening. Occasionally she would risk a glance through the open window, and it seemed, at least to her, that every time she did, her grandfather was pushing another vowel across the table to the blandly smiling Gayoso. *Zut! Do they never tire of this silliness?* she asked herself disgustedly, as the hour drew near to midnight and still they showed no signs of growing weary of cards and liquor.

As the hours slowly passed, her lids grew heavy and she had to suppress a mighty yawn more than once. Sleepy and just a little bored, her thoughts drifted from the coming theft of the vowels and she wondered if her grandfather had indeed spoken to Monsieur Slade. Was he one of the men in the room? She took another glance inside the room, deciding that the florid, bluff, heavyset man across from

46

Gayoso could not possibly be Monsieur Slade—he was too old, at least forty . . . and fat! But the man with his back to her, was he possibly Monsieur Slade?

He was tall and his shoulders were broad. His hair was black, his head well-shaped—what Leonie could see of it— and his voice was deep and pleasant. She chewed at her lip a while and then decided against him. *Non,* he was not Monsieur Slade. And her reasoning? Last night Monsieur Slade had stopped the party when it became obvious her grandfather was too drunk to continue, but tonight, when her grandfather was just as obviously too drunk to continue, this man did not.

Leonie's reasoning was drastically wrong, because the dark-haired man with his back to her was, indeed, Monsieur Slade. And his reasons for not stopping the gaming were simple—upon closer association it was easily discernible that Claude Saint-André was clearly a habitual drunk, a compulsive gambler, and a man who did not take kindly to the interference of strange young men, if his sometimes belligerent attitude this evening was anything to go by.

Ordinarily, though, Morgan still might have made some effort to see that Saint-André was not taken advantage of by Gayoso, but his mind was on other things. More specifically his thoughts were dwelling on the bluff, heavyset man that Leonie had so unflatteringly dismissed only moments before—General James Wilkinson of the United States Army.

Wilkinson's inclusion in the evening's entertainment had been a decidedly unpleasant surprise for Morgan. He had not been aware that the general was in New Orleans, and if he had known he certainly would not have accepted under any conditions, Gayoso's invitation, knowing full well that eventually it would result in a social meeting with Wilkinson—a meeting Morgan would have done much to avoid. He might have a certain wariness in dealing with Gayoso, but so far as Wilkinson was concerned, Morgan trusted the man no further than an inch; in fact he cordially disliked the general for a number of reasons. If some of Gayoso's dealings didn't bear close scrutiny, there

47

wasn't one of Wilkinson's schemes and double-dealing that didn't eventually produce a most noxious odor.

Wilkinson's appearance at the Spanish governor's residence here in New Orleans and the obvious air of intimacy between the two men—in view of Gayoso's outspoken hostility towards Phillip Nolan, Wilkinson's reputed protégé—only increased Morgan's suspicions that Wilkinson was up to no good. Or was it Gayoso who was up to no good? Morgan couldn't quite decide, but behind the deceptively lazy gaze of those vivid blue eyes his keen brain was effectively weighing up the situation, trapping every movement, every look, every nuance of the conversation for later consideration.

Gayoso had given the distinct impression that Wilkinson's arrival at his home this evening had been entirely unexpected, and yet Morgan couldn't shake the feeling that the meeting between the two men had been prearranged. And if it had been, why were the two of them acting as if it hadn't?

Despite the general's presence, the evening was passing pleasantly for Morgan. Wilkinson *did* have an easy manner about him, Gayoso was always good company, and even drunk and occasionally surly Claude Saint-André proved to be enjoyable company. But as midnight came and went, if Morgan could have politely ended the evening, he would have. All three of his companions were several years his senior and he had little, if anything, in common with them.

Ruefully, Morgan admitted that it would have been wiser to have called upon his friend Jason Savage first, rather than the governor. Jason's brand of entertainment was far more to his liking. There was hardly a year's difference in ages between Jason and himself, and they had attended school together at Harrow; consequently Morgan would have been much more at ease in Jason's company. Tomorrow, he promised himself, he would diplomatically thank the governor for his hospitality and then efficiently remove himself to the Beauvais Plantation to stay with Jason, as he had originally planned.

The conversation among the four men playing cards was light and inconsequential, the sort of polite, aimless discourse that takes place between people who are not well-acquainted, and Morgan discreetly swallowed a yawn as the tall clock of marquetry in the corner of the room struck the hour of two. Claude Saint-André, by now almost too drunk to function, was nodding over his cards, and Morgan felt pity stir within himself.

Throwing down an indifferent hand of cards, Morgan rose to his feet and said abruptly, "I hate to be the one to end what has been a pleasant evening, but I think I shall seek out my bed." Casting a considering eye towards the befuddled Saint-André, Morgan added, "I think that Monsieur Saint-André wishes to retire to his bed also."

Claude jerked up at mention of his name and blearily regarded the tall young man across the table from him. His brain moving in an alcoholic daze, the thought occurred to him that there had been something important he had wished to discuss with this young man, but what it had been temporarily escaped him. Staggering to his feet, Claude clutched the table for support and mumbled something about an enjoyable evening, thinking incoherently that tomorrow he must talk with this Monsieur Slade. It was important, that much he knew.

Gayoso, smiling as blandly as ever, rang for a servant and when the man arrived, requested that Monsieur Saint-André's servants be informed that their master was now ready to return home. There was idle conversation among the four men until Claude's servants were ushered in. Almost immediately Claude departed, his uncertain steps guided by the two Negro men who had done this task many a night in the past.

Wilkinson, his pale blue eyes contemptuous, said snidely, "I wonder at you, Manuel—keeping such company? Surely you could have found someone more worthy of our intellect than that poor speciman."

Gayoso's smile widened. "Perhaps, *amigo*, perhaps. But Monsieur Saint-André was once an extremely clever gambler, and I enjoy pitting myself against him." Almost smirking with satisfaction, one hand caressing the pile of vouchers, he added, "Sometimes he even wins, but"—with a laugh—"this is infrequent."

Wilkinson nodded his head knowingly and Morgan's

lips twisted in distaste. Hiding his emotion, he said carelessly, "Well, gentlemen, I must bid you good night." Then cocking his head in the direction of Wilkinson, he continued, "It was a pleasure meeting you again, sir." And lying even further, he finished, "I hope we shall meet again during my stay here in New Orleans."

"No doubt we shall, my boy!" Wilkinson returned jovially. "Some other time you can tell me about the latest happenings in Natchez."

Morgan gave a polite smile and turning once more to Gayoso, said, "Good evening, sir."

Gayoso, a knowing twinkle in his dark eyes, murmured, "It has been a dull evening for you, I think." And at Morgan's courteous denial, he added slyly, "But I can arrange for the remainder of it to be most enjoyable. A woman to warm your bed, perhaps . . . ?"

Morgan, intent upon leaving the room, made some noncommittal reply and the governor laughed and said, "You are very diplomatic, *amigo*. But I think, nonetheless, that I shall . . . later send along a little something to enliven the night for you, *si*?"

Morgan was smiling as he left the room, uncertain whether to accept the governor's offer or not. Stifling a yawn and thinking of the comfortable bed that awaited him, he decided he would let events take their course. The way he felt at the moment, when the woman did arrive, if she did, she would probably find him sound asleep, but one never knew. . . .

In the room that Morgan had just vacated a curiously hostile silence fell, and with a deliberate movement Gayoso took a sip of his brandy and then said, "Well, *amigo*, now that my guests have departed, it is time you and I had a serious discussion, *si*?"

Wilkinson, a wary expression in his eyes, muttered, "Do we have something serious to discuss?"

Gayoso's polite mask slipped, and making no effort to hide his displeasure, one fist smashed down on the table with a loud bang. "Yes, we do, *amigo*, as you well know! I think you forget that my country pays you very handsomely for the information you give us, and you have been attempting to cheat us . . . sending your *own* protégé, that Nolan, into our territory to spy on us! Explain yourself!"

The sound of Gayoso's fist on the table woke Leonie from her fitful doze outside the window, and with a jerk she came wide awake, the great cat eyes blinking in the darkness. Realizing with dismay that she had fallen asleep, she took a quick, surreptitious glance through the window. With relief she found that Gayoso and only one guest still remained—her grandfather and the other man must have departed while she slept. Anxiously she searched for the much-desired vouchers and the sight of them still in an untidy heap in front of the governor caused her heart to race uncomfortably. Soon, now, she must find a way into the governor's house and steal that pile of papers.

Inside the room, the Governor and Wilkinson eyed each other angrily across the table. Gayoso's swarthy face was flushed with temper as well as with the effects of the enormous quantities of liquor that had been consumed through the course of the evening, and there was a slight slur to his voice as he questioned harshly, "Well? Do you deny that Nolan is spying for you? And will you protest that Nolan's horse-hunting is really so that he can explore the country for you? To map it so that you might invade us?"

A brief look of fury crossed Wilkinson's face, but he veiled the telltale emotion so swiftly that Gayoso never saw it. Forcing himself to display an amicability that he didn't feel, Wilkinson leaned his large bulk back in his chair and said smoothly, "Come now, Manuel, you can't possibly believe that. I have been a good friend to Spain for years. Why would I want to jeopardize the gold your government so generously pays me? *Think,* man!"

Thoughtfully Gayoso viewed the other's ruddy features. Wilkinson *had* been a good friend to Spain in the past—he had passed on valuable information concerning the capabilities of various American forts along the borders between American and Spanish territory, he offered much advice on American politics, and he had even tried to break Kentucky away from the United States to have the state unite with Spain. Oh, Wilkinson had *indeed* been a good friend! But was he *now?* Gayoso wondered.

Reflectively, Gayoso admitted, "It is true you have aided

my country for a number of years, but I think only if it is to your advantage."

Wilkinson bristled. "Upon my honor, Gayoso! What sort of man do you take me for? My word is my bond and I have sworn to serve Spain! How can you doubt me?"

There was a note of sincerity in Wilkinson's voice and Gayoso was torn with indecision. Perhaps Wilkinson was innocent of any plotting; perhaps Nolan was the only culprit. His mistrust still obvious, Gayoso asked, "Do you deny that Nolan has been sending you information? Information that could be used to guide a large force of men through our lands? Information that a person interested in wresting huge tracts of land from Spain might find useful?"

Hiding his alarm and rage at the amount of information Gayoso seemed to have acquired, his jowly face the picture of outraged innocence, Wilkinson roared dramatically, "What a dastardly plot! Who dares to connect my name with such infamy? I tell you, Gayoso, I *will not* have it! My honor is well-known . . . and I will defend it with my life! Let me know the name of the blackguard who dares to besmirch not only my name but my honor as well and I shall prove to you who is really the villain!"

It was an impressive speech and Wilkinson did it well, his blue eyes sparkling with righteous indignation, his full cheeks bright red with the force of moral wrath, but Gayoso was not particularly awed. He had seen Wilkinson do the same thing on many another occasion, occasions when the good general had been lying through his teeth.

Outside, still propped against the wall, Leonie gave a mighty yawn and then sighed impatiently. *Mon Dieu!* Would those two *never* stop babbling and leave? The conversation came to Leonie as a low murmur of voices, except when she was actually looking in the window or when the voices of the two men inside were raised in anger, but it meant little to her. And as time passed, she grew more and more restless and disappointed. It was beginning to appear that her vigil had been in vain.

She had just taken another quick look and was almost on the point of admitting defeat when Gayoso picked up the pile of vouchers and his brandy snifter and, followed by the other man, disappeared through a doorway to Leonie's left. Galvanized into action, she swiftly ran along the side of the house until she came to the next window, and to her relief, once again had Gayoso and the vowels in view. Apparently this was his office at home; a huge, kneehole desk was placed near the wall farthest from Leonie, and from the litter of papers on the desk, it was obviously where the governor did a great deal of work. The room was attractively furnished with a thick carpet in tones of russet and olive-green covering the floor, and tall, channel-backed chairs in Spanish leather arranged here and there. The walls of the room were broken by the window, through which Leonie risked an occasional peek; the door near her, through which the men had entered from the card room, and another door next to the governor's desk that must lead to the main part of the house.

As Leonie dared another look, she saw the Governor lay the vowels on the corner of his desk and then pick up a nearby piece of paper. Almost contemptuously Gayoso thrust the paper at Wilkinson.

His eyes hard and unyielding, he demanded, "Will you deny that this was intended for you?"

Wilkinson glanced at it and then carelessly tossed it on the pile of vowels. "Absolutely! I don't even know what it means! I think it's *you*, Gayoso, who should do some explaining!" Wilkinson returned agressively. "I am an honorable friend of Spain, and *you* have made some vile implications . . . implications, I think, *you* should either prove or apologize for!"

Gayoso stiffened, and his voice hard with anger he snapped, "I do *not* apologize!" Controlling himself with an effort he said tightly, "Very recently, we have intercepted a messenger from Nolan and have discovered that he has been sending out information to someone in the United States." That Gayoso was certain Wilkinson was the person receiving Nolan's information was quite clear.

Glaring at the impassive Gayoso, Wilkinson's face was livid. Stuttering with outrage, he finally got out, "A-and y-you believe that I am the man he is sending this information to? Impossible! *I will not have it!*"

Gayoso looked at Wilkinson and asked mildly, "You are sure you do not recognize the map I just handed you?"

Wilkinson appeared to glance at the paper indifferently. Blustering he said, "It may be Nolan's work, but it has nothing to do with me!" And turning the attack he demanded, "What makes you think it was intended for me?"

Gayoso smiled thinly. "Everything, my dear General. Your fondness for Nolan is well-known, even if of late you have claimed differently."

Wilkinson continued to look outraged, and deciding it was time to let the general know just how much they knew of Nolan's activities, Gayoso murmured softly, "I think you should be aware of the fact that for the last three months I have had a spy in Nolan's midst." At Wilkinson's start, Gayoso continued dulcetly, "And my spy had informed me that he has seen Nolan making maps and that Nolan has spoken often of his important friend, General Wilkinson. He has even boasted that Wilkinson will decide the fate of Spanish land west of the Sabine River."

Wilkinson looked as if he were about to burst, his chest swelling out the front of his blue, gold-trimmed jacket, the buttons of his striped Marseilles waistcoat straining against the threads. His face was bright red and his voice trembled with fury as he snarled, "Ridiculous! This is all a pack of lies! It is the most errant nonsense I have heard in my life!" Staring hard at Gayoso he demanded, "You can't believe this farrago! My God, man, it is beyond belief!"

"We shall see," Gayoso replied imperturbably.

Genuinely frightened and disturbed, Wilkinson leaned over Gayoso's desk and exhorted him. "Believe me, Manuel, I know nothing of this! You must believe me!"

Gayoso looked pensive. "I really don't know what to believe," he said at last. "You are a devious man, I think."

Leonie taking a swift peek through the window was cheered to see that the conversation seemed to be ending. *Bon!* Surely they would part now? *And oh, please, dear God, let the governor leave the vowels precisely where they are,* she prayed fervently.

Her prayers were answered. Gayoso stood up from his desk and began to walk towards the door near Leonie. She crouched down again, her blood beginning to race.

54

Gayoso stopped at the doorway and said to Wilkinson, "I shall have to consider all the facts before I make my report to the viceroy. But at this moment, I should warn you that I do not think it will be favorable to you." Gayoso continued into the card room, his voice drifting back to the infuriated Wilkinson.

Wilkinson stood silently by the desk for a moment, his face twisted by hate and fear. Covertly he eyed the map near the vowels and, unable to prevent himself, he swiftly reached out and grabbed it, stuffing the map hastily into his vest pocket as Gayoso stuck his head through the doorway and asked, "Bring me my brandy, will you? It is there on the desk, and then come here and explain to me further why I should believe you."

The direction of Wilkinson's hand changed slightly and almost viciously he grabbed the delicate snifter of brandy. For a second he stared at the brandy swirling in the bottom of the glass, and then, with an ugly smile twitching his small mouth, he reached inside his vest pocket and stealthily brought out a little white packet. He threw a quick glance to the doorway where Gayoso had disappeared and then emptied the contents of the packet into the brandy. Giving the snifter a few twirls he walked slowly towards the doorway. Write the viceroy, would he? Destroy his reputation with Spain, would he? Wilkinson smiled. *No.* The governor was about to learn that *no one* crossed Wilkinson!

Hearing no more sounds from the room, Leonie took another look and seeing the empty room, felt her spirits rise. At last, her moment had come! *Grand-père's* gaming losses for tonight were as good as hers!

Holding her breath, she cautiously tested the window and to her delight discovered that it was unlocked. Slowly she pushed it open and then silently, her heart pounding frantically in her breast, she nimbly climbed into the room.

She let out her breath in a small gasp as she realized she had to walk past the open doorway where she could see the governor and the general still talking. For a minute she stared at the two men. The governor seeming to be acting strangely, his face contorting as if in great pain, but the fat man seemed unconcerned.

Tearing her eyes away from the scene in the next room, she crossed her fingers and quick as a cat she slipped passed the doorway. No cry of discovery followed her and with legs that trembled she hurried to the governor's desk. With fingers shaking so badly she could barely control them, she snatched up the pile of papers and stuffed them into her reticule.

Elation shot through her body. She *had* the vouchers! A grin beginning to curve her mouth, she had just started towards the window when, to her horror, she heard someone approaching the door that was between her and her avenue of escape.

Terrified she looked around for a place to hide. There was nothing to hide behind, and giving into sheer panic, she bolted out the door by the governor's desk into the main hallway of the house.

Her eyes wide with apprehension, her heart lodged somewhere in the vicinity of her throat, and the reticule clutched tightly in her hands, Leonie glanced wildly about, seeking either escape or a hiding place. Neither appeared immediately at hand.

Being in a long corridor and afraid to stay there, she took off in what she hoped was the direction that would lead her to the rear of the house. Her feet made no sound as she scampered down the carpeted hallway; the light from the candles in the carved and painted wall sconces guided her way. The hallway seemed to go on forever with turnings this way and that, until Leonie was thoroughly disoriented.

Mon Dieu! I am lost inside the governor's residence, she thought with a nervous, frightened giggle. She finally stopped her headlong rush, some modicum of common sense returning.

Think, Leonie, think! she told herself. *How are you to get out?* She had passed several shut doors but was reluctant to see what was on the other side, for obvious reasons. And yet she dared not stay forever in the middle of the governor's hall.

The sound of an opening door behind her decided the

question. Without thinking, her mouth dry as dust, Leonie simply leaped blindly through the doorway of the room nearest her. *Pray God it is empty,* she thought earnestly.

5

It wasn't. But Leonie didn't know that as she stood with her back against the door, her heart pounding painfully in her chest.

The room was in darkness, a pitch-black gloom meeting Leonie's gaze. She let her breath out in a long, shuddering sigh, giving up a small prayer of thankfulness that her luck had held and she had found herself in an empty room. An empty room with a pair of French doors, which seemed to offer an avenue of escape. She had just taken one step towards the doors when a man's voice froze her in her tracks.

"I was wondering if Gayoso had forgotten about me," Morgan said lazily as he reached out to touch Leonie, thinking she was the woman that Gayoso had offered.

Sleep had been the only thought on Morgan's mind when he had entered his room, but after stripping off his evening clothes and lying naked on the bed in the darkness, he had found his thoughts straying down a forbidden path. Stephanie's face swam in front of his eyes, her mouth laughing at him, her body taunting him, and then horrifyingly, Phillippe's dead form was suddenly there before him. With a curse, he had risen from the bed and slipped on his black velvet robe.

A stiff brandy from the decanter on a small table near the French doors did little to soothe the ache in his heart or to calm his anger against his dead wife. With a vicious movement he poured another brandy and swallowed it swiftly, the slow burn of the liquid as it slid down his throat helping to drive out the unwanted memories.

Sleep was impossible for the moment, and needing some way to vent the bitter emotions that ate at his vitals, he wished for the first time that he had told Gayoso to send a woman. A woman had caused his pain; another woman could give him temporary oblivion.

He had just set the brandy snifter down and had walked across the room to put on some clothes and go in search of company, when Leonie had entered the room. Morgan had no clear picture of her, just a glimpse of tawny hair and a firm bosom bursting from the confines of the dark gown she wore. It was enough, though, in his present state of mind—whores did have their uses, he thought cynically as he walked towards the woman and had spoken the words that sent Leonie's heart leaping in her throat.

Precisely what he had meant, Leonie wasn't certain— she only knew she wanted out of this room and out of the governor's residence *immediately!* Clutching the reticule tightly in her hand, she made a desperate, valiant attempt to bluff her way clear. Stammering in her nervousness, she stammered out, "Oh! *M-m-monsieur,* y-y-you frightened me! I-I-I think I must be in the wrong room. I-I-I shall leave at once."

Morgan's hand reached out of the darkness and lightly touched Leonie's shoulder, and she nearly jumped out of her skin. He felt the start she gave and he laughed softly, "Don't be nervous, *petite,* I won't hurt you. And believe me, if Gayoso sent you, you *are* in the right room." He started to turn away from a paralyzed Leonie, saying, "Let me light a candle so we have some idea who we're talking to."

Leonie's strangled, *"Don't!"* stopped him instantly.

Swinging back to her in the darkness, he put his hands on either side of her shoulders and murmured softly, "Well, that's fine with me, if you prefer it." His voice suddenly growing husky at the memory of the sight of those tempting white breasts above her gown, he said, "You prefer to remain a mystery woman, then?"

Leonie swallowed painfully, too conscious of the man in front of her and of his hands that could so easily hold her prisoner. Still fencing for time, still not quite certain where this curious conversation was leading, she muttered, "Believe me, *monsieur,* I am a mystery woman, and I shall always be one. If *monsieur* will allow me, I—" Leonie had intended to inform Morgan that she would leave, but Morgan wasn't interested in talking and his mouth found hers.

Leonie's mouth was soft with surprise and astonishment as Morgan's lips slowly explored hers, but then as the impact of what he was doing suddenly exploded through her brain, she jerked her head back and burst out with a shocked, *"Monsieur!* What do you think you are doing?"

If Gayoso hadn't implied he would send a woman to his room, if Morgan's head had been clear of the alcohol he had consumed during the evening, and if he hadn't just been thinking of his dead wife, the fact that this woman was acting extremely oddly for a whore might have occurred to him. But as it was, he was certain she was merely playing a game with him, teasing him for her own purposes, and jerking her into his arms he said against her mouth, "I think we've wasted long enough on the introductions. Remain a mystery if you wish, but for God's sake quit acting so damned coy!"

Leonie didn't have time to give her indignant reply, for Morgan's mouth came down on hers once more and this time there was no escape, his lips ruthlessly parting hers as his tongue, like a dart of flame, plundered her unprepared mouth. Stunned by the intimacy of the kiss— nothing in her life, so far, having given her any indication that this was the way of a man with a woman—Leonie stood momentarily motionless, her hands trapped between their bodies. She had never had this close contact with a man before in her life, and as Morgan's mouth possessed hers, his hands holding her prisoner against him, she became conscious of a number of things about a man. For one thing, he was infinitely stronger than a woman, which she discovered instantly when she tried to free herself from this unwelcome embrace; for another, he smelled faintly of tobacco and brandy, and for another, soft hair grew on his muscled chest—she could feel it brushing her breasts where they rose above her gown.

As this stranger in this darkened room of the governor's residence hungrily possessed Leonie's mouth, his arm slipped around her waist, pulling her even closer to his warm body, and his other hand slid up her neck, his fingers deftly undoing the pins that held the tawny mane captive. Released from its confines the bright hair cascaded down around her shoulders, and leaving her mouth for a moment, the man buried his face in the sweet-smelling strands of hair.

"Lovely, lovely," he murmured into the soft curls, his hand gently, persuasively kneading her neck. His lips traveling back across her cheek, searching for her mouth, he muttered, "Jesus! Am I grateful that Gayoso sent you to me! Come along, sweetheart, let's see just how pleasantly we can spend the rest of the evening."

Most of what this unknown man said made little sense to Leonie, and she was so frightened and bewildered by what was happening that for just a few minutes she had been almost paralyzed with shock, her brain numb with fear. But when he suddenly swept her up in his arms and began to carry her across the room, she was instantly galvanized with terror and determination. *"Non!* Monsieur put me down! There is some mistake . . . you do not understand," she cried angrily, some of her fear evaporating as her ready temper rose.

The man laughed. "The only mistake, *petite,* would be if I didn't do precisely what I intend to. And the only thing I don't understand is why you persist in this game." He kissed her hard on the mouth and added, "But it is a delightful game; play it if you wish."

The darkness of the room hid their features from one another, Leonie was aware only that the man was tall and strong, his skin was warm to her touch, and his voice was cultured and deep. A pleasing voice, she would have thought under different circumstances, but just now, when one of his hands strayed to her breasts and took shocking liberties, she was both frightened and furious. As for Morgan, he had an advantage over Leonie—he had seen a brief glimpse of her hair and body before she had entered the room, though he had no idea what her face looked like. She was soft, she was small, and the feel of her in his arms was incredibly desirable, his body hardening as she struggled against him.

One hand slipped inside the neckline of her gown and, finding her nipple his fingers gently rolled and caressed it, the feel of a man's hand on her breast sending an odd

61

quiver through Leonie's entire body. *"Mon Dieu!"* she gasped. "What are you doing to me?"

Morgan laughed, and leaving her nipple his fingers were suddenly busy with the fastenings of her gown. Before Leonie guessed what he was about, she discovered her gown was being swiftly and efficiently taken off.

Everything was happening too fast for her to comprehend quickly; new emotions were fighting with the urge to escape and the fear of discovery. She was frightened, she was angry, and she was being plunged into sensations she wasn't prepared for. And being Leonie she reacted the only way she knew how—she fought.

Unfortunately, her opponent was too intent upon possessing the firm young body that strained against his to question her struggles and he was far too strong to be stopped by her frantic thrashing and poundings. His robe had joined her gown and chemise on the floor by the bed and in a matter of seconds his hard warm body was pressed intimately against Leonie's.

For Leonie it was a disturbing experience. She was frightened, she was furious, her emotions were in a jumble—one part of her curious at her body's reactions to the intimacies this strange man was taking, another part of her horrified and repulsed, and yet another part strangely aroused by his touch.

What precisely went on between a man and a woman had never been explained to Leonie. Who had there ever been to tell her—the cook at Château Saint-André? her grandfather? But that didn't mean she didn't have some idea what was happening. She had grown up exploring the swamps near Château Saint-André and she had seen the spring matings of the animals that inhabited the watery woodlands, as well as the procreation of the livestock at the plantation. But that scant knowledge did nothing to prepare her for what this stranger was doing to her.

His mouth seemed everywhere, even on her breasts, and his hands were even more bold and brazen as they roamed her body. Her struggles to free herself seemed to please him rather than the opposite; as she arched up against his chest to escape the caress of his hand, it traveled down her back to curve around one firm buttock and pull her even closer to him. With amazement and shock Leonie felt a warm shaft of flesh press insistently against her stomach, and despite the welter of emotions that rioted in her breasts, she felt a queer jolt of pleasure shoot through her veins. *What is happening to me?* she wondered in a daze. And then she stiffened with shock when one of his hands slipped between her thighs and touched her gently there, where her thighs joined her body.

Morgan was a practiced lover and knew what he was doing, and as his fingers caressed and explored Leonie there, a small pant of pleasure and surprise escaped from her. "Ah, *monsieur* . . ." she cried softly, and Morgan knew he couldn't wait much longer before taking her.

His lips caught hers in a deep, probing kiss and gently he shifted his weight, his knees nudging hers apart as his body slid between her thighs. His hands lifted her hips slightly, and then with a groan of pleasure, he buried himself in the soft, warm flesh of the woman beneath him.

Leonie felt one sharp stab of pain, which instantly subsided into a dull ache as the man moved upon her, his body thrusting urgently into hers. Stunned, almost unable to believe what was happening to her, she lay with an unnatural placidness beneath him, so staggered and devastated by what was taking place that she could no longer fight this unknown man who had just taken her virginity.

That the woman didn't respond while he took his pleasure came as no surprise to Morgan—few whores did more than just lend their bodies for a man's use, and he assumed that was what this particular whore was doing at the moment. But her body was so warm and sweet that he didn't want to believe that of this one, and with a strange compulsion his lips crushed hers even more passionately, his hands tightening with exquisite enjoyment around the firm young hips.

The initial shock and horror of this forceful taking of her body was fading, and when Morgan's hands tightened around her hips, Leonie began to struggle once again, her body surging up to meet his, to throw him off of her if she could. Frantically she tried to free her mouth, twisting her head from side to side, but it was no use; then furiously she beat her small fists against his bare shoulders, but that too was no use.

For Morgan, the thrashings of the warm, silken body beneath him were suddenly more than he could bear, and with a long, shuddering moan, he released himself into the woman. Satiated and yet curiously dissatisfied, he slid off her body, wondering if he would ever again experience the exquisite fulfillment that had been his during the first years of his marriage. Then his mouth hardened and he cursed under his breath. God damnit! Would he *ever* stop thinking of Stephanie?

And because he was angry and disgusted with himself, his voice was harsh as he said, "You can leave now. There is some gold on the chest near the door, you can have it all."

Leonie was already in motion before Morgan spoke and she slid from the bed, scrambling frantically around in the darkness for her clothes. Finding them, she dragged the clothes on with shaking fingers and wasted just a moment longer to grope around in the blackness for her reticule with the precious vowels, which had fallen to the floor when this abominable blackguard had swung her up into his arms. As for his gold . . . with a glitter in the sea-green eyes, she stalked to the chest and blindly reached for the coins that were there. Her fingers closed around the gold and with short, jerky movements she came near the bed again.

She could barely make out his dark shape as he lay there on the bed, but taking good aim, she flung the coins with all her might in the direction of his face and spat, *"Keep your damned gold! You haven't enough to pay me for what you did!"* Then spinning on her heels, she tore over to the French doors, wrenched them open, and ran out into the night.

The coins stung as they hit his face, and with a snarl of pain and growing anger, Morgan sprang up and raced to the French doors through which the woman had disappeared. She was nowhere in sight as he looked out into the courtyard, and shaking his head, he walked slowly back to his bed. *Who could understand women?* he thought with puzzlement. The amount of gold on the chest had been more than generous so it wasn't because he had underpaid her. So why?

Almost absently he lit a candle that was on a small table near his bed and surveyed the room. His robe lay in a black heap where he had thrown it, but it was the gleam of the fine gold chain against its darkness that drew him. Bending over he picked up the chair and discovered an intricate, unusually fashioned crucifix hanging from it.

Thoughtfully he regarded it, and remembering the struggle as they had undressed, he decided it must belong to his little whore. He smiled, remembering her fit of temper, and was intrigued in spite of himself—whores did not refuse money, and few wore costly gold crucifixes. He came to the conclusion that he would like to see this increasingly fascinating little creature who had briefly shared his bed.

He turned away, intending to snuff out the candle, when his gaze fell upon the bed, his eyes widening with shock as he surveyed the telltale bloodstains. *Well, I'll be damned,* he thought half-angrily. *A virgin! No wonder she didn't take the gold!*

Then he frowned. What the hell was Gayoso doing providing virgins for casual guests? And why had the girl agreed to it, only to throw his money back into his face?

The thought that he had so carelessly taken the girl left Morgan unsettled and vaguely regretful. He hadn't been particularly brutal in his lovemaking, but if he had known she were a virgin, he might have taken more time and been less concerned with his own pleasure. And then again, if he had known, he might not have taken her at all—virgins being firmly connected in his mind with marriage. He was definitely not the type of man to roam the countryside with a view to deflowering every maiden who appeared on his horizon. If anything he held the opposite view—an experienced woman was far less trouble and could give a man a far more enjoyable evening. No, Morgan definitely did not hunger after virgins, his one virgin until tonight having been his wife, and he would have been perfectly content to keep it that way.

Feeling somehow that he had been betrayed, Morgan snuffed out the candle and went back to bed. *Jesus, but I'll be glad to leave here and see Jason tomorrow! And Gayoso is going to have some explaining to do,* he thought sleepily.

But in the morning when Morgan woke, he discovered that Gayoso was never going to explain anything to anyone again—the governor had died during the night.

Dumbfounded and disturbed by the news, any thought of a novice whore vanished from his mind. Feeling decidedly *de trop* in the face of Gayoso's unexpected and tragic death, as soon as he had paid his condolences to the governor's grieving widow, Morgan had vacated the premises and headed immediately to the Beauvais townhouse on the chance that Jason was staying in the city. He wasn't, but that news didn't perturb Morgan—he had been fairly certain that his friend would be at the Beauvais plantation. Without further waste of time, he hired a carriage and made arrangements for his things to be picked up at the governor's residence and delivered to the Beauvais plantation. Then riding a hired hack, he set out for Beauvais himself.

A long drive, lined with moss-hung oaks, led to Beauvais, the trees ending suddenly before the tall, white-columned mansion. At Morgan's arrival, a small Negro boy ran up and grabbed the reins of his horse, holding the animal still as Morgan dismounted.

After tossing the boy a coin, Morgan asked, "Is Mr. Savage at home?"

Before the boy could answer, another voice rang out, *"Mon Dieu!* You certainly took your sweet time getting here!"

His dark face lit by a grin, Morgan turned to find his friend Jason Savage standing at the top of the broad steps that led to the cool galleries of the house. Morgan nodded his head ruefully, admitting, "I know, I know. But damnit, Jas, I made the mistake of calling upon Gayoso as soon as I reached the city, and what does he do but insist I stay with him for a few days." His grin fading, he said bluntly, "He's dead. He apparently overindulged himself with liquor last night and died. It gave me a shock, I can tell you!"

"What?" Jason cried, his lean face revealing the shock of Morgan's news. "But he can't be. Good heavens! I spoke with him only last week."

66

"I know," Morgan said slowly. "But it's true. I was with him last night playing cards, and he seemed fine then." His expression distasteful, he added, "Our friend Wilkinson was there and I'll admit there was some heavy drinking, but nothing that seemed more than usual to me." He shook his head. "One never knows though, does one?"

Jason's heavy brows met in a frown over clear emerald eyes. "Wilkinson? I wonder what he was up to."

Morgan shrugged and, interjecting a lighter note, asked plaintively, "Are you going to invite me in, or must I stand forever out here in the hot sun?"

A shout of laughter greeted his words, and coming down the steps in a single lithe bound, Jason threw his arm about Morgan and said, "Ah, *mon ami*, it *is* good to see you! Your family, they are all well?"

As Morgan readily filled in Jason on the latest news from Natchez, the two young men walked up the steps and entered the house.

It was cool inside the spacious, elegant interior, and leading Morgan to a masculine room at the rear of the house, Jason offered him refreshments. After these were served and both men were seated comfortably, he began to ask more about the governor's death and Morgan's trip to New Orleans.

The two young men were similar in several ways—both were tall, Jason perhaps an inch taller than Morgan; both had the blue-black hair associated with a Creole parentage; both were dark-skinned, and each was attractive in his own way, though neither was classically handsome. Jason's nose was an arrogant blade in a hard face, while Morgan's chiseled features were too pronounced for perfect male beauty.

Their backgrounds were alike, both coming from wealthy plantation families with roots in New Orleans. Yet there were differences between them: Jason was the only child of his parents, and it was well-known that Guy Savage and his wife Antonia could barely abide the sight of one another and seldom did; Antonia lived in New Orleans, Guy on his estate in Virginia, named Greenwood. Jason also had relatives in England; his uncle was the Duke of Roxbury. The two young men had met at Harrow, and their friendship had lasted ever since.

Busy with their own affairs, their paths seldom crossed, but whenever they were in each other's neighborhood, it was understood the other *must* call and plan to stay . . . or else! There was an easy relationship between them and they shared many of the same pursuits—cards, liquor, horses, and women, although at twenty-six, Jason had so far escaped the trap of matrimony, saying with a crooked grin that with his parents as an example he rather thought he would forego the pleasure. It had been through Jason that Morgan had met Nolan, and as they conversed, it was inevitable that Nolan's name would arise.

"Have you heard anything from Nolan?" Morgan asked some time later.

Jason shook his dark head and said lightly, "No . . . but that doesn't mean anything. Philip is a secretive man, and believe me, as much as I admire him, he has secrets I would just as soon not know."

Morgan nodded. It was true, there was something about Philip Nolan that made one wary of being too close. Nevertheless Jason was an intimate friend of Nolan's and knowing how close Jason was to the man and the adventures they two had shared together, Morgan asked, "You went with him on one of his earlier trips . . . hunting for horses, I think . . . didn't you?"

A peculiar expression crossed Jason's handsome face. "Yes," he admitted slowly. "When I was seventeen. You remember my Indian friend, Blood Drinker?" And at Morgan's nod he continued, "Blood Drinker and I went with Nolan to trade for horses with the Comanches." His green eyes dancing, he said, "It was like nothing I've ever experienced, I can tell you that—and Blood Drinker refused to discuss it!"

Morgan smiled at Jason's reference to his Cherokee friend. He asked after Blood Drinker, and so the afternoon went, the two men eagerly and happily conversing the day away.

Armand, Jason's grandfather, wandered in at dusk, and after greeting Morgan with open affection, demanded to know if the two of them intended to remain cloistered in this room forever. Did they mean to ignore him *entirely?* Laughing, they denied the charge and the evening passed.

It was only when Morgan was undressing for bed that last night's affair with the tawny-haired whore returned to his mind. His frock coat had been thrown off, and he was just removing his waistcoat and checking his various pockets when his fingers encountered the gold chain and crucifix.

There was little chance of his being able to return it, in view of Gayoso's death, and yet he found himself strangely reluctant to get rid of it. *A momento of a night of passion,* he thought with a cynical smile. Perhaps. And not even certain why, he decided it would make an excellent charm. At any rate, everytime he saw it he would remember that women were ever deceivers—even whores!

Leonie missed her mother's crucifix almost as soon as she reached home. Slipping breathlessly in the side door that Yvette had left unlocked for her, she had instinctively reached up to touch the cross in thankfulness for having at last returned to the safety of the house, and with a soft cry of distress, she had discovered its loss.

In view of what had transpired this terrible evening, to lose her one tangible link with her mother seemed the final, punishing blow, and whether she cried for her lost virginity or the loss of her treasured crucifix, she was never quite certain. Unaware of the tears trickling down her cheeks, she slowly, painfully made her way to her bedroom, wondering if the damned vowels had been worth what she had suffered.

Throwing herself down on the bed, she decided that they hadn't been—*grand-père* could just go out again tomorrow and sign away more. Her spirits lower than they had ever been in her young life, for the first time Leonie allowed herself to be swamped by the thought of the dismal future. *Grand-père* was going to cause them ruin; he was going to force her to marry a man she had never met . . . and everything *she* had done would have been for nothing!

Her entire body ached, her mouth throbbed from the stranger's ravenous kisses; beneath her eyes were purple smudges of exhaustion and between her legs there was a dull pain that would not go away. Tiredly she removed her brown dress, and the sight of a blood-streaked petticoat brought an anguished moan from her. She was ruined! And for what? she thought with a sudden violent spurt of temper. *Grand-père's* gaming debts! With a flash of hatred, she glared across the room to where she had flung the old reticule that contained the vowels. I must have been mad to think of such a scheme, she decided with a burst of returning spirit.

Leonie was a strong, resilient young woman, and while the rape she had suffered tonight would scar deeply, she was fast recovering her usual fire. The taking of her virginity had been neither brutal nor cruel, and Leonie admitted reluctantly that the stranger had not known what he was doing. It didn't make it any easier for her to accept and she found herself growing even more furious as she thought of it, but she was an honest enough young woman to admit that she had been partially at fault for what had happened. If she had never gone to the governor's, and if she had not been slinking like a criminal through the house, she never would have met the man in the darkened room, and he would never have mistaken her for the whore Gayoso had apparently meant to send to his room.

Her face twisted in the darkness of her own room. Did women truly offer their bodies to men that way? To a complete stranger, she had never met and would never meet again? Thinking of confronting in the revealing light of day, the man who had possessed her body this night, Leonie shuddered.

She never wanted to meet that particuliar man face to face. Intrepid as she was, her cheeks flamed hotly at the idea of standing in front of the man who had so intimately explored her body. *Mon Dieu! I would die of shame or claw his eyes out!*

A faint scratching at the door brought her up with a jerk; she crossed the room and opened the door to find Yvette in a long cotton nightdress, her face white with anxiety.

"Oh, Leonie, you are home at last!" she cried in a low tone. "I have been so worried."

Leonie shushed her, and sending a wary glance down

the hall where her grandfather's room was located, she pulled her half-sister into the room. "I just arrived not many minutes ago," she admitted.

"I know—I have been checking your rooms every little bit," Yvette confessed. "I meant to wait up for you, but when your *grand-père* came home, he ordered me to bed. I was afraid for him to catch me by the door, so I contented myself with sneaking down here every now and then to see if you had returned." Almost hesitantly she asked, "Did you get the vowels?"

With an airiness she didn't feel, Leonie replied, *"Mais oui!* And it was as simple as I told you it would be."

Leonie didn't even stumble over the whopping lie, but there was a hard glitter in the sea-green eyes and a suggestion of strain about the young face. Peering at her closely in the gloomy pre-dawn light, Yvette ventured, "You seem strange. . . . Are you positive you are all right?"

Leonie snorted. "Bah! You worry overmuch. I am fine, and at least we have the satisfaction of knowing that tonight will not plunge us deeper in debt."

"But how long do you think you can do what you did tonight?" Yvette asked reasonably. "You cannot follow your *grand-père* out every night. Nor will you always know who he owes. I think you were very lucky tonight, but . . . well, you might not be so lucky another time."

Leonie bit back the hysterical choke of laughter that bubbled in her throat. *Lucky!* If Yvette only knew! But after a few more questions which Leonie answered easily enough, Yvette seemed satisfied with the account of the evening, and a moment later she slipped out the door and disappeared down the hall to her own room.

Thankful, Leonie climbed back into bed, exhausted both physically and mentally from what she had suffered this evening, and the moment her head touched the pillow she fell into a sound sleep. This night, and what had happened this night, would haunt her dreams for years, but for now the arms of Morpheus welcomed her eagerly.

It was well into the afternoon when she woke, and though one part of her was still devastated by what had happened the night before, some of her natural spirit and spunk had returned. Purposely she blocked out the time

71

spent in the strange man's arms and stubbornly refused to think about it. It had happened and it was over, she decided grimly as she bundled the brown gown in a ball and methodically ripped the telltale petticoat to shreds. Stuffing them into a cloth bag, she hurried out a back door and tossed the bag into the pit where refuse from the house was disposed of. If only she could dispose of the memory of what had happened that easily, she thought with a fierce scowl as she walked back to the house.

She went in search of Yvette, her mind busy with the vowels still in her reticule. What should she do with them? Destroy them? She didn't know, but she'd have to make some sort of decision about them soon, she admitted to herself. Their possession, once the theft was discovered, could be dangerous.

As the day passed if Yvette noticed that Leonie seemed oddly silent, she kept the information to herself. But there was something different about her half-sister, *that* she could tell for certain. Some spark was missing and she wondered, not for the first time, if Leonie had told the truth about what had happened the night before. It was unusual for Leonie not to be flushed with triumph when she had accomplished a task she had set for herself, and Yvette had been frankly surprised that Leonie had not been crowing with elation about her escapade.

Claude had not noticed anything different about his granddaughter when he had spoken with her briefly after he had arisen, not long after Leonie had, but then, that was not unexpected. He had his usual headache and the pain in his head did not sharpen his wits one bit.

But by four o'clock that afternoon he was feeling much better, and, determined to speak with Monsieur Slade while he was sober and before they became involved in another night of gambling, he toddled off to the governor's house. He was stunned at the news of the governor's death, but it must be admitted that his greatest sorrow came when he asked after Monsieur Slade and was told that the young man had left that morning. No, the servant did not know where Monsieur Slade had gone. The only thing he could tell Claude was that a carriage had called to pick up his personal belongings and that Monsieur Slade had given his condolences and then departed.

Depressed, Claude walked aimlessly away from the governor's residence. *Mon Dieu, what shall I do now?* he thought. *Monsieur Slade would have been so perfect!* Shaking his head sadly, he began to walk toward his favorite café, the Café des Ameliorations at Rampart and Toulouse Streets, intending to drown his disappointment in brandy.

He never made it this particuliar afternoon. Claude had not gone two blocks, when he caught sight of a tall, dark-haired young man heading down Royal Street. Monsieur Slade! Increasing his stride, he turned off of Toulouse Street and went in hot pursuit, catching up with the young man just as he was about to enter one of the many popular coffee houses that abounded on Royal Street.

"Monsieur Slade! *Morgan Slade! Attendez!*" he called out.

The young man stopped and glanced over his shoulder, his face showing no sign of recognition. "Yes?" Ashley Slade asked politely, neglecting to inform Claude immediately that he was not his cousin Morgan. Blue eyes, identical to Morgan's, swiftly summed up the slim, aristocratic old man, guessing to within a penny the cost of the well-cut, striped jacket Claude wore. His voice warmer, he added, "How may I help you?"

6

It never occurred to Claude that he was not speaking to Morgan Slade. Ashley could have passed for Morgan's twin, if one did not know either man well. Unfortunately, Claude did not, having met Morgan only twice and having been under the influence of alcohol on each occasion. Ashley, of course, decided to hold back his identity until he knew what he might gain from a mistaken impression.

Ashley's foray into the New World had not been pleasant, and he had cursed a dozen times a day the whim that had brought him from England to the North American continent. Money was hard to come by, unless one was willing to work for it, and as Ashley abhorred such an idea, he had drifted from frontier town to frontier town around the Gulf of Mexico, charming credit and hospitality where he could, and gaming and cheating where he couldn't.

Thinking that by now his father would have gotten over the anger that had driven him from England, and determined to return home and to familiar haunts, Ashley had at last reached New Orleans. He hoped to raise the money for passage back to England and escape from what was becoming an increasingly dangerous situation.

He had avoided Natchez out of necessity—Morgan would be certain to stop any nefarious scheme he might originate to gain money; he also knew he would find no welcome with his uncle and his sons, so he had not traveled that far up the Mississippi. He had spent some months in the small city of Baton Rouge and it had been upon his arrival there that he had written his father, telling him that eventually he planned to be in New Orleans. Writing his father had been a calculated move—Asheley needed money and he wanted to return home. Casually letting his father know where he was situated would eventually bring relief of some sort.

Ashley might have remained indefinitely in Baton Rouge, for he had charmed his way into the affections of a wealthy widow who was happy to support him if he had not run afoul of her relatives. His liaison with the woman had become blatant, and concerned relatives had decided it must stop. In order to protect his comfortable income, Ashley had challenged one of the woman's nephews to a duel. He had killed the unfortunate young man, and not unnaturally, the remaining members of the family were out for his blood. Ashley had quickly departed Baton Rouge, but not before filching several pieces of jewelry from his one-time love.

The money from the stolen jewels had given him a bit of breathing room, but upon arriving in New Orleans a week ago, he had recognized that time was running out. The money wouldn't last him long, not the way Ashley spent it, and his whereabouts in the city would soon be discovered by relatives of the young man he had killed.

Ever ready to take advantage of any opportunity, when the old Frenchman approached him, calling him by his cousin's name, he swiftly decided to see if there were a way for him to profit from the error.

The two men adjourned to a private table in the coffee house and over strong coffee, liberally spiked with rum and brandy, they conversed cautiously for some minutes— Claude, thinking of a diplomatic way to bring up his most ardent desire, and Ashley, carefully concealing his true identity.

They spoke of the governor's sudden death, and through the conversation and a few clever questions, Ashley was able to ascertain that Monsieur Saint-André had met his cousin only twice. Relaxing just a little, although the news that Morgan was in the city was most unwelcome, Ashley settled back to enjoy his role as Morgan, his penchant for iniquitous intrigue thoroughly aroused.

After several minutes of polite conversation, Claude found himself with very little to say, except what was foremost on his mind, and so, taking a fortifying sip of the steaming coffee, he began bluntly, "Monsieur Slade, I did not accost you merely out of politeness. . . . I have a proposition to lay before you."

Ashley's interest intensified. If there was money in it, he was *most* interested! Languidly he said, "Yes, and what might that be?"

Claude hesitated. Ashley might look incredibly like Morgan but he was *not* Morgan, and Claude was having some reservations about this young man. On closer acquaintance and when liquor was not blurring his thoughts, Claude wasn't so certain that his first impression of Morgan Slade was correct. There was *something* about *this* man . . . his eyes were hard, even calculating, and there was a hint of self-indulgence about the full mouth that Claude didn't remember. Pulling himself together and sneering at his own thoughts, he stated baldly, "I have a young granddaughter whom I would like to see married. I would like you to be her husband."

Ashley could have sworn with fury. What good did marriage do him? Hell, he could have married any number of times in the past few years—even an heiress or two—so why should he consider it now?

Claude supplied him with the answer. His eyes fixed on the black coffee in his cup, Claude said, "She has a large dowry and when I die, which my physician has told me will not be too far in the future, she will inherit hundreds of acres of fertile land some miles up the river from here. I know you are a wealthy young man yourself, but I also know that most men prefer a wife who brings something besides herself to the marriage bed." Looking up, his old face suddenly very tired, he asked softly, "Would five thousand doubloons in Spanish gold be enough for you?"

Ashley took a long, delighted breath. *Jesus Christ, is five thousand doubloons enough? I should think so! It's a bloody fortune! But how can I get my hands on it . . . without getting a wife hung around my neck? Or rather how can Morgan do it?*

To give himself time to think, his brain racing furiously, he took out a thin cigarillo, lighted it, and puffed a few minutes, staring out into space. Not wishing to appear too eager, and yet unwilling to let this unexpected opportunity slip by, Ashley said slowly, "I might consider it."

Flicking an ash from his cigarillo he went on, "Of course, it depends on your granddaughter. If we are to become relatives, perhaps I should first know something about the woman I *may* marry."

Relieved and yet finding this conversation strangely distasteful, Claude proceeded to tell him about Leonie. He did not of course, explain the true state of the Saint-André fortunes and tended to dwell more on Leonie's many attributes: her youth, her beauty, and her docile manner—the latter a blatant lie.

In spite of himself Ashley was intrigued, but he was also smart enough to realize that if the girl was everything her grandfather claimed and if he was as wealthy as he appeared to be, suitors would be fighting madly for her hand. So why did the old man want Morgan?

Letting that particuliar question wait for a moment, and needing to know if there really was some way he could profit by this meeting, Ashley asked smoothly, "If you and I come to agreement, say this evening, how soon would you wish the marriage to take place? Do you want a long engagement? Or is there some reason for urgency? And when would you turn over the dowry?"

There was something about this affair that was bothering Claude, but he couldn't put his finger on it. During their earlier meetings, Monsieur Morgan had not seemed either cold-blooded or mercenary, and Claude was troubled, wondering if he had greatly misjudged his man. But Ashley, as if sensing he was not imitating Morgan very well, suddenly flashed Claude a charming smile and murmured, "How very businesslike this must seem to you. Believe me, I am not normally so blunt, but then," with a depreciating gesture, "no one has ever offered me his granddaughter in marriage before."

Some of Claude's misgivings abated. Smiling warmly across at the handsome young man, he replied, "And I have never acted as a marriage broker before—so, we are even, *non?*" Feeling a little more at ease about the situation, Claude answered candidly, "I will be truthful with you, monsieur . . . if I could arrange the marriage for tomorrow I would! And the gold will be paid to you the day you marry my Leonie."

Ashley let out his breath in a whistle of surprise and asked curiously, "Why are you in such a hurry to see the girl married?"

Claude's face tightened and he said stiffly, "The number of my days are set. When I die, Leonie will be alone in the world. I should like to go to my grave knowing that her future is secure."

"I see," Ashley replied slowly, his cunning brain busily assessing how best to use this information. He *might* just be able to get his hands on the gold and get rid of the girl, he thought with growing confidence. Sending Claude a wide smile, he said affably, "I know you would like an answer immediately, but I must have some time to consider your proposition." A note of cajolery in his deep voice, he added, "The decision to give up one's freedom should not be made lightly." Glancing at the gold watch he took from a small pocket of his embroidered yellow vest, Ashley suggested, "Give me a few hours to think about our discussion. Would it be convenient to call upon you this evening at your home?"

Claude nodded, for some reason not as elated as he had thought he would be if Monsieur Slade had seemed agreeable to the proposition. Somehow Monsieur Slade was not reacting as Claude had imagined he would, nor did Claude find him quite so charming and impressive as he had at the governor's. *I must be getting old,* he told himself. The young man was certainly handsome in an arrogant way, his dark blue eyes gleaming brightly in the dark, handsome face, but Claude had found the face far more attractive when they had played cards than he did now. Sighing at his own lack of enthusiasm for what had been his most longed for accomplishment, Claude said aloud, "If you could come to call at, er . . . say, nine this evening?" And at Ashley's nod, he added, "If you give a favorable reply, I will introduce you to my granddaughter at that time."

Again Ashley nodded, inwardly aware of a feeling of smug satisfaction. By God, if I have my way, that gold will be in my hands before the week is out—and I'll be on a ship for England!

The two men parted, Claude to return to the house on Toulouse Street and Ashley to make some discreet inquiries about Claude Saint-André. What he heard made him smile nastily and understand why Saint-André had chosen to approach a stranger. No one, it seemed, wanted to shoulder the Saint-André debts, which were scattered indiscriminatly throughout the city. And no one, it seemed, had ever heard of the five thousand doubloons.

When Leonie was informed that there was a distinct possibility that she would meet her future husband within a matter of hours, she was torn between tears and fury. The day had brought her little solace, her body and mind still in a state bordering on shock after last night's assault. With the rape still raw in her mind, to be faced with a prospective husband was almost more than she could bear, and for one wild moment she considered running away. But then, her fiery mettle and valiant spirit came surging up, and Leonie knew she could never run away from any fight. She would face this man and, somehow, find a way to save herself, Yvette, and her grandfather in spite of himself.

Without enthusiasm, she allowed Yvette to arrange her hair in a neat cornet of braids, and then Leonie reluctantly put on the apricot gown she had worn the day before when she had quarrelled with her grandfather. It was her only decent gown and it fit her young figure admirably, the high waist and straight, slim skirt giving her a regal air. Slippers of white satin were on her feet, and Yvette, a born romantic, had insisted that Leonie let her pin a spring of jasmine in the tawny hair.

Viewing herself in the spotted mirror in her room, she stuck out her tongue at her image. "Bah! It doesn't matter what I look like—it is only the dowry that interests Monsieur Slade!"

She couldn't have been more correct, but neither she nor Claude knew that fact. The dowry drew Ashley like a shark after blood. Having decided that if the gold did exist, he might as well have it as Morgan. Ashley presented himself at the Saint-André townhouse at nine that evening. What did it matter to him, if Saint-André owed a mountain of debt? He wouldn't be around when the truth was discovered—Morgan would be! Let *him* sort out the problem!

Inquiries into the state of Monsieur Saint-André's finances had not been all that Ashley had seen to in the short time since he had bid Claude good-bye. A quick check of the ships in the port of New Orleans had revealed that the *Scarlet Angel* would sail for England the following Friday, just one week away, and he intended to be on her—with a trunk full of gold!

Consequently, Ashley was at his most charming, adroitly soothing Claude's growing suspicions that Monsieur Slade was not the man he had first thought him. The two men conversed in the room with the cream carpet, and burgundy chairs and drapes, the only elegant room in the house; in the soft candlelight, the obvious deficiencies were hardly noticeable.

Despite his earlier reservations, Claude was delighted when Ashley, with a nice air of deference, conceded that if Monsieur Saint-André found him suitable, then he would be honored to marry his granddaughter, and just as soon as Monsieur Saint-André could arrange it. The two men drank a toast with a bottle of excellent French brandy that had been saved for just such a momentous occasion, each feeling very pleased with the bargain.

Leonie wasn't. Ushered into the room a few minutes later there was a rebellious sparkle in the sea-green eyes and a determined slant to the small, firm chin. There had to be a way out of this coil and she was going to find it even if it meant throwing herself on Monsieur Slade's mercy!

Ashley was enchanted with the appealing sight she made in her apricot gown, the candlelight turning her hair the color of fine golden sherry. It really was a shame he hadn't the time for dalliance—and for a brief moment he actually considered the possibility of taking his supposed bride to England with him. But then, with a mental shrug, he dismissed the idea, too aware of the pitfalls in such a scheme. He was running a great risk as it was, so why risk more?

Leonie disliked Ashley on sight. Prejudiced against him by the fact that she was being forced to marry him in the first place, she saw more clearly the dissipation that marred his face than did Claude. The assessing blue eyes beneath the heavy black brows did not cause her heart to beat with pleasure, nor did the full sensuous mouth with its indulgent curve make her wonder how it would feel against hers—after last night she was quite, *quite* certain she never wanted a man's mouth on hers again. He was handsome in a rakish sort of way, she conceded, but there was nothing about him that made her want to marry him.

Claude beamed when they were introduced, and Leonie, mindful of her manners, suffered Monsieur Slade to take her small hand in his and gently brush his lips across it. Looking at Claude, Ashley asked affectedly, "May I keep this lovely little hand, monsieur?"

Despite the gravity of the situation, Leonie glanced quickly away and had to bite her lip to keep from giggling. *Mon Dieu! How silly!*

Claude was charmed. Smiling genially at the tall young man standing so close to Leonie, he said graciously, "Nothing would give me greater pleasure than to have you do so, Monsieur Slade."

Ashley turned to look into Leonie's face, his hard blue eyes wandering almost possessively over her features. "And you, my dear, will you accept me as your husband?" Ashley asked. The words were mere formality as far as he was concerned, as the girl would obviously do as her grandfather wished—and he could almost feel the gold in his hands! Certainly he hadn't expected an answer—a blush, or a shy glance or a small nod was the most he expected by way of reply. Unfortunately he didn't know the mettle of the young lady in front of him and her words came as an unpleasant shock.

Unwilling to meekly submit to fate, a defiant expression flickering over the sultry features, Leonie replied cooly, *"Non!* Why should I?"

Ashley was clearly taken aback and Claude was furious. *"Leonie!"* he thundered. "Have you forgotten our conversation about Yvette?"

Some of Leonie's defiance wavered. But then her mouth set mulishly, although there was a wary glint in her eyes, and she said with composure, *"Non, grand-père.* But before I accept Monsieur Slade's offer, I think I should be allowed to speak with him privately. It is only fair, *n'est-ce pas?"*

Both men appeared decidedly uneasy but for entirely

different reasons. Claude was aware that Leonie was going to fight every inch of the way to the altar in spite of her earlier capitulation, so he didn't trust her—with good reason! As for Ashley, he was infuriated! How dare this little slip of a girl upset his plans? He was counting on that money and the pleasure of bedding his innocent bride before he sailed for England, and it was a most aggravating surprise to discover that there might be some impediment to his plans.

Knowing how stubborn his granddaughter could be, and yet unwilling to meet her head on when things were moving so smoothly, Claude reluctantly acceded to her request. "Very well. It is proper and only right that you have a few minutes alone with your husband-to-be. But"—his face darkening and the threat of retribution obvious in the brown eyes, he ended harshly, "do not forget what I promised you! And, Leonie, I shall do it, if you deny me this."

Leonie's mouth tightened. "Of course. Now, may I speak with Monsieur Slade . . . alone?"

One fist clenched helplessly, but not willing to continue the argument in front of a stranger, Claude gave in. Looking apologetically across to the silent Ashley, he murmured, "She is a bit headstrong occasionally, you understand? And perhaps it would be best if you have a few words with her without my presence. I shall return shortly."

Leonie hadn't known what she was going to do with her few minutes of privacy with the monsieur, but it gained her a moment to think. Her thoughts were not pleasant, and deciding that the only way she could escape this marriage was for Monsieur Slade to withdraw his offer, Leonie swung in Ashley's direction and burst out passionately. "Monsieur, I mean you no insult, but I have no wish whatsoever to marry you!" Her eyes very big and pleading, she begged, "Could you please tell my *grand-père* that you do not think we will suit, after all? Please? It is very important to me."

Rather thoughtfully, Ashley regarded her. It was apparent she was not the docile creature her grandfather had led him to believe. It was also apparent the grandfather held some threat over her. Now, how might he make that work for himself? Wishing to know more about the situation and playing for time in the process, he asked bluntly, "Are you in love with someone else? Someone your grandfather does not approve of?"

Leonie let a small smile flit across her face. *"Non,* monsieur, I just do not wish to marry." Anxiously she added, "You do understand?"

Ashley didn't, but he relaxed slightly. At least there wasn't some annoying puppy in the picture, he thought slowly. And if the chit was telling the truth and it was a case of her simply resisting the idea of marriage, it was possible he could still get his hands on the gold. A coaxing note in his voice he said, "I would make no demands upon you, my dear. Your life would change hardly at all. Why, the only difference would be that you would have my name and I would have your dowry." Seeing that he had her attention and that she appeared to be actually considering what he was saying, he expanded further, "It would truly be a marriage of convenience between us. You could live here in Louisiana, and I would spend my time in Natchez. It would be a strictly business arrangement."

The expression in the cat-shaped eyes thoughtful, Leonie asked curiously, "Why marry at all then?"

Realizing that a certain amount of honesty has its uses, Ashley took a gamble and admitted blandly, "Well, you see, I don't really wish to marry either."

"Then why offer for me?" she asked reasonably. And as Ashley hesitated, cursing her forthright manner, her eyes suddenly widened with sympathy, and with a note of awe in her voice, she inquired, "Are *you,* too, being forced to marry?"

Seizing upon the reason offered by her innocent question and playing upon the sympathy evident in the small face, Ashley contrived to look both embarrassed and appealing as he muttered, "That's exactly the case, my dear! My father has cut me off without any funds until I return to Natchez with a bride."

"But *if* we do not live together, how will marrying me satisfy him?"

Hurrying to cover the mistake, he rushed, "Well, actually I don't have to precisely present you to him, just

83

inform him that I have married . . . and a copy of the marriage certificate would be sufficient." He smiled conspiratorially, "He never said anything about having to *live* with my bride . . . just that I *acquire* one."

"And you find *me* suitable?" Leonie asked in a dry voice.

"Why not?" Ashley returned easily. "You have a commendable dowry, and"—he let his eyes glow with appreciation and just a hint of desire—"I find you very beautiful. I must admit it was your availability and your dowry that first interested me, but having met you and seen your loveliness, I find that I—"

Leonie snorted in the face of his compliments. "Bah! Monsieur, I liked you better when you were honest. Do not, I beg you, talk foolishness!"

His face hardening, Ashley crushed the urge to slap her. Little bitch! Who did she think she was, snubbing him that way? Growing angry with the situation, feeling that Claude had entirely misled him about the *docility* of his granddaughter and furious at the thought of the gold slipping through his fingers, he snapped pettily, "Then, what do *you* suggest?"

For a moment Leonie hesitated, the barest glimmer of an idea coming to her. It might work, provided this Monsieur Slade meant everything he had said so far. Finally, deciding she had nothing to lose and a great deal to gain, she said slowly, "Monsieur, neither of us wishes to marry . . . but for various reasons it would be to our advantage to do so, *oui?*"

Ashley's eyes narrowed in speculation and he nodded his head.

"Then, monsieur, I propose a bargain to you. We will marry as my *grand-père* wishes, but—" and she held up her hand at Ashley's broad smile—"it will be a true marriage of convenience." The little face suddenly grim and haunted, she said, "You must promise me that you will make *no* demands upon me whatsoever, and that we will live *separately,* as you said earlier."

Ashley shrugged his shoulders. Why not? What did it matter to him? One week from today he had every intention of sailing for England . . . if he got his hands on the gold. Aloud he agreed, "But of course, my dear. As soon as we are wedded, I will return immediately to Natchez to inform my father." His brain leaping, he added, "We will tell your grandfather that my journey up river to Natchez is to prepare for the arrival of my bride. For his information, we will say I plan to return in the shortest possible time to fetch you. How does that sound to you?"

Leonie sent him an approving smile, tamping down the faint hint of guilt she felt in deceiving her grandfather. *"Bon!* That would do very well, I think." Her gaze suddenly uncertain, she began slowly, "Monsieur, this is a difficult subject for me, but it is one I feel I must discuss with you." At Ashley's encouraging look, she took a deep breath and said with an embarrassed but determined rush, "I will have need of my dowry eventually, and I do not believe it is fair that, for merely lending me your name, you should keep it forever. After all, you are a rich young man, and you have as much need of me as I have of you. Why should you keep my dowry too?"

His feeling of smug satisfaction fading once more, and not liking this sudden turn of events, he demanded, "What exactly do you suggest?"

Leonie frowned, trying to figure out a scrupulously fair bargain. "I suggest, monsieur, that you consider the dowry a *loan.* You may have it for a certain period of time, but at the end of that time, you will repay me, *oui?"* And at the balky look on Ashley's face, she continued, "It is only fair—I will make no demands upon you, and you will have the use of the money for the time being." Leonie felt she had offered him a more than fair exchange. She didn't believe he should have her dowry at all, but then she acknowledged that he was going to provide her with an escape from *grand-père's* edict and that she was willing to pay him for his troubles. Granted, he was also gaining, but knowing he could have the choice of any number of young women, she wished to make the bargain as appealing as possible.

Ashley nodded as she finished speaking, smiling cynically to himself. Stupid bitch! Did she really think he would return the money?

But Leonie was not stupid, and after sending Ashley a long thoughtful look, she said with deceptive sweetness,

"And you will, of course, be willing to sign an agreement that states all of these things? Yes?"

Ashley nearly choked in surprise. The little slut did have some brains! But it didn't make him like her any better, and if he hadn't wanted that gold so damned badly, he would have stalked from the room and left her to whistle for a husband—but the gold was too alluring! So, in a polite voice he murmured, "Naturally," adding almost pompously, "It is what any honorable man would do."

"Bien! It is decided. When my *grand-père* returns, we can tell him that we are both agreeable to this match." She sent him a searching glance and added, "It will be up to you to see a lawyer and have him draw up the agreements between us. And, monsieur, do not think that if the agreements do not set out precisely everything we have discussed, I will go along with this marriage. I will not, and you should know . . . I *keep* my word!"

His palm itching to slap her soft cheek, Ashley nodded curtly. "Of course. I shall see a lawyer tomorrow."

Leonie did not like the note in his voice, and risking a glance at the dark face with the hard blue eyes, she was suddenly very glad she was not going to share a normal marriage with Monsieur Slade. She did not like him, but he offered her the one chance to circumvent her grandfather's demand.

When Claude entered the room a moment or two later, he discovered to his surprise that Leonie and Monsieur Slade were quite in charity with each other. Feeling a weight lift off his chest, he suggested another round of toasts and allowed Leonie to have a glass of sherry, so that the three of them could drink to the engagement.

Leaving the house shortly thereafter, Ashley was feeling very pleased with himself. What did it matter what he agreed to? It was Morgan's name that would be on all documents, and Ashley smiled nastily. By the time Monsieur Saint-André grew suspicious of Leonie's excuses for her husband's extended return to Natchez, or that little bitch Leonie decided to call in the loan, he would be in England, and there would be no one to connect him with what he considered his cleverest scheme to date.

There were pitfalls ahead, even Ashley in his smugness

admitted that. He had to make certain Morgan's unexpected appeerence in New Orleans didn't upset the boat
too soon, and for a moment, in the privacy of his room on
Rampart Street, he considered that aspect of the situation.

Morgan was obviously in the vicinity of New Orleans.
But his cousin had just as obviously changed his place of
residence without informing Monsieur Saint-André. It had
been a mere chance meeting between Morgan and Saint-
André in the first place and Morgan might not even still be
in the city. Ever a gambler, Ashley decided he would take
the risk of Morgan suddenly finding himself in Monsieur
Saint-André's company. Besides, it might prove amusing
to watch Morgan try to extricate himself from this entan-
glement, Ashley thought maliciously.

The next obstacle was the marriage itself. He could wait
no longer than Thursday for the ceremony and somehow
he had to convince Saint-André to approve of such indecent
haste.

The agreements didn't worry him a bit. He would have
agreed to anything Leonie demanded, simply because he
had no intention of keeping his word. It was Morgan's
name that would appear on everything and thinking of
that, Ashley decided that on the morrow he would purchase quill and ink and spend a few hours perfecting the
excellent imitation of Morgan's hand, which he had used
before for his own gain.

The wedding night was the one problem he hadn't resolved. Surely Leonie must know that her grandfather
would insist the newlyweds spend *one* night together. It
was unthinkable, even Ashley conceded, that he depart
out of his bride's life immediately following the ceremony.

This had also occurred to Leonie. So when Monsieur
Slade dined at their house on Sunday night, she snatched a
moment alone with him and suggested that he tell her
grand-père that they wished to spend their first night together in one of the finer hotels in New Orleans. Separate
rooms, naturally! Blandly, Ashley agreed.

Luck seemed to be smiling on Ashley, because even his
greatest worry, the need for the wedding to take place almost immediately, was taken care of by Monsieur Saint-
André himself.

Claude, full of brandy and elation, had gone to bed late that night of the engagement. The next morning, he had experienced an agonized clawing of heart—his breathing was suddenly, frighteningly labored, his chest was filled with unbearable pain, and the objects in the room were moving in a black haze. This mortal terror made him frantic to have the marriage take place. Explaining to Monsieur Slade what he had experienced, he begged that the other man understand his need for haste. He wanted to see Leonie married while he was still alive.

Nothing could have pleased Ashley more and he instantly suggested Thursday for the wedding. Claude was painfully grateful, thinking his grandson-in-law-to-be was a prince among fellows.

Ashley had the agreements between himself and Leonie drawn up with no trouble, and the evening before their wedding he managed to slip the signed and witnessed documents to her. He needed nothing from her, and as he was the one who'd had to agree to everything, it had been a simple task to accomplish.

With the agreements in her hands, Leonie felt a huge wave of relief sweep through her, for until now, she actually hadn't been certain that Monsieur Morgan would keep his word. It appeared he had and she was ashamed of any doubts she may have harbored against him. Events seemed to be moving at a frightening pace and despite a fierce little vow not to worry, Leonie had been doing just that. The feel of the two documents in her hands reassured her—until she read the one concerning repayment of her dowry . . . and *then* she was furious!

Ashley had faithfully had the document drawn up as they had agreed, but when Leonie had said the money would be his to use for a reasonable amount of time, she had been thinking of a year or so—not the *five* years stated in the document!

He had been very clever, she decided as she lay in bed staring blankly at the ceiling. The wedding was the next day, so he must have known that she wasn't going to disrupt everything simply because the date the money due her was later than she had expected. But it showed he was not to be trusted, that he was quite capable of trickery, and

88

with that in mind she slipped from her bed and walked through the sleeping house to her grandfather's study.

The study was seldom used these days, most of the furniture having been sold, but his huge old desk was still there and in the second drawer was the case that held his prized dueling pistols. Leonie had no real idea how to fire a pistol, but Monsieur Slade did not know that; if tomorrow night, when they were in their suites at the hotel, he thought to demand his conjugal rights, he would be very much surprised.

Feeling a bit more comfortable, with the pistol tucked in the new reticule *grand-père* had bought her, Leonie went back to sleep.

The reticule had not been the only new item of apparal that *grand-père* had presented to her these past few days. He had made the supreme sacrifice and sold one of the two magnificient geldings he had managed to retain, even in face of his mounting debts. The gelding fetched a more than good price, and with the ready money, Claude had been able to bribe, beg and cajole three new gowns and other items of clothing from a modiste who had known him in the old days when the Saint-Andrés had had money and then some.

The clothes meant nothing to Leonie, but Claude was determined not to send her to her new husband in outgrown rags. His conscience pricked him just a bit whenever he thought of the crumbling state of Château Saint-André. Ah, well, Monsieur Morgan was a rich man, he would receive an impressive dowry, and most importantly, he would have Leonie for his bride. What more could any man ask for?

Ashley, sipping a glass of whiskey before retiring that night for bed, could think of nothing. Monsieur Saint-André was still convinced he was dealing with Morgan, and fortunately Morgan had not appeared to show the old man his mistake. Also, Ashley had taken great care to lie low and to avoid any of the spots Morgan might conceivably be. All the meetings with Saint-André had been held at the Saint-André townhouse, and when he had not been at the townhouse, Ashley had remained in seclusion in his rooms on Rampart Street, counting the hours until the dowry was in his hands and he boarded the *Scarlet Angel*.

The day of the wedding dawned hot and humid, and at four o'clock in the afternoon of July 26, 1799, Leonie Saint-André was joined in holy matrimony with a man she and her grandfather both thought was Morgan Slade of Natchez, Mississippi. And Morgan—his nefarious cousin Ashley and the old Frenchman Saint-André being the last people in the world he was thinking about—spent the day happily fishing for catfish with his friend Jason Savage.

7

The wedding was necessarily small and private. Naturally none of Monsieur Slade's relatives could attend, considering the haste with which the event had taken place. Leonie had looked very lovely in a demure gown of soft rose satin, and Ashley, posing as Morgan, had been very handsome in a form-fitting coat of dark blue superfine and black velvet pantaloons. There were few witnesses, only Claude and Yvette, and two black-robed nuns from the Ursuline convent, as Leonie said the words that joined her to the tall, dark-haired man at her side.

Ashley had explained to Claude his intention to return immediately to Natchez to prepare his home and his parents for the coming of the new bride. Claude had been a little disturbed that Slade did not plan to take his bride with him, but because of the hastened circumstances he made no demur.

Pleased and satisfied that he had done all a guardian should to insure a granddaughter's future, after drinking several toasts to the couple, he had departed for the Saint-André townhouse. *It is done,* he told himself with satisfaction. *Leonie is safe.*

Leonie was anything but safe. They had eaten dinner together in the privacy of the rooms Ashley had reserved. Ashley for obvious reasons had not wished to mingle with the wealthy, aristocratic crowd in the dining room, and Leonie had no desire to be seen by anyone. As the meal progressed, Ashley's eyes had roamed with increasing hunger over Leonie's round, creamy shoulders. Her hair was in shining curls that cascaded about the striking little face, and as his gaze rested on the swell of the small bosom against the rose satin material, he felt himself harden with desire.

My God, but she was a lovely little piece, he thought lustfully. An ugly gleam entered the hard blue eyes as he reminded himself that for all practical reasons she was also his wife. Why should he deny himself a wedding night? Besides he wanted to prove to the little bitch that it wasn't wise to deny a husband his rights under the law. Alone in the bedroom, her bloody precious agreement wouldn't be worth the paper it was written on!

Leonie had not missed the gleam of lust in his eyes and her stomach recoiled. *Mon Dieu, but I am glad I did not trust him,* she thought scornfully. There had been little conversation between them, and just as soon as the meal was finished, Leonie excused herself and escaped into her own room.

It was one of the most comfortable rooms Leonie had ever seen. A thick blue and wheat colored carpet flowed throughout the room; in one corner was an upholstered chair in a deep rose fabric and two small tables of polished oak had been placed on either side. The bed was equally charming, draped in yards of filmy white mosquito netting; the windows had curtains of gay chintz.

Leonie took a child's delight in the room and almost lovingly carressed the bright quilt on the bed. *It is all so welcoming,* she thought with pleasure. But then she shrugged. Tomorrow she would be back at the townhouse and by the next day on her way back to the Château Saint-André.

But first, she had to get through this night. Without thinking to ring for the maid her grandfather had spared from the townhouse, she had gone to the huge, mahogany wardrobe, and found the new nightdress that *grand-père* had insisted she have. The nightdress was a very daring garment and after putting it on, Leonie was shocked when she stared in the tall, cheval glass mirror that was in the room. She giggled nervously. . . . *What a wicked thing to wear to bed!*

The gown was of the sheerest, flimsiest material Leonie had ever encountered, and through the sea-green color of the gown the points of her rose-tipped nipples were very obvious, as was the sweet curve of the narrow waist and the slender length of the golden legs.

Deciding that she would feel infinitely less depraved if she were covered by the bedsheets, she had just approached the bed when the door that connected her rooms with Monsieur Slade's flew open.

Ashley had been drinking steadily since Leonie had bid him a chilly good night, and the more he thought of it, the more he was certain he was owed a wedding night. After all, he had gotten the wench out of a fix, hadn't he? If he hadn't come along, where would she be?

A petulant curve to his full mouth, he had poured himself another drink and proceeded to his own bedchamber where he stripped off his clothes and pulled on a vulgar dressing gown of gold satin that rioted with scarlet dragons. He eyed his empty bed with disfavor and after fortifying himself with another shot of whiskey lurched through the door to Leonie's room.

For a moment he stood there swaying, the dark blue eyes glittering with the hard sheen of desire as his gaze took in the enticing picture Leonie made in the revealing gown. He felt a tightening in his crotch and, almost licking his lips in anticipation, took a step towards Leonie.

But Leonie was not to be caught unprepared. Without a second's hesitation, she swiftly reached for her reticule lying on the table near the bed, and with a calmness she didn't feel, she grasped her grandfather's small pistol and swung it in Ashley's direction. Her heart beating so fast she thought she would suffocate, she put her other hand on the pistol and staring unblinkingly at Ashley's stupified expression said cooly, "Monsieur, if I remember correctly, we *do* have a bargain . . . do we not? It states that you will make *no* demands upon me. I trust you mean to *keep* that bargain."

Ashley's face darkened with rage, and in that moment there was nothing handsome about his features. Vain and greedy he might be, but he was not so foolhardy as to attempt the rape of a woman armed with a deadly looking pistol. "You'll pay for this, you French bitch!" he snarled before he turned on his heels and slammed from the room.

Her hands trembling, her entire body shaking from re-action, Leonie sank down on the bed. *Merde! but I was frightened,* she thought. She swallowed painfully, know-ing what she would have suffered if she had not taken the precaution of bringing her grandfather's pistol. The thought of the monsieur's mouth on hers and his taking the liberties the stranger at the governor's had taken only last week filled her with revulsion. Almost fondly she eyed the weapon lying loosely in her hands. *I must have* grand-père *teach me how to shoot it,* she decided grimly. *The next time I will not be bluffing!*

Leonie did not sleep much that night. She sat curled up against the headboard of the bed, her gaze fixed unwa-veringly on the door between her room and Monsieur Slade's, the pistol held firmly in her small hands. Occa-sionally sleep would prove too much for her and she would nod, only to come awake with a jerk, her heart thumping madly in her breast for fear Monsieur Slade had taken ad-vantage of the moment's weakness and had crept into her room.

In view of the night they had spent, when the newlyweds met the next morning it was with little pretense of affec-tion. Besides suffering from the worst hangover in his life, Ashley was thoroughly enraged that a mere chit of sixteen had outfaced him. As for Leonie, though she had never had a high opinion of men in the first place, Ashley's blatant attempt to disregard their bargain had been the final blow—men were such unscrupulous beasts!

She greeted her husband of one day coolly, her contempt obvious in the sea-green eyes. As for Ashley, he could barely stand the sight of her. With the exception of his cousin Morgan, no one had ever gotten the better of Ashley Slade, and he was furious that a mere slip of a girl had been able to beat him at his own game. What words he sent her way as they ate their breakfast were surly to the point of rudeness.

One of the slashing eyebrows quirking upwards, Leonie finally said, "Monsieur, we have only a few hours more to endure each other's company, and I think it would be wisest if, for that period of time anyway, we at least treated each other with politeness. I can well do without your profanity!"

Ashley snarled something ugly, but her point was well-taken. Until he was actually on the ship and it had left the port of New Orleans, he would take no further risks.

Consequently when they arrived at the Saint-André townhouse, no one would have suspected the true state of affairs. Claude noted the purple smudges beneath Leonie's eyes, but he assumed it was from a night spent in her husband's arms, so it gave him little alarm.

Ashley, ever the chameleon, played his role faithfully, smiling fondly at his young bride and bemoaning his imminent departure for Natchez. When at last the moment arrived, he swept Leonie into his arms and muttered maliciously, "I think you owe me *this*, at least!" the second before his lips came down hard and plundering on hers.

With her grandfather watching benignly, there was nothing Leonie could do except let Monsieur Slade have his way . . . but she made a grim little vow that he would *never* catch her in this position again!

Ashley took full advantage of the situation, his arms crushing her up against his hard masculinity, his tongue brutally raping her warm mouth. Just when she thought she could stand it no longer, when a hot tide of revulsion and temper was surging up through her body, Ashley released her, a smug, satisfied smile on his weak mouth.

Leonie's eyes hated him, and with the golden flecks very apparent, she spat in an undertone, "If I ever see you again, monsieur, it will be one day too soon!"

Ashley only smiled, his breathing faster than usual. He had enjoyed kissing her, enjoyed the softness of her body next to his, and he cursed the fact that last night he had not known fully the secrets of her slender body. Ah well, the gold of her dowry would buy women enough for him, and he would derive a spiteful enjoyment from the irony of it all. For just a moment, he pictured Morgan's face when Leonie appeared demanding her dowry.

Controlling the urge to chuckle at his own cleverness, Ashley finally took his leave from Leonie and her grandfather. By the time darkness fell, he was happily ensconced in his cabin on the *Scarlet Angel*, drinking a toast to his good fortune as the ship slowly sailed away from New Orleans.

Leonie drank no toast that night; instead she crawled gratefully into her own bed and as soon as her head hit the pillow she was sound asleep. It had been a difficult twenty-four hours for her, but at last it was over. She was married, it was true, but Yvette was safe—too, she had the precious agreements, which should protect her from her husband in the future, and in time she should receive her dowry back. The return of the dowry worried her just a little—Monsieur Slade had shown, to her at least, that he was *not* an honorable man, and even with the signed agreement, she felt fairly certain, she would have a fight on her hands when the time came. But for tonight, she would not dwell on the problems that might arise in the future.

Claude rested easily that night also, and in the morning when Leonie suggested that they return to the Château, he raised no objections. He was feeling tired and listless these past few days and the delights of the city held no allure for him.

The following morning the townhouse was closed and everyone returned to Château Saint-André. As most Creoles avoided the city in the summer, Claude, for once, seemed in no hurry to return to it. Gayoso's death had shaken him, making him accept for the first time inevitability of his own death, and with Leonie's future safely taken care of, it was as if he was simply marking time, waiting for the grim reaper to take him too.

The weeks immediately following her wedding were a good time for Leonie. *Grand-père* was staying at the Saint-André plantation and not running up more debts, and she had the satisfaction of knowing that sometime in the future there would be money to put back into the Château . . . *when* she got it from Monsieur Slade!

Claude, his brain cleared for the first time in years of brandy and liquor, took a casual interest in the plantation and for Leonie it was sheer heaven. Perhaps, she told herself hopefully, he has realized how desperate we have become and means to help salvage what we can.

Leonie and Claude grew very close during those weeks as August gradually gave way to September, and Claude

96

mourned the years that he had ignored his granddaughter's lively, enchanting presence. *If only I could call back the time,* he thought sadly. But then his mood lightened. *At least I have seen that her future will be safe—soon Monsieur Slade will return and my sweet Leonie will have a fine husband to care for her.*

Claude had noted that Leonie did not speak of her absent husband, but it didn't disturb him. *She is probably still angry at the way I forced her to marry him,* he decided with a smile, *and is not about to let me know that she finds him attractive.*

Of course Leonie had found nothing attractive about Monsieur Slade, but if she had met the real Morgan Slade, she might have felt differently. Certainly, the young woman that he was dancing with at the ball Armand Beauvais had given the night before he was to leave for Natchez thought he was prodigiously attractive. *No man,* she thought bemusedly, *should be allowed to have such wicked blue eyes and such curling black lashes,* as Morgan's gaze rested mockingly on her mouth. Almost despairingly Raquel Dumond said softly, "Must you leave tomorrow? Couldn't you stay for a few days longer?"

Morgan smiled teasingly. "So that you could ensnare me further, sweetheart?"

Raquel blushed, uncertain whether to laugh at his accuracy or stamp her foot in embarrassment. Laughter won out, and with amusement peeping in the brilliant dark eyes raised to his, she murmured, "Perhaps . . . one never knows what the future holds."

"For me, it holds a journey to Natchez . . . tomorrow," Morgan replied easily, not so ensnared with her Creole charms that he couldn't bear to leave them. Raquel had been a pleasant way to spend a few evenings, but with the departure looming in the forefront of his mind, he was restless and in no mood to play the gallant.

It had been a successful trip for Morgan, despite Gayoso's sudden death, and he had been able to secure the use of the wharves and warehouses that were so important to his family's plantation. His friendship with Jason Savage had helped, as well as the gold that had been discreetly passed from one Spanish palm to the other.

At Jason's insistence, he had made Beauvais his head-quarters and had only ventured into the city when business had called. The remainder of the time, he had spent at Beauvais, relaxing and visiting with Jason and his grand-father Armand. It had been a most pleasant time, but now he was anxious to return to Bonheur, even though he knew that once there, somewhere else would call to him.

It had only been as the end of his stay at Beauvais drew near that he had thought of his uncle's letter and his cousin Ashley. He and Jason had spent a few hours in late August scouring the city only to discover eventually that Ashley had sailed on the *Scarlet Angel* for England at the end of July. He and Jason had exchanged looks and then burst out laughing. "Why didn't I think to check with ship departures before we started combing the city?" Morgan had asked with amusement.

"Because, *mon ami*, you enjoyed slumming in those de-praved dens of sin that you claimed your cousin was sure to inhabit." Jason had replied mockingly.

Ashley dismissed from his mind, Morgan had busied himself preparing for the journey to Natchez. The next day dawned sunny and hot but there was the hint of a thunder-storm on the horizon, and eyeing it, Jason had said, "Are you certain you don't wish to delay your departure for a few hours?"

Morgan grinned. "My dear friend, what flimsy excuses you present to hold me here. I am not made of sugar, I as-sure you, and a little thundershower will not melt me!"

Jason had laughed, their hands meeting in a tight clasp; then, astride a prancing, chestnut gelding from the Beau-vais stables, Morgan had ridden away, heading up the river for Natchez. Attached to his watch fob was the little gold cross from a virgin whore.

He had looked at that little gold cross more than once during the past weeks, wondering about its owner. A dozen times, he had cursed the darkness that had hidden her fea-tures, cursed the circumstances that had allowed the girl to vanish from his life as quickly as she had appeared. And the fact that he thought of her often, that he had almost desperately wanted to know more about her, that he had regrets about that particuliar evening, annoyed him. What the hell—she was a whore, he had reminded himself repeatedly, ignoring the taunting voice in his mind that wouldn't let him forget that *he* had initiated her into her profession. Nor could he forget the feel of her in his arms, the sweet mouth beneath his, the soft body pressed next to his. He was grimly aware that if he could have found her, if his attempts to learn her identity from Gayoso's servants hadn't been fruitless, that he would be taking her with him now as he left New Orleans.

If she had been determined to sell herself, he reasoned that he might as well be the one to take advantage of it—she would have found him a generous protector. A discreet house in Natchez, a stylish carriage, blooded horses, clothes, jewels, servants, he would have gladly provided them all, and as his mistress she would have been safe.

Now why did I think of that? he thought sourly, as his horse trotted along the river road. Safety wasn't what she had wanted and he was angry that she could even now, weeks later, arouse a curious feeling of protectiveness within him. Scowling at the darkening sky, he angrily tried to push her out of his mind. But it was useless; a mile down the road, he caught himself wondering where she was now and what was she doing. And why the devil had she thrown his money back in his face?

The thunderstorm broke a half hour later, and to Leonie it seemed only fitting that the heavens should weep with her. For the past two weeks she had tried to ignore the signs, had tried to tell herself that nothing was different about her body, but this morning when she had arisen and the nausea that had been with her the last few days had attacked again, she knew it was no use pretending otherwise. She was to have a child . . . a child fathered in darkness and by a man whose name and face she had never known . . . and would probably *never* know!

PART TWO

FORTUNE'S PROMISE

"What! wouldst thou have a serpent
sting thee twice?"

The Merchant of Venice
William Shakespeare

8

The Saint-André family graveyard was nestled in a shady green glen about half a mile from the main house, and whenever Leonie came here, she was filled with a feeling of tranquility, of sadness—and yet not sadness, more a bittersweet nostalgia. There was an air of timelessness about the tiny graveyard, as if it had existed forever and would endure long after its inhabitants had faded from the memory of those who had known them in life.

Letting the peace of the place seep into her bones, Leonie's gaze traveled slowly around the area. Over there, under the marble seraph with its wide outstretched wings, was buried her great-grandfather, who had come from France, and next to him, his wife. To the left were tiny headstones of the three infants that had been born to them but had not survived the first years of childhood. Her parents' grave was marked with a pair of weeping angels, and *Grand-mère* Saint-André's final resting place was noted only by a starkly simple obelisk of startling white marble. All of the tombstones were aged, except one . . . *grand-père's,* and even it was beginning to reveal the soft ravages that five years time had wrought.

Leonie slowly walked over to where Claude was buried, and sinking gracefully to her knees, she gently laid the spray of fragrant yellow and white honeysuckle which she had brought for his grave. She had come here often in the five and a half years since his sudden death in October of 1799. It was tragic, but she found it easier to talk with him as he slept in his grave than she ever had when he had been alive. She came often to sit by his grave and talk of events that had taken place, or to discuss the various difficulties that beset her. Today was no different.

103

The huge, twisted live oaks that ringed the graveyard formed a leafy green umbrella, and the pink and coral roses, which persisted in clinging to the small white fence that enclosed the graveyard, filled the April air with their sweet fragrance. Absently, her eyes fixed on some distant spot, Leonie plucked a pink rose and unthinkingly began to strip its petals as she talked softly to Claude's grave.

"Justin is five years old today, *grand-père.*" A small little smile flitted across the expressive face. "You would be proud of him! He is a true Saint-André—stubborn, obstinate, and determined to have his own way!" Her face clouded for a moment, regret surging through her slender body that Claude had not lived to see his great-grandson's birth in 1800. And she repeated again, "You would have been proud of him."

Thinking of her son, her thoughts drifted for a time. Oh, how she had hated the idea of bearing that unknown man's child! There had even been times during the early stages of her pregnancy that she had struck her swelling stomach with helpless fury. It was so unfair—she had been left alone to bear the fruit of a night she would give anything to forget! It had been intolerable and there were times Leonie had thought she would go quite, quite mad. Yet, as her pregnancy progressed, as the child began to move inside of her, some of her fury lessened, and eventually she ceased to rail against her unwanted state and gradually came to realize that what had happened was no fault of the child that grew in her womb. And when her squalling son was placed in her arms, her heart had been so filled with sudden, fierce surge of love that she had feared it would burst from her breast.

The news of Leonie's marriage had not been well known in New Orleans. The Saint-Andrés no longer mingled in society as they once had; only their closest neighbors and friends were even aware Leonie was married. She certainly didn't wish to dwell on it. Claude's death occurred soon after the family had returned to Château Saint-André; that sad event effectively ended further speculation about Leonie's sudden, almost secretive, marriage.

The time which had passed since Claude's death and Justin's birth had not been pleasant, but somehow Leonie had struggled to retain possession of the main house and a hundred acres of land that surrounded it. Everything else—the townhouse, the two thousand or so fertile acres that had been part of the original plantation, and even *grand-père's* one remaining thoroughbred and carriage—had been sold to pay off the bulk of his debts.

But it hadn't been enough. Some people had been kind, many of his old friends simply burning the gaming vowels and shaking their heads that a man who had once been such an astute landowner could have let himself fall so deeply in debt. Others, of course, were not so kind, but with the sale of the townhouse and the two thousand acres of prime, loamy land, Leonie had been able to placate most of those who had clamored for repayment.

When all the debts that could be paid had been paid, there was still a sizable sum of money owed, and just when Leonie had thought she would lose everything and be thrown homeless and penniless to face the world, one of her *grand-père's* old friends came to her rescue. Monsieur Etienne de la Fontaine was their nearest neighbor; he and Claude had grown up together, and hiding the pity he had felt, he had gently suggested to Leonie that if she would put up the Château and the remaining lands as collateral, he would pay off the remaining debts. Gratefully, the sea-green eyes huge in her pinched face, Leonie had agreed. It had been a very one-sided bargain, for what Claude had owed, even after the sale of the townhouse and other lands, was well above what the Château and the hundred acres were worth. But Monsieur de la Fontaine was a kind old man and Leonie's plight distressed him. Besides, he told himself and others—someday, her husband might redeem everything and he would be well repaid.

Justin, Yvette, Leonie and the half-dozen slaves that clung so tenaciously to her skirts had lived a hand-to-mouth existence in the years that followed. They had farmed the land to obtain most of their food, and with all of them working on the remaining acres from dawn until dusk, until their backs were aching and stiff, their bodies almost exhausted, they had planted and harvested sugar cane as a salable crop for the things they couldn't provide themselves—salt, spices, materials for clothes, and shoes.

But they had survived. Until now—Monsieur de la Fontaine had died last month and his heir, Maurice, was demanding either payment of the note or the forfeiture of the lands and the house.

Staring blankly into space, the striking little face pensive, Leonie sighed. *Mon Dieu,* but life was hard. It was out of the question that she pay off the note, and so, she and the other inhabitants of the house must leave by no later than the fifteenth of May. Maurice de la Fontaine, a smirk on his dark thin face, had been adamant about that.

It was the most frightening situation of her entire life. No matter what had happened to her, her one solace had been the Château Saint-André, her home, her fortress against the world, and now in a matter of weeks, that was being wrested away from her.

Her fingers suddenly crushing the mangled rose, she thought viciously to herself, if Monsieur Slade had repaid me my dowry last year, as promised, all would be well. Damn him for the liar and cheat that he is!

She supposed she should be grateful that he had at least kept one part of their bargain and had not intruded into her life again. But in view of the child that had resulted from her desperate attempt in New Orleans to stave off more of her *grand-père's* debts, she was thankful indeed for her marriage papers. At least no one will call Justin a bastard, she vowed fiercely.

Leonie would not have been human if at times she didn't consider the possibility of appealing to her husband for aid, but her own fiery pride and a deep abiding mistrust and dislike of Monsieur Slade had stilled the notion. She would die and let the worms eat her flesh before she accepted his help. But he *owed* her the dowry, and time and circumstances were forcing her to go after it.

She sighed again, wishing there were some other way she could support herself and her little family. But there was nothing—Yvette's needlework would bring in little, Leonie herself was untrained for any work except the running of a household, and Justin and the blacks that remained with them could earn little money. Her mouth twisting derisively, she admitted there was one other way: Monsieur Maurice had intimated that he might find it agreeable not to foreclose if Leonie would be more accommodating. For obvious reasons, Leonie had scornfully thrown his offer back in his face. No, they would go to Natchez and demand that her dowry be repaid as had been promised.

A brooding expression in the cat-shaped eyes, she gazed at the soft, green mantle of grass that covered Claude's grave and said bleakly, "*Grand-père*, I didn't come here today just to tell you that it is Justin's birthday . . . soon we will be leaving for Natchez and I do not know when we shall be back . . . if ever."

She felt the sting of tears in her eyes and swallowing painfully she added, "I must get Monsieur Slade to repay me my dowry, and I do not know if I will receive the money in time to prevent Maurice from foreclosing. I have spoken with him and he has implied he would give me until the first of July before he accepts any offers for our home. But, *grand-père*, you do understand that I might not be able to meet the deadline? Monsieur Slade has proved himself a dishonorable man, and I may have to take him before a magistrate to get my money. That will take time . . . too much time, I fear."

An empty silence greeted her words, until in one of the oaks a mockingbird's clear song rang out in the warm April air. Leonie twisted around to find the source, and spying the cocky gray and white bird amongst the leafy green branches overhead, she smiled to herself. The mockingbird's song was a gay sound, and listening to the merry notes, she felt her spirits rise. She *would* succeed! She had expected no sign from the grave, but somehow, that happy warble drifting through the lazy spring air encouraged one to step forth with a lighter step . . . and to momentarily feel that the future might not be so bad after all.

Leonie stood up and shook out her faded blue gown. She took one last look around and then with an odd little wave of her hand, whispered, "*Adieu*, all of you who sleep here . . . perhaps one day I shall return."

Without a backwards glance she left the graveyard and walked quickly down the oak-lined dirt road that led to the Château Saint-André. The oaks ended and the Château, like a once beautiful woman who has fallen upon hard

107

times, rose up before her, the graceful lines still very apparent, yet also the signs of age and added wear. But Leonie would not see them today; today she wanted only to see the house as it must have looked when she was born, the pale blue paint glowing softly in the sun, the railings and slender colonnades glistening white against the blue background of the house, the lawns in front a neatly scythed green velvet, and the carriageway smooth and unrutted. She closed her eyes tightly, blocking out everything except the picture in her mind . . . and for one long minute she let that picture form and possess her. Then with a little shake, she opened her eyes and faced reality. *Ah, bah! I am a sentimental fool to mourn an old, decrepit house!* she scolded herself briskly and hurried on her way.

She had barely reached the house when a small tornado came racing around the corner of the house, crying excitedly, "Maman, maman, come quickly, the cat had had her *bébés!* Four of them, and I found them!"

At the sight of Justin, the last vestige of her unhappy thoughts vanished, and an impish grin breaking across the bewitching features, she replied, *"Bon!* We will take them with us when we leave, *oui?"*

Justin was a handsome little boy, even at five years of age showing signs that one day he would be a tall man. His unruly mop of hair was black as midnight, and already the sweet boy's face revealed the beginnings of a firm jawline and an alarmingly masculine nose and chin. It was, even now in childhood, a strong face, and Leonie often stared at it, wondering what his father had looked like. Had he been a handsome man? A tall man? She rather thought so—the Saint-André's had never been noted for their height, and while the Saint-Andrés had been passably good-looking, none of them had ever had quite the handsomeness this child possessed. The chin and jawline, she decided reflectively, must have come from his father, for they did not resemble any of the Saint-André physical traits.

Leonie never thought of Justin's conception. And yet occasionally, in spite of herself, she found herself wondering about the man who had fathered her child. What sort of man had he been? A kind man or a cruel one? As unscrupulous as Morgan Slade was? Or perhaps one who was gentle and concerned like old Monsieur Entienne de la Fontaine had been? She liked to think it would have been the latter, but she rather gloomily suspected the former. But if they had met under different circumstances and if he hadn't been an absolute monster, would she had been drawn to him? Perhaps he would have been attracted to her? She sighed wistfully. If only she hadn't gone to the governor's residence that fateful evening . . . mayhap they would have met socially and who knows—they might have fallen in love with each other, and then Justin would have a *real* father not one that existed only on a legal document!

Suddenly aware of Justin staring up at her, she angrily pushed aside her silly thoughts and smiled down at him. And staring into his much-loved features, she couldn't honestly say that she regretted any longer that night at the governor's residence. But she didn't like to think of it. She had buried that night so deeply in her mind that it was almost as if she had created Justin all by herself. He was *her* son and hers alone!

Justin's impatient tug of her hand caused her smile to widen. How like her he was—always impatient, forever in motion! Laughing at him, hand and hand they both ran off towards the dilapidated stables to view mother cat and her newborn kittens.

Seeing the two of them running together, Leonie's bare legs flashing in the sunlight, one might be forgiven for thinking them brother and sister; Leonie's tawny hair was streaming down her back in wild curls, and with her slender body and bare feet, she hardly looked her twenty-two years of age—she certainly didn't look like the mother of the sturdy little boy at her side. It was only upon closer viewing that one noticed that there was indeed a great deal of difference between this Leonie in 1805 and the Leonie of 1799.

Five, almost six years ago Leonie had been a child, but she was a child no longer. It was true her body was still slim, but there were changes—the firm breasts were fuller and thrusted against the gown she wore; the hips were still slender but more rounded and womanly; it was unconscious, but there was a decidedly provocative sway to her walk; her face had changed the most, the sultry promise of sixteen fulfilled at twenty-two—all signs that this was no child. This was a woman.

There was now cynical knowledge in those great sea-green eyes with the golden flecks, knowledge and mockery that danced in their depths, taunting and yet luring a man. The fine bones of the triangular-shaped face had matured, the jawline both firm and enchanting, the pointed little chin showing clearly the determination and stubbornness of which she was capable. The attractive hollows under the high cheekbones made the face more striking, the slanting green eyes seemed even more mysterious between their gold-tipped lashes, and the sweet curve of the lush coral lips were a blatant challenge that a man might find almost irresistible. Leonie would never be truly lovely, but hers was a face and a form that, once seen, a man did not easily forget. It was the face of a bewitching, untamed dryad, and to anyone looking into those mocking eyes, Maurice de la Fontaine's offer wouldn't be in the least surprising.

At twenty-two she was a curious mixture of innocence and cynicism. She had known a man's passion once, she had borne a child, and yet, she had almost lived the life of a nun. Her dealings with men had not been pleasant—her grandfather had been a selfish wastrel, she had been raped by an unknown man who had treated her like a whore, and her husband, forced upon her by her grandfather, had been certainly less than honorable. It was no wonder that when it came to men she was cynical and suspicious; even old Entienne de la Fontaine's kindness had been canceled out by his son's insulting proposition. And yet Leonie knew little of men. She had been raised away from men and their haunts and habits, and for all she had suffered at the hands of men, she might as well have lived behind the walls of a convent.

Since Claude's death, Château Saint-André had been a household of women, the only men being the black ex-slaves Saul and Abraham; Justin, Abraham, and Mammy's child, Samuel were mere babies yet and didn't count as men. And through necessity, Leonie had been forced to be the leader of the family. She had to be the strong one, the wise one, the one who made the decisions. It was to her

110

that Saul and Abraham came for their orders; it had been she who made all the hard choices that affected their lives, and she who ultimately had to provide a way of life for all of them.

Leonie had freed the slaves when Claude had died and had steeled herself to watch them go, leaving her and Yvette to face the future by themselves. But while they had eagerly enough taken the papers that freed them, no one had seemed inclined to leave the Château Saint-André and life had gone on as it always had. As Mammy had said crisply, "What good it do us to go somewheres else? This is home!"

Leonie had found the argument both heart-wrenching and irrefutable, and as she had been desperate for their help, she had not fought as strongly as she might have to persuade them differently. Even now, when they must leave Château Saint-André, Mammy and the rest were just as determined to go with her—they all belonged together. "It ain't fitting for you to go traipsing off by yourself," Mammy had informed Leonie indignantly, the big black eyes flashing with outrage. "Your *grand-père,* he would skin us alive if he knew we was to let you do this foolish thing. We is family and family stays together!"

And that, Leonie had thought with a tight throat full of tears, *is that!*

Consequently, some three weeks later on a bright sunny day in May of 1805, Leonie, Justine, Yvette, Mammy, and the rest set out for Natchez, Mississippi in two old wagons pulled by four tired-looking brown mules. The cat and her kittens rested safely in a big basket of straw in the back of the wagon in which Justin rode, and his absorption in them lessened the pang he might have felt at leaving his home and birthplace. Leonie did not look back; her face was set towards the north. Silently she vowed that Monsieur Morgan Slade was going to pay back her dowry as promised, or she was going to make his life so miserable that he would wish he had never laid eyes on her!

At that particular moment, on that particular morning, Morgan Slade was idly sipping coffee on the east veranda of Bonheur, wondering why he had come back. *It never*

111

changes, he thought vaguely to himself . . . *the fields grow and the crops ripen, papa grows a little grayer, maman a little plumper . . . and life goes on as it always has.*

It was a cynical thought, but then, Morgan had grown a great deal more derisive and jaded in the past years. He was a restless man, never content to stay long in any one place, and always his gaze was on the next horizon, wondering what excitement and danger might lie over the next ridge, the next mountain. And yet he couldn't deny that his birthplace called to him, and no matter where he had been, he found himself always returning, only to become bored and restless within an appallingly short period of time. And also as always, there was maman telling him tartly that if he had a wife and would settle down and start another family, he wouldn't find life quite so full of ennui. Thinking of her comments last night on that same subject, a sardonic grin slashed across the dark, rakish features. *Perhaps if maman didn't push quite so determinedly, I might find myself agreeing with her,* he thought. *Or perhaps I should simply go away and stay away. . . .*

The first time that he had left on one of his restless searches for something even he couldn't name, there had been a furious argument with his parents—an argument all the more serious because until then, despite his iron will and certain wild traits his parents preferred to ignore, Morgan had been an exemplary son. It was true he lived his life as he saw fit, not taking kindly to their well-meaning interference, but he had never done anything that had truly dismayed or distressed them . . . until he had left to follow Philip Nolan into Spanish Texas.

Reflectively Morgan stared at the contents of his cup, thinking of the changes that had occurred in the world since that day. The Louisiana Territory had passed in quick succession from Spanish hands to French and then to American. President Jefferson was in his second term of office and just last summer, the Vice-President of the United States, Aaron Burr, had shot and killed the leading Federalist, Alexander Hamilton, in a duel. In Europe, Napoleon had been crowned Emperor of France this last December and war was raging on all fronts with the French winning on the land and the British holding the seas.

112

For just a minute Morgan's thoughts stopped, and he briefly considered the possibility of going back to England and going ahead with his original plan to purchase a commission in the British Army. Fighting a war as a soldier instead of a spy might still this reckless disregard of life and constant search for adventure. But then he shrugged; at thirty-three he had matured somewhat, and in view of his narrow escape from Europe earlier this year, he dismissed the idea for the dangerous whim it had been.

But had it been any more dangerous than the whim that had taken him with Nolan in the winter of 1800? Morgan rather thought not, and he smiled at himself. Nolan had returned safely in November of 1799 from his trip to Spanish Texas, and for a time had seemed ready to settle down. He had married Fannie Lintot that December and the wedding had been a notable event in Natchez, for the Lintots were wealthy and well-known. But marriage, a new bride, and even the expectation of a child couldn't hold Nolan, and though denied permission to enter Spanish Texas, he had gone ahead and gathered a party of men and secretly crossed the Sabine River into Texas.

Morgan had accompanied Nolan, and it was only Morgan's restless nature that had saved him from losing his life or finding himself imprisoned deep in Spanish territory. Nolan and his little band of men had passed into the open country beyond the Trinity and the Brazos, where Nolan had elected to camp and begin capturing wild horses. They had fared well in the beginning, and if Morgan wondered how long the Spanish would let them stay unmolested in their territory and without permission, he kept it to himself. He also quickly grew bored with catching wild horses, and when a band of Comanches came to trade horses for goods that Nolan had brought with him, Morgan went with them when they left.

Morgan had lived almost two years with the Comanches, spending the time hunting buffalo, existing like a savage, fighting and raiding Comanche enemies. If he had been a hard man to begin with, he came back from the Comanches harder and tougher. It was in that Spring of 1803, at Natchez, that he learned of Nolan's death at the hands of the Spanish in 1801, and a chill had snaked down his spine. If he had stayed with Nolan. . . .

He found that Natchez held little interest for him, and taking advantage of the Peace of Amiens that existed then between England and France, he had boarded a ship for England. He arrived in England in May, and within days of his arrival, England had once again declared war on France.

Unwilling to remain idle on the sidelines and finding himself even more bored and restless amongst the dandies and simpering, marriage-minded young ladies he had, after a discussion with his uncle, the Baron of Trevelyan, called upon the Duke of Roxbury, Jason Savage's uncle.

Morgan had met the Duke of Roxbury on more than one occasion in his youth, but he was always wary of him— Jason's firm opinion that the Duke's sleepy gray eyes were *not* quite so sleepy, echoed his own. And in this instance both young men were proven correct. Morgan had come to the duke about the possibility of a commission in the army, but before the evening ended, he found himself agreeing to carry messages to spies in France and to turn his hand at a little spying himself. As Roxbury explained it, it seemed perfectly sensible—he spoke French like a native, thanks to a Creole mother, and also thanks to her, there were probably relatives in France who could and would provide him with information. Besides, Roxbury had added with a sly gleam in those gray eyes, it would be much more exciting than the army. Indeed it had been, Morgan thought with a grim smile. More than once in the past eighteen months he had thought it was perhaps a bit *too* exciting. His risky occupation in France had been ended rather abruptly by the unwelcome discovery that his cousin, Ashley, was working for the *French* in England! The instant a French officer had accosted him on a street in Paris, calling him by Ashley's name and wanting to know what new secrets he had brought to the Emperor, Morgan had known, that not only was he in a dangerous predicament, but also that the resemblance between himself and his cousin had made his continued usefulness to Roxbury impossible. Back in his rooms, he had sent a cipher message to Roxbury that he would try to get out of France before someone realized that he *wasn't* Ashley Slade. There was no doubt he would be killed if the truth were discovered, and as it was, he barely escaped out of the country. A company of dragroons had been on his very heels when he had boarded the American privateer that had brought him home.

But the brush with death in France had lessened some of his reckless urges, and today, even though he disliked the idea intensely, he seriously considered his mother's solution to his aimless wanderings. *Perhaps I* should *marry again,* he thought reluctantly. But then the memory of Fannie Lintot came to him, and cynically he admitted that marriage and child hadn't stopped Nolan from seeking his fate. It was an unpleasant thought and Morgan pushed it away.

That evening, as happened several times since he had returned to the United States two months earlier, the Marshall family came to dinner, and Morgan, seated across from their only child, a lovely blue-eyed creature by the name of Melinda, was in no doubt why they were found so often at Bonheur. Melinda's name was the one mentioned the most frequently whenever his mother brought up the subject of marriage. Since the Marshall estates adjoined Bonheur and Melinda was considered quite an heiress in the district, there was no doubt, Morgan mused, that it would be thought a good match.

Idly Morgan let his gaze roam over the girl across from him. She was a pretty thing, he admitted, with those big blue eyes and soft golden curls. But she didn't have a brain in her lovely head, he told himself wryly. Conversation with Melinda consisted of wide-eyed admiration and open-mouthed astonishment. All very prettily done, and he supposed some men might find it quite enchanting; unfortunately, it bored him. And yet in a wife, did a man truly need brains? One of the things he had admired about Stephanie had been her quick wit and intelligent conversation—and look where that had gotten him!

Melinda gave him a shy smile and sardonically Morgan returned it. He happened to glance around a moment later and noticed the pleased expressions on his parents' faces. *Ah, but they do have marriage on their minds, don't they?*

His eyes swung back to Melinda, noting the soft mouth and the alabaster shoulders above her demure pink gown. *Well, why the hell not?* he suddenly decided the sapphire blue eyes suddenly very bright and filled with mockery. *Why the hell not?*

9

If Morgan could have seen Melinda three hours later, he would not have been quite so complacent, and he certainly wouldn't have been seriously considering marriage with her. Locked in the fervent embrace of Gaylord Easton, Melinda was only vaguely aware of her effect on that young man, her thoughts still pleasantly lingering on the evening.

It was only when a somewhat breathless Gaylord, his soft brown hair disheveled from Melinda's absently caressing fingers, lifted his head and shook her slightly that she came back to the present. "Will *nothing* deter you from this foolish path?" he cried desperately. "Doesn't the fact that I love you mean anything to you?"

Gaylord Easton was a handsome young man, in a wild, dark way. He had a pair of fine, flashing brown eyes that had caused havoc among the young ladies of the neighborhood since he had been sixteen, and at twenty-four their brilliant darkness was even more potent. Gaylord was the youngest son of a fairly wealthy planter in the Natchez district, and while he had grown up with nearly his every whim granted, his father had recently made it clear that it was time Gaylord thought about his future. The elder Mr. Easton had stated firmly that while he did not object to paying Gaylord an allowance, and would never see his youngest child in want, Gaylord must stop playing the dilettante and start earning his keep.

Wasn't it time that Gaylord took an active interest in the small estate given to him at his majority? Did he think his father would support him in a lavish style all his life? It was time, Mr. Easton said grimly, that Gaylord learned

117

what a hard day's work consisted of. No more of this sleeping till noon, then joining friends for horses and drink and the like. No more of this careless, aimless pursuit of pleasure!

It was extremely unpalatable news for Gaylord, and shuddering at the thought of working, even if the work consisted of nothing more arduous than overseeing the twelve or so slaves that had also become his when he turned twenty-one, Gaylord had immediately set about seeking another way to feather his pocket. His fine dark eyes had fallen on Melinda Marshall for a variety of reasons. He had always admired her, for she was a beautiful girl, and now with money at the forefront of his mind, her inheritance made her even more beautiful.

Gaylord had begun his calculated courtship some months ago, but somewhere along the line, he had made the mistake of falling madly in love with Melinda; and until the return of Morgan Slade, he had thought he was winning Melinda's capricious heart. Morgan's advent on the scene had been a nasty setback. During the past several weeks, he'd had to sit back and watch with pain and impotence as his love meekly followed her parents' dictates, and his heart was filled with rage and jealousy.

If Gaylord hadn't fallen in love with Melinda, he could have shrugged aside her sudden deflection and looked around for another heiress—certainly there were plenty of them in Natchez—but Melinda's melting blue eyes had stolen his heart and he was in jealous agony. He was furious, yet understanding of her parents' obvious angling for marriage with Morgan Slade. After all, Slade was a far richer man than himself, and Gaylord did have a reputation for wildness and lack of steadiness. There had been one or two incidents that the elder Easton had very quietly hushed up, but even so, Gaylord's reputation was such that most parents might view him with a jaundiced eye. Of course, no one but Gaylord and Melinda knew that their affair had gone quite beyond what was acceptable. This midnight rendezvous was nothing new, nor was the fact that Gaylord had kissed Melinda more than once and had even daringly caressed her smooth white bosom. Gaylord

118

had taken Melinda's consent to meet him as a positive sign and his heart had leaped with joy, but while she consented to these shocking clandestine meetings, she always became rather vague when he pleaded with her to let him approach her father with an offer.

Unfortunately for young Mr. Easton, Melinda had been only testing her feminine wiles on him, and while she had found him exciting at first, and the daring of meeting with him secretly had been most enjoyable, since meeting Mr. Slade, she'd begun to find Gaylord's protestation of love something of a bore. His kisses were very nice, of course, and it was most thrilling when his eyes glittered with suppressed passion and he was nearly shaking with the emotions she aroused, but she had discovered she had suddenly grown weary of it all. Now, Mr. Slade was something else again, she mused dreamily. He wouldn't tear his hair with rage and sulk like Gaylord did when she had slapped his hand for taking liberties. Oh, no, she thought with a delicious shudder, he wouldn't stop so easily.

"Melinda, haven't you heard a word I've just said?" Gaylord said roughly, and blinking her blue eyes like a sleepy kitten, she looked up at his dark, tormented face.

"Yes, of course, I have," she answered sweetly, "But it doesn't change anything. Mr. Slade is calling on father tomorrow morning, and if he makes an offer, I intend to accept."

"But Melinda . . . !" Gaylord cried with anguish, his arms reaching out for her.

They were in the rose garden at the side of Marshall Hall, and Gaylord's voice carried clearly in the still night air.

Almost sharply, Melinda said in a lowered tone, "Oh, hush! Someone might hear!"

Gaylord threw a harassed eye towards the majestic white house, the huge pillars gleaming ghostly in the moonlight, the tall oaks and magnolias appearing almost black against the lightness of the house. It was silent, no sound breaking the stillness, and his voice a hoarse whisper, Gaylord got out, "You can't marry him! You must let me speak to your father first!"

119

Her blue eyes reproachful, Melinda stared at him. "Do you wish for me to be unhappy?"

"No, of course not!" he replied instantly.

"Could you take me to Paris? Could you give me a house as large and wonderful as Bonheur?" she asked reasonably.

His young face uncertain, he said slowly, "No, not at first, but . . ."

Melinda let a tear form in the blue eyes. "You would want me to live in that horrid old house you have on that meager amount of land you own?"

Nonplused, Gaylord looked away. He had never planned for them to live there—he'd meant for her father's money to provide them with something considerably more suitable, but he could hardly tell her that. And he writhed at how mercenary he had been. In a barely audible voice, he muttered, "No, but . . ."

"With Mr. Slade, I shall travel and have lots of lovely clothes. I shall have all the servants I want, and I shall have babies . . . and the biggest, most beautiful home in the area," Melinda said happily, a pleased gleam in the blue eyes. Looking at Gaylord's dark face, she asked, "Could you give me all that?"

"No, but . . ." he began helplessly.

"Then how can you say you love me? And that you want me to be happy, when you don't want me to have the things that I need to *be* happy?" she asked with a pretty pout.

His fine dark eyes flashing with the intensity of his emotions, Gaylord said passionately, "Melinda, I *love* you! I thought you loved me! How can mere *things* compensate for our not being together?"

Melinda let her breath out in a sigh. "I don't know, Gaylord . . . I only know that mother and father want me to marry Mr. Slade, and that he can give me all the things that will make me happy. I will miss you, and I know I will cry at night when I think of your sweet kisses . . . but I think I had better marry Mr. Slade."

"Melinda!" he nearly shouted with helpless fury. "Stop and realize what you are doing. *I love you!*"

Her lovely chin set at an obstinate angle, the golden

curls gleaming softly in the moonlight, Melinda said with paralyzing practicality, "Well, if you love me, you'll want me to be happy. And I think it is very selfish of you to want me *not* to marry Mr. Slade. You said you didn't want me to be unhappy." She hesitated, and then looked so adorably soulful that Gaylord's heart ached as she added, "I should be so very unhappy if I were poor, Gaylord. I couldn't bear it!"

There was no argument Gaylord could offer to change her mind, and with a mixture of love, pain, and a strong desire to strangle her, he watched her slip through the gardens to the house. Knowing his heart was breaking, he turned away, his thoughts heavy and dispirited. He felt it was ironic justice that the woman he loved should want to marry someone else for money, in view of the fact that he had once thought to do that very thing himself. And unfortunately, he didn't even have the solace of thinking she was being forced into the match— she'd made it abundantly clear that she found the idea of being Morgan Slade's wife more than a little appealing.

Melinda wasn't quite as mercenary as she appeared. But when Morgan had made the assessment that she hadn't any brains, he hadn't been far wrong. Melinda had all the intelligence of a spoiled, petted child of ten. There wasn't a mean bone in her body and she was at heart a gentle person, if singleminded in the pursuit of her own happiness. She had been fond of Gaylord in her fashion, and if he had been rich, she would have very happily married him and settled down to be a loving wife and mother. But she also looked out for her own comfort, and while Gaylord's dark eyes had once attracted her, Morgan's mocking blue ones did now. Completely oblivious to the hurt she had inflicted upon Gaylord, she happily made her way to her room and once in bed proceeded to sleep deeply, her dreams full of Morgan's dark, ruthless face.

To Melinda's immense satisfaction and delight, Mr. Morgan Slade did come to call upon her father the next morning, and that afternoon in the same garden that had seen the death of Gaylord's hopes, she very prettily accepted Morgan's offer. She looked lovely in the golden sunshine, her flawless face protected by a wide-brimmed straw hat, and her high-waisted blue gown trimmed in delicate lace intensifying the blue of the big eyes. Politely kissing the soft white hand that had been extended, Morgan smiled to himself, thinking that perhaps life with this sweet, undemanding child might be quite enjoyable. He gallantly pushed aside the thought that it would also be boring . . . very.

The two families were jubilant, and in the evening there was a small dinner party to celebrate the betrothal. It was decided that on the first of June there would be a large formal party at Marshall Hall to announce the approaching nuptials, and Morgan had found himself agreeing to a marriage in August. He also found himself curiously disinterested in any of the plans that were discussed. Stifling a yawn, his face very dark above his white linen shirt and his blue eyes full of mockery, he finally excused himself from the talk of wedding gowns, food, and drink, and wandered outside.

Walking slowly around the wide veranda of Marshall Hall, glancing occasionally out at the well-kept gardens, the color and vibrancy of the shrubs muted in the moonlight, Morgan let his thoughts drift. Stopping at the broad steps that led to the massive double doors at the front of the mansion, he lit a thin, black cheroot and savored for a moment the aroma of good Virginia tobacco.

The double-breasted evening coat he was wearing tonight fit his broad shoulders expertly, and in the moonlight the dark blue color appeared black, his linen shirt a white blur in the shadows of the night. The tip of his cheroot gleamed whenever he raised it to his lips to take a deep, satisfying drag, the smoke curling like an ever-changing mist near his dark head.

Blankly he stared out across the wide expanse of lawns, his thoughts far away from the tranquility and peacefulness of the night, and he was suddenly assailed with an aching longing for the seemingly endless acres of tall, waving grass of the plains of Texas and the sound of the wind's mournful keen as it swept across the prairie. He took an absent drag of the cheroot, one hand resting in the pocket of his nankeen breeches, and glanced at the full moon. *A Comanche moon,* he thought to himself, *a raiding moon,* and the yearning for the wild, savage days of those two years with the Comanches swept over him. He sighed and grimaced in the darkness. *Why do I always seem to want to be where I am not?* he asked the night silently. He hadn't always been this restless, reckless seeker, he admitted to himself. *No,* he thought bitterly, *not until Stephanie and Phillippe's death.*

Time had dulled some of the pain of Phillippe's death, but it had done nothing to lessen his contempt and cool indifference to the women who sought his attention. Even having agreed to marry Melinda, he couldn't say that his ideas about women had changed. Absently his fingers lightly touched the little gold cross that still hung from his watch chain after all these years—women were deceivers ever, he reminded himself. And for the first time in a very long time he found himself thinking about the virgin whore he had taken that night at the governor's residence in New Orleans. Where was she now? Morgan wondered idly. And would she still be as desirable as she had been that night? Or had time and the life she had chosen transformed her vibrant young body into that of a worn hag all too soon? The thought disturbed him, especially since he could remember vividly the feel of her in his arms, and he moved uneasily. *She haunts me even now,* he admitted wryly. It must have been the mystery, the curiosity about her identity and the reasons behind her actions that made him recall her so clearly, he decided slowly. What other reason could there be?

I should have tried harder to find her, he concluded grimly. Once seen in the clear light of day there would have been no more mystery about her to taunt and tantalize him. And who knew—once seen, once her identity was established—he might have decided to make an honest woman of her. Why not? She had come to him a virgin and he would have had no doubts about her purity . . . at least at first. She had been young, very young, of that he was certain, and he could have molded her to suit him precisely. Morgan laughed harshly under his breath. Oh, yes, that's exactly what he should have done—married his virgin whore and brought her home to Natchez.

A burst of laughter from the house intruded into his thoughts, and taking one last drag of the cheroot, he pitched it into the darkness and it made a flaming arch against the blackness of the night. *My little betrothed awaits me,* he told himself grimly and then turned to go into the house, only to be brought up short by the sight of his younger brother Dominic leaning negligently against one of the huge, white pillars of the house.

Dominic spoke first. Pushing himself away from the pillar, he said, "I've been watching you the past few minutes, and I'll be damned if you give the impression of a man on the verge of embarking upon the happy state of marriage. More like someone who's received a death sentence."

Morgan smiled and cocked one thick, black eyebrow. "And you have made an extensive study?"

"No, but despite the separations, I do know you, and you're not in the best of moods at the moment . . . and I wondered why."

Dominic had grown into a tall, slender young man during the past five, almost six years, and while he didn't yet have the broadness of shoulders that his older brother possessed, he would have in a few more years. The childish softness that had been his at seventeen had vanished and left a face that wasn't precisely handsome, and yet there was something about the laughing mouth and dancing gray eyes that made one think that Dominic at twenty-three was *very* handsome. He walked slowly towards his brother and added, "The thing that has me puzzled is why, out of all the belles in the district, you chose that ninny-hammer!"

Cool amusement glittering the dark blue eyes, Morgan replied dulcetly, "True, but think how undemanding she will be. As long as I give her a child every few years, and buy her gowns and take her to Paris now and then, she will be perfectly contented."

Dominic frowned in the darkness, not liking either the expression on Morgan's face nor his tone of voice. Studiously observing the toe of one highly polished evening

124

shoe, Dominic said slowly, "Morgan, I hesitate to mention this, but are you certain you're doing the right thing?"

Morgan shrugged his shoulders and replied wearily, "God knows! But I'm tired of wandering like one of the Israelites in the desert, and marriage seems one way of putting a stop to it."

Dominic said nothing for a moment and then very casually he murmured, "Did you know that up until you arrived home, Gaylord Easton had been paying very assiduous court to the fair Melinda?"

Sending his younger brother a level glance, Morgan reached into his waistcoat and pulled out another cheroot. Taking his time he lit it, and then just as casually he asked, "Old Lloyd Easton's youngest cub?"

"Hmm. The very same," Dominic answered noncommittally. "The gossips say that Gaylord needed a rich wife and that Melinda was his choice . . . until you came back. There's some who even say she wasn't averse to his suit either."

His voice without inflection, Morgan inquired, "Are you warning me about something, Dom?"

A picture of innocence, Dominic glanced up. "Me? Of course not! I just thought you might find it interesting." Dominic turned away and started towards the house and then stopped. Over his shoulder he added, "I'd be careful of Gaylord, Morgan—he doesn't have the best reputation, and I would wager he's not going to take Melinda's betrothal well . . . or without trying to do something to stop it."

Without another word, Dominic strolled back into the house, leaving Morgan alone with his unpleasant thoughts. Dominic hadn't been exactly subtle, and the knowledge that Melinda had been involved with another man just prior to his arrival sat ill with Morgan—especially in view of what had happened with Stephanie. He wasn't jealous, and if the involvement had been an old affair, he would have dimissed it. But Dom had obviously felt the need to warn him, and as his brother was not given to gossip, Morgan took heed of the words. Had Melinda's heart been involved with Easton . . . and were her parents pushing her into a more advantageous match?

125

During the days prior to the public announcement of their impending nuptials, Morgan made several attempts to discover just that, but to all his gentle probings, Melinda returned a sweet smile and began to speak of something entirely different—usually her wedding gown or their plans for the future. She was particularly insistent about wanting to go to Paris, once the horrid war between England and France was over, to buy an entire wardrobe, and Morgan was left with the bitter reflection that marriage was *not* going to be the answer to his restless state.

Gaylord Easton had lived up to Dominic's prophecy, and Morgan had found himself delicately treading a line between the desire to laugh out loud at Easton's ridiculous behavior and a strong inclination to give the young man the fight he was obviously spoiling for. Gaylord made no secret of his blighted hopes, and while most people were inclined to smooth over his wild accusations that Morgan had used unfair tactics in gaining Melinda's hand and heart, there were a few who nodded their heads in agreement and encouraged young Easton to make a complete fool of himself. Things came to head two evenings before the grand ball at which Morgan and Melinda were to be toasted and honored.

Seeking some relief from the talk of the wedding and the rapidly approaching ball, Morgan had escaped to King's Tavern, which was located on a slight hill on the outskirts of town. The place was not precisely fashionable, but Morgan liked its simple good cheer and comfort.

The well-known tavern was situated at the end of the Natchez Trace, and travelers usually stopped here either traveling up or down the Trace. Consequently, it was a busy place and there was generally a pleasant hum of activity about the tavern. The lower floor was bricked and it was here that the taproom and kitchen were located, while the second story, constructed of wood with a narrow porch and slim wooden columns, consisted of private rooms for the weary travelers.

Stepping inside the taproom with its thick wooden beams and narrow doors and windows, Morgan was reminded of similiar places in England and France—the air was blue with smoke from the cigars and cheroots; the smell of ale and whiskey and the appetizing aroma of roasting beef and baking hams assailed his nostrils. He recognized a few people from town, but most of the patrons were strangers to him, as was to be expected. Finding a small oak table in a secluded corner, he settled back comfortably in the wooden chair and prepared to relax and watch his fellow patrons. After ordering a glass of Monongahela rye whiskey, he lit a cheroot and glanced idly around the taproom, his experienced eye appraising and judging the other inhabitants, the obvious travelers, the merchants from town, and the few young bucks who preferred the easy atmosphere of the tavern to exclusive places in town.

He had just taken his first sip of the strong rye whiskey when Gaylord and two companions lurched into the taproom. It was obvious that Gaylord had been drinking as could be seen from the unsteady sway in his gait when he approached the bar that ran along one side, and Morgan cursed under his breath. Gaylord Easton was the *last* person he wished to meet tonight! So far, he had managed to avoid a direct challenge from that hot-tempered young man, but judging Gaylord's condition tonight, he rather doubted that a confrontation could be averted if Gaylord spotted him.

Gaylord didn't see Morgan in the murky gloom of the taproom at first, and as he and his companions took a table on the other side of the room, Morgan hoped he would escape detection. For a while, it appeared he might. Gaylord's back was to him, and as that young man seemed intent upon drowning his sorrows in glass after glass of whiskey, Morgan relaxed slightly, thinking he could either outwait Gaylord or slip out unnoticed. He didn't want to have to kill the young fool in a senseless, unavoidable duel.

Unfortunately, his chance for escape was foiled when one of Gaylord's companions looked across the room and recognized him. The other man, a fair-haired youth of about twenty, instantly leaned over the table and said something in Gaylord's ear that caused him to jerk around and stare blearily in Morgan's direction. Morgan swore under his breath as Gaylord suddenly erupted to his feet and began a determined, if stumbling, walk towards him.

Thinking quickly, his mind working coolly as it had in the past when he had found himself in a tight position, Morgan decided that the one way to avoid bloodshed was to let Gaylord challenge him. As the challenged one, Morgan then had the right to choose weapons, time and place. If luck was with him, he could turn this dangerous, silly situation into a farce.

Gaylord reached his table and slamming both hands down hard on the table, he said aggressively, "You, sir, are a scoundrel and a blackguard!"

His blue eyes locked on Gaylord's flushed, handsome face, Morgan took a deliberate sip of his whiskey and then asked indifferently, "Oh? And why is that?"

Taken aback, Gaylord's dark young features expressed puzzlement "Well, because . . ." he began uncertainly and then stopped in confusion. He was very drunk and his thoughts were foggy, but he was quite certain he had just grievously insulted his successful rival. Why wasn't the man reacting? Deciding he hadn't made himself clear enough, he blustered, "You have stolen the heart of the woman I love! Only the basest dastard would do such a thing!"

Morgan sighed. What in the hell was he going to do with this hare-brained rapscallion? Even if his emotions were not involved, he wasn't about to have Melinda's name bandied about in a common taproom by a drunken fool. Eyeing Gaylord's gaudy yellow satin waistcoat with ill-concealed amusement, Morgan thought swiftly and then said coolly, "If I am a blackguard and a scoundrel, as well as a base dastard, what then are you? A trumpeting fool? Or perhaps just an ass-eared dunce?"

It was brutal, but it had the desired effect. Like one struck by lightning, Gaylord stiffened upright and burst out hotly, "And you, sir, are insulting! Name your seconds! I shall not let this *too* pass!"

Morgan leaned back further in his chair, and after flicking an ash from his cheroot, while Gaylord waited in simmering silence, he finally returned lazily, "Oh, I don't think that will be necessary. Seconds will not resolve this between us, will they?"

"By God, no!" Gaylord shot back furiously.

"Then may I offer a suggestion?" Morgan glanced up to the angry young man and at Gaylord's curt nod, he continued unhurriedly, "As the challenged man, I have the right to name the place and the time and the weapons . . . and what better place or time than here and now?"

Gaylord was too angry to think, but he did send a questioning look around the crowded room. "Here? In the tavern?"

His blue eyes glinting with mockery, and his face very dark and enigmatic in the gloom of the room, Morgan drawled, "Perhaps not right here—the garden adjacent should do very nicely, don't you think?"

"Absolutely! Name your weapons!" Gaylord said stiffly, the impending duel and the danger involved clearing his head rather effectively.

"Fists," Morgan said softly.

"Fists!" Gaylord repeated incredulously. "What are you, some kind of riverboat brawler? A gentleman doesn't fight a duel with his *fists!*"

The blue eyes suddenly hard and a dangerous smile breaking across the rakish features, Morgan murmured softly, "You've already said I'm no gentleman."

Gaylord gulped, instantly wishing he hadn't let the liquor plunge him into this predicament. He couldn't back out, and so taking a deep breath, he said with an attempt at bravado, "Very well. I suppose it is what I should have expected from your likes."

Now, Morgan had been very patient and to a certain extent he sympathized with the young fool—a broken heart is not easy to soothe—but his temper was beginning to soar and in a level tone he promised grimly, "One more word, and I'm afraid I might be compelled to kill you instead of merely teaching you the lesson you so richly deserve!"

Fortunately, Gaylord seemed disinclined to press the issue, and within seconds the two men, followed by Gaylord's companions, were standing at the side of the tavern. It was almost pitch-black outside, the waning moon only a thin curve of silver in the sky, but the feeble glow from the narrow windows of the tavern itself shed enough light for Morgan to see the others distinctly.

From the tavern came the occasional sound of a clinking glass and the rise and fall of conversation and laughter, but outside where the four men stood, there was a taut, tense silence. Gaylord was nervous, and it was apparent to Morgan that his two companions were definitely feeling ill at ease and slightly uncertain.

He didn't recognize the two other young men, but that wasn't surprising—he could probably give them a good ten years advantage, and in the last five or six years Natchez hadn't seen a great deal of him. They looked like what they evidently were, a couple of high-spirited youths out for any lark, but Morgan suspected there wasn't any real evil in them—for that matter in young Easton either. His summation proved to be correct, as one of the young men, a short, dark-haired fellow, said nervously, "Um, if it's acceptable to you, sir, I'll act as your second. The name is Blanchard, sir, Evan Blanchard."

Morgan nodded his head and replied, "That's very kind of you. And as that little technicality has been settled, shall we begin?"

Gaylord pulled uneasily at his starched cravat and blurted out, "What exactly did you have in mind?"

Thoughtfully, Morgan glanced around the area. It was fairly clear of obstacles, the ground packed from years of passage by human feet, and the only shrubbery a few straggling oaks. "I suggest we have our duel here. Fists shall be the weapons, Blanchard and your friend shall act as witnesses and seconds. Whoever draws first blood will consider himself satisfied. Fair enough?"

Gaylord gave a stiff nod, and as the first shock of finding himself actually challenging his rival for Melinda's hand was lessening, he grew more confident. A patronizing note creeping into his voice, he said, "I'm considered to be very handy with my fives . . . and you are at least ten years older . . . are you certain you wish for such a *physical* confrontation?"

Morgan stifled back a snort of laughter, and keeping his face perfectly straight he murmured, "Oh, I think I shall

130

manage. Thank you, though, for your concern." If the young fool thought that at thirty-three he was old and decrepit, Morgan would just have to show him the error of his ways. Barroom brawls and hand fighting were no strangers to Morgan—not with the dangerous life he had lived these past years. More than once it had been only his punishing right cross between himself and death or imprisonment, but there was no way he was going to explain that to this arrogant puppy.

The two men were fairly evenly matched—Morgan was perhaps a few inches taller, but Gaylord was more powerfully built—and in an increasingly tense silence, they prepared for the duel. Unhurriedly Morgan shrugged out of the elegantly cut gray jacket he was wearing, and just as calmly unhooked his watch with its gold chain from his white Marseilles waistcoat, the little crucifix dangling at the other end of the chain. Silently he handed the objects to the waiting Blanchard and then set about undoing the exquisitely arranged, starched cravat at his neck.

Morgan's movements were sure and deft, almost indifferent, whereas Gaylord performed the same sequence of disrobing with short, jerky bursts of angry energy, his sense of injustice growing with every moment. By the time both men were in their shirtsleeves and ready to actually begin the fight, Gaylord had whipped himself into a fine, raging temper, and, finally facing his enemy across the small space that separated them, he snapped, "You will not marry Melinda! She has promised her heart to me, and I shall not stand idly by and let you marry her!"

Inwardly Morgan sighed with exasperation and was very tempted to tell the young fool that he could have his bloody Melinda—any desire that Morgan may have had to marry that particular young lady had faded with every passing moment he spent in her prattling, empty-headed company. But essentially being a gentleman, he wasn't about to renege on his offer to marry, although he damned well wished he hadn't been *quite* so impetuous in asking for her dainty little hand—which was something he could hardly tell the angry young man across from him!

Hiding his growing impatience and distaste for the entire silly episode, he merely remarked quietly, "That remains to be seen. But in the meantime, I would remind you that the young woman's name you bandy about so freely *has* accepted my offer."

Gaylord gritted his teeth with sheer fury and snarled, "But she shall *not* marry you! You may think you have won for the moment, but we'll see whom she marries in the end!"

Morgan shrugged and raised one black eyebrow quizzically, "If you've finished with your harangue, shall we begin?"

"By God, *yes!*"

It was an uneven fight from the beginning. Gaylord may have had righteous wrath on his side and a more powerful, younger body, but he was no match for Morgan's iron sinews and steel-sprung muscles, as he soon found out. For a tall man, Morgan was swift and light on his feet; he was also deadly with his fists, and while Gaylord managed to land one wild swipe in a bruising blow to Morgan's lean cheek, Morgan brought the extraordinary duel to a quick end.

Dancing expertly out of reach of Gaylord's maddening swings, Morgan watched intently for the opening he wanted. It came within a few seconds of the start of the fight, and with lethal accuracy his right fist connected with Gaylord's handsome chin. The blow rocked Gaylord off his feet and sent him smashing to the ground, also splitting his lip, and staring at the blood that rushed down his chin, Morgan said evenly, "I believe first blood is mine."

Gaylord's dark eyes flashed up at him, and with fury and chagrin he growled, "You'll still not marry her! I tell you now, I shall do everything and anything within my power to stop you! Anything!"

Morgan smiled at him pityingly, wondering if he had ever been quite so young and impassioned. Then his face hardened. Yes, he had been . . . until a lying, cheating jade of a wife had shown him the errors of his ways. Shrugging into his jacket held reverently by an admiring Mr. Blanch-

132

ard, Morgan said cooly, "In that case I presume it behooves me to beware."

Gaylord sat up and wiped his bloody lip. Glaring up at Morgan, he spat fiercely, "You think I jest, but I *shall* stop you! You'll see, I'll *find* a way!"

10

The day of the betrothal ball dawned bright and clear. Standing at his window at Bonheur, sourly viewing the clear, cloudless blue sky, Morgan decided that the day's warm promise certainly did not reflect his inner feelings. The brief, ridiculous duel with Gaylord Easton had given him much to think about, and he knew now, had known from the moment he had offered for her, that the last thing in the world he wanted to do was marry Melinda Marshall. *Even that soft, white body can't tempt me,* he thought. There was nothing that Melinda could give him that would compensate for being leg-shackled to a woman whose one aim in life was to dress well and have babies . . . if, she had confided tranquilly to Morgan just yesterday, they didn't ruin her slim body!

Gaylord, my young, silly friend, if you can come up with a way to gain your heart's desire, you have my blessing! I'd even help you!

Gaylord wasn't going to need anyone's help in stopping his marriage, for Leonie Saint-André was about to burst on the scene. But of course neither Morgan, as he gloomily prepared to attend his betrothal ball that night, nor Gaylord as he miserably made his way to King's Tavern to drown his sorrows in whiskey, was aware of that fact.

Leonie and her little group had arrived that day in Natchez just as the sun was fading; having no idea where to locate her erstwhile husband, she had not sought a place to stay for the night. Trying to conserve her slim resources, Leonie had nervously skirted the squalor of Natchez-under-the-Hill, passed by the elegant and expensive inns and taverns on the bluff above, and finally settled her exhausted, travel-stained entourage in the homey, plain comforts of King's Tavern.

The journey from Château Saint-André to Natchez had been without incident, but it had also been a long, tension-filled trip for them all. Not one of the little group had ever been farther away from home than New Orleans, and as they pressed deeper and deeper into the wilderness the simple act of making one's bed on the hard ground in a strange, unfamiliar territory had been an ordeal.

Relief had almost been palpable when they had reached Natchez. Mammy, her round black face shining with delight at having arrived alive and unscathed at their destination after the long, lonely stretches of green wilderness, had said firmly, "That was the last time I leaves home!"

Leonie had smiled tiredly, unwilling to argue, and at that moment, all she cared for was a bath and a real bed. But by the time everyone had been settled in and she had bathed and put on a clean gown, her spirits had revived, and she was preparing to find Monsieur Slade. By eight o'clock that night, having seen that everybody was comfortably occupied for the night, Leonie sat planning quietly in the room she shared with Yvette and Justin. She would ask the proprietor if he knew of Monsieur Slade, and depending on what he told her, she would proceed from there. Looking across at Yvette who sat in a small, wooden rocker plying her needle, Leonie asked abruptly, "Will you be all right with Justin, if I leave you for a while?"

Yvette's lovely brown eyes were troubled as she glanced at her half-sister. "You mean to begin immediately searching for him, don't you?"

Leonie nodded her tawny head vigorously. *"Oui!* We haven't much time. What little money we have will not last very long. . . . I must see Monsieur Slade as soon as possible."

Justin, who had been sleepily playing with the kittens on the floor near Leonie's feet, looked up, and with a sparkle in the green eyes, so like his mother's, he demanded, "You are going to see my papa? I wish to come too!"

Leonie bit her lip and made some vague reply. Presenting Justin to Monsieur Slade was going to be dangerously difficult. Justin's conception was a secret that Leonie had

135

not shared, and everyone assumed he was her husband's child. For obvious reasons she had not seen fit to explain any differently, and Justin had grown up believing Monsieur Slade to be his father. What she had not counted on was Monsieur Slade seeing Justin, and now that the moment was fast approaching, she was understandably uneasy and terrified that the truth would come out. She could not bear for Justin to be labeled a bastard, and in some way, just precisely how escaped her, she intended to avoid that.

The only glimmer of hope she had was the fact that Morgan Slade had been *very* drunk their wedding night, and it was possible, if not probable, that if he found out about Justin's existence she could convince him that *he* had fathered the child. *Mon Dieu! but that is unlikely,* she thought angrily. It was far too probable that he was going to remember vividly how she had denied him her bed, threatening him with a pistol! *I shall just have to take a gamble,* she decided determinedly. *No matter what he says if he learns of Justin, I shall just stoutly maintain that Justin is his son.*

Shaking out the soft folds of her gown, she stood up, and then bent down and kissed Justin's cheek. *"Bon nuit, mon fils*—you will do as *tante* Yvette says, and go to bed soon?"

Justin made a face, but as he was an agreeable child, he nodded his dark, curly-haired head. *"Oui, maman.* You will not be gone long?"

Leonie answered him honestly. "Only as long as it takes, but I shall hurry, *mon petit.*"

Then with a swirl of her skirts, she was gone from the room. Unaware of the enchanting picture she made in the gown of lavender muslin, the long, unruly hair caught in a coil of braids at the back and short ringlets round her face, she hurried down the hall, intent upon finding the tavern's proprietor.

The lavender gown was one of the dresses her *grand-père* had bought when she had married Monsieur Slade, and despite being almost six years old, it was still quite fashionable with its high waist and slim, narrow skirt. It was a bit low-cut for Leonie's taste, but she had solved that problem by wearing a square shawl of cream silk across her shoulders and fastening it in the center with a cameo brooch that had belonged to her *grand-mère*.

A frivolous reticule of white lutestring spangled with silver hung from one slim hand; it contained the all-important agreements that Monsieur Slade had signed in the summer of 1799. Agreements he was now going to honor, she thought grimly as she reached the stairway that led to a small garden at the side of the tavern.

It was the same garden where two nights earlier Gaylord and Morgan had fought their ridiculous duel. As luck or fate would have it, Gaylord had wandered from the taproom and was brooding over the indignities he had suffered at Morgan's hands when Leonie came down the stairs. Seeing the young man standing there in the darkness, his form and shape faintly outlined in the light from the tavern, Leonie stopped instantly.

Since the night she had lost her virginity at the hands of a stranger, Leonie was not quite as foolishly intrepid as she had once been. This young man in his well-cut, brown jacket and buff breeches did not look dangerous, but she was not going to leave herself open to suffer a repetition of that night. She stood there indecisively, wishing he would leave, and had just decided to return to her rooms when Gaylord saw her standing there.

A polite young man under most circumstances, and not so drunk that he didn't recognize a lady when he saw her, he bowed politely and murmured, "Good evening, Ma'am. It is a pleasant evening, is it not?"

Still not leaving the safety of the stairway, tensed to run if he made any overt move, but slightly reassured by his elegant clothes and well-bred voice, Leonie replied just as politely, *"Oui*, monsieur, it is."

The soft French accent caught his attention, and walking slowly towards her, he asked, "Are you newly arrived here in Natchez? I couldn't help but notice your accent."

As he approached, Leonie surreptitiously moved farther up the stairs. She didn't mind conversing with strangers . . . provided they didn't get too close. *"Oui*, monsieur, my family and I arrived here just this evening."

Gaylord stopped at the newel, and looking up at Leonie, catching his first sight of the bewitching face with its high

137

cheek bones, slanting eyes, and sweetly curved mouth, he decided instantly that perhaps Melinda *wasn't* the most beautiful girl in the world. The dark eyes glowing with admiration, he flashed his most charming smile, and said softly, "I sincerely hope that you and your family plan on a long stay in Natchez. And would you think me very forward if I asked to be numbered amongst your first . . . and most honored acquaintances?"

Unused to the intricacies of flirting, Leonie shrugged and answered indifferently, "If you wish, monsieur." She frowned for a moment, and then sending him a considering glance she asked slowly, "Are you familiar with the people who live here in Natchez?"

Slightly taken aback at her cool reception to his practiced charm, he muttered, "I should think so . . . I have lived here all my life."

"Then, perhaps you could tell me where a Monsieur Morgan Slade lives?"

The simple words had an electrifying effect on Gaylord. He stiffened and the charming smile was wiped instantly from his handsome features. The hand resting on the newel tightened convulsively while his other hand closed into a fist, and in a harsh voice he demanded, "And what would be your business with Slade?"

Leonie's winged eyebrows rose haughtily at his manner, and in a cold little voice she answered, "I do not see that it is your concern, but he is my husband and I wish to find him!"

Gaylord's fine brown eyes nearly started from his head, and he burst out with great astonishment, "You're lying! He's not married!"

Not noted for her even temper, Leonie flushed, and the green eyes glinting with golden flecks, she spat, "And you, sir, are insulting! How dare you accost me and call me a liar!" She spun on her heels, intent upon returning to her room, but Gaylord wasn't about to have their confrontation end. Bounding up the stairs, he caught her arm and jerked her around to face him. "Now, just a minute! I want to talk to you!" he snapped.

Furious that this stranger would lay a hand on her, and just a little frightened considering what had happened the

138

last time a strange man had done so, Leonie smacked him soundly with her hand and gave him a robust shove that sent him tumbling backwards down the stairs. Her small bosom heaving under the silk shawl, she watched with satisfaction as he sprawled in the dirt at the bottom of the stairs.

Abraham, having been ordered by Mammy to check on the young mistress before they retired for the night, came around the corner of the tavern just then, and Leonie was never so happy to see his sad-eyed black face as then. "Abraham! *Mon Dieu!*, but I am pleased to see you! This creature attacked me!"

"Now, wait a minute!" Gaylord got out as he struggled to his feet. "I don't mean to harm you, and I would like very much to speak with you about—er—your husband."

Despite her anger and her fear, Leonie was curious to learn what this young man knew about Monsieur Slade. She slowly descended the stairs until she stood in front of him. Abraham lurked nearby, not certain whether to go for help or stay and defend his young mistress.

Gaylord glanced in his direction and said with difficulty, "I mean your mistress no harm." And then swinging back to Leonie, he added, "I apologize for grabbing you that way, but you startled me."

"*I* startled *you,* monsieur?" Leonie asked with obvious disbelief.

Defensively Gaylord replied, "Yes, you did. Are you certain that Morgan Slade is your husband?"

Leonie took a deep, angry breath, infuriated that a stranger would doubt her word about something so important. She dug around in the reticule and found the marriage license. Furiously she threw it at him and spat, "There, monsieur!"

Holding the paper in his hands, his mouth gaping foolishly, Gaylord read the legal words and stared at the bold signature of Morgan Slade. "My God!" he cried out distractedly at last. "My poor Melinda is about to commit bigamy! The devil! *That black-hearted monster!*"

Puzzled by his reaction, but still very angry herself, Leonie stood in toe-tapping impatience and demanded, "What are you talking about? *Who* is a black-hearted monster?"

139

Gaylord looked at her with sudden pity. She was an enchanting little creature . . . and to think that Morgan Slade had obviously deserted her and was on the point of announcing his betrothal to another woman. Frowning, Gaylord said bluntly, "I'm afraid your husband is, madame."

"Ah, bah! I knew *that!*" Leonie returned forthrightly. "But what of this woman Melinda, and bigamy?"

Drawing himself up stiffly, Gaylord announced dramatically, "Melinda is the woman I love—and your husband has stolen her from me! At this very moment they are announcing their betrothal!"

"Mon Dieu! This *cannot* be!" Leonie breathed. She had known that Monsieur Slade was not honorable, but to think that he would attempt to marry another woman was beyond anything she could have imagined. The vivid little face fierce with determination, she declared passionately, "We must stop them! He must not be allowed to do this dastardly act!"

Their previous disagreement forgotten, in a very few minutes Leonie and Gaylord Easton were speeding through the night in a hastily rented gig. Easton drove while Abraham glumly hung on to the rear. She might be in complete cordiality with Monsieur Easton at the moment, but common sense dictated that she bring along Abraham—her distrust of so-called gentlemen went too deep.

It was almost nine o'clock when the gig turned down the long drive that led to Marshall Hall. Gaylord was in a fever of impatience, and his heart was singing in his breast, for now his dear, sweet Melinda would never marry that bastard Morgan Slade—*he* would expose the man for the evil-hearted bigamist he was.

Leonie's outrage had not cooled as the miles had passed, and by the time Gaylord hauled the rented horse to a snorting standstill in front of the mansion, she was in a flaming fury. How dare Monsieur Slade take advantage of another defenseless young woman? Perhaps he made a habit of marrying unwary females for what money he could gain. It was an unsettling thought, considering the circumstances, but her main concern was that she save this Melinda Marshall from this horrid fate.

The impressive elegance of the huge house did not deter her, nor did the sight of the many carriages or the sound of voices and laughter that carried from the many lighted windows. It was going to be an embarrassing situation, but she was without fear or shame. Tightly clutching the reticule which contained the proof of Monsieur Slade's perfidy, she swiftly walked up the broad, white steps with Gaylord.

A butler in a black satin uniform and a pristine, white shirt looked them up and down, obviously dismissing Leonie's simple gown and Gaylord's casual dress of breeches and boots. In a voice cool with disapproval, he asked, "Your invitation, sir?"

Attacked with nervousness as he contemplated what he was about to do, Gaylord ran a trembling finger around the edge of his cravat and stammered, "Um, ah, we don't have one. But it is of the utmost importance that I speak with Mr. Marshall!"

The butler raised a haughty eyebrow. "If you will tell me the nature of your business, I shall see if Mr. Marshall is available."

Leonie had stood silently by Gaylord's side during this exchange, her temper rising with every passing moment. Deciding that Gaylord, for all his desire to expose Monsieur Slade, would dither forever, she caught both men by surprise as she stalked determinedly past the butler and said disgustedly, "Ah, bah! By the time you do that, it will be too late! I shall find Monsieur Marshall myself!"

The butler made an attempt to intercept her, but Leonie was not to be stopped. With Gaylord following uncertainly behind them, the butler breathing shocked protests, Leonie walked swiftly down the wide, gold and white hall, stopping only when she came to the wide, arching doorway of the ballroom.

The ballroom was full of men and women in silks and satins; the light from hundreds of candles in the crystal chandeliers above bathed the room in a golden glow. It was a handsome room of grand proportions; the highly waxed, wooden floor shone like amber glass in the candlelight. The women's gowns were vivid splashes of jeweled color as they moved about; the men were more somberly arrayed in

141

velvets and satins of dark blues, deep greens, and black. Soft music drifted across the room, and the sweet scent of roses and honeysuckle permeated the air. Satin-garbed servants discreetly darted about with huge trays laden with refreshments.

Leonie stood for a moment in the center of the arch, her eyes slowly scanning the room. The size of the fashionable throng disarmed her and she was instantly assailed by a flicker of doubt. *Mon Dieu,* how would she find Monsieur Slade in this crowd? But she didn't have to go looking for Morgan Slade, because Morgan found her.

The evening had been passing with paralyzing boredom for Morgan, and any small hope he had cherished that life with Melinda might not be quite as insipid as he feared had been put to flight by a walk in the garden with that young woman.

Melinda, he had to admit, looked lovely. Gowned in blue satin and lace, her guinea-gold curls framing her pretty face, she was indeed a sight to quicken a man's blood. Unfortunately, Morgan's blood did not quicken, and as they walked and conversed desultorily in the garden, he had wondered again how he could have been such a fool as to think marriage to an empty-headed moonling like Melinda would solve anything.

As they walked, Melinda had bemoaned the fact they would not be able to visit Paris for a honeymoon. A plaintive note in her voice, she had complained, "That terrible Napoleon—he is ruining everything! If only that horrid war would end, we would be able to go to Paris. I did so want to visit there."

Forgetting the intelligence of the woman he was with, Morgan had murmured teasingly, "Perhaps I should write him and request that he cease his hostilities long enough for us to have a Parisian honeymoon after all."

The big blue eyes wide with delight, Melinda had breathed admiringly, "Oh, *could* you? How absolutely splendid that would be!"

Realizing that she was in dead earnest, Morgan had looked at her with incredulity, and then strangling back the desire to laugh out loud, he had hastily suggested that they return to the house. *My God,* he had thought, torn between amusement and exasperation, *is there* anything *in her lovely head?*

As the evening progressed, it appeared there was not. By the time the hour approached to make the announcement of their impending marriage, Morgan was so bored with her company and empty prattle that he knew there was no way in hell he could face the rest of his life married to Melinda. *But how the devil am I going to withdraw my offer without causing an unholy scandal?*

Definitely a thorny problem, he admitted glumly, and it was compounded by his own reluctance to embarrass his parents and the Marshalls. It wasn't *their* fault Melinda was such a ninnyhammer! *Somehow,* he decided grimly, *I shall have to find an excellent reason for* her *to cry off. It should be simple enough to give her a distaste for me,* he thought with a grin—appearing foxed a few times in her presence, sporting a decidedly tyrannical air, and flaunting convention now and then should do the trick. *Just act normally,* my boy, he thought derisively to himself, *and you'll come about!*

It would have been easy enough for Morgan to put his half-formed plan into action that evening, but not even he was willing to put Melinda and her family, in addition to his own, through the embarrassment of watching the proposed bridegroom act the part of a rude, overbearing boor on the very night their betrothal was to be announced. *Tomorrow,* he mused slowly, *will be soon enough for me to show my disreputable colors and start revealing what an arrogant swine I can be.* Suddenly he smiled, thinking of the expression on Melinda's face when he, oh, *so* casually, informed her that he was considering the possibility of their settling in the wilderness somewhere along the Natchez Trace. *If that doesn't start giving her second thoughts, nothing will. . . .*

With that comforting notion, Morgan relaxed slightly, and weary with boredom, resigned himself to playing out his role for the remainder of the evening. Arranging his features in a deceptive mask of polite cordiality, he dutifully did all that was required of him, but he detested every false moment, longing intolerably for the entire affair to be over.

143

Finally, it was time for the announcement. With the two beaming families flanking them, Morgan and Melinda stood at one end of the elegant room as Mr. Marshall jovially called for everyone's attention. The musicians instantly laid aside their instruments, the babble of voices hushed—and it was in that moment that Morgan Slade caught his first clear sight of Leonie Saint-André.

What brought his eyes to her, he couldn't say, but one second his gaze was idly skimming the smiling crowd, and the next it was riveted on the dainty figure standing uncertainly in the archway. *Sweet Jesus, who is that bewitching little creature?* was his first thought, the blue eyes narrowing intently as they moved assessingly over the bright tawny hair and golden skin. So compelling was the pull of attraction that it was all he could do to prevent himself from closing the distance between them and demanding an introduction. Despite the occasion and the distance that separated them, the small slim figure radiated an irresistible appeal that trapped Morgan's attention, and he found himself unable to tear his gaze away from her. *It's the hair,* he told himself savagely a second later, *it's the same shade as Stephanie's.* But it wasn't that, and he knew it—the first sight of Stephanie's shining curls had not filled him with an almost overpowering desire to caress their silken softness, nor had it instilled a craving to bury his head in the unruly strands and breathe in the sweet perfume he knew was there.

Angry at this sudden surge of passion, his mouth tightened and the dark blue eyes hardened. Whoever she was, he was damn well going to avoid her—any woman who could arouse such powerful emotions at first sight was a damned witch and dangerous in the bargain. And yet, having decided that, he still couldn't tear his gaze away, as unwaveringly he stared at her, every nerve in his body aware of her—and furious because of it.

Leonie felt the steady, increasingly hostile blue stare, and as if drawn by a magnet, she looked at last in his direction. Across the space that divided them, she saw a tall, broad-shouldered man with a hard, arrogant face dressed in a well-fitting jacket of midnight blue velvet and black satin breeches that displayed the long, muscled length of his legs. The candlelight caught blue shadows in the black hair, and his skin was dark, the heavy, arching black brows very apparent in spite of the distance and people that were between them.

Time seemed to freeze; the rest of the room and the world faded away. There were just the two of them as their eyes met across the width of the ballroom. Then Leonie recognized him—or rather thought she recognized the man she had married nearly six years ago—and with righteous wrath blinding her to everything but his iniquity, she stormed toward him.

Gaylord was two steps behind her, his courage wavering at the ugly, embarrassing scene that was about to erupt. Cowardly, wishing he had suggested they wait until later and then have a private confrontation with Slade, he made one vain attempt to catch Leonie's arm and persuade her to postpone the confrontation.

It is doubtful anything could have stopped Leonie at that moment; everyone in the room was becoming aware that something was very wrong. Morgan's eyes had not left Leonie's slim, determined little figure as she made her way towards him, and naturally people began to turn to see who or what had his undivided attention at such an inopportune moment. Gaylord's presence alone caused a titter of curiosity to sweep the room, and Melinda's satin-slippered foot started to tap with an angry rhythm. *If he does anything to spoil my party, I shall never speak to him again!* she decided petulantly. Disparagingly, her gaze rested for a moment on Leonie and then dismissed her. *What a positively dowdy gown she is wearing!* was her only thought, as Leonie reached them.

A hush fell as Leonie, her vivid little face alight with rage, stopped directly in front of Morgan. Gaylord was at her side, and from the moment Morgan had spotted him, he knew there was going to be trouble, even if it hadn't been obvious that the young lady was harboring some great stress. What, he wondered with interest and growing wariness, was young Easton up to? And what part did this ravishing creature, standing so breathlessly before him, play in these machinations?

By God, but she was captivating, he thought detachedly,

one part of him mesmerized by the vibrant features that went beyond mere prettiness—the cat-shaped eyes which gleamed an intriguing golden-green between the long, spiky lashes; the high cheek bones, stained just now with a becoming flush, and the soft, provoking mouth that blatantly dared a man to taste its sweetness. Most of Morgan's attention was on Leonie, but he was also very aware of everything else that was going on in the room—of Mr. Marshall's blustering noises at the intrusion; of Melinda's tightening grasp on his arm; of Gaylord's half-conciliatory, half-defiant air, and of the curious hush that had fallen on the rest of the guests.

As for Leonie, she was aware of nothing but the man before her, and seeing his face up close for the first time in almost six years, she was baffled at how little he resembled her memory of the weak, unscrupulous man she had met in New Orleans. Had his eyes always been that piercing shade of blue, the oddly feminine, thick, black lashes intensifying the impact of their gaze? Had his jawline and chin always been so agressively masculine? The nose so arrogantly formed? And the mouth so frankly sensuous and yet slightly cruel in its shape? She didn't think she could have forgotten his harshly handsome face. . . . This man was the Morgan Slade she remembered, and yet, he wasn't—but any differences she detected, Leonie promptly put down to the passing years and her own faulty memory. After all, she had only seen the man three or four times and that had been six years ago. There were bound to be changes—she wasn't the same so why should she expect him to have remained untouched by time? The man *was* Morgan Slade, of that she was positive, even if his actual features did not bear an exact resemblance to the face of her memory. And he was undoubtedly a double-damned villain, she thought with a surge of rage.

Glaring up at him and ignoring the others, she burst out, "It seems, monsieur, that I have arrived just in time to stop you from carrying out your wicked plan! *Mon Dieu,* but I never dreamed you were such a scoundrel!" Not stopping to catch her breath, nor giving anyone a chance to speak, she turned to the openmouthed, goggle-eyed Melinda, and with a flicker of sympathy in the great golden-green eyes, she said contritely, "Mademoiselle, I am sorry to cause you distress this way, but you cannot marry this devil!" Earnestly she added, "You will thank me some day for my interference."

Silently applauding what he not unnaturally assumed was a clever bit of acting, and thinking that Gaylord had hired this enchanting little actress to play the part of a woman scorned, Morgan watched the scene unfolding before him with amusement. In time he would put an end to it and send Gaylord about his business, but for the moment curiosity, as well as a lively sense of humor, kept Morgan from calling a halt to what was for him a delightfully ridiculous descent into absurdity. *But why the hell does Gaylord think an accusation of villainy will cause Melinda to cry off?* he wondered derisively. *Surely there must be more to this farce than an outraged woman warning Melinda of my evil character.* Eyeing the red-faced Gaylord somewhat reflectively, the dismal thought occurred to him that if this was the best young Easton could come up with, then any hope he had of Gaylord acting as an unwitting ally could be discarded.

At Leonie's words, the guests began to murmur amongst themselves and glance questioningly at Morgan, waiting expectantly for his reaction. Morgan's face remained impassive, although a gleam of mockery danced in the blue eyes, and he had difficulty in keeping from laughing out loud at the scandalized and avid expressions of the people nearest him.

It was Melinda, though, who broke the silence. The big blue eyes darkening wrathfully, she rounded furiously on Gaylord. "How *could* you!" she cried angrily. "You've ruined my evening and spoiled everything! I hate you! Do you hear me, *I hate you!*"

Leonie stared at her, puzzled by the reaction. Why was this creature angry at Gaylord? She should be grateful to him, Leonie thought with perplexity. Perhaps the young lady didn't understand? And suddenly realizing that she had not made clear the depth of Monsieur Slade's perfidy, Leonie began gravely, "Mademoiselle, do not be angry with Monsieur Easton. He has only your best interest at heart. You should be thankful for his deep concern. You cannot marry Monsieur Slade. He is my—"

That was as far as she got, for Melinda flashed her a venomous look and snapped, "Oh, shut up! Don't tell *me* about Gaylord Easton! I don't know what the meaning of this is, but you were not invited to my party, and neither was he. I want you to leave immediately! Do you hear me, *immediately!*"

"Melinda, you must listen to her!" Gaylord instantly implored, finally finding his tongue. "She has something of the utmost importance to tell you. Listen to her!"

Her lip curling in a sneer, Melinda shot him a look that spoke volumes. "I don't want to listen to her. Why should I?" Clinging even tighter to Morgan's arm, she purred smugly, "I am going to marry Mr. Slade, and nothing you can say will change my mind! So there!"

Gaylord drew himself up with a hiss of rage at her stubbornness, and completely forgetting himself, in a voice that shook with righteous indignation, he shouted, "You silly ninnyhammer, you can't marry him—he's already married! *This is his wife!*"

11

There was a concerted gasp from the assembled guests and Morgan, feeling that the farce had gone on long enough, said in a deadly tone, "I think that's enough out of you, young man. I can sympathize with what you think is a broken heart, but that is no excuse for your offensive actions. Kindly take your little friend in hand, and the two of you find somewhere else to perform your less than amusing antics."

Melinda glanced up at him admiringly. "Oooh, I just love masterful men!"

Something that could have been distaste flared for a second in Morgan's eyes, but it was gone so quickly no one saw it but Leonie—and the only reason she did was because she had been staring at him with astonishment. *Eh bien!* This was something she had never expected. That he would try to weasel out of paying her the dowry, she had been prepared for, but that he would pretend ignorance of who she was had simply never occurred to her.

Enraged more than she had thought possible, with a violent motion Leonie dug in her reticule and with the green eyes spitting golden sparks, she thrust the marriage papers under his arrogant nose. *"Non!* We do not leave! Deny these if you will, monsieur!"

His face betraying only his growing impatience, Morgan unhurriedly took the papers from Leonie's hand. He glanced at them, the thick black eyebrows snapping together in a frown as the import of the officially worded lines and the boldly scrawled signature across the bottom sunk in. His lip curling up in a sneer, he turned a cold gaze on Gaylord and murmured dryly, "I see you have added forgery to your few talents, my young friend. But it won't

149

work. Now, as I said earlier, get yourself and this little harpy out of here!"

Matthew Slade, who had remained silent by his son's side, said quietly, "May I see them?"

Indifferently Morgan handed the documents to him, his eyes insolently meeting Leonie's furious ones. *Witch!* he thought with amused savagery. *Gaylord Easton may be the one who pays your bills now, but by this time tomorrow you're going to find yourself with a new protector . . . one who will make far better use of that impudent mouth than that young fool could ever dream of!*

Leonie did not like the look in his hard blue eyes, but she was not about to back down. Too many people were dependent upon her. She must have her dowry returned to her. *She must!* Not consciously planning it, she turned to the older man who had asked to see the marriage papers, and the small face alight with earnestness, she said softly, "Monsieur, I do not know who you are, nor do you know me—but I am not a liar, nor are those papers you hold in your hand forgeries. They are authentic. I am married to this man. I married him in New Orleans six years ago this July. I do not lie about this, it is the truth!"

Her words moved Matthew. That and the damning papers he held in his hands, as well as the sea-green eyes fixed so appealingly on his face. And yet, he couldn't quite believe that Morgan was capable of the perfidious acts that she claimed he had done. Obviously, though, this wasn't something that could be decided in an instant, and clearing his throat uncomfortably, not looking at his son, he said quietly, "I think we had better find a more private place to discuss this." Glancing apologetically at Mr. Marshall, who was beginning to gobble like a turkey cock, he added, "I am sorry for the embarrassment, but until this affair is cleared up, I do not think it would be appropriate to continue with these festivities."

Morgan may have found Gaylord's machinations amusing at first, but by now any amusement he might have felt had faded. And while the ending of his engagement to Melinda may have been his fondest desire, he did not like the sudden turn of events. For one thing, he *knew* he hadn't married the scheming little bitch in front of him, and for

150

another, he didn't like the implication that he was some sort of nefarious villain who went around marrying young women whenever the whim struck him. That his father would even for a moment believe the papers he held in his hands were real was infuriating, and as for the clever green-eyed witch who claimed to be his wife, he'd like to strangle her . . . or make violent love to her, he thought furiously, undecided which would give him more pleasure.

Stiffly, if unwillingly, Morgan acceded to his father's request, and in a blessedly short period of time he found himself, along with the conniving little baggage who claimed to be his wife and the others most concerned with the debacle, in the green salon of Marshall Hall. Leonie was the only woman present—Mrs. Marshall and Morgan's mother were too busy attempting to alleviate Melinda's shrieking hysterics.

The betrothal ball had ended rather abruptly. The guests had left with their curiosity unrelieved and speculation and gossip spreading like wildfire through their ranks. Tonight would not be quietly forgotten by anyone.

In reality, Morgan should have been pleased, as his marriage to Melinda Marshall was now out of the question. But he disliked having his hand forced and especially disliked being accused of a crime he had not committed. He particularly objected to being saddled with a wife he didn't want, and the expression in the blue eyes, as they considered Leonie, was unpleasant.

The entire situation was unpleasant and none felt it more than Leonie. With only Gaylord as her champion, and faced with growing suspicion and hostility by the other men in the room, her heart sank. Several things stopped her from turning tail and running out into the night: She knew she was telling the truth; she had a son as well as several others who were dependent upon her, and she had the agreement that Morgan Slade had signed promising to repay her the dowry given to him by her grandfather.

In addition to Morgan and his father, Mr. Marshall was present, as well as a young man whom Leonie took to be Morgan's brother; none of them looked particularly sympathetic. Mr. Marshall's plump features were so red and angry that she thought he might explode; the unknown young man was staring at her with hard, suspicious gray eyes; the older man, Morgan's father, had a worried, uncertain expression on his face, and Morgan, lounging carelessly against a tall, mahogany bookcase, was viewing her with open contempt.

As for Gaylord, he was having second thoughts; after all, what did he know of this woman? She could have been lying about the marriage, and in his eagerness to confront Slade, he might have made a terrible mistake. Hesitantly he began, "Um, I think I should explain how I came to meet this young lady."

"That won't be necessary," Morgan said bluntly, the blue eyes moving insolently over Leonie. "She has a tongue . . . one, I might add, she has used to good effect this evening. I'm certain she can explain everything to us." And suddenly deciding that divide and conquer might be used to their advantage, he added with deceptive indifference, "As a matter of fact, I see no real reason that you should be part of this meeting. You've played your part. So why don't you leave it to your discovery to finish this drama?"

The others agreed, and before he could protest Gaylord was firmly shown from the room. "Don't wait for the young lady," Morgan said sweetly. "I shall see that she is taken care of."

Relieved to be out of it, Gaylord did not demur, and within seconds after informing Abraham to wait for his mistress, he was driving swiftly away from Marshall Hall, torn between elation at having put a stop to Melinda's betrothal and the lowering knowledge that his part may have done him more damage than good. Melinda had been *furious,* and recalling the tears and tantrums that had erupted once the guests had left, Gaylord shuddered. She might never forgive him!

Back in the elegant room from which Gaylord had just been almost forcibly ejected, Leonie swallowed tightly, and in a voice that shook slightly with emotion she said tautly, "Messieurs, I regret the timing of my announcement, but nothing can change the facts. You have the proof of what I say in your hands. It *is* Monsieur Morgan Slade's signature, and he *did* marry me almost six years ago in New Orleans."

Morgan flicked one eyebrow upwards and murmured sneeringly, "If that is the case, why don't *I* remember it?"

It was one of the most difficult moments of Leonie's life. She knew she told the truth, and yet confronted by an outright denial by Monsieur Slade and the obvious disbelief of the others, she was both furious and frightened. *Mon Dieu,* what was she to do if she could not convince these gentlemen that she spoke the truth? Morgan Slade was apparently going to pretend they had never met, so her one chance was to convince the other men in the room.

The green eyes staring beseechingly at Matthew Slade, she said in a voice that trembled with despair, "Monsieur, what I tell you is the truth. I have no reason to *lie!*"

Matthew moved restlessly, his gaze dropping once again to the document he held in his hands. It had the look of authenticity as he had seen his son's bold, scrawling signature too many times not to recognize it. The slim girl before him had the look and air of a lady, and even more damning, there was a ring of truth to her words. He looked thoughtfully across at his eldest son. Could he have done such a thing? Married a young woman and then deserted her?

It wasn't something Matthew liked to contemplate, nor did he particularly like the answers that came to him. What did he actually know of this son of his anymore? Once, he could have answered without a doubt that no son of his would do such a thing, but now? Now he didn't know. Morgan had changed a great deal since Stephanie and Phillippe had died. It was possible that he could have married this beguiling young creature with some twisted thought of punishing her for Stephanie's sins. He didn't know. But what he did know was that the document appeared authentic . . . and so did the young lady.

Matthew asked quietly, "Will you please tell us how you came to meet my son, and the precise sequence of events that brought about this marriage you claim took place?"

Heartened by his slight softening, without hesitation Leonie told him the facts, her vivid face reflecting a variety of emotions as her young voice rose and fell in the room.

When she finished, there was a waiting silence, broken only when Morgan pushed himself away from the bookcase and said sarcastically, "A touching story, my dear, but one that I fear is patently untrue." Meeting Matthew's eyes, he stated in a hard voice, "I *did not* marry her, God damnit! Not even in a drunken stupor! For God's sake, don't you think I would remember?"

Staring intently at the tip of his shoe, it was Dominic who said softly, "But you were in New Orleans that summer. And you did play cards with Gayoso—you've told me that yourself. Did you by chance meet an old Frenchman by the name of Saint-André there?"

Morgan let out his breath in an explosive sound. The blue eyes glittering with fury, he snapped, "How the hell should I know? It was almost six years ago, and with the exception of Gayoso's sudden death it was an uneventful trip. I stayed with Jason, and I conducted the business I had gone down there to do. And *I damn well didn't marry anybody!*"

Where once Leonie had been the one on the defensive, it was now becoming apparent that at least two of the men in the room were giving her story some credence. A note of incredulity in his voice Morgan demanded, "You believe her?" And when neither his father nor brother would answer or meet his eyes, he turned on Leonie and snarled, "Why the hell did you show up now? *If* I married you six years ago, why did it take you so long to make yourself known?"

"Because, Monsieur, you and I made a bargain," Leonie spat back. "I promised to make no demands on you and you none on me, and at the end of five years, you were to pay me back my dowry. It is for the dowry that I have come— not *you!*"

"Oh, I see," Morgan replied insultingly. "I knew that there must be *money* involved somewhere. How much do I owe you, cat-eyes?"

Leonie stiffened at the tone of voice and two spots of color bloomed on the high cheek bones. "Do not call me that! And you do owe me the money!" Reaching once again

154

into her reticule, she pulled out another crumpled piece of paper and practically threw it at him. "There, monsieur! There is the paper you signed which promises you shall pay me my dowry back at the end of five years. Deny that too, if you dare!"

Frowning blackly, Morgan read the paper, his signature once again staring damningly up at him. "Jesus Christ, but you're a clever little bitch!" he finally bit out. "And I'd like to know how and where Gaylord found you so opportunely . . . or have you merely been waiting for the right moment to strike?"

Leonie didn't think, she was so angry that there was only one thought on her mind—stop his ugly accusations. Like a small tawny wildcat, she lunged across the room towards him, her hand connecting soundly with his dark, lean cheek. The sound of the slap was like a pistol shot in the room, and Morgan reacted instinctively, his right hand closing like a steel-sprung trap around her slender wrist before he yanked her arm behind her back, forcing her body up next to his.

The imprint of her hand burned a dark red on his cheek, and in a murderous voice Morgan threatened, "Don't ever do that again, or I'll break your neck!"

"*Morgan!*" Matthew thundered, more shocked than he had ever been by his son's actions. The violence that radiated between the pair was almost tangible, and Matthew was helpless. He was a gentle man and of the firm opinion that the ladies deserved only cosseting from a man. Morgan's actions were totally outside his comprehension, and the stunned expression on Matthew's face, as much as his tone of voice, made that more than apparent.

The sound of his name uttered in that shocked accent brought Morgan sharply back to the reality of the situation, and with a snarl he threw Leonie away from him. "Shall I apologize to the *lady,* father?" he asked in a dangerous tone. "She has accused me of the blackest villainy and has even gone so far as to strike me. For *that,* I am to meekly bow my head and say, thank you very much? Not bloody likely!"

Mr. Marshall, although angry and mortified, had remained an avid spectator to everything that had happened

155

and finally managed to break into the conversation. "Disgusting!" he said with affronted dignity. "Matthew, my friend, I do not wish to be insulting, but I cannot say strongly enought that after this violent exhibition of your son's temper, it would be out of the question for my little Melinda to marry him. Even if it turns out that this young lady is lying . . . which I seriously doubt!" Puffing himself up importantly, he added, "I have never been so embarrassed or insulted in my life as I have been this evening, and no matter what you say, the blame all lies at the feet of your son!" Looking at Morgan the same way he would a coiled snake, he ended pompously, "The only saving grace of this entire affair is that my daughter has been spared a life of what I am certain would have been unmitigated misery. How I could have been so mistaken by a man's character, I do not know! What a shocking evening this has been!"

While Matthew might have agreed with some of the statements made by Mr. Marshall—it *had* been a shocking evening—he didn't relish the other man's assessment of his eldest son . . . even if it might be proven true. His handsome face suddenly appearing older than his sixty years, Matthew said stiffly, "I cannot apologize sufficiently for this unfortunate incident, but until Morgan's guilt or innocence has been established, I would appreciate it, if for no other reason than our long friendship, that you refrain from casting slurs about my son."

Mr. Marshall sniffed and muttered peevishly, "Oh, very well, but I don't know how I am going to hold my head up again. My darling Melinda will never be able to meet anyone who was present here tonight without dying of shame! And the wasted food! My God—"

"If that's all that's bothering you," Morgan said nastily, "send the bills to me! As for your shame and embarrassment, you should have no trouble laying everything at my door . . . you have already begun to do so! And I'm positive that by tomorrow morning, friendship or not, you will be joining in with the hue and cry of the pack in shrieking my many sins to the heavens!"

Mr. Marshall shrank back slightly at the expression on Morgan's face, wondering how he could ever have considered Morgan Slade as a man worthy of his sweet Melinda, but then remembering all the broad acres and money that went with the heir to Bonheur, he had second thoughts. A man was entitled to a show of strength now and then—women seemed to like that sort of thing—and who was he to whistle down a fortune for his daughter? Besides, subsequent events might prove that Morgan was innocent . . . and then where would they be? Conciliatorily, he said, "Oh, come now, there is no need for such hot statements among friends. We are all under a severe strain, and I think it would be best for us all to have a good night's sleep and discuss it further in the morning. We, none of us, are at our best at the moment."

Morgan's face twisted into a sneer of disgust, but Matthew forestalled the inflammatory words his son was likely to fling by saying with more heartiness than he felt, "An excellent idea! I think by tomorrow morning we will all view this in a better light. Please ring for the servants to bring our carriage round, and have someone see if my wife will ready herself for the ride home."

Leonie, who had remained silent, unconsciously rubbing her wrist where Morgan's fingers had bruised the tender flesh, spoke up, "And me, monsieur, what of me? Am I to simply disappear overnight so that your lives will go on just as they have?"

Morgan walked over to her and with a tanned hand he tipped up her chin. Smiling, not a nice smile either, he drawled, "You, my dear? Well, you shall of course accompany us to Benheur. After all, we can't have all these questions unanswered, can we?"

Leonie tried to move away from him, but when she took a step backwards, she found herself up against a piece of furniture. Glaring up at his dark face, she agreed tightly. *"Non!* Of course not."

Still smiling that not very nice smile, Morgan purred with deceptive cordiality, "Fine. Then you will have no objections to riding with me in my curricle to the plantation. I'm certain we shall find several things to discuss on the way home."

Leonie felt her heart begin to beat very fast, and just a little frightened by the cold promise in those blue eyes, she blurted out breathlessly, "That is not necessary. I have taken rooms at a tavern here in Natchez and I shall stay there for the night."

"Oh, no, we can't have that," Morgan murmured softly. "It wouldn't be seemly for the woman who *claims* to be my wife to stay at a common inn."

Leonie swallowed nervously, deciding that she much preferred the furious man who had hurt her wrist to this calm, apparently polite gentleman who said all the right and polite things with his mouth, but whose eyes said something entirely different. He was standing too close to her, and there was such an air of menace about that big, powerful body that she knew the last thing in the world she was going to do was ride off into the night with him.

"Thank you, monsieur, but I would prefer to keep my own arrangements," Leonie said stubbornly. "If someone will kindly see that I have transportation back to King's Tavern, I shall be quite happy."

"But I won't be," Morgan drawled. "Having been separated from you for—ah, let me see, almost six years is it? I can hardly bear to let you out of my sight."

It was obvious he meant nothing of the kind, but Matthew, still not certain which one of them he believed, decided that it would be best if the young woman did stay at Bonheur until things were settled. Kindly he said, "My dear, while of late I seldom find myself in agreement with my son, in this case I believe he is right. You must make Bonheur your home until we straighten out this tangle. It will be much better for everyone."

Ignoring Morgan, who still stood too close to her for comfort, Leonie looked across the room to Matthew, her indecision clear. This was not how she had envisioned things. She had never meant to intrude into Morgan Slade's life beyond what was necessary to retrieve her dowry. Certainly she had never planned to live in his home or to take her place as his real wife—something that might very well happen, she admitted with a sinking feeling in her stomach, if Matthew Slade had his way. She sensed correctly that Morgan's father was leaning more and more in her favor, and while that should have elated her, it gave her instead a feeling of disquiet. Matthew Slade did not look

158

the sort of man who would calmly allow his daughter-in-law simply to disappear. If he decided she was indeed Morgan's wife, then he would insist she become one of the family—something Leonie had *no* intention of doing!

She hadn't wanted Morgan Slade for a husband six years ago and she definitely didn't want him for one now. *Mon Dieu!* Not after what had happened this evening. Even the thought of the last and final piece of paper she had that he had signed in New Orleans gave her no comfort. Risking a glance at his hard, lean face, she quickly dropped her eyes at the mixture of insolence and something else which she couldn't define that flickered in the depths of those dark blue eyes. *Non!* The piece of paper that he had signed waving away his rights of husband would prove a frail, if nonexistent, barrier to him, if he decided he wished to be her husband in fact as well as name.

As she hesitated, trying desperately to find a graceful way out of the situation, Morgan, who had been watching the vivid face intently, and mistaking the reasons for her hesitation, said dryly, "Not quite working out as you planned, is it, little witch?"

Leonie shot him a look full of loathing and admitted honestly *"Non!* It is not. . . . I did not expect you to pretend we had never met!"

Morgan's eyes narrowed, but any retort he might have made was forestalled quickly by Leonie. The delicate features framed enchantingly by her tawny curls, Leonie looked appealingly across to Matthew Slade. "Monsieur," she said quietly, "there is no need to take me into your home." And when Matthew seemed inclined to argue, she added reluctantly, "I am not alone, there are others with me besides my servants."

If there was anything besides the agreement concerning conjugal rights that Leonie wished to avoid revealing, it was Justin's existence. In one respect, Morgan's flat denial of ever having known her made it easier to claim Justin was his son, but on the other hand, she was very much afraid that if Matthew realized there was a child involved, he would be even more adamant about her remaining here in Natchez as Morgan's wife. It was an unholy dilemma. She had hoped that she alone could transact any business between them and that if she were lucky, she could leave Natchez and Morgan Slade behind . . . *before* he learned of the child.

But nothing was turning out as she had thought it would. A bald announcement at his betrothal ball to another woman certainly had not been considered. Nor had she thought to meet his parents, or any of his family for that matter. And now, his father was forcing information out of her she would rather not divulge.

"Oh," Matthew asked curiously. "I thought you said that your grandfather was dead? And that he was your only living relative?"

Morgan moved even closer to Leonie, and not even aware he did it, his hand closed around her slender arm, and almost jealously he demanded, "Yes, you did say you were alone in the world, didn't you? Forget something? Like a lover?"

Leonie flushed with anger, and vainly attempting to shrug off his detaining hand, she muttered furiously, "I do not have a lover!"

"Well, then?" Morgan inquired silkily.

Searching frantically for a way to keep Justin a secret, Leonie admitted unwillingly, "I have a female companion . . . almost a relative, she and I have grown up together. Yvette is like a sister to me. There are also two black families who are with us." Forcing herself to pretend Morgan was not standing so still beside her or that his hand wasn't firmly holding her arm, she smiled briefly at Matthew. "They are freed slaves, but they insist that they belong to me. I couldn't leave them behind."

Matthew's face broke into his first real smile since Leonie had met him. The fact that she had a companion and old family retainers relieved his mind a great deal. A scheming hussy would not travel so, and wondering unhappily if perhaps his son didn't have a lot of explaining to do, Matthew said warmly, "I see no reason why they should cause any trouble." Glacing at his gold pocket watch, he murmured with surprise. "Well! It is not more than half-past ten—if we do not waste any more time, I think within the hour we can have all of you settled at Bonheur."

160

"Monsieur," Leonie began desperately, but at Matthew's questioning look, she said lamely, "I—I would rather not stay at Bonheur." And grasping at straws, anything to stave off the revelation of her son, she added earnestly, "There seems to be some doubt in your mind about what I have told you tonight, and until that is resolved, I would prefer *not* to partake of your exceedingly kind offer of hospitality."

Matthew couldn't honestly say that he had decided she was telling the truth, but the evidence *was* damning and while still hoping that there was a logical explanation for her accusations, he was aware that with every passing moment that her story took on more credibility. Aloud, he merely said calmly, "I can understand your feelings, my dear, but I feel it will be much better for all of us if you and your party stay at Bonheur. Tomorrow we will all discuss the matter further and between us, we shall thrash out this affair."

"But, monsieur . . . !" Leonie protested frantically, feeling as if her entire life was being taken over. "You don't understand!"

"What doesn't he understand?" Morgan inquired dangerously into her ear. "That you hadn't meant for the game to go this far? Or that it is really the money you are after, and not the comfort and safety of a family?"

"Non!" Leonie burst out angrily, throwing Morgan a scathing look, the golden flecks burning so brightly in the almond-shaped eyes that their color was a molten golden-green.

"Then why the hesitation, cat-eyes? It's what you came after, isn't it?"

"My dowry only!" Leonie spat back. "Only what you agreed to give me . . . nothing more!"

Through cold blue eyes, Morgan assessed her flushed face, wishing he wasn't quite *so* aware of the bewitching features and the soft body so near his own. Now was a time for detachment, a time for cool, clever reasoning, and all he wanted to do was find a private place and discover if that mouth was as sweet and passionate as it looked. He was also icily furious at the way she was gulling his father. How dare this little charlatan rearrange his life this way!

161

And to think his father, and Dominic too from the look of him, gave credence to her story! Good God, what sort of a monster did they think he was? Barely holding his temper in check, Morgan snarled, "How easy for you to say that now . . . now that you have brought yourself to my family's attention and presented them with your filthy lies! Do you really believe my father, honorable man that he is, will let me merely pay you off and send you on your way?" Morgan laughed harshly, "You made a drastic miscalculation there, sweetheart, if that was your plan!"

"Morgan's right, my dear, even if I find his way of expressing it distasteful. I am not *un*convinced that you are telling the truth, and if your story proves to be legitimate, then I must insist you join our family and let the rest of us show you we have little in common with your husband other than name." Those were painful words for Matthew to say, but they accurately reflected his feelings. The more he heard and the more he saw, the more he began to believe Leonie. Morgan's actions tonight had shocked him, shocked him even more than the growing belief that his son had acquired a wife years ago and had been on the verge of committing bigamy. He had never thought to see a son of his manhandle a woman, much less ever hear him speak to her in this insulting fashion—he was ashamed and disillusioned. Sending Leonie a painful little smile, he added, "You must let us care for you, my child, until we have settled this matter."

"Isn't that my business?" Morgan asked tightly. "After all, it appears that everyone is positive she *is* my wife! In that case, her welfare should be left to me. I should be the one to take care of her."

"But you haven't done so in the past, have you?" Matthew returned sternly.

Morgan hadn't felt his face burn in years but it did now, and it didn't do him any good to know that he was innocent. God damn it! Had everyone gone mad? His father's words left him feeling defeated and helpless. Aware that further argument would be useless, he slowly released Leonie's arm and turned away, shrugging his broad shoulders.

"Well, now that we've settled that point," Matthew said

heavily, "I think we should see about removing ourselves from here . . . and then see to it that the rest of Leonie's party is transported to Bonheur."

Leonie swallowed painfully, knowing that the moment of truth was upon her. She *had* to tell them of Justin! Obviously she was not going to be able to escape staying at Bonheur, and it was just as obvious that there was no way she could hide Justin's existence any longer. Taking a deep breath, she licked her bottom lip nervously and got out, "Monsieur, there is one other person that I did not mention."

"Oh? And who might that be?" Matthew inquired.

She swallowed again and risked a quick, uncertain glance at Morgan's stiff back. "M-m-m—o-o-*our* son!"

12

Morgan whipped around, a murderous scowl darkening his brow. *"What?"* he ejaculated incredulously. "A child?" And at Leonie's defiant nod, he burst out furiously, "Now, just a goddammed minute! I would *know* if I'd ever bedded you, and I damn well haven't. I never laid eyes on you until you walked in with Easton tonight!" His voice full of implacable rage, he added, "Take heed, little harlot—you might have convinced my father that you are my wife, but there is no way in hell you're going to foist somebody else's bastard on me!"

Leonie's reaction was not nearly as spectacular as it would have been if she hadn't known she was lying, but even so, for this abominable blackguard to call Justin a bastard was like tinder to dry grass. "You will *not* call him that! He *is* our son and you will not deny him!" Leonie spat fiercely, the tawny curls nearly bristling with rage. "Call me names, monsieur, if that pleases you, but do not vent your bad manners and foul tongue on Justin!"

Morgan's jaw clenched, and feeling as if he had wandered into a nightmare, he snarled softly, "Point taken—whatever you are, your child, if he *is* your child, is not to blame. One thing I know for damn sure, though, is that he is not *my* child!"

Leonie held her head very high, and not meeting the furious glitter of Morgan's eyes, she said stubbornly, "But he is, monsieur . . . he was born almost nine months to the day after we were married. He is your son."

Smiling grimly, Morgan ground out, "I seem to have forgotten so many things—you, our wedding, our wedding night, everything. How can that be?"

Flushing at the insulting implication in his voice, Leo-

164

nie snapped hotly, "Because, monsieur, it was my dowry you were interested in, not me or our marriage!"

Matthew, growing more uncomfortable by being a party to this increasingly venomous and painful scene, cleared his throat loudly. Both combatants looked at him as if only now realizing that there were other people in the room. As for Matthew, the knowledge that there was a child was a stunning surprise. Though the existence of a child complicated an already complicated situation, this might also prove the key to the dilemma. A child that bore the unmistakable stamp of the Slades would be all the proof that Matthew would need.

Eager to see this child, this child that might possibly be his own grandson, eager to have the truth proven one way or another, Matthew said, "My dear, I think we have all said enough for now. Come, let us see about removing your son and the others to Bonheur before the hour grows much later. Tomorrow will be soon enough for us to thrash this out." Finally forcing himself to glance at Morgan's dark, angry face, he said coldly, "It would be best if you took your mother home. Dominic and I shall take the young lady to the tavern and see about bringing the others to the house."

There was, as Matthew had said, nothing more to be gained from this acrimonious discussion, and with a grimace of disgust and resignation, Morgan left the room. His mother was waiting in the hall, and sardonically he greeted her. "It seems that you are relegated to associating with the condemned man. Father and Dominic are going to King's Tavern to arrange for the removal of my little bride and son, and you, I suppose, are to see that things are made ready at the house. Shall we go, madame, or am I too far beyond redemption to have your company?"

"Morgan, *mon fils,* stop it!" Noelle said sharply. "Come, you must tell me what happened." Her eyes anxiously searching his shuttered face, she asked uncertainly, "Is it true? Is she your wife and does she have your child?"

An hour ago Morgan would have heatedly denied it, but after the buffeting he'd taken from his father, he was in no mood to continue to protest his innocence. "She claims she

165

is, and she has legal documents with my signature on them which would tend to prove her word true."

It was an uncomfortable ride home—Noelle wanted to believe in her son's innocence, but Morgan's hostile attitude made it difficult. He had put up a wall between them, and to all of her questions, he made glib, mocking replies that made her long to box his ears as she had done when he was a child.

Leonie's ride to King's Tavern was not *un*pleasant, for Matthew did his best to put her at ease, and Dominic, who she now knew as Morgan's younger brother, was also very polite, though still reserved. It was obvious that Dominic, like Matthew, had not quite made up his mind. He wasn't openly siding with either of them; he was assimilating the facts and weighing them.

Matthew's polite prattle proved soothing, and Leonie found herself relaxing slightly, the tight, painful knot of despair lessening in her chest. Smiling across from her in the gloom of the carriage, Matthew said lightly, "Staying with our family will be quite different for you, and we are such a large family that I hope our numbers do not frighten you."

Leonie sent him a small, strained smile. "Oh? Are there more than Dominic and M-M-Morgan?"

"Indeed yes, my dear! Robert, my son after Morgan, and the youngest children, the twins Cassandre and Alexandre, were also there tonight, but during the fuss I suggested that Robert take them home. You'll meet them tomorrow. There is also a daughter who is married and lives in Tennessee, and I suspect before the year is out, if you are indeed Morgan's wife that is, you will meet Alicia and her ever-increasing brood."

By the time they reached the tavern, Leonie knew the names and ages of all the Slades. All three of them discreetly avoiding even mentioning Morgan's name.

The Slade family sounded delightful and under other circumstances, Leonie would have enjoyed herself hugely, but as it was, she was exhausted emotionally as well as physically. It had been a long, tiring journey from Château Saint-André to Natchez, and she had not even been allowed to gather her forces before she had been vaulted into a situation that she had never considered. Like a little cat who finds itself in a strange place with strange people, and with at least one of those strangers treating her with hostility and the threat of physical violence, she was on her guard and extremely tense.

What questions Matthew and Dominic put her way, she answered honestly, if cautiously. Perhaps they were pretending to be her friends in order to trick her? It was possible, she thought, yet she had no choice but to trust them . . . until they proved unworthy.

She was apprehensive about the move to Bonheur, but that too, she was powerless to stop. She had been in charge of her life and the lives of everyone else in her small group for so long that she felt as if she was being stifled and smothered by the Slade family. At least at King's Tavern, she retained some control of their lives, but with every second that passed, they were all being drawn inexorably into the power and possession of the Slades. She was simply too confused and devastated by the night's ugly scenes to find a way to avoid moving to Bonheur. *Tomorrow,* she vowed silently to herself as they entered the tavern . . . .

Fortunately Yvette had still been up when they arrived, and the introductions had gone smoothly, Matthew and Dominic clearly blinded by her radiant beauty. Dominic's eyes kept straying back to the perfect oval of her lovely face.

Yvette was even more breathtakingly lovely than she had been at sixteen. Everything about her was exquisite. Her black hair was luxuriant, her eyes wide-spaced, long-lashed, and dark. Her sweetly shaped bosom pressed gently against the soft material of her gown, the small waist and slim hips prettily discernible beneath the soft drape of the narrow skirt—Dominic felt completely besotted just looking at her.

Yvett's shy smile and unassuming manner were delightful, Matthew decided warmly, and his certainty that Leonie was Morgan's wife increased. It was inconceivable that these two utterly charming young women could be involved in anything deceitful. Morgan, he thought heavily, has much to answer for!

Whatever suspicions Matthew might have had concerning Justin's parentage, were put to flight the instant he laid eyes on the sleeping child. He would have known the child as a Slade anywhere and most particularly as Morgan's. The small masculine features were a vivid reminder of Morgan's at the same age; the jaw and the already arrogant shape of the nose reminded Matthew unmistakably of his eldest son.

Dominic, who had followed his father over to the bed, looked hard at the boy, but he could see no striking resemblance; of course he hadn't been born when Morgan was five years old and so he couldn't recognize the similarity. Justin was just a black-haired, attractive child to him, although he would admit that the boy *could* have been Morgan's. But then again . . . Unconsciously Dominic shrugged his shoulders; what the hell did he know of children?

But Matthew was positive, and with an incredibly tender expression on his face, he stood staring for several moments at the sleeping child. Then with a softer note in his voice, he turned to Leonie and said, "Forgive me, my dear, for ever doubting your story. Justin is all the proof I would ever need."

Only by the greatest of will power did Leonie hide her astonishment. *Mon Dieu,* but this was unexpected! Was Monsieur Slade mad? Anyone could see that her handsome son bore no resemblance to that hard-faced, hawk-eyed scoundrel who had called her such names tonight!

Deciding Matthew Slade must be the type of man who convinces himself of what he wants to believe rather than accepting the facts, Leonie made some light reply. But watching the older man's face as he bent over the child, at the wondering expression of tenderness that crossed his features, she was racked by a sudden stab of guilt. It was very bad of her to let this man think Justin was his grandson, but she could not very well at this point baldly state that she had *no* idea who had fathered her child.

Matthew's easy and instant acceptance of the child only added to Leonie's increasingly unhappy dilemma. On one hand, for Justin's sake, she was elated that Matthew assumed the boy was his grandson, but on the other, it cre-

168

ated hazardous problems that had never occurred to her before. Should she let this apparently kind man begin to love Justin when she had no intention of remaining in Natchez? How could she allow him to think this was his grandson when she knew Justin wasn't? It seemed unbearably cruel to deceive Matthew, but she agonized even more about what it would do to Justin. Was it fair to let him think this man was his grandfather? To let him believe that the other members of the Slade family were his relatives? To have him learn to love the Slades only to wrest him away from them? Her thoughts were so painful that for the moment Morgan and the problems he represented faded away. Her one thought was of her son—Justin *must* not be hurt by this situation.

But during the next half-hour or so, Leonie was so busy with their immediate removal to Bonheur that she had no time to think of anything but the present. Fortunately, there was not a great deal of repacking to do, so in a remarkably short time they were all on their way to Bonheur.

Leonie, Yvette, and the sleeping Justin rode with the two Slades, while Mammy, Abraham and the others followed in the two mule-drawn wagons. It was only then, with Justin's small dark head resting on her bosom, the coach swaying lightly on its well-sprung chassis as it moved unhurriedly through the black night, that Leonie thought again of Morgan Slade.

Sitting quietly in the coach, she bit her lip thoughtfully as she reviewed the evening. Anyway she viewed what had transpired, it had been disastrous. And her resentment and dislike of Morgan Slade grew with every passing mile. He was indeed a scoundrel, and she questioned angrily how her grandfather could have so misjudged a man.

But even more than that, she puzzled over how her own memory could have played her so false. She had thought of him as a weak man, but there had been no sign of weakness about him tonight, and remembering that hard, dark handsome face, she trembled slightly. Those were not the features of a weak man!

She was certain she detested him, despised him in fact, and yet she was unwillingly aware that had she not known

169

his true character, she would have found him overpoweringly attractive. She frowned blackly in her corner of the coach, wondering viciously how such a thing could happen. She was not some silly *jeune fille* susceptible to a handsome face! But despite all that had happened that evening, during every moment of it, she had been acutely conscious of Morgan's tall, lithe body as she had never been aware of another person in her life.

Even when he had touched her in anger, something deep within her had responded to the feel of those strong hands against her skin, and she was both angered and bewildered by that knowledge. Surely she was not *attracted* to this monster? Such a thing could not be! she thought confusedly. He was a liar, and an dishonorable man, so how could she even feel the slightest stirring of attraction?

I must be overwrought, she decided firmly. *Or perhaps it was the sherry I had before dinner.* At any rate, she stubbornly and resolutely put the disturbing idea from her mind. *Bah!* She was not going to waste time thinking about *him!*

Morgan's absence when they arrived was conspicuous, but Noelle was waiting for them in the huge, elegant entrance hall. She greeted Leonie and Yvette with cool civility. Good breeding demanded that she be polite, but she could hardly bring herself to do more than acknowledge their presence. Whatever the truth of the matter, this young creature had caused Morgan a great deal of discomfort and embarrassment, and Noelle would not easily forget it. Still, since it appeared her husband at least believed the story, she could not and would not show the girls any unwarranted rudeness, regardless of her own thoughts on the matter.

Actually, Noelle had no firm convictions either way— she had no illusions about what her son might be capable of, and he had made no attempt to deny the marriage. But then, she also knew Morgan rather well and knew that if he had been hurt or falsely accused, he was far more likely to throw caution to the winds and defiantly refuse to speak in his own behalf, hiding his lacerated feelings behind a sneer. He was stubborn and proud, she admitted unhappily.

170

Matthew followed behind the two young women; Justin, sleeping that hard, deep sleep of the very young, was motionless in his arms. Meeting his wife's questioning eyes, Matthew said simply, "You can see for yourself."

Moving across the wide hall, Noelle approached her husband and gazing down into Justin's face as he lay sleeping in Matthew's arms, she felt her heart twist in her breast. Thus had Morgan looked as a baby. *Mon Dieu, it must be true,* she thought reluctantly.

Thawing slightly, she swung around to look more closely at Leonie. "You must be exhausted, *ma chèrie,* with all this upheaval. Come with me, I have had several rooms prepared for your use. Your servants will be shown to their quarters by our butler, so have no fear about them."

A very few minutes later, Leonie was sleeping soundly in the most comfortable bed she had ever lain upon in her life. Yvette was in the room next to hers, with Justin sleeping in a small alcove off of it. Leonie had wanted Justin in with her, but Yvette had said practically, *"Petite,* you are fatigued beyond reason. Tomorrow, Justin will wake early and I'll take care of him until you are fully rested. Go to sleep now and do not argue with me—you know I am right!"

Leonie had been too tired to fight over such a trivial thing and had meekly capitulated. And even though she had slid into bed with the set intention of waking early, the day was half gone before she opened her eyes.

For just a moment, she didn't know where she was, but then with unwelcome clarity, the events of last night flashed across her mind. She was at Bonheur, the Slade family estate, and shortly she was going to have to face her unscrupulous husband again.

It had been a tactical error on Leonie's part to sleep in so long, because while she had slept dreamlessly, a great many things had been happining. For one thing, it gave Morgan time to put some plans of his own in operation . . . plans that were *not* going to find favor with Leonie!

If Leonie had slept dreamlessly, Morgan had not. He lay in his bed in a room several doors down the hall from her room and stared sightlessly at the ceiling above him, alternately damning Leonie for the lying jade he thought

171

she was, and his father for being fooled by a pair of bewitching green eyes.

Morgan could not remember a time in his life that he had been as furious as he was at the moment, or a time when he had felt as helpless as he did now. He wasn't quite certain which enraged him more—Leonie's clever attempt at extortion, or the fact that his family for the most part believed him capable of such chicanery. And to *know* that he was innocent was galling beyond belief.

It had been no accident that he had not been there to greet Leonie when she arrived at Bonheur. He had purposely kept himself out of the way, afraid that if he laid eyes on that lying, conniving little bitch he might not be accountable for his actions. *God* damn *her!* he thought viciously, his hands unconsciously clenching into white-knuckled fists. *Lies, lies, and more lies! But how to prove it!*

She had the legal documents with his name on them and she was enlisting supporters, oh, so ingeniously, by using her feminine wiles to good effect—a wide-eyed appeal here, a hint of a quaver in her voice there; and when that didn't seem to be gaining the objective, outrage so magnificently expressed that it sounded authentic. Oh, Jesus! What the hell was he going to do?

Too angry and infuriated to sleep, Morgan at last gave up the pretense and slid naked from his bed. Shrugging on a robe of sapphire blue silk, he carelessly knotted the belt about his lean waist and then unconsciously began to pace the confines of his room like a caged panther.

The more he thought about the evening and what had transpired, the angrier he got—and he'd been blazing mad to start with!

Pacing the floor didn't seem to help, and dwelling on the past evening only served to add more fuel to what was rapidly becoming ungovernable rage. Realizing that he was gaining nothing by stalking back and forth across his darkened room and thinking about the crafty little viper who had insinuated herself in his family, he pulled on a pair of old breeches and boots, and after slipping on a linen shirt and hastily buckling a wide belt about his waist, he left his room.

A few minutes later, Morgan let himself out a pair of

French doors at the side of the house and was on his way to the stables. Moments later he was astride his favorite mount, a powerful, long-legged, blood-bay stallion with black points and named Tempête—a name that suited the animal's temperament admirably. Tonight, though, beyond snorting affectionately and cavorting playfully for a few seconds, Tempête did not live up to his name and responded eagerly to Morgan's commands.

Morgan did not bother with a saddle. Riding the horse bareback through the silence of the night brought back memories for Morgan—memories of his life with the Comanches and many a moonlight raid.

How long he rode, Morgan didn't know. He took a turn off from the main road to Bonheur and then followed a narrow, overgrown path that gently angled downward, and after a while he found himself riding near the edge of the roiling, hissing, mighty Mississippi River. He rode for some miles, staring vaguely out into the darkness, not even aware of the roar of the river; his thoughts were far away from the trauma and disagreeable situation that awaited him upon his return. And as he rode silently through the blackness of the night, the sky gradually began to turn that soft purple that comes as the stars fade and the sun seeks to establish itself once more in the heavens.

The ride brought Morgan a sense of peace, his rage and furious resentment fading for the moment. By the time the first pink and gold fingers of dawn were streaking across the sky, he was able to view the problem that Leonie and her precipitous advent into his life had created, with less emotion and more of the cool, unruffled intelligence for which he was noted. For the first time since she had erupted so violently into his life, he was able to put aside the completely natural desire to furiously shout aloud his innocence, and, instead, to turn his powerful mind to the problem of finding a way to expose this clever schemer for the lying, conniving bitch she was.

Just the thought of her, and Morgan felt scorching, scarlet rage boiling up inside of him, but he swiftly brought it under control. Raging and ranting would gain him nothing. He had to fight the little witch on her own grounds, he

173

decided slowly. He must find a way to turn this situation against her—somehow, those very legal-looking documents that she had so neatly trapped him with must be made to work against her. But how?

Turning Tempête from the river, Morgan eventually found the path he had taken down and slowly retraced his ride, his mind occupied with the search for a solution. It was obvious that her main reason for seeking him was to extort money.

Then why, he wondered idly as he urged Tempête along, had she chosen such a public and dramatic way of announcing their ostensible relationship? Gaylord? That could be, he admitted reluctantly.

A patch of blue to the right caught his eye, and seeing the beckoning glitter of the dawn sun on water, he guided Tempête toward it. Pushing their way through the wild, luxuriant undergrowth, they came eventually to a spot Morgan hadn't visited since a child.

A small, gurgling creek ran around the edge of the Bonheur estate before it plunged over the high bluff to the river below, and here and there as it meandered over the acreage, it widened into deep, blue pools—pools where Morgan had loved to swim. This particular one had been his favorite because it was the one farthest from the house; the deepest one with the clearest, sweetest water; and because of the small waterfall that splashed over the small rocky abutment at one end of the pool.

Staring at the cool, clear depths, Morgan gave into an impulse. Dismounting Tempête and tying the reins to a nearby bush, he walked to the edge of the pool.

It took him only a moment to strip off his clothes, and then with a clean, strong dive, he plunged into the clear water. The water was cool and pleasing along his skin, and settling down to a steady pace, he swam from one end of the pool to the other, then back again, his mind once again seeking a way out of the trap Leonie Saint-André had sprung on him. His body moved effortlessly through the water, the muscled arms and legs propelling him without conscious thought, leaving his brain free to concentrate on more important things.

What part *did* Gaylord Easton play in her plans? he

174

wondered as he swam. Or was it Gaylord's plan and Leonie only his tool? Somehow, Morgan doubted that. Leonie Saint-André had not left him with the impression that she would be anyone's tool.

Pushing himself forcefully away from the rocky abutment, he did a precision turn, and then with his arms cutting cleanly through the crystalline, blue waters, he swam back and forth, his mind fully on Leonie Saint-André. He did not like what he was thinking either. *She's too damned attractive,* he admitted savagely, knowing he wouldn't have let her disappear out of his life even if she hadn't brought herself so summarily to his attention. Which left him where? Drawn irresistibly to a woman he perceived to be an unprincipled bitch?

God damn it, no! he nearly shouted aloud, his stroke faltering a bit. But Morgan knew he lied, and stopping abruptly in the center of the pool, he treaded water, shaking his wet dark hair from his eyes. All right, so he'd like to bed the wench, he couldn't deny that, but despite his desire for her, he still wanted the little vixen exposed for the liar she was.

Suddenly losing his pleasure in the swim, he left the pool and dragged his clothes on over his wet body. Seating himself at the base of a huge magnolia tree near where Tempête leisurely cropped tender spring grass and clover, Morgan plucked a blade himself and idly chewed on it as he continued to search for a way out of this snare.

If it *was* money she was after, then of course, the easiest solution was to have her name her price and give her the damned money, he conceded. But that solution rankled. He hadn't married the bitch and wasn't about to be harrassed into meeting her demands. Besides, paying her the money wouldn't solve his problem—with her gone he would still have to convince everyone else that she had lied and that the entire preposterous incident had merely been a scheme to bleed money from him.

No, she was going to find out that Morgan Slade was not the easy gull she had first thought, he decided grimly, and that meant he had to play along with her until he had the proof he needed. He tossed away the mangled blade of grass, and feeling as if he now had a glimmer of a plan, he

175

swiftly remounted Tempête and headed back towards the house.

And so it was, as he rode along the narrow, tree-shaded little patch through the woods near Bonheur, that one way of turning the tables on Mademoiselle Saint-André occurred to him. The path ran in front of a large clearing, and glancing at it, Morgan's hands tightened unexpectedly on the reins, causing Tempête to dance angrily.

A miniature of Bonheur sat serenely in the clearing, the forest flanking it on all three sides, and staring at the house Morgan suddenly smiled. Of course, Le Petit Bonheur.

Le Petit Bonheur had been constructed three years earlier by Matthew in the hopes that a house separated from the main estate would encourage one of his bachelor sons to marry. Robert was thirty-one, Dominic already twenty-three, and Alexandre and Cassandre sixteen, rising seventeen, and Matthew was optimistically planning for the future. Someday, he hoped there would be several homes scattered across the thousands of acres of Bonheur, all of them housing the growing families of his sons, and Le Petit, as it was called, was the start of that very fervent hope. But so far, none of his three eldest sons seemed inclined to take advantage of the elegant little house. Until now, Morgan thought with a dangerous glitter in the dark blue eyes . . . until *now*. . . .

13

Leaving the path, Morgan approached the front of the house, staring at it thoughtfully. Le Petit was about half the size of Bonheur, and while it duplicated the broad columns, the wide verandas and the architecture of the main house, it had a charm of its own, the soft yellow glow of the walls and the glistening white columns pleasingly different from the cool green of Bonheur.

Speculatively, Morgan rode slowly around the house, noting the kitchen, constructed as usual some distance from the building, and the stables that nestled under the verdant growth of the pines, oaks, and tupelo trees. Servants' quarters of brick were further along in the forest, each with its cleared little space for whatever food crops the blacks wished to grow for themselves. Turning Tempête back towards the main house, Morgan glanced interestedly at the latticed summerhouse that could be seen through the trees at the right of the house. Beyond it, he caught a glimpse of the same stream that formed the pool he had just left. Guiding the restive stallion around to the other side, he discovered a terrace and a boxwood garden, as well as another building just inside the forest line which he correctly took to be the office.

Nudging Tempête into a brisk trot, he rode back towards the path, and stopping there, took another long look at the house. A fairy-tale house, in a fairy-tale setting, he thought sardonically, and a smile of pure deviltry lit his face. *I wonder,* he mused with unholy amusement, *how my new bride will like it!*

Le Petit had given him the idea for a partial solution to block Leonie's further intrusion into his family. If he brought her here, she would be isolated from the rest of the family and would have fewer chances to work her wiles on his parents. She had claimed to be his wife; everyone seemed to believe her, so why not appear to give in gracefully? Precisely what sort of excuse he was going to offer to explain his reasons for denying her existence so vehemently last night, and supposedly deserting her, escaped him for the moment, as did any sort of explanation for his behavior with Melinda, but he was certain something would occur to him. Leonie Saint-André was going to discover she wasn't the only one who could lie through her teeth, he decided coldly.

Appearing to acknowledge the validity of her claim was risky, even he would admit that. He would be branded a liar as well as several other more unpleasant things, but momentarily there was no other choice. As long as he denied her accusations, she would gather sympathy and supporters, but if he coolly conceded defeat and did *not* deny her story, might that action disconcert his charming little wife?

Somehow he rather thought it would, certain she'd had no intention of actually taking her place as his spouse. It was money that she was after, not social position, and he'd be willing to wager his inheritance that the last thing she wanted was a husband hung around her pretty neck. Something she was going to get with a vengeance, he promised with a nasty smile.

It would also give him time to put someone to work on discovering exactly who this little bitch was and why she had chosen him for her scheme. Acknowledging her as his wife deftly took the offensive away from her and gave it to him, leaving her the one to then find a way to get herself out of the trap *she* had fallen into.

The more Morgan thought of the idea, the more intrigued by it he became. There were, he reflected cynically, several aspects to having a wife that he was certain he would enjoy—that challenging mouth, for one and that delectable, slender body for another.

A mocking smile on his lips, Morgan finally kicked Tempête into a gallop, suddenly eager for the commencement of battle—and a battle, he was certain, it was going to be!

All of his earlier rage had disappeared, if not the bitter hurt and sharp disappointment of having his parents think him capable of villainy, and he was in a more normal, confident frame of mind. As for his parents, his current plan couldn't wound or distress them more than they already had been. They believed the worst of him, so who was he to deny it? The scandal and gossip currently flying from one plantation to another he dismissed contemptuously—next week there would be something else for the residents of Natchez to discuss, and the unexpected appearance of Morgan Slade's wife at his betrothal ball to Melinda Marshall would fade into the past.

He might furiously damn Leonie Saint-André for disrupting his life, but he was more alive and full of enthusiasm than he had been in months, perhaps even years. For the first time in far too long, he was actually looking foward to something, actually planning something instead of allowing weary disinterest to take him where it would. The tedious boredom that had been his constant companion was gone, and in its place there was a burst of excitement surging in his bloodstream and a pleasurable sense of expectancy that went to his head like vintage wine.

Morgan was almost happy when he reached Bonheur—not quite, but almost—for, after all, he had always enjoyed a good fight, and the one shaping up gave all the appearances of being the most treacherous and yet exciting fight of his entire life. He was going to greatly enjoy crossing swords with Mademoiselle Saint-André!

The house was stirring now, and when he approached the stables, he was met by Jeremy, the head groom. Tossing Tempête's reins to the man, Morgan sent him a carefree grin and slid lithely from the back of the stallion.

"He's had a good run, but I'd have him walked before turning him loose in the pasture," Morgan said by way of explanation.

Leaving Jeremy to stare after him with curiosity, Morgan walked swiftly to the house, whistling as he went. He passed several servants busy about the house and greeted them cheerfully as he made his way towards his room. Behind him, looks of surprise and perplexity were exchanged —perhaps Master Morgan was happy his wife had come?

179

Entering his room, Morgan began to strip off his shirt, calling for the very correct and very English valet he'd acquired during a trip to England years ago. "Litchfield, have someone prepare a bath for me, will you? I've been riding and can't go to the breakfast room smelling of the stables."

Litchfield appeared from the dressing room, and his long, sallow face expressing disapproval, he said haughtily, "I assumed as much, sir, and took the liberty of ordering one some minutes ago. It should be ready any moment."

"Is one permitted to know what led to that assumption?"

Litchfield gave a condescending nod. "Of course, sir. I am, as you know, well acquainted with your wardrobe, so upon ascertaining what was missing and upon a further inquiry to the stables if one of the horses was missing, and having that confirmed, it was simple enough to come to the conclusion that you had gone riding."

"I see. And have you also, er, ascertained what I am to wear this morning?"

A scandalized look crossed Litchfield's face. "Naturally, sir! I have laid out the appropriate clothes on your bed."

The hot water for the bath arrived just then, and a few minutes later Morgan was pleasurably immersed in warm, soapy water in the large brass tub which had been set up in his dressing room. A thin, black cigarillo was clenched between his teeth as he scrubbed, and glancing over at Litchfield's impassive face as the other man moved unobtrusively about unnecessarily straightening things, Morgan asked, "Have you heard the news?"

Litchfield stopped his incessant fiddling and looked at Morgan. The two men had been together for over ten years, and except for those times when Morgan went haring off after adventures or simply did not want his services, Litchfield saw him daily. They shared a good relationship—Morgan delighting in finding ways to shake Litchfield from his stolid, almost pompous attitudes, and Litchfield equally delighting in rising above Master Morgan's unbecoming and ungentlemanly antics, determined not to betray by so much as a flicker of an eyelash anything but polite disdain.

The valet was some fifty years old, and as he frequently relished informing Master Morgan, he had trained in the Duke of Leighford's household. He did his job well, and despite assuming a look of insulted reproachfulness, he had upon occasion acted as Morgan's butler—necessary to discourage a certain clinging mistress who could not believe that Mr. Slade had grown tired of the association—and he had even deigned to cook for the master when they had been stranded in an abandoned cottage on the Cornish coast during a raging storm when Morgan had been unable to make contact with the smuggler who would take him to France. And it had frequently been Litchfield whom Morgan relied upon to relay his messages from France to the Duke of Roxbury concerning the movements of Napoleon's troops. Morgan was unwilling to trust anyone but Litchfield, who always acted as if he were grievously offended at being asked to do something other than the normal duties of a gentleman's gentleman.

Litchfield was not an imposing figure, being only an inch or two above average height, and was inclined towards stoutness. His hair was dark but had begun to thin, and his large, round eyes were a pleasant, unremarkable shade of brown. A long nose and a small, prim mouth completed the picture—all in all, a most forgettable face if it had not been for the expressive quality of those features. As Dominic had once remarked, Litchfield could sour an apple with a glance.

At the moment, Litchfield's face expressed rigid distaste as he looked at Morgan. "My dear sir, I could hardly avoid it. The entire household is fluttering with it."

Morgan removed the cigarillo from his mouth and to Litchfield's intense annoyance idly flicked the ash on the floor. "Believe it?" Morgan asked curiously.

One thin eyebrow soaring disdainfully, Litchfield sniffed dismissingly and said simply, "No."

Morgan made a face. "Well, you my friend, are about the only one!"

"Indeed, sir?"

Taking a puff of the cigarillo, Morgan blew a cloud of blue smoke in the air. "Indeed, yes, Litchfield," he said cheerfully. "And you are about to be shown the error of your ways." Looking across at his valet, he said deliberately, "For the time being, I think you and I are going to find ourselves saddled with a household that comprises not only my wife . . . but apparently my child!"

"Indeed, sir?" Litchfield repeated dryly, his face impassive.

Morgan shot him a grin. "Yes, indeed! And you had better start packing my clothes—I'm going to have us all cozily settled in Le Petit by tonight."

Litchfield merely nodded his head in acknowledgment and murmured imperturbably, "Naturally, sir. I shall see that everything is taken care of."

Having set the plan in motion, Morgan wasted little more time with his bath. Not fifteen minutes later, suitably attired in a superb fitting, olive green jacket and nankeen breeches, he walked purposefully towards Dominic's room. Not bothering to knock, he pushed open the door and finding Dominic still soundly sleeping, crossed the room and cheerfully flung back the heavy drapes to let the bright sunlight cascade into the room.

The light fell right across Dominic's face, and with a muttered curse, he turned on his stomach and pulled one of the pillows over his head; but Morgan would not let him off so easily. Just as cheerfully as he had opened the drapes, he pulled Dominic back over, shaking him ungently as he did so, and drawled dulcetly, "Wake up, little brother. I have need of you."

Groggily, Dominic regarded him. "Morgan, do you realize what time it is?" he growled.

"Mmm. Shortly after eight, I believe," Morgan replied.

Dominic groaned and attempted to hide from the sun again, but Morgan would have none of it. A hint of laughter in his voice, he said, "Dom, wake up! I need to ask you a few questions about last night. And I haven't much time."

Knowing further sleep was going to be impossible if Morgan was determined to talk to him, Dominic capitulated. Muttering under his breath, he turned over and sat up in bed, pushing a huge, white pillow behind him. Rubbing the sleep out of his eyes and then running a hand through his rumpled black hair, he said resignedly, "All right, what is it? What do you need to know?"

Morgan sat down on the edge of the bed and said simply, "Tell me your impression of my . . . er . . . wife."

Suspiciously, Dominic studied him. "Why? What are you up to? What are you going to do?"

A glitter in the blue eyes that made Dominic decidedly uneasy, Morgan replied innocently, "Do? Why nothing, my dear brother, except acknowledge my wife. What else would I do?"

Dominic's black brows so like Morgan's, lowered in a scowl. "I thought you said you'd never seen her before." At the expression on Morgan's face, he added hastily, "*If* you married her, you should know more about her than I do!"

"*If*, Dom? You have doubts?"

Uncomfortably, Dominic said, "She tells a convincing tale, Morgan. On the other hand, I find it difficult to believe you would do as she claims. I don't really know which one of you to trust, and so for the moment, I'm giving you both the benefit of doubt."

"Generous, Dom!" Morgan said dryly.

"Well, God damn it! What else can I do? She had the bloody papers, Morgan!" Dominic snapped furiously. "And it's your damned signature on the bottom of them. She's not just some little tart, either. She's a lady born and bred—anyone can see that!" Almost sulkily he finished, "And father thinks the child is your very image at the same age!"

Morgan shrugged. "Father would! Especially if he's made up his mind that she *is* my wife!"

"I'll grant you, you're probably right about that, but it still doesn't explain the marriage papers or the agreement to pay her back the dowry."

"No, it doesn't, does it?" Morgan agreed amiably. "Which is why I need your help, little brother. What else did you learn of her—besides the fact that she is . . . a lady born and bred?"

Aware that Morgan wasn't going to be deterred Dominic said grudgingly, "Not too much. She seemed rather reluctant to talk much about herself, but apparently, as she told us all at Marshall Hall, her grandfather arranged the marriage when he learned he hadn't long to live. She says she met you at Gayoso's and decided you were the proper man

183

to entrust her future to. I understand she wasn't given much choice in the matter and that she didn't precisely want to marry you, but her grandfather, more or less, forced her into it." Dominic stopped abruptly and glared at Morgan. "Why in the hell am I telling you this? You were there—you heard what she said!"

His face infuriatingly bland, Morgan said with suspect diffidence, "Oh, I merely wondered if my recollection of last night tallied with yours. And I was hoping that perhaps once I was no longer present, that my dear, er, wife might have mentioned a few other things that she neglected to speak of in front of me."

"Like what?"

Morgan shrugged carelessly. "Like why she waited until now to reveal herself. Why now, after all these years, does she want to take her place as my wife? Why didn't she find me after the child was born?"

Dominic sent him a long thoughtful stare. "She doesn't want to take her place as your wife now. Even I gathered that from last night! What she wants is for you to repay the dowry you recieved from her grandfather, and that, according to her, is the only reason why she has come to Natchez."

Looking as innocent as he dared, Morgan murmured pensively, "Money, eh? You think if I repaid her, she'd go out of my life just as quickly as she entered it? Doesn't that smack of blackmail to you?"

"Morgan, she has a child to support and her home is being taken away from her. For God's sake have a little pity. She's responsible for several other people besides herself, and the only way she could think of was to ask for her dowry back. That doesn't leave *me* thinking blackmail." Dominic looked away and said flatly, "If anything, it leaves me wondering about you."

Morgan's hard-won tranquility fled and his face froze. "I only needed *that!*" he ground out between clenched teeth. "Thank you very much, brother! I'm surprised you even conceded to speak with me!"

Miserably, Dominic reached out and touched Morgan's rigid shoulder. "Morgan, I'm sorry. It's just that everything is in such a tangle . . . and I don't know what to think. . . . *No one* does!" Searching his brother's implacable features, he said earnestly, "None of us wants to believe that you did as she said, and yet she has irrefutable proof!"

"Signatures can be forged," Morgan replied stonily.

"Yes, that's true, but Leonie herself is not hard to believe. And when you add the two together, plus the fact that you were in New Orleans at the time she said the marriage took place . . . ."

"Very well, then," Morgan said stiffly. "I see that there is nothing else for me to do but to claim my wife. Good morning, Dominic."

"What do you mean to do?" Dominic asked with a note of apprehension in his voice, not liking the expression on Morgan's face.

"Do?" Morgan snarled. "Why, I am going to confess everything! If you wish to view the condemned felon's admission of guilt, I suggest you dress yourself and join the family in the breakfast room."

"Wait!" Dominic yelped, but Morgan had already stormed out of the room.

All of his earlier rage had come back to the surface, and knowing it would gain him nothing, Morgan brutally fought to bring his temper under control. *My God,* he thought furiously, *if you're going to leap on the high ropes the first time someone speaks ill of your supposed action, you're going to scuttle your own plans!*

But that unfortunate loss of control held a vital lesson, and Morgan knew it—under no circumstances was he to forget the role he had chosen to play. If he could run a rig for Napoleon' agents, he could damn sure act his way through this little farce!

Still, he needed a few minutes more to recover himself before bearding the others, and instinctively he headed out of the house. He didn't go far, just to the edge of the forest that encroached near one side of the house. Taking in a few deep breaths and staring blankly into the cool, green growth, he let the peacefulness seep into his bones and grimly forced the angry tide of injustice that swelled within him to subside.

He was not a man who often lost control of himself or a situation, and his present predicament was at once infuriating and unnerving. Nor was he a man used to having people think ill of him, and while he had always considered himself impervious to the opinions of other people, he discovered that the pain of his family's defection went deep. *And for* that, *little wife, you're going to pay dearly,* he promised harshly!

With an effort he wrenched his mind away from thoughts of retribution against his lovely tormentor, and instead, concentrated on regaining some of the tranquility and almost light hearted confidence that had been his before his interview with Dominic. If this unpleasant facade was going to succeed, he was going to need all his wits and every bit of self-control that he possessed. *No more tantrums for you, my friend, if you are wise!*

Smiling with wry amusement at his own words of wisdom, some of the earlier pleasurable anticipation that had been his came flooding back. *Think of it as a game,* he told himself. *Enjoy it and, for God's sake, stay unruffled! Let Leonie have the tantrums!*

Feeling in control once again, he gave the towering pine tree he was standing next to a hearty slap and then spun on his heel, and for the second time that morning, entered the house with a cheerful whistle on his lips. Reaching the door that led to the breakfast room, he hesitated for just a minute, wondering if some other solution existed. No, he rather thought not—as long as he denied the marriage, the more adherents Leonie would gather to her banner, but take that weapon away from her and she was at *his* mercy. *Jesus Christ, but I am going to enjoy watching her try to wiggle out of my trap!* he decided savagely. Then taking a deep, fortifying breath, the light of battle gleaming in the dark blue eyes, he pushed open the door and sauntered cooly into the breakfast room.

As it was still too early for most of the inhabitants to be up, especially after last night, Morgan found only his father and Robert seated at the table. That they had been discussing him was more than obvious from the abrupt halting of the conversation that had been taking place between the other two men.

Ignoring the sudden silence, Morgan said lightly, "Good

morning! I trust you all slept well after last night's contre-
temps?"

"You apparently did," Matthew replied heavily, his
shadowed eyes clearly revealing that *he* had not slept well
at all.

Helping himself to a rasher of bacon and some scrambled eggs from the oak sideboard, Morgan murmured casually, "As a matter of fact I haven't slept at all. But I found
that a dawn ride and a hot bath can do marvelous things
for one's sagging spirits . . . you should try it."

"I'm pleased *you* can recover so quickly!" Matthew
snapped.

"Well, I'll admit it was a facer when Leonie first showed
up, but upon reflection I have decided that having a wife
might be a very good thing. After all," Morgan said reasonably, "I was on the point of leg-shackling myself to Melinda, so it isn't as if I were opposed to the married state."

Openmouthed, his father stared at him, and Robert, who
had been looking more and more confused, blurted out,
"How can you tease about such a serious matter?"

Morgan glanced at him. "My dear fellow, *must* marriage
be a tragedy?"

"Well, no, but that isn't what I meant! I meant—"

Blandly interupting him, Morgan said dryly, "I know
what you meant, Rob."

Matthew recovered himself, and staring hard at Morgan's dark face, he asked sharply, "Does this mean what
Leonie told us is true? Are you admitting that she is your
wife? That you lied when you claimed you'd never seen her
before?"

"I'm admitting that she has all the proof to lay claim to
the dubious title of my wife, and that if she wants to be my
wife . . . well, then I have no objections."

It was a very unsatisfactory answer and Matthew glared
at him. Letting his breath out in a long sigh, he demanded,
"Is that young woman your wife or not?"

His face expressing only mild surprise, Morgan drawled,
"I thought everyone had agreed on that."

Matthew drew himself up angrily. One clenched fist
resting on the table, he snapped, "Stop this nonsense! I
have seen your child, Morgan, and I have seen the mar-

187

riage papers with your signature. I believe her, but I find it difficult to credit you with the sort of reprehensible actions that must have taken place to bring about this situation. Have you nothing to say in your defense?"

Morgan toyed idly with the spoon that rested on his saucer and, for a moment, considered once again of professing his innocence. But it would be useless, even he could see that, and remembering the role he had chosen to play, he returned lightly, "Only that at first I really had forgotten about her . . . and all these years I had assumed that the marriage had been terminated. I didn't know about the child."

"What do you mean?" Matthew questioned swiftly, his eyes fixed keenly on Morgan's face.

Morgan had wondered what he would say when he was asked that question, but now that the moment was upon him, he found that the words came easily enough. "As I recall, it was a whim of mine . . . old Saint-André caught me at one of those times when I was ripe for anything, and before I realized it, I found myself married to the chit. It was only the morning after the wedding that I came to my senses and recognized the fact that I had been a bloody fool." Staring intently at the spoon as he continued to toy with it, and hating the lies he was spinning so effortlessly, he continued slowly, "I decided then that the quickest solution would be to divorce Leonie quietly, without any fuss, and to go on with my life." Wryly, he added, "The thought of a child never occurred to me, and after I saw a lawyer there in New Orleans, I left instructions for him to facilitate a divorce as soon as possible. He was to notify Leonie when all the legal documents had been completed." His mouth quirking in a derisive smile, he said, "Obviously, the lawyer pocketed the gold I left with him and did nothing."

As Morgan spoke, Robert's face began to clear, and when Morgan stopped speaking, he turned to his father eagerly. "See! I knew Morgan couldn't be an out-and-out blackguard! I told you there had to be some sort of reasonable explanation!"

"So you did," Matthew replied thoughtfully, not quite as willing as Robert to accept Morgan's glib explanation. It did explain several things, but Matthew didn't like it. Divorces were not that easily obtained, especially after one had been married by a Catholic priest. There was a note in Morgan's voice that he distrusted, something about the pat recital of facts that bothered him. And yet what did he want? Morgan to continue to deny the marriage in the face of all the evidence? Aloud, Matthew asked dryly, "And the dowry? Why wasn't that repaid?"

Morgan looked over at his father and smiled sweetly. "My lamentable memory, you know. Five years is a long time, and I'm afraid it simply just slipped my mind."

"Quite a few things seem to have slipped your mind."

Undaunted by the skeptical note in his father's voice, Morgan returned imperturbably, "I know, it is most vexatious, but now that I have a wife, I suppose things will improve. Women do tend to remind one of so many things . . . don't they?"

Matthew regarded Morgan with unnerving penetration for several moments before inquiring expressionlessly, "And last night? Would you mind telling me why you denied ever having met Leonie? Denied all knowledge of the marriage?"

His face the picture of innocence, Morgan admitted ruefully, "I was completely taken off guard! And quite frankly, I had put what happened in New Orleans out of my mind. I had assumed the divorce had been completed and I was a free man. It was only last night after the ball, when I began to rack my brain for some clue that would explain what had happened . . . that I realized who Leonie must be."

"Did you now?" Matthew commented interestedly. "And having realized who Leonie is, what exactly do you plan to do?"

If the situation had not been so serious, Morgan would have been enjoying himself. It was apparent his father didn't believe a word of what he had been saying but could find no other logical explanation for what had happened. A mocking glint in the dark blue eyes, Morgan answered with unwonted meekness, "I thought, perhaps, that Leonie and I could set up our household temporarily at Le Petit."

Matthew took a sip of his coffee and gave Morgan another long, assessing stare. Reluctantly, he said, "I can see no objections, but I don't think that Leonie will consent to it."

Morgan smiled angelically. "As my wife, she really doesn't have any choice, does she?"

14

Having cleared the first and most dangerous hurdle without incident and having received Matthew's reluctant consent to use Le Petit, Morgan wasted little time. Leaving Robert and Matthew to explain the extraordinary details of his marriage, Morgan immediately set about preparing the house.

Fortunately, he discovered that Matthew had left orders for the house to be aired and cleaned regularly, and walking slowly through the elegantly furnished rooms, Morgan smiled to himself. His father had left nothing to chance—the house was in excellent order, needing only foodstuffs, linens, and the like to be ready for occupancy.

Litchfield was already upstairs unpacking Morgan's clothes. Servants had been no problem as Matthew had very generously given Morgan permission to borrow indefinitely a dozen or so from Bonheur, and Morgan had unhesitatingly accepted. He had also gone around and met with Leonie's servants; Abraham, Mammy, and the others were at the moment once more unpacking their meager belongings in two of the brick cottages that Morgan had suggested they use.

Mammy had made it clear that they were Leonie's servants and free people; but Morgan could be overwhelmingly charming when he chose to be, and in short order Mammy had found herself agreeing happily to work for the new master. The others followed her lead and had decided that while Le Petit wasn't Château Saint-André, it would serve very well.

It was a busy morning, but Morgan was well organized; with dozens of hands to carry out his orders, Le Petit was rapidly taking on a lived-in look. Several horses, including

191

Tempête, now resided in the stables; Mammy and two assistants were busy in the kitchen; little black children played in front of the row of brick cottages; and from inside Le Petit came the sound of voices as the other servants moved about, putting away items as they arrived from Bonheur.

Consequently when Leonie finally woke, she was greeted with the horrifying news that the only thing needed to make her new home complete was the presence of herself, Justin, and Yvette! It was Justin who happily broke the news to her as he at last escaped from Yvette's watchful eye and burst impatiently into his mother's room.

"Maman! Maman! Wake up! We are to have a new house with papa! Oh, maman, *do* wake up!" he cried exuberantly as he jumped playfully up and down on Leonie's bed.

Yvette had managed to keep him occupied most of the morning in their room, but Justin was an active little boy who longed to be outside exploring. At first he had been very well behaved and had been content with Yvette's explanation of how they had arrived here while he slept. He had spent a great deal of time hanging out the tall windows that overlooked the front of the house, admiring the long driveway and watching with fascination the various comings and goings.

But that had soon palled, and Yvette had been at her wit's end trying to think of ways to amuse him when the summons to meet with his grandparents had come. She had purposely kept Justin inside the room with her, because she had been too shy and uncertain to leave its safety. Even the kindness and courtesy of the servants, who had seen to their breakfast trays and who seemed to take such a delighted interest in Justin, did nothing to alleviate her nervousness. Almost as much as Justin, she wanted Leonie to wake up; Leonie would see that everything went right in this houseful of strangers.

The request to bring Justin to the drawing room to meet with his grandparents threw Yvette into a panic, and she almost rushed into the other room and woke Leonie herself. But gathering her composure, she set her chin at an angle she had often seen Leonie adopt, and with an outward serenity that hid all her inward trepidation, she took Justin's hand in hers and followed the servant to the drawing room.

The ordeal wasn't as bad as she had feared. Only Matthew and Noelle were in the charming blue and gold room, and since Morgan had apparently confirmed Leonie's story neither one of his parents were inclined to treat Yvette with anything but politeness and friendliness—besides Justin had their undivided attention.

Justin thoroughly enjoyed himself. He was the center of attention and like all children, reveled in it. Grandmother Slade gave him a sugar plum, which made him decide then and there that grandmothers were rather nice to have, and he had shrieked with uninhibited laughter when Grandfather Slade had swung him up high in the air. All in all, Justin was having a grand time.

It was Grandfather Slade, who told Yvette and Justin about the proposed move to Le Petit, and while Yvette was surprised and just a little concerned about Leonie's reactions, Justin was hugely pleased. His slanting, golden-green eyes opening very wide, he had asked eagerly, "We are to live with my papa? We will have our own house, *oui?*" And ever the opportunist, he added hopefully, "And papa will buy me a pony?"

Matthew had laughed and nodded his head. "I think something can be arranged." Seeing the child again stilled his doubts, even if Matthew didn't quite believe the story Morgan had spun out for them this morning. But it was far easier to think that his son had acted irresponsibly than to think that he had deliberately deserted a young wife with a child. His actions had been crass, there was no denying it, but they had not been those of a scoundrel who had preyed upon an innocent young maid.

Oddly enough, Noelle had accepted the story without question. Yes, it had been reprehensible of him, it was true, but he had tried to set things right, hadn't he? It wasn't Morgan's fault that the lawyer had not done as instructed, was it? Besides it had worked out for the best, hadn't it? If the lawyer had done his work, they would never had known about Justin, and that would have been a shame, wouldn't it? "And," Noelle had finished tell-

193

ingly, "I think I much prefer young Leonie to Melinda Marshall after all."

Matthew had quirked an eyebrow at her. "The hysterics, were they very bad?"

Noelle had shuddered. "Very bad, *chèrie!*"

Everyone seemed to be happy with the way things were turning out, even if there were some reservations on the part of a few people. Dominic, for one, flatly refused to believe the story, although he kept his opinion to himself, and Mr. Marshall, who had arrived smartly at ten o'clock this morning for the express purpose of mending the damage done last night, was another. Of course, in Mr. Marshall's case there was a great deal of self-interest—sober reflection on the wealth and power of the Slades had made Morgan seem just as desirable a partner for his daughter as he had been before that deplorable interruption at the ball. But he had become outraged when Morgan and Matthew had gravely explained Morgan's lapse of memory. Unfortunately, it wasn't the improbablity of the tale that outraged Mr. Marshall, but the fact that the heir to the Slade estates had just slipped out of his grasp.

Nevertheless, Mr. Marshall was soon forgotten in the rush of preparing Le Petit. Justin was perhaps the most excited of them all at the prospect. Matthew had no sooner told him about it than Justin had tugged enthusiastically on Yvette's hand. "Hurry! We must tell maman!"

Laughing at Justin's pleasurable excitement, Matthew had opened the door and said, "By all means, do go tell your maman. It should please her!"

Nothing of course could have been farther than the truth, but the full import of Justin's happy prattle didn't immedately sink into Leonie's brain. She had been lying there in the huge, silk-draped bed wondering what the day would bring when Justin burst into the room, and for the next several moments, they were too involved in playing the special game that had been theirs since Justin had first learned to walk and crawl into Maman's bed.

It was part of their morning routine, and the familiarity of having Justin clambering away from her as she tackled his wiggling little body was so achingly normal that she momentarily forgot everything but the joy of playing with

194

her son. Unmindful of anything but the sheer fun of giggling and wrestling with Justin, the two of them soon had the bed in an untidy shambles. They had gone from chasing one another under the covers to a pillow fight; Leonie, her tawny mane curling in delightful disorder about her shoulders, the bewitching green eyes alight with mischief and merriment, and her entire face glowing with laughter, looked not ten years older than her son. She had slept in an old, cotton shift and the soft, worn fabric clung to the slender body, hiding none of the beauty of the small, impudent breasts or the slim, narrow hips, as she sat gracefully back on her heels and deftly avoided Justin's pillow. Two slender straps were all that held the shift up, and Leonie's shoulders gleaned an enticing shade of pale gold as she gleefully attacked Justin with her pillow.

"Dolt! How dare you treat me so, *mon fils!* I shall beat you soundly and lock you up in the barn for such behavior!" Leonie threatened teasingly as Justin's pillow caught her on the side of the head. "But first, I shall tickle you for an hour, *oui?*"

Her mouth curved in a lively smile, she lunged for Justin, and Justin, squealing with laughter, met her halfway across the bed as he threw his arms about her neck. "Ah, maman, *je t'adore!*" he said impulsively.

Leonie was kneeling, her arms about her son, as Justin hugged her, the black head and the tawny one very close together. "And I love you too, *mon fils!*" she said in a suddenly husky voice.

Justin moved his head slightly away from hers and asked with a slight note of anxiety, "Papa will love us too, *oui?*"

Leonie hesitated, longing to reassure him, but the words she might have said never came, for Morgan's voice stunningly provided the answer to Justin's question.

"I don't see how he could resist," Morgan said oddly from the doorway where he had been watching them for several moments, unashamedly taking pleasure in observing their uninhibited antics.

Leonie stiffened, the gaiety dying out of her face, the green eyes suddenly shuttered as she glared at him. He was lounging casually against the doorjamb, his arms folded across his chest, and the unexpected sight of the tall, manly form and the dark, lean face, as much as his astounding statement, caused her heart to race at a frantic pace.

Morgan had noted the instant change in her demeanor, and he was aware of a painful stab of regret that the enchanting creature who had gamboled so delightfully with her son only a moment before had disappeared, and had left in her place a fiercely hostile young woman. He had just arrived back at the house and had come upstairs for the express purpose of mockingly informing his wife that their new home awaited them, when he had been transfixed by the sight of Leonie and Justin romping across the rumpled bed. He remembered with pain that Stephanie had not liked Phillippe to disturb her in her bedroom and had disliked intensely having her hair mussed or to be in disarray of any sort. As Morgan watched them almost enviously as they played, something stirred deep within him, an emotion he had long thought never to feel again. But he would have furiously denied any such feeling if he had been conscious of it—his heart and emotions being safely armored against the dangerous wiles of a woman. Yet Justin's artless question had breeched his defenses, and consequently he had been unable to make the scathing reply he might have.

Morgan's words seemed to hang in the room for a second, and then Justin, his eyes widening as he stared at the tall, handsome man leaning in the doorway, asked breathlessly, "Are *you* my papa?"

Leonie's eyes flew to Morgan's, and the fierce plea in the golden-green depths, as much as his inability to hurt the child, caused Morgan to push away from the doorjamb and to say softly, "So I have been led to believe. Would you like to be my son?"

Justin, completely unaware of the tensions that swirled between the two adults, cocked his head to one side and said cautiously, "It might be pleasant, *oui?*"

Morgan grinned at him and walked closer to the bed. Reaching out a careless hand, he gently ruffled Justin's mop of unruly black hair and murmured, "I think so. Shall we try it?"

Justin was not a shy child, nor had he yet learned to mistrust strangers, and so with an engaging grin of his own, he replied, "Oh, *oui!*" Adding with devastating simplicity, "I have never had a papa before!"

No matter what Morgan might think of his mother, he simply could not resist Justin's appealing personality; his own son Phillippe had not been much younger than Justin when he had died. And Morgan, despite the impenetrable barrier he had placed around himself, invariably found himself painfully affected whenever he saw a sturdy, dark-haired little boy of Phillippe's approximate age. It was not in him to harm the child simply because his mother happened to be a scheming little bitch.

Justin was very pleased with this tall stranger, and completely oblivious to his mother's frozen form, he asked with unaccustomed shyness, "Would you like to play with us? We were having a grand fight with the pillows. They are most full, not like ours at home."

Leonie was suddenly galvanized in action by Justin's invitation, and also becoming uncomfortably aware of her state of dishabille, she said hurriedly, *"Non!* Your papa is busy, and I must dress."

A mocking glitter in the blue eyes, Morgan calmly sat down on the edge of the bed and drawled, "Oh, but I think I would enjoy joining you!"

Justin was delighted, but Leonie shot Morgan a look that spoke volumes, her soft mouth tightening with annoyance. "Not this morning," she said cooly, wishing that her detestable husband would go away and allow her to dress in privacy. She had never been so conscious of her body before, and the expression in those blue eyes as they roamed assessingly over her slender curves did nothing to stop the increased beating of her heart.

But Morgan was enjoying her discomfort, aware that if the child were not present she would not be quite so polite or show such restraint. Of course he took full advantage of it. Throwing himself backwards on the bed, his hands behind his head, he smiled sweetly up into Leonie's outraged features and murmured mockingly, "Oh, but I protest, dear wife. It has been years since I've had such a delightful invitation . . . would you deny Justin and me our pleasures?''

Leonie swallowed tightly, quelling an urge to take the pillow in her hands and violently smash it against that taunting mouth. Justin displayed no such compunction and with a whoop of excitement, launched himself on Morgan's prone form, his pillow hitting Morgan full in the face.

There was a muffled shout of laughter from Morgan, and then the next few minutes were chaotic as he promptly and efficiently retaliated. In the ensuing, noisy battle that followed, Justin did not seem to notice that his mother had removed herself from the scene of violent activity, but Morgan, even fending off Justin's determined attack, was very much aware of her still form as she shrank against the elaborate headboard to avoid coming in contact with Morgan's lean, muscled length.

A gleam of pure devilment in his eyes, Morgan lunged for Leonie, and before she could guess what he was up to, he had twitched her pillow from her hands and had pulled her down on the bed next to him. Half-lying, half-propped up by his elbows, he grinned down into her furious face and said lazily, "Good morning, wife." And ignoring the battering Justin was giving his back, doing as he had wanted since he had first laid eyes on her, he bent his head and kissed Leonie full on the mouth. Morgan didn't hurry, he took his time, his lips warm and compelling as they explored her soft, surprised mouth, his entire body suddenly suffused with an unexpected surge of desire, entwined with a queer tenderness, at the heady sensation of that provocative mouth under his.

Leonie was too surprised to react instantly, and before she did finally begin to struggle, she discovered two rather terrifying facts: her body acted with a will of its own, instinctively curving closer to Morgan's, and she didn't find his kiss at all repulsive! Horrified by what was happening to her, she stiffened in his embrace, her hands pushing frantically against Morgan's chest.

Immediately she was free, Morgan's mouth reluctantly leaving hers and his body rolling away from her. Like a frightened animal she scrambled away from him, her

198

breasts heaving beneath the thin, cotton shift. With wide, dazed eyes she stared at him. "Monsieur, you should not!" she gasped.

"Why not?" Morgan asked softly, his mocking gaze fixed intently on the soft quivering mouth. "You're my wife, aren't you?"

Leonie's answer to his question was lost as Justin, deciding he had been ignored long enough, threw himself on Morgan's chest, laughing with glee. "I have you, papa! I have you now!"

Knowing this was not the time for further conversation between them, Morgan turned his attention from Leonie and grinned at Justin. "So I see, young man! And what do you demand as your tribute?"

Justin's smile faded just a little and with a slight frown, he asked, "Tribute? What is tribute?"

Morgan glanced cynically at Leonie before looking back at Justin. "Tribute, Justin, is the reward for winning." He spoke to the boy, yet Leonie had the curious conviction that he was really talking to her. "And," Morgan went on easily, "as you have won, you can demand that I give you whatever you wish."

Justin regarded him silently for a moment. Then tentatively, "A pony?"

Morgan smiled. "I think that can be arranged."

"One black as thunder?" Justin questioned eagerly.

"Thunder is a sound, not a color."

"But it is a very *black* sound, *oui?*"

Morgan laughed out loud. *"Oui!* A very black sound!"

"We will go and get him now?"

"Not right now," Morgan replied as he sat up, taking Justin with him. "Right now, you and your mother have got to get ready to move to our new house."

"What?" Leonie demanded, an odd trembling starting in the region of her stomach.

Lazily, Morgan turned to survey her. "Our home. Did you think we would live all the time with my parents?"

Her face wearing an expression of utter horror, forgetting Justin's interested presence, Leonie got out frantically, "But, monsieur, you misunderstand! We do not plan to *remain* here! I only came for my dowry. We promised not

199

to interfere in each other's lives . . . it was understood between us."

Morgan smiled nastily. "But you *have* interfered in my life, haven't you?"

There was no answer to that, and Leonie looked away, flushing. Before anyone could say anything else, Yvette, having decided that Justin had played long enough with his mother, came into the room but stopped abruptly at the sight of the tall, handsome man sitting on the edge of Leonie's bed holding Justin in his arms.

Embarrassed at having interrupted such an intimate scene, a small gasp escaped her and hearing the sound, Morgan glanced curiously over in her direction.

No one had thought to mention to him Yvette's positively dazzling beauty, and for a moment, like Dominic, he stared as one besotted at the perfectly formed, delicate features. Even gowned as she was this morning in a simple frock of yellow muslin, the midnight black hair in neat little curls near her creamy cheeks, she was breathtaking. Letting his breath out in a sigh of appreciation, he rose politely to his feet and asked softly, "And who in the name of all that's holy might you be?"

Leonie had never once envied Yvette her exquisite beauty, but in that moment, seeing Morgan's obvious bedazzlement, she felt a stab of something that came perilously near to envy . . . and jealousy. She did not like it at all that her husband found Yvette quite so attractive. Angry at the foreign emotions that had pierced her body, she said coldly, "She is my companion, Yvette Fournier."

"Ah, yes, the companion," Morgan murmured with an odd note in his voice. What he had expected he didn't know, but somehow, while Leonie had so cleverly projected the image of a damsel in distress, he hadn't been prepared for the companion to also show the unmistakable stamp of breeding. It was disturbing, and Morgan began to see how his father and Dominic could have come to believe Leonie's lying tale. *She doesn't make one wrong step, does she?* he thought viciously, suddenly forgetting the role he meant to play.

Justin, still held carelessly in his arms, felt the nearly imperceptible change in him, and almost anxiously tugged at Morgan's collar and asked, "You do not like *Tante* Yvette? She is very nice . . . and I love her best next to maman!"

Morgan recovered himself instantly, and grinning into Justin's puzzled features, he said easily, "I don't see how I could not, especially since you seem so fond of her."

Justin giggled and wiggled out of Morgan's hold. Scampering across the room to grasp Yvette's hand, he pulled her towards Morgan. "Come, *Tante* Yvette and meet my papa! He is to give me a pony!"

Shyly, Yvette approached him, just a little apprehensive at finally meeting Leonie's mysterious husband. "How do you do, monsieur," she murmured softly, the dreamy brown eyes like huge velvet pansies.

Morgan returned a polite greeting, and having recovered from the first shock of Yvette's startling beauty, he decided that while she was beautiful beyond belief, he rather preferred a lion-maned little cat with golden-green eyes. Glancing over his shoulder at Leonie's rigid form, his gaze slipped mockingly down the length of her and he drawled, "It seems that I am to play host to *two* lovely ladies. I am certain that after all my lonely bachelor years I shall find it a most pleasant experience."

He watched with amusement for a second the angry clenching of Leonie's fist, and then swinging back to Yvette, he said, "I must bid you all good day for the present, but I look forward to seeing you in just a short time at Le Petit. Until then . . ."

He bowed politely, sent Leonie an infuriatingly mocking little smile and sauntered out of the room. Morgan had barely passed through the doorway when Justin flung himself on Leonie's bed and begged, "Oh, do hurry, maman! I want to see our new house . . . and to make certain that papa gets my pony!"

Leonie gave him a strained smile and made some placating reply. She could not, it appeared, avoid moving into the new house with her husband any more than she could have avoided coming to Bonheur last night. Her emotions and thoughts in a jumble, she pulled off the cotton shift and then began to dress in the gown she had worn yesterday.

Yvette, like Justin, seemed to be taken with Morgan, and as Leonie did her brief toilet at the marble washstand and furiously dragged a brush through the unruly mane, she had to endure listening to the two of them speak in rapturous tones about her beastly husband. It was galling, all the more so because she could not and would not disillusion either of them about him or his unscrupulous manners.

And yet she was intensely grateful for the way he had treated Justin; too easily he could have made some disparaging remark or have been cruel to the boy. That he had not surprised her and made her just a little uneasy. This Morgan Slade was *not* acting as she had assumed he would.

But what was worse than that was her own traitorous reaction to him. Too well could she remember the suffocating leap of her heart at the sight of him standing in her doorway, and even worse, the memory of the warm wave of shocking pleasure that had coursed through her body when he had kissed her. It should have disgusted her, filled her with repulsion, but it had not; and she found it nearly impossible to believe that her own body and senses had betrayed her so treacherously. *Mon Dieu, I am going mad, I think!*

With a sort of helpless fury, she watched as Mercy, whom Morgan had sent over to Bonheur to help Leonie pack, moved busily about the room, deftly putting into Leonie's small, worn valise the few things that had been taken out last night. Mercy was full of Morgan—how handsome he was; how kind he was; how tidy the little houses were that he had assigned to them; how charming was Le Petite, and most of all, how lucky was the little madame to have a husband such as he. Leonie gritted her teeth and bit back the furious retorts that tangled in her throat. It was all she could do to keep from screaming with rage that she did *not* want to be Morgan Slade's wife!

But for all her thwarted anger, Leonie was deeply puzzled and appalled that now, after all these years, and after even going so far as to deny her existence last night, this morning he appeared resigned, almost eager to claim her as his real wife. The Morgan Slade that she had met in

New Orleans had made it very clear that a wife was the *last* thing he wanted, and after their aborted wedding night, she had been certain that she would be the *last* woman he would want as his wife. Perhaps *he* was mad? Or, the thought occurred chillingly, could it be that he was going to avenge himself on her?

Morgan was quite, quite sane, but it can't be denied that he was harboring thoughts of revenge . . . and enjoying himself far more than he had in years. But if Leonie was puzzled and angry so was Morgan. He had found the child, Justin, an irresistible little scamp, but he wondered disgustedly what sort of unscrupulous bitch would make her own child a party to such a nasty, sordid scheme as she was undertaking. And yet, she had not looked like an unscrupulous bitch as she had played so enticingly with Justin, nor did Yvette appear to be the sort of hard-faced, calculating creature one associated with this type of ruse. The servants too all seemed authentic, and still trying to find a chink in her tale, Morgan spent the next several minutes talking with Abraham as the lanky black man moved about in the stables, happy after so long a time, to be, working once again amongst the spirited, clean-limbed animals that occupied the various stalls.

The conversation with Abraham gained him little, as did the one with Mammy, busy in her new kitchen, or the one he had with Saul, as Saul had explored the spacious grounds of the house which would be his province from now on. Growing more frustrated by the hour, Morgan sought relief in the small office he had spied earlier that morning.

Already his father had sent over a few things to make it even more comfortable, and opening the door, Morgan discovered that the room, like Le Petit itself, lacked nothing. A pair of tall windows looked towards the woods, while another set faced the boxwood gardens. A long leather sofa was against one wall, and a huge oak desk with a chair stood near a pair of French doors that opened onto a small, secluded courtyard, where presumably the master of the house could take in a breath of fresh air when the demands of the estate became too much for him. The courtyard had also been furnished; a white iron table with four matching chairs had been placed in the center. Morgan stood in the middle of the French doors, gazing out at the pleasant scene.

Turning back towards the inside of the office, he noted the fireplace near the sofa and the two tall-backed chairs, covered in a pleasing shade of gold, that sat nearby. A pair of mahogany bookcases were behind the desk, and a writing table and a chair of oak rested under one of the sets of windows. The floor was covered with a carpet in a soft russet as were the curtains that lined the windows, and taking another long glance around the room, Morgan decided that under other circumstances he would have found the room more than adequate for his needs.

Seating himself behind the desk, idly his fingers played with the quill and inkwell that rested on its polished surface as he mulled over all that he had learned this morning—which was damned little, he decided with frustrated anger. Everyone backed up Leonie's story. By God, but she had planned this cleverly and primed them all well in their parts, he conceded with a sort of reluctant admiration.

But more than that, all of them *looked* the part, right down to their clothes and possessions. As he had talked with the various blacks, he had made a mental note of the bedraggled mules and the condition of the two wagons, as well the cherished, well-worn copper pots that Mammy had insisted upon using in the new kitchen. Their clothes were clean and presentable, but it was obvious that they were old and threadbare. Even during the brief time he had spent in Leonie's room, he had unconsciously gathered certain impressions—Leonie's night shift, for one thing, was certainly not what one would expect a conniving adventuress to wear. Nor were Justin's clothes much better than those of the blacks, as they too had show signs of being well-worn and, even more tellingly, of not having been of the first quality when they had been new. Even Yvette's gown, while charming, showed that it had never been expensive or particularly stylish, and Morgan was rather well versed in the cut and cost of women's wearing apparel; he had paid the dressmaker's bill for too many gowns for the various women in his life not to be.

So, what did that tell him? he wondered sardonically. That his little wife had planned well? That she had left nothing to chance? That every word that came out of that sweet mouth could be reinforced by her cohorts? Morgan snorted disgustedly. It did rather look that way.

Which left him where? *With a goddamned wife I don't want!* he thought explosively. *And a son, too,* he reminded himself. A son he knew was *not* his!

Oh, he could see where his parents might think that Justin resembled him, but then, that black hair and decided chin could have come from any number of other men—an aggressive jawline and a jutting, masculine chin were not the sole property of the Slade family!

For the moment, he would have to play the game as the cards were dealt to him. He would let Madame Leonie run her length, and when the noose tightened, he'd be there to see her brought down.

In the meantime, it would behoove him, he decided slowly, to send someone to New Orleans to double-check her background and the story she told. Maybe he would get lucky and there would be some tiny mistake that she had made, thereby giving him the leverage to explode her clever little tale for the pack of lies it was. *And for the present*—Morgan smiled—*for the present, I shall enjoy all the rights and pleasures to which a husband is entitled!*

15

Five days passed. Five days of tranquility and peacefulness on the surface, but underneath a seething cauldron of suspicion, and wariness. Fortunately, only Leonie and Morgan were the guardians of those emotions; everyone else, from Morgan's parents on down to Justin, were aware only of the pleasant veneer that the other two showed the world.

Justin was most ecstatic. Within two days of their moving into Le Petit, a pony, "black as thunder," arrived, and from that moment on Justin was Morgan's adoring slave. Everything that papa did met with his full approval, and Morgan could hardly take a step without finding Justin tagging along behind him.

For Leonie, the sight of Justin happily scampering behind Morgan's tall form as he went about his not-very-arduous duties was a knife thrust in her heart, and her mistrust and suspicion of Morgan Slade grew. Only he and she knew the truth of their abortive wedding night, and Leonie wondered uneasily more than once why he had so casually and effortlessly acknowledged the child. He *had* to know that Justin was not his, and yet he actually appeared to *like* the child. Certainly he did not discourage Justin's blatant desire for his company; of late, too often had Leonie seen Justin dart after Morgan crying, "Papa! Papa! Wait for me!" Morgan, his lean features lightened with a warm smile, would stop and catch Justin up in his arms, and with Justin happily perched upon his shoulders the two of them would wander off to the stables, or to the office or on secret little rides of their own, Morgan atop the snorting, cavorting Tempête, and Justin merrily astride the newly named Thunder.

The others, Yvette and the blacks from Saint-André, were all happily settling in at Le Petit as if they planned to live there forever. With every passing day, Leonie felt they were slipping away from her, as if they had somehow mysteriously become aligned with the despicable Morgan Slade. No one, it seemed, gave a thought anymore to the possibility of their returning to Château Saint-André, and as time passed and she was still no nearer to reclaiming her dowry, Leonie had to admit that it seemed the Château was to be lost to her forever.

Thus far, Leonie herself could not say that she was *un*-happy. It would be hard for anyone to remain in misery in such charming surroundings, and as Morgan had not as yet made any overt move toward her, she was almost able to relax and enjoy herself. . . . Almost.

The house itself was lovely; the spacious rooms with their elegant furnishings would have delighted any young bride, and to someone like Leonie, who had grown up and lived in the faded splendor of Château Saint-André, it was particularly enjoyable to wake up in the large, handsome set of rooms that she had been shown the afternoon she first arrived at Le Petit. She had her own sitting room, dressing room, and bedroom; each was large and airy, and full of light from the wide, tall windows that overlooked the latticed summerhouse and the pair of French doors that led onto the upper veranda. The decor for the most part was a charming mixture of cream and rose, the walls were hung with a delicate shade of rose silk, the carpet was a gorgeous blending of cream rose and green, and soft drapes of cream velvet lined the many windows.

In the sitting room, the sofa and chairs were upholstered in a beautiful tapestry print that combined the cream and rose colors, and the small tables were of satinwood; in her dressing room and bedroom, the wardrobes and other pieces of furniture were of the same gleaming light wood. Her bed with its high, delicately carved headboard was draped in yards and yards of rich ruby satin which formed a swirling canopy overhead before drifting in billowing curtains down the sides.

But while Leonie took a certain amount of pleasure in

207

these elegant surroundings, she was always conscious that this was Morgan Slade's home. It was his food that she ate; his money that paid her servants; his stables that housed her mules. She also knew that eventually, whether or not the others followed, she and Justin *must* leave Le Petit.

Of Morgan Slade and his effect upon her emotions, she dared not think. He was too overpowering, too male, too virile, and too attractive for someone like Leonie, who had lived most of her life away from men. Time and time again she tried to recall the dislike and disgust she had felt for him in New Orleans, but instead she would find herself staring dreamily out the window, remembering how he had smiled at her at breakfast, or the flicker of something exciting in the depths of those dark blue eyes when he looked at her. *He is being* too *nice,* she decided at last. *Much too nice. He is up to something, of this I am positive.*

Morgan *was* up to something. He was cooly stalking Leonie, but she was too innocent to realize it. He had held off forcing his way into her bedroom, enjoying instead the pleasure of the chase. It was a lazy game to Morgan; he advanced and she retreated, and just when it ceased to be a game, even he wasn't sure. It could have been the morning that he looked across the breakfast table and noticed the almost childish delight she took in the flaky croissant Mammy had served; then again, it could have been the evening that Dominic and Robert had come to call, and while they all, including Yvette, were sitting outside in the summerhouse, Leonie had given her charming gurgle of laughter at something Dominic had said, the sea-green eyes slanting bewitchingly with amusement. Morgan was never sure precisely when it happened, but sometime in those five days, despite the suspicion and distrust which existed between them, the fierce emotion he had experienced that night when he had first looked up and had seen her standing in the archway . . . that emotion took root and began to grow. He was unaware of it and would have furiously scoffed at the ridiculous idea that he could be falling madly in love with a lying little jade like Leonie. He told himself that it was simply proximity—seeing Leonie everyday, it was only natural that he would often find her in his thoughts. Perfectly natural, he reassured himself time and time again.

But if that were true, why did he take such delight in simply watching her? The play of emotions across that expressive little face? The grace of that slender body as she ran across the expanse of lawn with Justin? Or, for that matter, why did that enchanting ripple of laughter that was so particularly hers fill him with such pleasure?

Despite the spell Leonie was unconsciously weaving about him, Morgan retained enough hardheaded common sense to finally sit down and write the letter that he had been putting off for too many days. Further thought on the subject of finding out the truth about Leonie Saint-André had made him decide that rather than send someone to New Orleans to investigate, he would write to his friend Jason Savage and have Jason discover what he could. And thinking of Jason, Morgan smiled to himself, for the first time seeing a glimmer of sanity in this entire insane situation. Jason could verify that Morgan had been with him at the time he supposedly married Leonie Saint-André. But Jason's word wouldn't be enough, Morgan conceded ruefully—their friendship was well-known and it was only logical that Jason would substantiate his story whether it was true or not.

Oddly enough, he had deliberately avoided writing the letter, but once it was sealed and had been sent on its way, he felt at once positive and yet queerly depressed. Perhaps he didn't want to know the truth about Leonie Saint-André. And yet the simple act of writing that letter stirred something deep in his mind. Something about that trip to New Orleans that he should remember . . . something that might provide the clue which would explain everything.

The sending of that letter reminded him forcibly of the fact that no matter how attractive or bewitching Leonie was, she *was* a liar who had embarked upon a dangerous masquerade. It was time, he thought with a grim sort of anticipation, to show her that there was more to their supposed marriage than just sharing a house.

Leonie sensed the difference in him almost immediately. During the time that had passed, and her mocking, deceitful husband had made no attempt to force his attentions on her, Leonie had been lulled into a false security. She told herself optimistically that he must mean to abide by the agreement he'd signed—the one agreement that had not yet been mentioned. She assumed that his own masculine vanity kept him from bringing it up, and while she was suspicious of his motives, she couldn't help but breathe a sigh of relief that he appeared willing to honor at least *one* of their two agreements. And perhaps this was an indication that in time he would repay the dowry. Leonie sincerely prayed so! For as soon as she had received her dowry, she and Justin and the others would be off to try to regain their home. And that, Leonie vowed fiercely, would remove them from Morgan Slade's influence!

But apparently not soon enough, she thought uneasily, when she happened to look up and see him astride Tempête and watching her and Justin as they walked barefoot in the creek. She told herself it was the surprise of seeing him so unexpectedly, surprise and not the look in those brilliant blue eyes that sent a shudder of apprehension down her spine.

Leonie and Justin had been alone at the edge of the creek, and Yvette, finding the increasingly warm afternoons too debilitating, had retired to her rooms to rest. As Leonie and Justin were perfectly happy to be alone, they had forgotten everything except the sheer pleasure of exploring the rippling cool creek. They were out of sight of the house, just inside the green, shadowy forest when Morgan came across them. And as had happened the first morning he had found them playing on the bed at Bonheur, they were completely absorbed in their own activities and were unaware of him.

Leonie's skirts were rucked up about her waist, and small droplets of water sparkled on her golden legs and thighs as she and Justin splashed in the creek, attempting to catch a little green frog. Her hair had come loose from its haphazard chignon and cascaded in a curling mane about her slender shoulders. The gown was an old one of a soft shade of green, and staring at her, at the slim golden

210

arms and the laughing, bewitching face as she turned to Justin when she caught the frog, Morgan felt as if he had never seen anything quite so temptingly lovely in all his life. She was a wild, fey thing . . . a forest nymph that he had caught by surprise. Unconsciously he held his breath, his hands tightening on the reins that controlled Tempête so effortlessly, afraid that the slightest movement would make her vanish in the green, sun-dappled forest like a mirage.

It was a secluded place where they were, the trees and vines hiding them from the house, the little creek edged here and there with wildflowers—wild hyacinth and sweet-scented violets. And as she stood there, the lovely shape of her legs clearly revealed, a shaft of sunlight turning the tawny curls to molten gold, Leonie exuded an almost irresistible, earthy sensuality that Morgan found difficult to ignore.

He was instantly conscious of the blood flowing hot and thick in his veins and of the heavy, sweet ache that suddenly flooded his loins. Only Justin's presence stopped him from urging Tempête into the stream and reaching down to swing her up into his arms. The fierce, hungry desire he felt was obvious in the blue eyes, and he made no attempt to conceal it when Leonie happened to glance up and saw him and the big, blood-bay stallion.

He was very handsome as he sat with insolent grace on Tempête, his white shirt carelessly opened to his waist, the buff breeches fitting snugly along his powerful thighs. The thick black hair brushed the collar of his shirt and one willful lock displayed a tendency to dip across his broad forehead, giving him a rakish air. His feet were bare, an oddity, but then he had been on his way for a private swim when he had come across Leonie and Justin. There was an unconscious arrogance about him, and the blatant expression of sexual desire which blazed in those dark blue eyes forced Leonie backwards, a half-frightened, half-defiant look on her face. Suddenly aware of the naked length of leg exposed to his gaze, an angry blush staining her cheeks, she hastily pulled her gown down and asked breathlessly, "Did you want us, monsieur?"

The "monsieur" made Morgan smile. Even pretending to be his wife, even living in his home, she refused to call him anything but "monsieur," and he was conscious it was her way of keeping a barrier between them. A barrier, he decided in that instant, he was going to enjoy smashing.

"Not exactly," he said slowly as he urged Tempête to the edge of the creek. Glancing briefly at Justin, he commanded easily, "Run along, will you, Justin? I want to talk to your maman . . . alone." Before Leonie could countermand the order, Justin had already begun to run towards the house, the little frog clutched triumphantly in his hand.

Alone, the two adults faced each other. The hard sheen of desire still glittering in his eyes, Morgan murmured softly, *"You,* not us, I want."

"Non!" Leonie spat, her small body rigid with rejection. "You will not touch me, monsieur! I have a paper that says you will not!"

Morgan grinned at that, for a moment real amusement dancing in the vivid blue eyes. "Have you really, sweetheart? You must show it to me sometime. But not," he said thickly, "not now."

Leonie made a valiant effort to escape, picking up her skirts and spinning on her heels with the fleetness of a doe, she raced down the creek and deeper into the woods. And it was only as she plunged into the concealing green of the forest that she realized, she should have run *toward* the house, not *away* from it. Dodging and darting, running as fast as she dared through the trunks of the trees, skirting the smaller clumps of brush, desperately she tried to work her way back towards the house.

Behind her she could hear Morgan's smothered laughter and the thud of Tempête's hooves as the stallion easily followed her. Her breath was coming in gasps and her heart was beating as if it would burst from her breast, but still she ran on, the long golden legs flashing in the occasional rays of sunlight that permeated the thickness of the forest. She ran with grace, and though she tried trick after trick to lose her pursuers, she was no match for Morgan's determined chase or Tempête's speed.

212

The uneven chase had only one end, and Morgan having let her run as far as he wanted, suddenly kicked Tempête into a gallop and swiftly bore down on the slim figure. Coming alongside her, he captured her in his arm and swung her up in front of him. Leonie still fought, twisting in his hold, her soft body like a sweet intoxicating flame wherever it touched. Angrily she panted, *"Non!* Monsieur, I tell you, *non!"*

"And I tell you, yes!" Morgan breathed against her soft mouth before his lips stopped hers.

Leonie strained desperately away from him, but it did no good as his hold on her tightened and his mouth took liberties that reminded her vividly of the night she had lost her virginity to a stranger.

Bur Morgan was no stranger, and his probing tongue seemed to fill her mouth; his lips were hard against hers as he deepened the embrace, his arms forcing her slender, resisting body up next to his until her breasts were crushed against his chest and she could feel the desire that drove him.

Whatever control Morgan may have had over his emotions, whatever good intentions he may have had, vanished the instant his mouth touched hers, and with a groan of sheer sensual pleasure, his lips and tongue slowly, caressingly explored the warm honey of her mouth. He held her firmly against him, reveling in the exciting twistings of her soft body as she fought to escape, and half-blindly, half-knowingly he guided Tempête farther away from the house and deeper into the forest.

It was a singularly erotic ride for both of them. Morgan could feel the horse's powerful movements beneath him as Tempête moved easily through the gloom of the woods, and there was Leonie's provocative body in his arms, her breasts brushing warmly across his naked chest where his shirt hung open, her soft thighs thrashing across one of his and with half her hip, half her stomach pressed against his groin, he thought he would go mad with longing.

For Leonie, it was just as evocative. There was something wickedly exciting about being held so close in his strong arms, to be aware of the horse beneath her and of

213

the hard body of the man who held her captive, his mouth teaching hers the pleasures that his drugging, passionate kisses could bring. She fought, and yet as they rode deeper into the silent, sun-dappled forest, she discovered she was fighting her own treacherous body as much as she was him.

As they rode, passing towering oaks and pecan trees, the occasional willow and myrtle, and the stands of pungent pine, Morgan's mouth never left hers. He continued to kiss her so hungrily, so devastatingly, that a burning wave of excitement and pleasure swept through Leonie's body, draining away her urge to escape. A delicious languor seemed to invade her limbs, and instead of beating against his broad back, her hands betrayed a deplorable tendency to tangle in his thick, black hair, to pull his head down closer to hers, her mouth softening and eagerly accepting the invasion of his.

When Tempête finally stopped of his own accord, it was several moments before Morgan became aware that the stallion was no longer moving, and reluctantly raising his mouth from the sweet challenge of Leonie's, he glanced around in blank surprise, every fiber of his being having been engrossed with the enchanting body in his arms.

The sight that met his eyes brought a pleased half-smile to his lips, and sliding lithely from the stallion, he pulled Leonie with him, saying huskily, "M'lady's bower awaits her."

Like one coming out of a trance, Leonie glanced dreamily around, not quite noticing the beckoning crystal blue of the water with its tinkling waterfall at one end. She was too conscious of Morgan's warm, muscled length next to hers to pay any attention to her surroundings—only half-aware of the clearing in which they stood, only partially aware of the remainder of the forest that gently encircled them, turning the pool and waterfall into a place of enchantment, a garden of Eden.

Unhurriedly, Morgan took her into his arms, his mouth once again seeking hers, his strong arms crushing her pliant, unresisting body up next to his. For Leonie, reality vanished; this was her husband who was

214

kissing her, her husband whom she had thought she despised, and yet with every touch of his mouth and hands, something deep within her struggled to be free. It was not hate that fought so desperately to break free of the chains she had imposed upon it, but an emotion far stronger and more enduring.

Sweeping her up into his arms, his lips moving urgently over her mouth and slender throat, he carried her under the shady umbrella of a huge, spreading sycamore and gently laid her down on the soft, spring clover that grew beneath it. Lowering his body next to hers, his mouth slid down her warm skin to taste the soft flesh that rose temptingly above the old, green gown.

The material proved a frail barrier and with insistent hands he eased the gown from her shoulders, baring the loveliness of the small, proud bosom, his warm fingers softly caressing the rosebud nipples until they were throbbing and rigid under his touch. Unable to help himself, his lips moved like a scorching flame up to her mouth, once again kissing her with all the demanding passion that blazed within him. His hands cupped the small breasts, delighting in the satiny feel of the smooth skin, and needing the taste of her, his head dropped, and gently his mouth closed over a tempting nipple.

Leonie's breath caught in her throat at the touch of his warm tongue curling so intimately around her breast, and instinctively she arched her body up to his mouth, the desire he had evoked destroying the control she had on herself. There was no reality at that moment, there were just the two of them in that secret, welcoming glade—Morgan's mouth, hands and body being all that existed in this sensual world into which he had taken her.

For Morgan too nothing mattered but that the lovely body so near his respond to his touch and that the dark magic that seemed to flare between them continue forever. His clothes became an obstruction he would not tolerate, and with an almost angry motion he lifted his head and ripped off the confining shirt. The breeches would have gone then, but Leonie, unaware of anything except the fact that he had stopped his intoxicating caresses, gave a small

215

moan of distress and instantly Morgan lowered his body to hers once more.

The touch of his hair-roughened chest against her breasts was deeply erotic, and with an odd little sound of pleasure, she pressed her body even closer to his, longing for him to continue to caress and touch her, to give the pleasure she only half-sensed he could. All the sweet passion of which she was capable had been fully aroused for the first time in her life, and she was like someone half-drunk, her body instinctively seeking more of the exquisite sensations.

Her response to his caresses was everything Morgan could have wished for, and driven by the increasingly urgent hunger that ate at his loins, with trembling hands he lifted her and in one sure moment swept the hindering clothes from her body. His own followed, and blindly he pulled her naked body next to his, groaning with pleasure at the softness of her stomach and thighs against his hard, muscled length.

Leonie could feel the cool softness of the sweet-scented clover against her nude body, and it, combined with the warmth of Morgan's body as he leaned over her, was a sensual delight. Errant shafts of yellow sunlight through the wide-spreading branches of the sycamore caressed their naked bodies and the hum of honeybees droned in the background as his hands explored her slim, golden body.

Morgan took his time, delighting in the silken warmth of Leonie's skin beneath the palm of his hand. She was so lovely, he thought with awe, as he raised his head and glanced along the slender length of her, noting the rose-tipped nipples, the narrowness of her waist, the gentle flare of her slender hips, and the delicate golden curls at the junction of her long, slim legs. Bringing his gaze back to her face and seeing the half-closed, cat-shaped eyes drowsy with desire, the tawny hair spread out like a golden-brown cloak of curls against the green clover, and the passion-bruised softness of her mouth, with a groan he buried his lips on her throat and muttered, "Witch you may be, but God help me, I want you . . . no matter who you are or what you've done."

His words made little sense to Leonie; she was in the

grip of the first awakening of her deeply passionate, sensual nature. And aware only of the stirrings and demands of her body, she gave herself up to him eagerly, freely, holding nothing back. Her fingers clenched pleasurably in the crisp blackness of his hair, and unconsciously brazen, she brought his mouth back to hers, wanting to know again the sweet fierceness of his kiss.

Morgan did not deny her, his mouth devouring hers hungrily, his hand leaving her breast to travel lazily down the flat stomach to the golden, beckoning triangle between her thighs. With a soft growl of anticipation, his hand slid through the soft curls and then gently sought out the place he hungered for, his fingers seeking and exploring with blatant intimacy the most secret part of her.

Leonie stiffened when she felt his hand between her legs, her body racked with a delicious surge of pleasure and yet mingled with fright. The last time a man had touched her so, it had hurt, and in that second, the enormity of what she was doing suddenly burst in her brain. With a whimper half of disgust, half despair, she made an attempt to free herself, but Morgan would have none of it.

He was too aroused to think coherently, and his only thought was that he was moving too fast for her, that she wasn't quite prepared for him yet. His lips against her mouth he whispered thickly, "Don't close your legs against me, Leonie. I won't hurt you, sweetheart."

Unerringly, Morgan had chosen the right words to soothe Leonie's fear, and with his mouth and hands holding her prisoner, there was no escape anyway. Intent upon pleasuring her, his teeth teasingly grazed her throbbing nipples and his hand brought her unimagined pleasure as he knowingly caressed her. With a shudder of surrender, Leonie stopped her feeble attempts to free herself.

The probing touch of Morgan's hand was a sweet agony, the gentle motion of his fingers creating a feeling of such intense, aching pleasure that Leonie thought she would cry aloud with the physical gratification they gave her. But it wasn't enough, she wanted more, wanted something she could only guess at, and as the tormenting longing for more seared through her blood, unconsciously her hips be-

217

gan to move in a dance as old as Eve and she pushed up frantically against Morgan's hand, her body trembling with the force of the emotions that he had unleashed.

But Morgan deliberately held back, fighting the screaming demands of his own body to take her, to lose himself in the hot, satiny sheath he knew waited for him. It was an exquisite torture for him, his manhood ripe and swollen with desire, and yet he denied them both the pleasure their joining would bring, wanting first for her to know the exploding sensations of release his hands could give her.

Like a wild thing, Leonie twisted under his probing caresses, her blood surging madly through her veins, every nerve shrieking aloud for relief from the tight, almost painful knot of pleasure that seemed centered under Morgan's hand. And then, just when she thought she could bear it no longer, when she was certain she had gone mad, there was such an explosion of pleasure that her entire body arched uncontrollably with it, a moan of astonished delight escaping from her.

Dazed by what had happened, she lay on the soft clover staring up at Morgan's dark face. There was an intent hungry look in his eyes, and the full, chiseled mouth was frankly sensual as he stared back at her. He had never before wanted to please a woman as much as he did this one, and both satisfaction and a queer possessive excitement blazed in his eyes as he noted the soft, surprised expression that was obvious in the slanted, drowsy green eyes.

Her mouth was half-parted and unknowingly provocative, the high cheekbones of the delicate features giving her a catlike look of satisfaction, and as his eyes fastened hypnotically on those rosy lips, Morgan could restrain himself no longer. With a soft groan of impatience, he eased his big body between her thighs, knowing he must possess her soon.

Still half-dazed by what he had done to her, Leonie was only vaguely aware of what he was doing at first, the weight of his body pleasant as he rested gently on her for a moment, the hair of his chest teasing her nipples. Insistently, his knees nudged hers apart, his hands slipped under her hips to lift her to him, and then with a sensation of stunning pleasure, she felt her body widening, stretching

218

to accept the hard, warm length of him. Their bodies were
locked together, and in a welter of confusion and spiraling,
heady emotion, Leonie felt her body burst once again into
flames as urgently Morgan began to move her, his body
thrusting hungrily into hers.

His hands held her hips prisoner to him as he drove
deeply into her silken softness, and compulsively his
mouth caught hers, his tongue filling her mouth even as
his body filled hers. Lying beneath him, unbearably conscious of the heat of his chest as it pressed against her
breasts, of his warm hands as they cupped her buttocks,
and of the seductive movements his body made as it moved
on hers, Leonie was staggered to feel her own body respond
wildly to him. With helpless abandon, she arched to meet
the thrust of his body into hers, moaning with pleasure as
he pressed urgently deeper within her. Incredibly, the
same spiraling sense of exquisite, aching ecstasy, seemed
to form in her stomach again, and softly sobbing her gratification, she once again felt her own body contract and leap
with pleasure.

Lost in a world where nothing existed except himself
and the soft, arching body beneath him, Morgan was
aware that he could not bear the pleasure she gave him
much longer. His entire body ached with the need to release the pent-up desire that surged through him, and
when Leonie's body trembled and leaped with the force of
the shattering sensations which exploded within her, he
could hold back no longer. Kissing her even more deeply,
his hands tightened convulsively around her hips, his
movements became almost violent as he too at last knew
ecstasy.

Leonie was only dimly conscious of what happened to
Morgan, but as she drifted hazily in the new sensual world
he had taken her, she was aware of his body lying next to
hers, his hands still lightly caressing and touching her.

Time seemed suspended as they lay there together in the
leafy glade, the sunlight gilding their bodies while the
blue pool of water shimmered in the distance. Dazedly,
Leonie looked up into Morgan's dark face as he leaned over
her, almost as if she were seeing him for the first time.
How could I have ever thought of him as weak, she won-

dered confusedly, her eyes lingering on the hard, chiseled mouth and strong, almost arrogant chin and jaw. The prominent cheekbones and the proudly jutting nose reinforced the impression of power and ruthless vitality, and staring into that dark, harshly handsome face, she was suddenly overwhelmingly conscious . . . conscious that against her will, she had, somehow, fallen in love with her husband!

16

The remainder of that afternoon passed in a blur for Leonie. She vaguely remembered that Morgan had carried her to the pool and tenderly washed her body in the cool, reviving blue waters. A blush staining her cheeks, she remembered too the way he had helped her with her gown, his hands displaying an alarming tendency to wander over her body. The ride back to the house was hazy. She knew he held her in front of him on the big, blood-bay stallion and that he had kissed her with devastating intensity just before the stallion had left the forest and they had approached the house, but beyond that, the entire incident had taken on a dreamlike quality.

And in the familiar surroundings of her rooms much later that afternoon, she stared intently at her naked body in the cheval glass, puzzled that there were no outward changes to reveal the shattering metamorphosis she had undergone in her husband's arms. She had known a man's passion once before in her life, and yet Leonie had been completely unprepared for the exquisite pleasure Morgan's fervent lovemaking had given her. The abandoned reaction of her body bewildered her, almost as much as the knowledge that somehow, incredibly, she had managed to fall in love with Morgan Slade. Which event astonished her more would be difficult to decide, and the confusion she felt was obvious in the depths of the golden-flecked green eyes as she continued to peer at herself in the mirror, almost as if seeing herself for the first time.

The tawny mane curled and tumbled about her shoulders, one gleaming strand resting on the nipple of her breast, and remembering Morgan's mouth on that same nipple, Leonie's cheeks were red with embarrassment. Almost tentatively she touched her small breast, aware of the warmth and satiny texture of the smooth skin, wondering with a curious tingle in the pit of her stomach if Morgan would want her again. To her astonishment, she discovered that just thinking about him and what they had shared provoked a wild response within her as a warm wash of anticipation flooded through her body, her nipples hardening even as she stood in front of the glass.

Suddenly shy at what was happening to her, she spun around and hastily shrugged on her soft, white chemise and then put on the same lavender gown she had worn the night of Morgan's aborted betrothal to Melinda Marshall. The limitations of her scanty wardrobe were becoming obvious even to Leonie; there were only so many ways in which to disguise that one was wearing the same gown to dine in night after night. She and Yvette were both in the same position, and even trading off gowns and shawls and what little jewelry and bits of frippery they owned could alter their appearances only so much.

It had never bothered Leonie before that she possessed the barest essentials when it came to clothes, but tonight as she dressed to join Morgan for dinner, she wished passionately that she had something else to wear. None of her well-worn, everyday gowns would be suitable, and for reasons she could not even identify, she had put off wearing the dress she had been married in. As a matter of fact, *both* girls avoided the beautiful, rose satin gown, Yvette steadfastly refusing Leonie's generous offer of the dress. The brown eyes faintly puzzled, Yvette had said time and time again, "But it is your *wedding* gown, *ma petite!* I could not wear it! It would be bad luck, *non?*" Leonie didn't agree, but she could not *force* Yvette to wear the gown, and consequently in languished in shining splendor at the back of Leonie's meager wardrobe.

Usually Mercy attempted to help Leonie dress, and Leonie found it infinitely amusing that after all these years of doing practically everything for herself, including some rather back-breakingly hard work, that now she had at her disposal a servant whose only task was to see that her mistress was properly attired. Considering the size of her wardrobe, Leonie found it almost silly for Mercy to wait around the room, acting as if there were any choice in what she would wear that evening. Tonight, she had not even waited for Mercy's unnecessary help and was already dressed. She was just brushing a final curl into place when Mercy arrived.

Mercy eyed the lavender gown with disfavor, but she did not immediately launch into her accustomed argument about Leonie's avoidance of the rose satin gown. Instead she chose to be offended that Leonie had not waited for her services and muttered dire threats about what fates befall certain young ladies who had gone against the wise advice of their trusted servants. Leonie grinned at her, blew a kiss, and skipped out of the dressing room.

It wasn't quite time for dinner, and finding herself strangely unsettled, she walked through the French doors in her room which led to the veranda. Blankly she gazed out over the lush, newly scythed carpet of grass and the neatly trimmed shrubs of Le Petit, suddenly longing for the untidy, scraggly and dearly beloved grounds of Château Saint-André. Le Petit was everything that any woman could wish for, and yet sometimes Leonie longed unbearably for the unkempt, faded glories of her home. And perhaps it wasn't so odd that tonight of all nights she yearned for it with a fierce intensity.

Château Saint-André had been her bulwark against the world, and in time of trouble or uncertainty it had given her the peace and solace she needed. Tonight, she would have given much to be there, to have the reality of her own past about her, to remember who she was and why the journey to Natchez had been so vital.

Certainly, it had not been for love! Nor had it been to be engulfed and swamped by the Slade family. Day by day she could feel herself becoming further enmeshed in life here, and it frightened her . . . almost as much as the thought of loving Morgan Slade did.

Staring out into the gathering darkness, Leonie's thoughts were in a turmoil with images of Château Saint-André, Morgan, Justin, and even the dowry moving in a chaotic blur. She was the most unworthy creature alive to forget, even for a moment, the real reasons why she had come to Natchez, why it was imperative to have her dowry.

223

Château Saint-André was *home!* That was Justin's heritage, not this pretty doll's house! And her dowry would give Justin back what was his; the precious gold would allow them to restore the Château to great beauty, to turn it into a home as lovely or lovelier than Bonheur.

And yet, how could she bear to tear herself away from the man who had begun to mean so much to her? Justin too must be considered, and thinking of the way he followed Morgan about, of the growing affection she knew the child bore the man he thought was his father, Leonie writhed with self-abasement . . . she should never have deceived her son that way.

But what else could she have done? she wondered with anguish. It would have broken her heart to have Justin labeled a bastard. Not for herself did she care, but for Justin—he wasn't going to grow up with people sneering and sniggering behind his back, making sly remarks about his parentage. She simply could not and would not allow it!

Perhaps, she thought painfully, that was when she had begun to lower her guard against Morgan Slade's mocking charm. The way he had so carelessly acknowledged her son that morning he had found them pillow-fighting had disarmed her completely, and for the first time since she had met him in New Orleans, she had felt something more than mere mistrust and dislike for him.

In the days that had followed as she and Morgan lived in close proximity with one another, that initial disarmament had continued. She had seen him express a seemingly natural affection for her son; her servants had been completely captivated, and even Yvette had confessed shyly that she thought Leonie was very fortunate in her husband. Leonie also had found herself drawn to him, liking the wicked gleam of amusement that danced in the vivid blue eyes, the sound of his laughter when he and Justin played together, and the easy kindness and courtesy with which he treated them all.

He certainly seemed very different from the man she had married in New Orleans, and that difference disturbed Leonie. This man she liked, might actually have begun to love . . . but the man she had known in New

224

Orleans had aroused no such emotions. And yet, she was still full of doubts and questions.

The story he had given concerning his reasons for denying her accusations at the ball had sounded reasonable when she had finally heard them from Matthew, but something didn't ring true. She mistrusted the tale of a divorce that was *supposed* to have taken place . . . and he *had* denied ever seeing her before. Even if she could accept the fact that he had thought he was divorced, that still didn't explain why he had not repaid her the dowry—his excuse of poor memory had found even less favor with Leonie than it had with his father. Or why he now seemed prepared to open up his arms to them all—to take not only a child he knew wasn't his, but also the rest of Leonie's little entourage into his home. *Why? Why? Why?* she wondered, unconsciously biting her lower lip.

It had been clearly understood between them that they would make no demands upon the other, and yet, in spite of everything, here she was with her son and the others living in his house and partaking of his generous bounty. The Morgan Slade she had married in New Orleans had never struck her as generous.

But even more unsettling than those inconsistencies was the fact that she was very much afraid that she had foolishly allowed herself to fall in love with him. Instantly she rebelled at the idea, denying the thought. *Mon Dieu,* it was impossible! She could *not* love such a man!

A dozen questions about the future filled her head. Did this afternoon *truly* change anything? Was their marriage to become real? Not just a business arrangement? And what of Justin? Sooner or later Morgan would demand the truth. And the dowry; did she just forget it and allow her husband to support her?

Something in Leonie rebelled at that thought. She had been independent too long, had managed her own affairs too long, to let someone run her life. No, Morgan must pay back what was hers. It was, she decided stubbornly, the principle of the thing, not so much that she wanted the money if she was to take her place as his wife. She must provide for Justin's future; if she and Morgan had children

225

of their own, their father could provide for them, but Justin's future was her responsibility.

The idea of bearing Morgan's child made her heart beat very fast, and she realized with a shock that she was actually contemplating remaining in Natchez to live as Morgan's wife. Château Saint-André tugged at her soul, but Leonie knew that bricks and lumber could never give her the joy that living out her days with her husband at her side could. But with the dowry it could be saved for Justin, she thought confidently, and knowing that her son would one day walk the land of their ancestors eased some of the ache in her heart. Soon, she must talk to Morgan about the dowry and explain why it was so necessary for her to have the money immediately. The first of July was less than a month away, and Maurice de la Fontaine was not likely to wait longer than that for his money. . . .

Tomorrow, she concluded firmly, *tomorrow I must talk with Morgan and see that he takes the necessary steps to repay my dowry.* Feeling more at ease within herself, if suddenly shy and yet excited at seeing her husband again, she left the veranda and made her way downstairs to join the others for dinner.

As had been the case since they had moved into Le Petit, Robert and Dominic had joined them for dinner, and the meal that followed was lively with teasing conversation among the three brothers, as well as a radiant Yvette and an oddly tremulous Leonie. Every time she glanced up and caught Morgan's bright blue eyes on her, her composure deserted her, and in confusion she would look hastily away.

Morgan looked at her often that evening, unable to do otherwise. He would try to ignore the steady, almost violent appeal she held for him and lose himself in talking animatedly with his brothers, but time and time again like steel to a magnet, his eyes were drawn inexorably back to her. An expression of possession and speculation in his gaze, his eyes would rove slowly over her face and shoulders, lingering appreciatively for a moment or two on the soft fullness of her mouth or the gentle rise and fall of her breasts beneath the lavender gown.

He wanted her, Morgan admitted slowly to himself. But

though he found her incredibly desirable, he also was positive that he wasn't insane enough to fall in love with her. And yet, all afternoon he had been unable to get her out of his mind, remembering too well the taste of that sweet mouth under his and the delicious warmth of her body as it had writhed under his. But more than just sexual images had crossed his mind during the hours since they had last seen one another. The memory of how she had looked standing in the stream with her skirts rucked up about her waist came back to him, as did the jubilant smile that flashed across her face when she had caught the frog for Justin. She was absolutely enchanting, and Morgan was uneasily aware that he was in danger of allowing himself to forget the reasons behind the charade they were playing.

Inexplicably, in less than a week Leonie and her son had become part of his life, and he was bewildered by the ease with which it had happened. With an effort he had to remind himself repeatedly that underneath the pleasant surface presented to the world, there was a deadly battle being fought . . . that they were "the enemy." Not the child, for Justin could not be blamed for his mother's schemes, but Leonie herself was definitely his sworn adversary, and staring hard at her across the long, white table, his thoughts were suddenly unkind as he reminded himself forcibly that no matter how enticing he found her, she was still a liar and a fraud.

Mentally, he ticked off her sins: she claimed to be his wife and he knew very well that she was not; she claimed he had promised to pay her back a dowry he had never received; and she was passing off a child as his he knew he had never fathered. Not a pretty list of activities, he thought savagely, as Yvette and Leonie prepared to leave the room so that the gentlemen could enjoy their cigars and brandy. Nevertheless, despite the chicanery he implacably believed her capable of, he found that she still had the power to arouse emotions in him that he had thought never to feel for another woman again. Not just passion—passion was something he had felt for a number of women—but with this one, there was some other emotion en-

227

twined, an emotion he vehemently denied and would not name.

He and his brothers did not linger long over their brandies, and in a very short time, they had joined Yvette and Leonie as the two young women conversed idly in the main salon. Broodingly, Morgan watched Leonie through heavy-lidded eyes, wondering at the paradox she presented.

She looks so damned genuine, he admitted angrily. The tawny curls were caught in a neat chignon at the base of her neck, a few unruly locks escaping to frame her lovely face, giving the high cheekbones and straight little nose a patrician cast. Her manners were impeccable, as was her speech, and she handled herself just the way one would expect a young woman of good breeding . . . except, Morgan thought with a sudden grin, she held wild pillow fights with her son and chased frogs in the creek like a hoyden.

Dominic interrupted his thoughts just then by asking him a question, and with an effort Morgan brought himself back to the moment at hand. Aware that now was not the time to delve into the mystery Leonie Saint-André represented, for the next few hours Morgan pushed the problem aside, and it was only as he undressed for bed later that his thoughts returned to Leonie's presence in his life.

She was definitely an adventuress, he finally decided. No matter what reasons she had for doing so, she was lying through her lovely little mouth every time she claimed to be his wife. And more damningly, she had gone to a lot of trouble to have those clever forgeries made up. And who, he wondered suddenly with a painful clutch in his gut, was Justin's father? Why hadn't she sought help from the boy's father?

The thought of another man possessing that vibrant, young body was exceedingly unpleasant, and he forced himself to think of something else. It was then that something even uglier occurred to him. Perhaps there was one person he hadn't met yet . . . the mastermind of the entire plot, the man in Leonie's life . . . the father of her son.

His mouth filling with bitter bile, Morgan's hands clenched. Of course. It wouldn't be the first time that a scheme such as this had been tried on a wealthy man. It had to be a man who had decided which pigeon they would pluck, a man who had made the forgeries and had done all the necessary investigations to make certain that no hole could be found in her story. Perhaps her grandfather wasn't even dead. Perhaps he was behind it.

They could all be in on it, he decided viciously. Family servants were notoriously loyal, if they *were* family servants, and if they stuck to their tale, the story would be impossible to disprove.

He was almost positive he had stumbled across the truth. Leonie had never made any secret of the fact that it was her dowry, her *money* that she was after. Most men sucked into such a sordid little plot would have found it easier to simply pay the money and have Leonie disappear out of their lives—presumably after giving the poor dupe some "proof" that could be offered to his friends and neighbors to explain away the entire unpleasant situation. And then with the merry jingle of gold in their pockets, Leonie and her partner would look around for their next victim.

Oh, yes, how easily it could be done. The child, the servants, even the incredibly lovely companion Yvette, all part of the rig. Together they formed an aura of such truth and authenticity that it was almost impossible *not* to believe them.

Standing at his window overlooking the boxwood garden, Morgan smiled tightly to himself. It had probably worked very well for them in the past . . . but not this time, he promised savagely. *Not this time!*

Sickened by the thoughts that were running through his head, he turned away from the window and with leadened steps crossed the room to his bed. Were Leonie and Justin truly part of such a despicable plot? Even as he coolly admitted that they could very well be, his every instinct cried out a fierce denial.

But until he heard from Jason, he thought with angry frustration, there was nothing he could do but allow the situation to continue. Further questioning of the servants would gain him nothing, and Leonie herself certainly wasn't going to make any mistakes . . . the lying little bitch hadn't put one foot wrong yet!

It was very late when sleep finally overtook him, and while there had been a moment when he had considered seeking out Leonie and losing himself in the pleasures her body could give him, he had instantly dismissed the idea. In the mood he was in at present, he decided harshly, he was far more likely to strangle her than make love to her.

Morgan's nonappearance in Leonie's bedchamber left her with mixed emotions. On one hand, in spite of her newly discovered emotions regarding Morgan Slade, she was relieved not to be forced too soon into a relationship she had such reservations about, but on the other hand . . . Lying alone in her bed, unwillingly remembering Morgan's passionate kisses over her body, she felt her senses stir and her blood began to race in her veins. *Ma foi!* This is most unseemly, she thought uncomfortably. It is very bad of me to think such lustful thoughts—the devil will have my soul!

After a brief struggle with shockingly sensual fantasies, resolutely she focused on her need for the dowry and fell asleep planning the conversation she would have with Morgan in the morning. Leonie might have been able to control her conscious mind but she had absolutely no power over the subconscious, and as she slept images of Morgan and herself in the forest glade engulfed her; she woke in the morning with the memory of his mouth on hers, his strong arms crushing her to him.

Dressing in her second best gown of yellow linen, Leonie decided that it was imperative that she speak with Morgan about the dowry. His reactions to her request could conceivably resolve some of her reservations about him. She might have been foolish enough to think herself in love with him, but she was also uneasily aware that he was definitely not quite the charming lover and father he had played this past week.

The memory of her initial dislike and mistrust in New Orleans came back too strongly at times to be ignored, and while she hoped those feelings were merely the result of a young girl's resentment of being forced into a marriage she hadn't wanted, she couldn't forget them. And Morgan hadn't exactly followed any of the agreements he had signed—he had not paid back the dowry and yesterday afternoon's events certainly were not in keeping with the promise not to exert his conjugal rights.

The more she thought about it, the more confused she became. Had she truly fallen in love with a man whose word was meaningless? Was he as dishonorable as he appeared? Capable of lies and deceit, his only thought his own pleasures? She stopped in bewilderment, aware that the only real thing she did know was that Morgan Slade had many faces, and she longed to know which was the real man.

Walking slowly down the stairs on her way to find Morgan, every ambiguity of the situation hit her. They had agreed to live separate lives and yet here she was in his house, living as his wife. Her son was not her husband's, but thus far her husband had made no comment on that fact and blandly accepted the boy. Perplexed, she shook her head as if to clear the paradoxical thoughts that churned there.

The dowry seemed to be the one thing that would reveal the real man—if he paid, as promised, *voilà!* It would prove that he was at heart an honest man. But if he did not, she decided with a tightening of the firm, little jaw, if he did not. . . . If he did not, *then* she would know him for the *villain* he had first appeared to be!

17

Morgan was working in his office when Leonie finally found him. She was shy about entering what was predominantly masculine territory, and although she had been in the office once, when she had been shown over the grounds of Le Petit, until now there had been no reason to seek him out as he worked.

When Leonie knocked lightly on the door, he was idly browsing through some account books Matthew had thought would bring him up to date with the affairs the sprawling estate. His mind had not been on the neat columns of figures and concise entries, though, and to glance up and find the object of his thoughts hesitantly pushing open the door in answer to his command to enter came as a distinct surprise.

For a long moment, they stared wordlessly at each other, Leonie very conscious of him as a man—a man who was her husband and a man who had awakened instincts and responses she had never dreamed she possessed. Her original reason for seeking him out had been straightforward, but now that she found herself alone with him, the impact of his blatant masculinity on her newly discovered senses left her curiously tongue-tied and self-conscious.

He was half-sitting, half-lounging on one edge of the big desk, his knee swinging carelessly over the corner while the other long leg was stretched out to the side propping him up. The account books were spread haphazardly at his side, and the one he had been perusing so indifferently rested lightly on the strong thigh of the leg that swung freely from the desk, the lean fingers that held it open appearing very dark against the pale gray binding.

He was dressed much more formally than Leonie had seen him lately, the dark blue coat fitting his broad shoulders expertly, the starched, elegantly arranged cravat of white linen contrasting pleasingly against both the jacket and the darkness of his face. Form-fitting nankeen pantaloons hugged his long, pwerful legs, and gleaming, high-topped boots of dark brown Spanish leather were on his feet.

A tense little silence permeated the room as they stared at one another, and assailed by a foreign surge of cowardice, Leonie suddenly wished she had not sought him out in such an isolated, private place. It would have been better, she decided with belated hindsight, to have spoken with him in the company of somebody else or at least at the house where there were others nearby.

Now why that thought should have occurred to her, she didn't know, she only sensed that once again, Morgan had changed personalities on her. There was something about this man that disturbed her. He looked the same, but this morning there was a hardness about the sapphire blue eyes she hadn't seen lately and a forbidding grimness to the full, mobile mouth that she was certain hadn't been there yesterday. A sudden flush crossed her face. No, definitely there had been nothing grim or forbidding about that mouth yesterday afternoon.

Morgan noted the flush and his eyes narrowed. Snapping the account book shut with a sharp movement, he tossed it aside and asked unencouragingly, "You wanted to see me?"

"*Oui,* monsieur, there are some—some things that I wish to discuss with you." Leonie answered with more confidence than she felt, wishing helplessly that he was not so attractive and that just the mere sight of him didn't start her heart pounding erratically in her chest. *Mon Dieu, but I am acting like a schoolgirl.* Just a little angry with herself, she added more briskly, "There are things that must be decided between us. We cannot continue as we are."

Morgan's foot continued to swing slowly, his face expressionless as he looked at her. She was, he admitted unwillingly, absolutely charming as she stood before him, the old, yellow linen gown intensifying the color of the golden skin and tawny hair. The sea-green eyes with their bewitching golden flecks were wide with a beguiling sort of entreaty, but Morgan detected a hint of stubborn determination as she met his steely regard.

Leonie's advent into his private sanctuary had startled him, but now that the initial surprise had faded, and in view of the ugly thoughts that had kept him sleepless the night before, surprise had been surplanted by wariness . . . and a cold, deadly desire to trap her and the shadow man he was certain existed. Underneath his calm exterior, he was furious, furious that he had allowed his hunger for her body to further abet a scheme he firmly believed had been planned for the express purpose of separating him from his money, and furious that even for one moment he had allowed passion to rule him. There was another reason too for his fury: For the second time in his life he had come perilously close to allowing himself to be beguiled by an enchanting, lying little slut, and that knowledge was like salt on a raw wound.

Yesterday, the sight of her standing so demurely in front of him would have filled him with a queer delight, and he would have taken wicked enjoyment in continuing the exciting, treacherous game of wits between them. But that had been yesterday, yesterday when he had been so stupidly blind to the snare around his very feet. Today, he was very much aware of the snare, and had cursed himself a dozen times this morning for letting the demands of his body overrule the cool logic of his brain. He had almost forgotten the lesson Stephanie had taught him so brutally, but now his defenses were in place and there was no way in hell he was going to forget that this desirable little slut was only after money.

Precisely how he was to repair the damage done by so rashly acknowledging her as his wife hadn't yet occurred to him, but he was certain that sooner or later he would think of something. And in the meantime he could take a certain pleasure in knowing that if he had entangled himself foolishly in their net, the scheme wasn't working out as his opponents had planned either.

The fact that Leonie had sought him out alone gave him a curious feeling of savage satisfaction. Her opening words increased the notion that perhaps at last there would be some plain speaking between them, and Morgan was torn between the fierce desire to have things out in the open and the bitter, galling knowledge that he wasn't quite prepared for her to leave his life.

Insolently, his eyes ran over her slim shape. No, not yet. She owed him something for all the trouble she had caused, and by God, before he was finished with her, she was going to pay dearly. If it was going to cost him a great deal of money, and he suspected it might, he was damned well going to get some pleasure out of it.

Thinking the silence had lasted long enough, Morgan finally made some comment to her earlier statement. A mocking smile curving the full mouth, he murmured, "Oh? I'm afraid I don't understand. I thought things were going along just fine . . . especially yesterday afternoon."

Leonie blushed a fiery red. Suddenly disliking him intensely, in a tight voice she said, "I did not come here to discuss what happened yesterday. It was, I realize now, a mistake. A mistake that will not be repeated, I assure you, monsieur!"

"But surely," Morgan purred gently, a dangerous glint in the blue eyes, "you don't intend to deny me the rights of a husband? After all, I am your husband, am I not?"

"And that is what we must discuss, monsieur!" Leonie said hotly, deciding she had been a fool to think even for one moment of loving Morgan Slade or remaining here as his wife. *Dolt!* she thought angrily to herself. *He is every bit as detestable as he was six years ago.* Aloud she said fiercely, "I never intended to remain here as your wife! My one reason for coming to Natchez was to receive the money you owe me . . . and for nothing else!"

"Ah. Of course, the money," Morgan murmured dryly. "I wondered when you'd finally bring that up."

Feeling as if she were dying inside, Leonie said with as much composure as she could muster, "I'm sorry if you think I have imposed too long on your hospitality before

235

broaching the business between us, but you will remember, monsieur, that I mentioned it the first night I arrived in Natchez."

"So you did. How stupid of me to have forgotten. You made it quite, quite clear, didn't you?" Morgan's voice was harsh as he spoke, Leonie's every word only confirming his earlier thoughts. He *had* disrupted their plans, of that he was now certain, and growing impatient with the way things were going, they must have decided not to waste any more time before applying pressure on him to pay them the money they wanted. Furiously he wondered how many other men had been taken in by this scheme, coldly curious if any of the others had made any attempt to catch Leonie and her partner in their own trap. Somehow, he rather thought not . . . it was just bad luck on their part that they had finally chosen someone who *wasn't* going to play the game their way.

The green eyes flashing with rising temper, Leonie answered his question. *"Oui,* monsieur, *very* clear!" Adding scornfully, "There was no other reason for me to come here—we had promised not to interfere in each other's lives, if you will remember!"

Morgan's face didn't change, although Leonie noticed a muscle that jumped in one lean, dark cheek. His eyes were hard and contemptuous as they met hers, and sickly, she admitted that it was as if the past days had never existed, as if what had happened between them yesterday afternoon had never been. They were precisely where they had been that first night at the Marshall ball. All that was needed to make it even more agonizingly the same was for Morgan now to claim again that he had never married her, she thought with a wave of pain and anger.

But Morgan wasn't about to make that claim. No, he was beginning to think that he might not have made such a blunder as he had first thought. Accepting her as his wife had now put the pressure on her and the others, and he couldn't say he was displeased with the result. At least, he mused viciously, the little bitch is finally showing her colors. Ignoring her last statement, he asked bluntly, "And if I pay you this, ah, dowry, you claim I owe you, what happens then?"

Her throat aching with unshed tears, Leonie glanced away and replied in a low tone, "We will all leave." It was what she had wanted so desperately at one time, but now she was devastated at the thought of never seeing Morgan's dark, handsome features again.

"I see. It's a rather cold-blooded arrangement, don't you think? I pay you the five thousand in gold and then, you disappear. Your marriage vows certainly don't mean very much to you, do they?" he snapped.

Leonie's head jerked up at that, hot rage singing through her veins. *"Non,* monsieur, they do not! They never have! And at one time, they didn't mean very much to you either. You were certainly willing to agree to everything I asked—and you admitted that marriage was not what *you* wanted either! It was to be for our mutual benefit, but so far," she finished angrily, "I think you, monsieur, are the one who has had the benefit. And if you do not pay me the money within the week, then I shall be forced to seek out a magistrate and put the entire matter in his hands!"

"Why, you little bitch!" Morgan burst out explosively. Rising from the desk in one lithe, dangerous movement, his fingers closed punishingly around her slender arm and he violently jerked her body up next to his. "Don't overplay your hand, madame," he snarled softly. "Push me too hard, too quick, and you're likely to get much more than you bargained for!"

"I want nothing from you!" Leonie spat furiously, clawing at the steel-fingered hand that held her arm captive. "I want only what is rightfully mine, and I will do anything to get it!"

Her body was warm against his as she struggled wildly to be free of his grasp, and to Morgan's astonishment, even as enraged as he was, as disillusioned and contemptuous of her as he was, he felt his own body instantly react to the nearness of hers. Her features were flushed and angry as she glared up into his face, but Morgan thought she had never seemed lovelier. His eyes going irresistibly to her mouth, he said thickly, "Anything, sweetheart? Even submitting to the embraces of your husband?"

"Non!" Leonie retorted hotly, twisting helplessly in his

237

increasingly painful hold. "I am not a whore to be bought, monsieur! The money is mine and you must repay it! You *must!*"

"Perhaps I will . . . someday," he muttered under his breath, "but first, I intend to discover again exactly what it is I will be paying for."

Reading the intent in the glittering blue eyes, Leonie fought even more fiercely, her free hand balling in a fist and striking his shoulder repeatedly. But Morgan was too determined to taste the sweetness of that soft, provocative mouth again to be deterred, and almost cruelly his other hand tangled in the tawny curls, holding her head steady as his lips found hers. A shudder shook her body at the touch of his mouth against her lips, but stubbornly, unwilling to surrender to the traitorous flame of desire that swirled through her body, she kept her mouth tightly closed and refused to let him deepen the kiss.

Morgan was aware of her resistance, and his fingers tightened painfully in the golden-brown mass of hair, forcing Leonie's head further back.

"Open your mouth to me," he said huskily against her lips. "I want all of you. I want the taste of you on my tongue, the scent of you in my nostrils . . ." Lightly his mouth slid down the white column of her throat, planting fiery little kisses wherever it touched, and stopping at the base of her throat, his tongue gently moved against that spot where her pulse pounded madly despite her determination to remain unmoved. Feeling that betraying movement and aware of how his own body suddenly ached with the need to join with hers, he muttered wonderingly against her skin, "A moment ago we were at each other's throats, but now that I have you in my arms, I find that all I want is to share what we had yesterday, to have you naked against me, to feel your breasts against me, and to have your body filled with mine."

Leonie trembled at his words, the images they conjured up too powerful and erotic to resist. With a small sigh of defeat, when Morgan's mouth again sought hers, she denied him nothing, the soft lips opening helplessly under the demanding force of his.

Morgan kissed her deeply, his tongue sensuously exploring her mouth, deliberately exciting both of them, deliberately arousing the primitive passion they had shared yesterday. There was no longer any need to hold her head captive, and his hand cupped her breast through the soft fabric of the yellow gown, his thumb moving rhythmically over the nipple until it was hard and throbbing under his touch.

The sharp rap on the door, as well as Dominic's voice demanding entrance, was like a douche of icy water and just as effectively destroyed their increasing intimacy. Leonie instantly froze in Morgan's embrace, and with a muffled curse Morgan reluctantly released her. A crooked smile on his face, he murmured, "Perhaps it's as well my brother is tactless. Another few minutes and I'm certain he would have interrupted a far more embarrassing scene."

Flushing scarlet with shame, Leonie would not meet his eyes and said painfully, "Monsieur, this changes nothing between us. Now is not the time for us to talk, but we must straighten things out between us before much longer."

Dominic knocked again louder, and with a frown of annoyance crossing his dark features, Morgan snapped, "Come in, Dominic, for God's sake! Don't just keep pounding on the door!" Glancing back at Leonie, the passion that had ruled him only a second ago gone as if it had never existed, he said coldly, "I don't think anything can be settled between us with mere conversation. And certainly, the current situation is not going to be resolved either swiftly or easily. So resign yourself, my dear, to several more weeks of being my wife!"

Leonie would have refuted that statement hotly, but Dominic walked in and the opportunity was lost. Throwing Morgan a fulminating look, she made some brief remark to Dominic and promptly left the office, her anger very apparent.

Dominic looked after her thoughtfully for a minute and then at his brother. "Interrupted something, did I? I thought it took you a hell of a long time to answer the door."

"Oh, shut up, Dom, I'm in no mood for your teasing," Morgan snapped irritably, his eyes on the door Leonie had just flounced through.

"Excuse me! Shall I return at a later time when your highness is in a better mood?"

Morgan laughed reluctantly, and a hint of apology in his blue eyes, he said honestly, "I'll admit I'm in the devil's own temper, but it has nothing to do with you. And I'm a boor to snap at you so. Forgive me?"

Dominic waved a careless hand. "Nothing to forgive. But if I have come at an inconvenient time, I'll come back later."

"No." A grin on his face, Morgan added, "Better you came when you did than five minutes later—then, I would have cheerfully murdered you for intruding."

"Ah. Like that, was it?"

"Yes, like that," Morgan said flatly, his grin fading. Seating himself again on the corner of the desk, he asked, "What can I do for you?"

"Nothing really. No, that's not true," Dominic admitted reluctantly, shooting Morgan an uncertain glance. "I want to have a conversation with you . . . about your marriage."

Morgan cocked an inquiring eyebrow at him. "Oh?"

Not meeting Morgan's curious gaze, Dominic walked over to the doors that led to the small courtyard and said, "Been doing a lot of thinking the past few days. Thought about all the things I know about you, and a couple of things hit me between the eyes."

He hesitated as if searching for words, and gently Morgan prodded him. "And what precisely is it that has, ah, hit you between the eyes?"

Encouraged, Dominic said bluntly, "Never knew you to lie before. Never even knew you to tell a half-truth. And I've begun to think that while you may not have been lying the night of the Marshall's ball, you sure as hell have been lying through your teeth these past days." Throwing his brother a challenging look over his shoulder, Dominic added, "Don't ask me how I know, or why I now believe you really didn't marry Leonie, but I've a gut feeling that you're running some kind of rig . . . playing for time or something."

An admiring expression on his face, Morgan said lightly, "Why Dominic! You positively unman me!"

Dominic scowled. "Don't play games with me, Morgan! I might have been confused at first, everything happened so damned quick. But once the initial shock died down and I really began to think about what happened, I'd swear on my life that you'd never seen Leonie before she exploded like a cannon right underneath your feet that night!"

"And?"

"And, damn it, I want to apologize for not believing you, and also, to tell you that *whatever* the game is, I want to be dealt a hand. A man can always use an ally when his back is against the wall."

Morgan regarded him intently for several seconds and then said slowly, "You're right, I could use an ally. God knows it's been difficult lately pretending to be content with the way things have worked out." His face hardening, Morgan said in a harsh voice, "On my honor, Dominic, such as it is, I never laid eyes on Leonie Saint-André until Gaylord Easton brought her up to us. And I sure as hell never married her or fathered Justin."

"Somebody obviously did," Dominic returned tartly.

"Precisely," Morgan agreed with a nasty smile.

"Oh-ho! I think I begin to see a glimmer of what is going on."

"Well, it occurred to you quicker than it did me," Morgan muttered. "It was only last night that I realized there was at least *one* piece of the puzzle missing—Justin's father!"

Briefly and succinctly, Morgan told Dominic what he suspected, and Dominic, willing to follow his lead, could find no fault with his reasoning. It all made sense. And even though they discussed the possibility that Leonie was doing it all on her own, both men dismissed that idea. No, both felt there had to be a man in the background. They discussed the idea of Claude Saint-André still being alive but decided against it. The plot had the feel of a younger man, a lover, or a pimp. Definitely a clever man had supplied the forgeries and had selected Morgan as the present candidate for plucking.

"If we can find him," Morgan said grimly, "I think we can expose the entire charade."

"The servants and Yvette all tell the same tale?"

Ruefully Morgan admitted, "Hell, yes. I questioned them as closely as I dared, but they all say the same thing. I've tried every way I know, without arousing their suspicions, to trap just one not conforming to the story, but so far they've proved cleverer than I am."

Dominic looked at him disgustedly. "Knowing you're not married to her, why the hell did you go ahead and acknowledge her?"

A wry smile on his face, Morgan said bluntly, "With you and everyone else believing the worst of me, with Leonie waving those damned marriage documents with my signature on them under my nose, with the parents positive that Justin is my very image at the same age, what in God's name could I do? Besides"—Morgan suddenly grinned—"if you've taken a truly assessing look at my dear, little wife, I think you'll understand completely why I wasn't averse to accepting the rights of a husband."

"Odd, but that thought *had* occurred to me. She's damned, appealing, I'll grant you that." Shooting his older brother a speculative glance, Dominic asked, "Well, what do we do about the situation?"

"At the moment, I don't know," Morgan confessed bitterly. "I've written to Jason in New Orleans, hoping that, perhaps, he can find out something down there. I have the queerest feeling that the truth, if there is any truth to discover, lies in New Orleans." Morgan let out a sigh and said baldly, "Dom, I have never felt so helpless in my entire life. I *know* she's lying. And, fool that I am, by confirming her story, I've dug an even deeper pit for myself than the one she prepared. My only hope seems to be to find the man, *if* there is a man—sometimes, I even wonder about *that*—and shake the real truth from him."

"What about Gaylord Easton?" Dominic offered slowly.

Morgan grimaced. "I've thought of him, but . . ." Morgan's voice trailed off, a frown creasing his forehead as he reconsidered the idea. Thoughtfully he mused, "It could be, Dom, it just could be. It was Gaylord who brought her to the hall. Gaylord who supposedly met her at King's Tavern. And if anyone had reason to wish for my discomfiture, it was young Mr. Easton."

"Of course! Morgan, that has to be it!" Dominic said quickly, the gray eyes flashing with excitement. "Who would suspect him? And it's well-known he needs money. For all we know, Leonie has been his mistress for years. After all, gentlemen don't go around flaunting their whores, or their bastards for that matter. Certainly he would have been discreet and kept her and the child nicely tucked away . . . and you could damn well wager your last penny that she wouldn't be introduced to polite society. Gaylord has a reputation for being a bit of a wild one, so why not? Why couldn't he be the man behind it?"

"He might not be the mastermind, *if* such a figure does in fact exist, but I do think it behooves me to have a long conversation with Mr. Easton, don't you?"

"By God, yes!"

Unfortunately, when Morgan called at the Easton ancestral mansion that afternoon, he was met with the unpleasant news that young Master Easton had decided to visit with relatives in Baton Rouge and wasn't expected home for several months. Gaylord's absence seemed sinister, almost as if having set the plan in motion, he now removed himself from the source of danger . . . or had he gone to meet with the *real* mastermind? Morgan wondered sourly.

Some judicious questioning by Dominic of a few of Gaylord's cronies, shortly after Morgan returned with the news of Gaylord's departure, elicited the information that the elder Eastons, upset and distressed by his part in the ugly scene at the Marshalls' ball, had literally ordered him to remove himself for several months from the district.

"They want everything to die down before the darling boy shows his face again. Or, I should say, that's the tale they're telling," Dominic said dryly.

"You think it might not be true? Or merely convenient?" Morgan asked quietly as they sat in his study that evening before joining the ladies for dinner.

"Damned convenient, if you ask me. He wants to lie low for a few months, and his parents providentially furnished him with a perfect excuse to leave Natchez." Glancing over at his older brother as Morgan absently sipped a glass of well-aged Kentucky whiskey, Dominic inquired, "What are we going to do now?"

"You," Morgan said slowly, "are going to remain here and make certain that my dear wife and son don't suddenly disappear, and I—well, I think that I shall take a brief trip to Baton Rouge. It *was* Baton Rouge where Gaylord went, wasn't it?"

PART THREE

WHISPERS ON THE WIND

> There was never any yet that wholly
> could escape love, and never shall there
> be any, never so long as beauty shall
> be, never so long as eyes can see.
>
> *Daphnis and Chloe*
> Longus

18

It was a fast, grim trip that Morgan made down the Mississippi River to Baton Rouge that June of 1805. Litchfield, after a certain amount of argument between Dominic and Morgan, went with him. As Dominic had heatedly pointed out, and Litchfield had swiftly agreed, they had no way of knowing precisely what Gaylord was doing in Baton Rouge. It *was* possible he had gone to meet with another member involved in the charade—the man who might be the mastermind, and if by chance this was true, Morgan might find himself in need of protection.

Time was of the essence, as much because Morgan had a growing need to have things settled as because he feared that Leonie might somehow escape Dominic's watchful eye and disappear as swiftly as she had appeared. It had been decided to tell no one of his trip until after his departure so that no one could interfere. It also gave him a headstart if Leonie tried to send any messages warning Gaylord. Naturally not a breath of his real reason for traveling so suddenly and unexpectedly to Baton Rouge came to light. Dominic stoutly maintained the ridiculous fiction that Morgan had decided that he wished to move his newly acknowledged family to his own property, Thousand Oaks, and had gone to inspect it and see that work was begun to make it comfortable for his bride. Noelle looked at Dominic closely, and Matthew's lips thinned with displeasure, but no one challenged him.

Predictably, Leonie had been furious when Dominic had broken the news to her that morning. The ugly scene with Morgan the previous day had hardened her resolve to resist the attraction he held for her and to forge ahead with her original plan.

After the things he had said to her in his office, and the way he had treated her, it was painfully apparent to Leonie that her first assessment of him had been correct. *He is,* she had thought scathingly the previous night as she had lain sleepless in her bed, *a handsome, dangerous serpent! Mon Dieu, that I should have been fool enough to believe even for one moment that he might have changed.*

Growing angrier by the second, as much at her own folly, as at his trickery, it wasn't surprising that when she did finally fall asleep she slept badly and woke like an enraged tigress. Intent upon at last letting Monsieur Morgan Slade know *exactly* what she thought of his tactics and of settling things between them once and for all, when she learned from Dominic that Morgan had left at dawn to make ready a house she had no intention of ever setting eyes on, she was engulfed with fury.

Dominic had been in the breakfast room at Le Petit when Leonie entered. She was taken aback at first, but as she had grown used to Dominic, as well as Robert, more or less running throughout the house at will she hadn't thought much about it; she wasn't going to let Dominic's presence interfere with what she had to say to his brother.

They exchanged greetings and then almost casually Dominic informed her of Morgan's departure. There was a thunderstruck silence in the charming little room and then with one small foot tapping with ominous rhythm, the golden flecks in her eyes glowing dangerously, she regarded Dominic unnervingly for a long moment. In a tight voice she demanded, "He has left already? For Baton Rouge?"

Dominic smiled mockingly and gave her a correct little bow. "That is correct, madame. He wished to tell you himself, but the boat was leaving at dawn and he was certain you would understand."

Holding on to her rising temper by a slender thread, Leonie took a deep breath and asked levelly, "When will he return?"

Dominic shrugged his shoulders. "I really couldn't say. I suspect it depends upon how long it takes him to get things in order at Thousand Oaks. He might be gone for only a week . . . or a month. It all depends."

"A *month!*" Leonie burst out appalled, the devastating thought occurring to her that if Morgan did indeed remain away from Le Petit for that period of time, any hope of regaining Château Saint-André would be shattered. Almost despairingly she added, "But he can't be gone that long. Not a month!"

Up until this moment Dominic had found the confrontation going as he had expected, but the stricken expression that had flitted swiftly across her lively face disturbed him, and suddenly he didn't find himself quite so aloof. "Is something wrong?" he felt compelled to ask.

Recovering herself, unwilling to let one of the detestable Slades see her pain, Leonie sent him a bitter, proud little smile. "Wrong, monsieur? Now why should you think that?"

At a loss, Dominic muttered, "I don't know, you looked . . . you looked *hurt.*"

Again furious, Leonie snapped, "Does it matter that I might be hurt, monsieur? Does it matter that because your brother has proven himself a dishonorable man that I may lose the only home I have ever known? I never wanted to be his wife! *Never!* It wasn't to take my place as his wife that I came to Natchez. It was only to receive what was mine, what was promised to me when I agreed to marry him." Taking an angry step nearer to him, her cheeks flushed with the emotion that ran deep within her, she said fiercely, "I never wanted anything from him but what was mine, and I didn't even want that for myself. I wanted it to save my home, the home my great grand-*père* carved out of the swamps, the home where my *grand-père* was born, where my father was born, and where I and my son were born. It is our *home,* can you understand that? Château Saint-André is dear to me, *dearer* to me than Bonheur is to your family!" The golden-green eyes shimmering behind a veil of tears, she spat, "I had until the first of July to repay the debt on it and now by your brother's cowardly act of running away, of reneging on his debt to me, he has deprived me of any chance of saving it. And you dare to say I look *hurt!*" Mortified at her outburst, choking back the tears that threatened to spill, she whirled on heels and fled the room.

"Well, Jesus Christ!" Dominic said to the empty room. "I wonder if Morgan knows this."

Morgan, of course had heard something to that effect during his questioning of the servants, but he hadn't paid a great deal of attention to that particular information, and the blunt truth of the matter is that even if he had, it wasn't likely that he would have done anything any differently. Leonie's oddly moving little admission he would have put down to being simply another ploy to get the money out of him. The initial scheme wasn't working, so why not try tearing at his heartstrings? Unfortunately, as Morgan would have told Leonie bluntly, his heartstrings had been torn out long ago.

The trip down the river was without incident and Morgan might have enjoyed it under other circumstances, but to his intense annoyance he discovered that absence did not lessen Leonie's hold upon him. She drifted like a beckoning, tawny temptress into his every thought, her slender form seeming to dance seductively around each curve and bend of the mighty Mississippi River, her soft laughter ringing in his ears. It was at night that she truly haunted him; time after time he would wake up abruptly, the feeling of her in his arms so strong, the taste of her on his lips so real, that for several seconds he didn't realize he had been dreaming again. With a virulent curse, he would fling himself over on his side and force himself to sleep, only to have the same insidious dream weave itself through his subconscious.

Morgan also discovered that it wasn't only Leonie who had insinuated herself into his thoughts; he found that he missed Justin intolerably. In the short space of time he and Justin had been together, he had grown rather used to the boy's exuberant greeting in the morning as, his green eyes alight with enthusiasm, he came flying down the stairs in search of his "papa." The boy was hard to resist, Morgan admitted to himself, knowing that he had taken more than a little pleasure in those rides around the estate with Justin following happily on Thunder. It would be so easy to accept Justin as his real son, so easy to love the boy as he had Phillippe. So *damned* easy!

250

In the short span of barely a week the two of them have possessed me, he reflected furiously. Just the fact that he even gave Justin a thought revealed how entwined his life had become with the Saint-Andrés. And the nights, the nights were proof of how completely Leonie had invaded his entire being.

At least the journey gave him something constructive to do, he told himself repeatedly. And Gaylord Easton could conceivably hold the key to the entire puzzle, the information he might learn from Gaylord effectively ending the mockery of marriage he shared with Leonie.

The certainty that there was another man involved somewhere had grown even more firmly in Morgan's mind as he and Litchfield came nearer to Baton Rouge. He had some reservations about that man being Gaylord Easton, but Gaylord was the only other link to Leonie that he had at the moment. Obviously someone had fathered the child, and it seemed reasonable that Justin's father would be the man who governed Leonie's actions. Whether that elusive shadowy man was Gaylord Easton remained to be seen. Morgan did have some doubt that Gaylord was Justin's father, but surveying the murky waters of the Mississippi as they approached Baton Rouge he admitted that he should have questioned Gaylord immediately, instead of having so blithely dismissed him.

Baton Rouge had been one of the earliest French settlements in Louisiana but was now considered part of West Florida. Controlled by the Spaniards, it was a bustling port city situated on a pleasant bluff on the left bank of the Mississippi. Finding a comfortable set of rooms proved no obstacle and, leaving Litchfield to unpack their few necessities, Morgan sought out a livery stable and bought a pair of horses. He and Litchfield would need them for the journey home. That business accomplished, he set about finding Gaylord Easton.

After a few questions, Morgan learned that a family named Easton lived some five miles north of Baton Rouge. From what he had gleaned, they sounded as if they were the relatives that Gaylord had come to visit.

Morgan was up early the next morning impatient to find Gaylord, but he restrained himself from calling upon the

Michael Easton family until the respectable hour of ten o'clock. He found the house, an elegant three-storied white mansion, with little trouble and he hoped he would find Gaylord with equal ease.

Luck was with him, for these were indeed the relatives that Gaylord had come to visit. And, fortunately, from Morgan's point of view, Michael Easton, a bluff hearty man of some fifty years, proved to be an easy agreeable fellow.

"Want to see my nevvy, do you?" he asked interestedly, his shrewd brown eyes quickly sizing up Morgan's tall elegant form. At Morgan's nod, he added, "Well, I hope you can take him from the path he is on! Since he's arrived from Natchez he's done nothing but drown in my best whiskey and moan and blubber over some chit by the name of Melinda. Says if he had it to do over again, he'd go ahead and let her commit bigamy. Says he never thought she'd blame *him* for the broken engagement! Can't say as though I don't agree with him. All the boy did was the right thing, and I'm afraid I don't see how this Melinda hussy can say it's his fault when all he did was save her from making a damned fool of herself."

Morgan smiled slightly and murmured, "I doubt anyone can stop Melinda from making a fool of herself."

Michael Easton cocked a rusty-brown eyebrow at him. "Oh-ho, like that is it? Well, I can't say as I'm surprised. Sounded like a Canterbury tale to me!" Nodding to his left, he continued, "You'll find him in the *garçonnière.*"

Walking away from the elder Easton, Morgan was extremely thoughtful. From the remarks dropped by his uncle, it seemed Gaylord was deep in the throes of self-pity and certainly not involved in any scheme with Leonie.

Entering the *garçonnière,* a small two-storied building that was a greatly reduced replica of the main house, Morgan found Gaylord in his rooms on the second story.

Gaylord was drunk, sprawled in a large overstuffed leather chair, when Morgan walked into the room. Blearily Gaylord gaped at him, the stubble on his face and chin giving him a decidedly unsavory appearance, and the red-rimmed eyes were more than adequate proof that his uncle had not exaggerated the situation. A glass full of what

Morgan assumed was whiskey was clasped loosely in one hand and as Morgan stopped just inside the doorway, it suddenly slid from Gaylord's slackened hold and shattered on the floor.

"You!" Gaylord blurted out with loathing and astonishment, ingoring the shattered glass and widening ring of liquid on the floor. "Isn't it enough you have taken the only woman I shall ever love from me? Must you hound me too? Melinda will not even speak to me! And do you know why?" Rising clumsily to his feet, his hands clenched into fists, he snarled, "Because I saved her! I *saved* her from you and now she hates me! I begged her forgiveness for the way I ruined her ball; I've pleaded with her to understand that my one thought was to protect her; I've admitted I shouldn't have created such a scandalous scene. But good God, what could I do?" His fine dark eyes full of dull misery, he said bitterly, "When I met your wife that night at the tavern I couldn't believe my luck! I was so *damned* excited, I never thought of anything but of saving Melinda from your dastardly clutches." He threw back his head and gave an angry shout of laughter. "What a jest! I think the *worst* thing that ever happened to me was finding your wife! Believe me, I wish now I'd never laid eyes on her!"

Morgan said nothing for several seconds as a number of things raced through his brain. After an intense scrutiny of the younger man's features, the first thing that struck him was that Gaylord bore no resemblence to Justin, and Morgan found himself uncomfortably relieved by this. Did it really matter to him who Justin's father was? He gave Gaylord another assessing look, deciding he must have been mad to think even for one moment of this poor besotted fool as a partner in an underhanded scheme to part him from his money. It was obvious that Gaylord was, for reasons which totally escaped Morgan, pining grievously for Melinda Marshall. It also appeared that he regretted bringing Leonie to the Marshall house that night.

But aware that it could be an act, Morgan proceeded to explore the matter further. Idly he murmured, "I can sympathize with your dilemma, but I wonder if you would mind explaining to me precisely *how* you came to so opportunely discover Leonie? It is something that has mystified me for some time."

The conversation that followed was acrimonious and mercifully brief. But Morgan was able to ride away from Gaylord Easton a short while later, confident in his own mind that while Gaylord was a hot-tempered fool, determined to waste his emotions on a silly chit not worth a moment's thought, his only connection to Leonie was a chance meeting at King's Tavern.

His mission accomplished, he and Litchfield left that very day for home. Riding swiftly towards Natchez Morgan couldn't say that his trip had been a success. He had eliminated Gaylord from whatever plot existed, but his notion of another man, a shadowy stranger in the background had only grown stronger. And he was precisely in the same position he had been when he had left Natchez—saddled with a lying jade who claimed to be his wife.

Through the humid heat of June he and Litchfield rode the narrow, curving trail that lead toward Natchez, arriving at Le Petit after midnight near the middle of the month. They had discussed camping another night on the trail, but both men had been eager to reach home and so, aided by the light of a half-moon, they had pushed on.

The house was in darkness, and after unsaddling their exhausted horses and giving them a scant rubdown, both men walked silently towards the house. They entered as quietly as possible, not wishing to awaken anyone, and might have managed to gain Morgan's rooms undetected if Litchfield hadn't stumbled over something in the blackness, and dropped the valise he was carrying.

The valise landed with an audible thump and there was a muffled curse from the annoyed Litchfield. In offended tones he said, "I believe, sir, that young Justin has left his wooden horse in the hallway."

Morgan grinned in the darkness, knowing that Litchfield would never have allowed such a deplorable incident to have occurred if he had been in charge while the master was away. Morgan started to make some teasing remark, when the door to the study suddenly flew open and Dominic, a pistol in one hand and a candle in the other, snapped,

"Hold it right there! Make one move and you'll be dead men!"

"Dom!" Morgan said with surprise. "What the hell are you doing here at this hour of the night?"

Recognizing Morgan's voice instantly, as well as his tall form in the candlelight, Dominic grinned sheepishly, and lowering the pistol, he said, "Oh! It's you!"

"Well, who else did you expect at this ungodly hour?"

"Housebreakers. While you've been gone several houses in the area have been robbed, and with no man in the house, maman has been worrying herself into a decline fretting over Leonie and the others." Throwing Morgan a resigned look, he added, "As you know, once maman gets something into her sweet little head she instantly takes steps to correct what is bothering her."

Morgan smiled in agreement. "Yes, but tell me why you aren't abed? Surely the house can offer something more than the dubious comfort of my study?"

Dominic pulled a face. "Well, yes. But you see if maman was determined that a man stay in the house, Leonie was just as determined not to have me stay!" Shaking his head, a rueful gleam in the gray eyes, he admitted, "There have been some stormy days while you have been gone, I can tell you that! Leonie is as stubborn, independent a little minx as I have ever met. She informed maman that she had managed to live the past five years without the protection of a man and she saw no reason why she should suddenly have herself saddled with someone who probably couldn't shoot as well as she could! Maman took exception to that, I can tell you! She decided that Leonie was casting aspersions on my ability as a marksman and for a few minutes there I was afraid I'd see blood spilt."

Morgan could well imagine the scene, and a hint of laughter in his voice he asked, "What happened?"

Litchfield forestalled Dominic's reply by saying in long-suffering accents, "If you gentlemen will persist in conversing in the dark except for one candle, and after the hour of two o'clock in the morning, might I be excused to find more refined comfort?"

Dominic smothered a snort of laughter and Morgan, amusement glittering in the dark blue eyes, turned to look at his valet. "By all means, Litchfield, *do* take yourself off. I shall see you in the morning . . . unless of course, you have other plans?"

Litchfield sent him a speaking glance and without another word disappeared in the gloom of the hall.

Swinging back to Dominic, Morgan said wryly, "He is right you know, we *could* find somewhere else more comfortable."

Dominic gave a silly little bow and murmured, "If you will follow me?"

A few minutes later they were both seated in Morgan's study sipping whiskey. The disappointing outcome of Morgan's trip to Baton Rouge and his meeting with Gaylord had been discussed, and for the moment they were simply enjoying each other's company. Morgan had shrugged out of his jacket and his shirt was half undone to the waist revealing portions of his bronzed chest with its whorls of fine black hair. Lounging comfortably in a red leather chair, his long legs encased in buff breeches, Morgan laid his head back against the softness of the leather and expelled a long relaxed sigh. "God, but it's good to be back!"

Dominic grinned at him. "Now that's an odd statement coming from you. Can you actually be thinking 'no place like home'?"

Morgan frowned. "I don't know. I only know that I'm damned glad to be here . . . and glad to know that my charming, lying wife hasn't managed to disappear behind my back."

Dominic's grin faded. A trouble expression on his dark young face, he said slowly. "I don't think she had the resources *to* disappear. I'd wager my entire inheritance that if it hadn't taken every bit of ready money she possessed to get them all here, she *would* have disappeared despite anything I might have done to stop her."

Looking thoughtful, Morgan sipped his whiskey. "How do you know it took all her money to reach here? For that matter that the lot of them really did come from New Orleans? We have only her word for it!"

"I know you're going to think I'm vacillating, but damn it, Morgan, there are times I actually believe what she says . . . or at least *some* of it," Dominic admitted uncomfortably. "I'm so confused I don't know what to believe anymore. You say you didn't marry her, and I'll take your word for it. On the other hand, there are things that Leonie says that I believe also."

"For instance?"

"Well, I believe that they did all live in that old run-down plantation she talks about." Glancing at Morgan he asked, "Did you happen to pay close attention to her clothes and hands before you left for Baton Rouge?"

His brow furrowed in concentration Morgan thought back, remembering the faded old green gown she had worn and the singular sameness of the gown she had worn for dinner. He tried to remember her hands, but the memory of her soft, impudent mouth got in the way and somewhat abruptly he answered, "The clothes can be discounted. It would be stupid of anyone telling the story that she is, to wear anything *but* old, worn clothing. As for her hands, no, I didn't pay them much attention. I generally do not make a study of a woman's hands." A sudden gleam of amusement flickering in the blue eyes, he added dulcetly, "They have such other interesting facets, you understand."

Dominic smiled faintly. "Agreed. And I don't usually notice their hands either, but in her case I did. If you'd have been around a bit longer before leaving for Baton Rouge I'm certain you would have discovered the calluses on her palms too. You won't see them as clearly now, but at first her hands showed plainly that she had worked, worked hard and not just the sort of lady's nonsense that maman does with a needle to amuse herself. I mean hard, physical work, Morgan. And when father talks of planting and the like, she has no trouble following him. Every other female I know, including maman, doesn't understand a word of farming and planting, but Leonie *does*. She even offered one or two suggestions about rotating the cotton fields that impressed father. She may be an adventuress, I'll grant you that, she might even be a scheming little cheat, but she also, I think, did do the things she claims to have done."

Morgan looked at him consideringly. After a long moment he asked caustically, "You will concede the fact, won't you, that she is obviously after money?"

257

Dominic flushed at Morgan's tone and stiffly he replied, "I'll admit that. But I'm not so certain that it's greed that motivates her." Fiddling with his glass, he added softly, "The morning you left, when I told her about it, somewhat gleefully I'm ashamed to confess, it was like I'd given her a facer. And it wasn't so much that you had left, but the fact that I implied you might not be back for weeks, instead of days, that disturbed her. She wanted the money, I can't deny that, and it all might have been a clever act to gain my sympathy, I don't know, but I'd swear she was genuinely upset by the news. Not because she couldn't get the money from you, but becuase of the fact that even if you gave her the money when you returned it would be too late to save the Château."

"Save it? I thought it was already lost . . . or has she changed her tale?"

"I don't know that she's changed her tale, so much as she's telling more than she did to begin with. Seems some old neighbor of theirs held a note against the place and when he died, his heir demanded restitution. She had nothing to pay him with but the Château." Meeting Morgan's skeptical gaze, he said bluntly, "That place meant a lot to her. There was a note in her voice—I don't know, something that made me think of how I would feel if Bonheur were sold to a stranger."

"That's hardly proof she's telling the truth, Dom," Morgan said dryly.

"Don't you think I don't know it?" Dominic burst out irritably. "That's what has me in such confusion. She damn well doesn't *act* like an adventuress!"

"And you, of course, have known so many," Morgan drawled mockingly.

Dominic glared at him. Then taking a hasty gulp of his whiskey, he said almost apologetically, "I'm not saying that she isn't still trying to get money out of you, I'm only saying that she might not be quite as black as we first thought."

Regarding his dusty food somewhat blankly, Morgan finally said, "You might be right. Perhaps she is telling none of those intricate tales of half-truth, half-lies—tales

258

that are damned difficult to disprove simply because they *are* half-true."

Eagerly Dominic sat forward on the edge of his chair. "That's what I think. And if we go on the premise that not everything she says is a lie, that she is partially telling the truth, won't that make our task easier? I mean won't we have something more to go by?"

Morgan sighed. "Hell, I don't know. Maybe. Maybe not. I forsee a trip to New Orleans soon, though. That's where this tangle started and that's where I'm afraid I'll have to go to sort it out."

Setting down his glass, Morgan ran a hand across his forehead. "Right now nothing makes sense to me. It was a wasted journey to Baton Rouge, and I'm not even certain now why I was so positive that seeing Gaylord was absolutely vital to unraveling this mare's nest!"

The door to the study opened just then and startled, both men turned to stare in that direction. Litchfield haughtily strolled across the room, and deposited on a table near the chair where Morgan sat a large silver tray heaped with slices of cold roast beef and ham, as well as golden brown biscuits and a large hunk of yellow cheese. His face expressionless he said coolly, "If you *will* insist upon remaining up for the night, I suggest that some sustenance is in order."

Aware of how hungry he was, Morgan sent him a slow, grateful smile. Affectionately he said, "Litchfield, have I ever told you that I'd sell my last horse before I'd let you leave my service?"

Litchfield looked down his long nose and sniffed disdainfully. "Frequently, sir, but usually only when you are in your cups." Turning away he marched from the room leaving Morgan and Dominic to stare helplessly at each other before bursting into laughter.

Biting into a slice of roast beef with relish a few seconds later Dominic admitted, "I can see why you sing his praises so highly, but damn, Morgan, he scares me to death!"

Morgan only grinned. "He takes a bit of getting used to, I can tell you that, but I'm not lying when I say I couldn't do without him." Pushing aside the remains of his repast, Morgan looked at Dominic and asked suddenly, "Are you ever going to tell me why I found you sleeping in my study?"

19

"Oh, that!" Dominic replied easily. "Well, it goes back to what I was telling you about the housebreakers and maman wanting a man in the house at night, and Leonie objecting to it. You know how maman will not rest until things are arranged to her satisfaction . . . ?" At Morgan's amused nod, he went on, "Maman wanted me here and Leonie didn't. So in order to keep both of them happy, for the past few nights I've been slipping in here after everyone has gone to sleep and dozing until dawn, before returning to Bonheur." Stifling a yawn, he admitted, "I'm glad you're back, because I don't know how many more nights I could go on. Or how long before Leonie discovered what I was up to." Giving a mock shudder, he said, "She'd have my ears for breakfast if she knew what I was up to."

"You mean she *doesn't?*" Morgan asked astonished.

Dominic grimaced. "I don't know. Sometimes I convince myself that I am so stealthy in entering the house that no one can hear me, and yet at other times, especially when Leonie looks at me a certain way, I'm almost positive she *does* know and is simply keeping quiet in order to avoid open warfare with maman."

"That bad, is it?"

"No, it's not really that bad," Dominic replied slowly. "I think both of them, after a few early skirmishes, have taken each other's measure and have decided that they've met their match. Maman won't admit it, but I suspect she likes Leonie, and Leonie is such a self-contained little thing that I can't tell for sure, but I think that under different circumstances, she would enjoy being friends with maman. As it is, she views all of us with such suspicion that she won't let herself like any of us."

"Suspicion?" Morgan enquired incredulously. "She's suspicious of *us*?"

"Uh-huh. She's made it quite clear that she believes that all of us are shielding you. If the situation weren't so damned serious I'd find it terribly amusing." Almost a note of awe in his voice, Dominic added, "She's by far and away the best little actress I've ever seen. If I didn't know you better, I'd swear she was telling the truth."

Morgan viewed his brother sourly. "Well, I *am* telling the truth! I didn't marry her! And Justin's not my son and I'm not going to be blackmailed into paying any money either."

Not meeting Morgan's eyes, Dominic said casually, "Might have to."

Ominously Morgan demanded, "And what, little brother, do you mean by that?"

"She's laid the entire thing before the magistrate,"

"What?" Morgan burst out wrathfully.

Dominic made a face. "Just what I said. Father tried to dissuade her, and the rest of us talked ourselves hoarse, but Monday she rode one of her mules into town and saw Judge Dangermond. Gave him the agreement and told him that she wanted justice done."

"She rode a *mule* into town?" Morgan asked, diverted, a spark of amusement glittering briefly in his eyes.

"Uh-huh. Proud little minx. Told us she could provide her own transportation, and that she didn't need any help from the Slades. Said all she wants is her dowry, and then the rest of us can whistle down the wind for all she cares."

His momentary amusement gone, Morgan frowned. "Has father talked to the judge?"

"Yep." Dominic answered inelegantly. "Did that the same day." Glancing at Morgan, he admitted reluctantly, "The judge says that unless you can prove she's lying, that the document is a forgery, and if she's determined to carry it further, that you're going to have to pay her the money. Told father that in the meantime he'd try to delay things. Good thing he's an old family friend."

"Does she know that?"

262

"Not yet, I don't think. But she's quick, I'll grant you that, and it won't take her too long to realize that Dangermond is in our pocket and that he is playing for time."

"She's *too* damned quick!" Morgan said furiously. "By God, if I had any doubts about her before, she's certainly laid them to rest—permanently!" His jaw tightening menacingly, he drawled in a softly dangerous voice, "So she's gone to the judge, has she?"

Made vaguely uneasy by Morgan's tone, Dominic asked, "Exactly what do you mean to do?"

Morgan glanced at him, an icy glitter in the sapphire blue eyes. "Do? Men have dealt with recalcitrant wives for centuries, Dom. I'm certain I shall prove no different in finding a way to change her mind."

Somehow Morgan's words didn't precisely reassure Dominic. Uncertainty in his voice he inquired, "You wouldn't harm her, would you?"

A nasty smile curving the handsome mouth, Morgan mocked, "Wouldn't I? At the moment I could ring her neck!"

Mildly Dominic said, "Might have a bit of trouble doing it. Somehow I don't think she'll take having her neck wrung very easily."

Reluctant amusement crept into Morgan's eyes. "I suspect you're right—and I doubt, though the idea is appealing, that I would be foolish enough to let her drive me to that extreme."

"She can be infuriating, I'll admit," Dominic agreed, and at Morgan's questioning look, he added, "I told you there have been some storms and quakes while you've been gone—Leonie is definitely a proud, prickly sort of adventuress."

His earlier fury gone, Morgan sipped his whiskey and asked interestedly, "Oh?"

"Well, let's see . . ." Dominic began reflectively. "I've told you about the mule ride, and I've told you about her little skirmishes with maman, so you have some idea of what has been going on. Leonie seems fairly content to live in your house and eat your food, but I think it's because she hasn't any choice. Other than that, she won't accept one thing more—not for herself or for any of the others." A faint smile on his lips, Dominic went on, "After you left, maman and father came over just about every day, didn't want Leonie to pine for you and of course, Justin holds a great deal of their attention. Anyway it didn't take too long before maman decided that it was ridiculous for your wife and son to continue to wear the same old clothes that they had arrived in, and she suggested to Leonie that they go to her seamstress and have some new gowns made for she and Yvette, as well as some new clothes for Justin."

Morgan nodded his head in agreement. "I can't see anything unreasonable about that. I may not wish to be cheated out of several thousand dollars, but I have no objection to clothing her, or the others for that matter." An unpleasant smile curving his mouth he added, "I am, after all, receiving a certain amount of pleasure in return."

"You might think it wasn't unreasonable, but Leonie acted as if maman had insulted her," Dominic said dryly. "Drew herself up like a furious kitten and said in the iciest voice I'd ever heard that she didn't need *charity* from the Slades. Said that if her husband would simply pay her what was owed her, she would buy their own damned clothes—her words, by the way—and even better, they'd all leave so maman wouldn't have to be offended by the sight of them in unfashionable clothing."

Frowning Morgan asked, "Was maman tactless about it? Did she call it charity?"

Dominic shook his head. "No. Maman was tact itself—she *likes* Leonie, and Morgan, you have to remember that she—along with the rest of the family—truly believes that Leonie is your wife. Maman was only trying to help, but Leonie will have none of it." His gray eyes contemplative, he finished, "She's determined not to take a damn thing . . . except her dowry. Wait, I take that back—she will allow maman and father to give Justin presents, but she also puts a limit on that. Doesn't want him to become spoiled, she says."

Morgan stared at his whiskey glass for a few minutes after Dominic ceased speaking. "She doesn't seem to be precisely what one envisions as an adventuress, does she?" he said finally.

"That's what I've been telling you," Dominic replied in-stantly. "She wants that damned dowry, I'll admit that, but Morgan, by heaven that seems to be the *only* thing she wants from you. She won't let us do anything for her—there's a perfectly good carriage and a spanking team to pull it, as well as a half dozen mounts suitable for a lady eating their heads off in your stables, but does she ride them? Hell, no! She takes a mule to town!"

The image brought no glimmer of amusement this time to Morgan's eyes. Slowly he mused, "She might be doing it for a purpose, did you ever consider that?"

Puzzled, Dominic demanded, "How do you mean?"

"Just that by not reaching out and taking what has been offered and by sticking so determinedly to her demand for the dowry, that she has only strengthened her position." Looking quickly over at Dominic, he said wryly, "You al-ready half believe her story. And by acting as one would expect a young lady in her position to behave, she makes it even more difficult to disprove her claims."

"I hadn't thought of that," Dominic admitted blankly.

"Think about it," Morgan murmured quietly. "If she were greedily demanding other things, taking with out-stretched hands everything she could possibly get, wouldn't that tend to support my statement that she *is* a scheming adventuress intent upon blackmailing me?" At Dominic's slow nod, he went on softly, "But by appearing to *object* to maman's kindness and all the other things she could have, doesn't that distort the image? Doesn't it make you se-cretly admire such apparently high-principled actions?"

Dominic moved uncomfortably in his chair, not liking the picture Morgan was fashioning. And yet, every state-ment Morgan made could be true and Dominic felt a faint surge of resentment against Leonie. She'd almost tricked him. Thank God Morgan wasn't about to be taken in by her clever act!

There was little more conversation between the two brothers, and a few minutes later, Dominic left to seek his own bed at Bonheur, while Morgan slowly walked up to his suite and entered his bedchamber. Signs that Litchfield had been there before him were evident—a candle flick-ered on the mahogany dressing table; a dark blue and black brocade robe was laid neatly across the sapphire blue coverlet on his bed, and a tray with a glass and a crystal decanter of brandy was on the night table. Morgan smiled to himself. What in God's name would he do without Litchfield?

That same thought was echoed again when he discovered the warmed water that had been left in a thick pottery pitcher on the dressing table next to the candle. Stripping off his travel-stained clothes, Morgan gave himself a hasty, refreshing wash and then with a sigh of pleasure slipped naked into his bed.

Exhaustion dragged at him like a sea-tide, but he discovered to his frustration that sleep would not come. Fragments of the conversation with Dominic buzzed endlessly around in his brain until finally he had a thundering headache.

He didn't want to think of Leonie, didn't want to begin to question his own reactions, to wonder if he had read the situation correctly, to even allow, for one tiny second, doubt in his own conclusions to creep into his mind. He believed implicitly every word he had spoken with Dominic and yet lying in the darkness of his room he found himself questioning his judgment, unaccountably wanting to find excuses for her behavior. And that, of course, infuriated him, making him aware of the power of Leonie's charms.

The news that she had done as she had threatened and laid the entire situation before a judge had shaken him as much as it enraged him. He hadn't really believed she would go that far, and it proved, at least to him, that she and those with her must feel that her story was damned near impossible to discredit. It also, he decided thoughtfully, revealed that they had realized that he wasn't going to be quite the easy gull they had first thought. Why else would they risk the thing being put to trial?

Morgan had no answers and after tossing restlessly, he abandoned any pretense of sleep. Shrugging into the brocaded robe, he splashed some brandy into the glass, walked over to a window, and stood staring out into the blackness of the night.

The brandy managed to relieve some of the tension that coiled inside of him and the throbbing of his temples lessened, but sleep still eluded him. He was now too tired to sleep, and while his body sagged with weariness and his eyes were scratchy from lack of rest, his brain was working furiously, unwilling to let sleep sweep over him.

Methodically, pushing aside his unwanted attraction to Leonie, Morgan went over the facts for the thousandth time, his thoughts just as confused when he finished as when he had begun. He was aware again of a nagging sense of something he *should* remember, some little, now forgotten, incident that had occurred six years ago that would give him the solution to the problem.

When he finally sought his bed, only one thing was certain: somewhere there *had* to be a man involved. That conclusion was inescapable, if only because of Justin's existence. So where was the man? And while Leonie might be perfectly capable of forging his signature, a gut feeling that couldn't be ignored made Morgan positive that a man, perhaps *the* man had forged those papers. And if that were true, where in hell was this man?

Morgan wasn't going to have to wait long before he found himself face to face with the man who had forged his signature on the marriage papers. At that precise moment, Ashley Slade was in the middle of the Atlantic Ocean on a French ship sailing for New Orleans, the sole purpose of his trip to find the little bride he had wed six years ago using Morgan's name.

The reconciliation with his father, the Baron Trevelyan, had lasted just as long as it had taken Ashley to become bored. Home hardly a week, he rode his father's prize stallion into the ground, carelessly destroying the magnificent animal if only because the horse *was* the pride of his father's stables. Next he had precipitated a cold-blooded, brutal fight with his younger brother, Miles, nearly blinding that pleasant young gentleman in the process. The baron tried to make excuses , but when' it was discovered some three months later that Ashley had deliberately seduced the young lady Miles had been engaged to marry, and that she had taken her life when he refused to save her from ruin was the final straw. Looking at his eldest son, his heir, with a loathing he had thought impossible, his handsome face working with both sorrow and anger, the baron had banished Ashley from the ancestral acres.

Ashley spent several months in London going through Leonie's dowry with a lavish hand, and it was only when the money was gone that he discovered that not only had he been banished from home, but that his father had no intention of either paying his mounting bills or making any sort of a settlement upon him. It was a disagreeable situation that Ashley had never envisioned.

For some months he managed to stave off his debtors and even tried his hand at card-sharking, but eventually he was forced to flee or find himself in prison. The possibility of having his father murdered in order to hasten the inheritance that would one day be his *did* cross his mind, but with regret he discarded it—the way his luck was running lately someone was certain to connect him with it.

Deciding a rich wife would be the solution to all his problems, Ashley cast his lures about, but unfortunately for him, his reputation had gone before him and the heiresses were all quickly hustled away whenever his handsome person appeared on the horizon. And after living the precarious existence of a highwayman for almost a year, Ashley finally came to the conclusion that his fortune was not to be made in England.

France called. Napoleon's star was on the ascendency and Ashley decided that any nation where a Corsican upstart could become the most powerful man in the country definitely held possibilities. Consequently in the summer of 1801, almost exactly two years after he had married Leonie under Morgan's name in New Orleans, Ashley found himself in French territory.

Due to the hostilities raging between England and France, his crossing had not been pleasant and he hadn't been certain of his reception in France, but the meeting with the smuggler who had sailed him across the channel to France proved to be propitious. The smuggler, and sometime spy for the French, Garret Penryn, was of an aristocratic background, and his history was not unlike Ashley's. Before Ashley departed the small sloop at Cherbourg, it had been decided that Ashley would turn his hand at spying.

Through Garret, Ashley was guided to the master spy, Joseph Fouché, the minister of police, and after several harrowing meetings with that ruthless, calculating gentleman, Ashley agreed to spy for France. Some six weeks later he returned to England, ostensibly a changed man.

Where before his scandalous life had been flamboyant, he now conducted his affairs with discretion; he now had money, money he claimed to have won in France; but more importantly, he seemed to have become fascinated by anyone in the military. He made it a point to make friends in high places in the Horse Guards and for several months he proved extremely adept at his new profession, supplying Garret with information about troops and supplies that was eventually relayed to Fouché in Paris.

The Peace of Amiens in the spring of 1802 annoyed Ashley—spying was proving to be a most profitable profession, but Fouché's fall from power that same year worried him. A trip to Paris was required.

Fortunately, Ashley discovered that *his* future was not in jeopardy, and more to the point, he was gratified to find that Napoleon was aware of the service he gave France.

Born with a natural grace and charm as well as a handsome person, Ashley managed, during the months that followed, to insinuate himself into Napoleon's circle, fawning and clawing his way into favor. He supplied the French government with information about the English, who now flocked to Paris during the Peace of Amiens.

The not unexpected outbreak of war between England and France in May of 1803 pleased Ashley, and he returned to England, his pockets full of French gold and his head filled with optimistic thoughts. And the future *was* very rosy for Ashley that spring—he had Napoleon's favor, an unlimited supply of gold, and the promise of further rewards in the distance.

The fact that he was betraying his own homeland bothered him not at all. He still rubbed shoulders with his old cronies and was still accepted by polite company; he was able to gamble and wench just as he always did, only now he didn't have to worry if the baron would pay for it. He lived just as he always had, the only difference being that

269

he passed along vital tidbits of information to the French and they paid him handsomely for this service.

Morgan's trip to England might have stopped this delightful state of affairs if they had chanced to meet. Fortunately, when Morgan arrived in England, Ashley was in France, and by the time Ashley returned to his familiar haunts, Morgan had crossed to France to spy for Roxbury and England. And if Morgan had barely escaped from France with a company of dragoons at his heels, Ashley, some three weeks after Morgan had sailed away on the smuggler for America, nearly fell into the hands of the excise men sent to stop his meeting with the English smuggler, Garret. The excise men, like the dragoons, were unsuccessful in catching their quarry and the spring of 1805 found Ashley again in France, this time with the door to England closed against him.

It didn't take Ashley very long to discover precisely *who* had betrayed him, and the knowledge that Morgan seemed to have bested him once more infuriated him and made him long to get the better of his detested cousin just once. *Someday,* he vowed viciously, *someday, my dear cousin, you will pay dearly for disrupting my life and my fortune.* The loss of his lucrative bargain with the French was a blow to Ashley's future, but he was resourceful and immediately reestablished himself within Napoleon's circle, the desire for revenge against Morgan momentarily put aside.

It was an unpleasant shock for Ashley to discover that the French were no longer receptive to his advances, and of course now there was no longer an unending flow of money —he no longer had anything that the French wanted. Fouché was once again in power, though, and Ashley quickly offered his services in helping to ferret out English spies in France. Ever the cynic, Fouché accepted his offer.

Eventually Ashley would have outlived his usefulness and probably would have ended up with a dagger in his back, except for two rather fortunate events.

The first came about quite by accident some weeks later, when he trailed a suspected English informant to the Loire Valley. The gentleman Ashley followed happen to visit with friends who owned a magnificent estate nestled against the gentle rolling hills, and like the good spy that he had become, Ashley grew curious about them. It was then that the first hint of the fortune that might be his came to light. The estate was named simply Château Saint-André and that name struck a cord of memory within Ashley. More questions revealed that the family had all died during the Terror, but one old woman vaguely remembered that a branch of the family had gone to America . . . to Louisiana.

Unable to believe what this might mean, Ashley retreated to a nearby country inn to do some deep thinking. Was it possible that the little chit he had married in the summer of 1799 was the heiress to this estate? And if she was, if he could prove it, how would that benefit him?

It was true that Napoleon, in an effort to weld the remaining aristocracy to him, to lure back the émigrés who had fled to England, had been restoring many of the grand estates confiscated during the Terror. Perhaps the great man might be willing to do the same for an émigré to America. Especially one married to a man who had proved himself a loyal patriot of Napoleon's new France. . . .

Deciding he needed more information, the suspected spy for the moment forgotten, Ashley discreetly questioned the inhabitants of the small village near the Château Saint-André searching for some proof of his suspicions. He found it finally in an old family Bible.

It was a miracle the Bible had survived, and it was only the fact that it had fallen into the hands of one of the loyal members of the Saint-André household that it had not been destroyed when the family had been dragged to the guillotine. The Comte Saint-André's valet had managed to save a few things from the house that terrible day and one of the things he had saved had been that Bible in which were recorded the births and deaths in the Saint-André family for the past hundred years.

Ashley wasn't interested in the past; it was the last entry that riveted his attention, the last entries that dealt with the branch of the family which had emigrated to America. Staring at the spidery, black ink in which Leonie's name and birth were recorded, Ashley's pulse quickened.

By God, what luck! The little bitch *was* the last Saint-

271

André! And he had married her! Under Morgan's name it was true, but *he* had been the one to marry her, not Morgan!

Gaining possession of the Bible proved a bit of a problem; the old valet, while willing to show it to this handsome gentleman, wasn't about to relinquish it. Ashley tried cajolery, bribes, and finally threats. Nothing worked, so he simply stole it.

The Bible safely in his possession, Ashley forced himself to turn to the task at hand—the possible spy staying at the Château Saint-André. But it was the family who lived at the château which now interested him. They would, Ashley reflected coldly, have to be displaced in order to smooth the way for his wife's claim to the estate.

Ashley found out little more on this trip. His quarry left for Paris the next day and Ashley had no choice but to follow him.

In Paris, Ashley reported to Fouché that he had come up with nothing new, and Fouché was not pleased. He was even less pleased when Ashley brought up the subject now dearest to his heart.

Fouché looked across at Ashley with cold eyes as they sat in his office. "Do you really expect me to believe that you are married to this Leonie Saint-André? And more importantly do you really expect that Napoleon is going to turn over to you an estate that has already been given as a reward to someone else? Especially to *you*—an *English* traitor?"

Ashley flushed and his lips tightened. "Napoleon thinks highly of me! And if I can prove that she is my wife, that she is the rightful heiress to the estate, why wouldn't he return it to her? He's returned several other such estates to the legal heirs."

"But not," Fouché said dryly, "estates that have already been disposed of. Forget it! Put your mind to business or you might find that I have no use for you."

Doggedly Ashley argued, "Suppose it turns out that the people who now own it are spies? That they and that young fool I followed are really, as we suspect, working for the English? What then?"

272

Fouché smiled thinly. "That would indeed put a different complexion on the matter."

And that was Ashley's second stroke of luck. With information which he obtained through bribery and murder it was discovered that the new possessors of the Château Saint-André, the family Cloutier, while not spies for the English, were part of an underground group who were planning to assassinate Napoleon.

Almost triumphantly he laid the evidence on Fouché's desk and murmured, "And now what do you say about my wife's claim?"

Fouché sent him a cool, considering look. "I would say, Monsieur Ashley, that *if* you can present Leonie Saint-André here in France, with proof that she is whom you claim—the last Saint-André *and* your wife—then perhaps it is possible that out of gratitude, our glorious Emperor might indeed bestow upon her the estates that had belonged to her family."

Ashley had smiled and bowed. "I leave tomorrow for America and when I return, I shall have everything that you require—the woman and the proof of my marriage and her identity. *Bonjour,* monsieur."

And so, about the time that Morgan had returned to Le Petite from Baton Rouge, Ashley had already been at sea for almost three weeks. Ashley's destination was America, his only purpose once he reached New Orleans, to find Leonie Saint-André and take her back to France with him. At least the finding of Leonie Saint-André was his only purpose until he remembered that he still had a score to settle with his cousin. Perhaps, he thought slowly, while in America, I might find a way to arrange an unpleasant surprise for Morgan.

20

When Leonie learned the next morning that Morgan had returned, she was assailed with a curious rush of pleasure. Instantly, she quelled the emotion and reminded herself sternly that Morgan was her avowed enemy and that he wasn't going to be exactly pleased when he discovered that she had struck the first blow in the battle between them by laying the matter of the dowry before a judge.

And yet, even knowing that, she couldn't quite control her wayward heart, and with fingers that trembled slightly, she dressed that morning with special care, a new sparkle in her sea-green eyes. Suddenly realizing why she was taking such care with her appearance, she immediately stopped Mercy from completing the elaborate arrangement of her curls and glared in the mirror. *Mon Dieu, but I am a fool!*

Ignoring Mercy's protests, she jumped up from the dressing table stool and agitatedly smoothed down her gown. "I've changed my mind—I don't want you to put my hair up after all," she said, angry with herself for caring how she looked to Morgan.

She had put on the pretty lavender gown which she usually wore in the evenings, not wanting to greet her returned husband in the yellow gown she had worn so often, but her anger with herself was such that she almost even changed into the old yellow gown. Only Mercy's shriek of outrage stopped her.

Flustered at her own contradictory actions, she dismissed the maid somewhat tartly, and crossly undid Mercy's half completed work with her hair. Brushing the thick wavy mass, she made a face in the mirror. Bah! What did it matter whether her hair was fashionably arranged or not? Who would care?

Putting down the brush and feeling a bit more in control of herself she readied herself to leave the sanctuary of her room, aware that she had deliberately dawdled overlong in the hope that she could quash the maddening bubble of excitement lodged in her chest. It apparently wasn't going to go away, but with a defiant toss of her head, she marched from the room.

Meeting Morgan with Justin in his arms just outside the door to her rooms did nothing to restore her equilibrium. Her breath catching in her throat at the unexpected sight of him, she barely managed to stammer, "M-m-monsieur, *bon jour!*" Then feeling foolish she rushed on, "Mercy told me that you had returned. Did you enjoy your trip?"

Morgan hadn't known what his reactions would be when he saw Leonie again, but he had been fairly certain that anger would definitely be one of his emotions. What he hadn't expected was the painful tightening of his chest and the shocking feeling as if his heart had suddenly ceased to beat.

When he had finally fallen asleep, he had slept deeply and soundly, waking to the exuberant greeting Justin usually reserved for his mother. As soon as Justin had learned that his papa was home he had burst into the room, confident of his welcome, and had proceeded to jump and bounce on Morgan's big bed with such cheerful enthusiasm that Morgan pushed aside the thought of further sleep.

Justin was so patently delighted to see him that Morgan stilled the reprimand which had hovered on his lips and instead had suddenly found his arms full of a squirmy little boy. Hugging Morgan in a stranglehold, Justin had confessed disarmingly, "Ah, papa, I have missed you *so!*"

A rush of emotion so fierce that it frightened him surged through Morgan's body as Justin hugged him, and hugging the child back he was conscious of how wonderful that warm, wiggling small form felt in his arms. How wonderful and how *right!* And in that moment he stopped fighting. Stopped trying to find reasons for keeping himself at a distance. Momentarily, he stilled the black suspicions that swirled in his brain and let himself be charmed by Justin.

And as he dressed, with Justin chatting merrily on a stool nearby, watching every move Morgan made, it occured to him he could simply stop fighting the entire situation. Why not give in, and see where it led? He was so *damned* tired of looking for hidden snares, of seeing something sinister in everything that Leonie did.

Why *not* give in to the attraction he knew existed between them? And, he reflected sardonically as he shrugged into a form-fitting coat of tobacco brown, wouldn't a seeming capitulation throw his little wife into disorder?

The decision had seemed so simple when he had made it that morning and yet now that he had set the plan in motion, now that he was on the brink of carrying it out, he had second thoughts. Leonie was so appealing and enchanting as she stood there before him, the tawny curls tumbling carelessly about her slim shoulders and the green eyes so beguiling between the thick silky lashes, that for at least a second, Morgan's mind went blank. Blank except for the startling knowledge that he was, he very much feared, on the brink of falling in love with this infuriating little baggage.

Unconsciously clasping Justin tighter in his arms, he said slowly and truthfully, "No, I didn't enjoy my trip." Sending her a searching glance, he added coolly, "It would have been much more pleasant if you and our son had been with me."

Leonie's eyes flew to his, puzzlement obvious in their depths. The deep blue eyes met hers steadily and she was suddenly aware of the thick, pounding beat of her heart. Shaken by what his words might mean, she swallowed nervously and hastily looked away from his compelling gaze, saying hurriedly, "Justin missed you. Not a day went by that he didn't wish that you were home."

Justin nodded in happy agreement, his little arms squeezing Morgan's neck uncomfortably. *"Oui!* Papa I *did* miss you so much!"

The strange moment of unexpected intimacy between the two had been shattered by Justin's innocent intrusion and conscious of the fact that he wasn't quite ready to examine his feelings or motives too closely, Morgan grinned at Justin and said, "And I, bratling, missed you!" Slanting a sly glance at Leonie, Morgan asked softly, "Did you perhaps miss me too, sweetheart?"

Leonie opened her mouth to return a scathing reply, but under Justin's interested stare she didn't dare and so in a gruff little voice, she muttered, *"Oui,* monsieur."

Morgan was aware of the reason behind her answer and smiling to himself, he took blatant advantage of Justin's presence, saying with a mocking gleam in his eyes, "I missed you too, my dear—there wasn't a moment of the time during which I was away that you and Justin weren't in my thoughts."

That his teasing remark had been closer to the truth than he would have liked annoyed him, but he didn't have to worry that he had revealed a weakness for her to use against him because the expression on Leonie's face made it glaringly apparent that she didn't believe a word of what he had said. But that she was perplexed by his actions was obvious from the uncertain, baffled look she sent him.

Suddenly feeling inordinately pleased with the situation, Morgan further destroyed Leonie's composure by saying, "Justin and I were on our way to find you. We have decided to try out the new gig that arrived while I was gone, and we would like you to come with us. I've even had Mammy pack a light repast to take along."

The refusal was on her lips in an instant, but again Justin, as Morgan had known he would, leaped into the fray, "Ah, maman, you *must* come with us, *oui?* It will be most fun, just you and me and papa! Yes, you will come?" he asked eagerly.

What could Leonie say? Throwing Morgan a fulminating glance she said with far more lightness than she felt, "Of course, *mon fils,* I will gladly come with *you."*

Justin let out a happy gurgle of laughter and wiggled out of Morgan's arms. "I will tell Abraham to bring the gig around to the front of the house, *oui?"*

"Yes, you do that," Morgan answered easily. "Your maman and I will be right behind you, and then we shall be off for the day."

Leonie barely let Justin disappear out of sight before she turned on Morgan. "You planned that!" she spat angrily, the sea-green eyes ablaze with golden flecks.

Morgan smiled seraphically. "But of course, my dear! Can you think of anything more pleasant for us all to do?" he said innocently. "After all, I have been gone for several days; isn't it logical that I would want to spend the day with my family after being away from them?"

Her eyes narrowed, she asked bluntly, "Did you see Dominic last night? Did he tell you that I have gone to see a judge?"

Some of Morgan's amusement fled and in a harder voice he returned just as bluntly, "Yes, I saw Dominic last night—I take it you did know he was sneaking into the house?"

Leonie gave him a scornful glance. "But of course, monsieur. I am not stupid!"

"No, I'll grant you that, but tell me if you will why you didn't confront him?" Morgan asked curiously.

Leonie shrugged. "If I had he would have found another way and it seemed simpler to let him think he was getting away with his little plan." Some of her anger fading, she asked uncertainly this time, "Did he tell you that I had been to see Judge Dangermond?"

Taking her arm politely and guiding her towards the stairs, Morgan replied noncommitally, "Yes, he told me."

Shooting him a considering glance, and seeing no sign of fury on the lean dark features, she blurted out with confusion, "And you're not angry?"

"No, I don't think I am," Morgan returned reflectively. "Enraged would be perhaps a better word."

Startled at how unemotionally he said the words Leonie nearly stumbled as they walked down the stairs, but Morgan's hand tightened on her arm preventing her from falling. The perplexity she felt written across her expressive little features, she said nothing for several seconds; then when it was apparent that he wasn't going to elaborate, she said helplessly, "You don't *appear* enraged, monsieur."

Morgan smiled down at her, the look in the dark-blue eyes causing her heart to race . . . and not with fear. There was a brief flicker of something in the depths of those blue eyes that made her suddenly conscious of his lithe tall body walking so easily next to hers, and she glanced away in complete bewilderment. What was he up to now? Why was he being so—so . . . charming? Too charming, she thought with a small spurt of anger.

Aware of the confusion she felt, Morgan continued to smile at her and replied calmly, "No, I don't, do I?"

Growing a little angry at the lightness with which he was treating their reunion, as well as the news that she had laid the business of the dowry before a magistrate, she demanded fiercely, "What game are you playing at, monsieur? What do you hope to gain?"

His smile fading, the blue eyes suddenly very hard, he said grimly, "I think those are questions you would do well to ask yourself! And I should warn you, cat-eyes, that no one has ever gotten the better of me!"

They were in the main hall of the house and the butler was just swinging open the wide double doors when Morgan finished speaking. Leonie threw her husband a look of utter loathing, but she remained silent as Justin, his face alight with excitement and pleasure, came bounding through the opened doors.

"There you are!" he said excitedly. "I thought you were *never* coming! Hurry, hurry, Abraham says the horses are restless and that we shouldn't keep them standing."

"Abraham . . . or Justin?" Morgan murmured, a hint of laughter in his voice.

Justin looked guilty, but then smiling sunnily, he said simply, "*I* wanted you to hurry."

Moments later the three of them were comfortably seated in the shiny new gig and riding away from Le Petit, Justin ecstatically ensconced between Leonie and Morgan. Conversation proved to be no trouble; Justin's happy prattle covered any awkwardness that might have existed between the two adults. And by the time his rapid-fire questions and exclamations had slowed to a more normal rate, Leonie had recovered her equanimity and was able to converse just as if there were nothing of any importance on her mind.

There was a great deal on her mind though, and she

279

couldn't help the perplexed glances she occasionally sent Morgan when she thought he wasn't aware of her. What was he up to? That question kept reverberating through her mind, even when she was smiling charmingly up at him or answering a question of Justin's.

Morgan handled the spirited pair of matched chestnut geldings effortlessly, his good mood such that he even set Justin upon his lap and let the child try his small hands at the reins. Justin was delighted and seemed disinclined to release them when Morgan had decided the road ahead required a firmer touch.

Giving Justin a smiling look, he murmured, "Soon enough, my son, you'll have your own pair but until then, you'll only drive when and for as long as I want you to."

A mutinous expression on his face, which reminded Morgan vividly of Leonie, Justin started to protest such high-handed treatment, but Leonie distracted him by saying, "Oh, look, Justin, there's a fox over there."

The possible squabble instantly forgotten, Justin watched with wide-eyed interest as a small red fox disappeared into the underbrush.

While they rode quietly down the tree-lined road, Leonie found herself relaxing more and more, a real smile now and then curving her lips at the teasing remarks Morgan directed towards Justin.

Their ride seemed aimless and after a bit Leonie asked idly, "Are we going anywhere in particular?"

"Eventually I have a destination in mind, but for the moment, no. For the moment, I am simply giving you and Justin a tour of Bonheur." Morgan answered easily.

It was a pleasant drive under the towering oaks and chestnut trees, the scent of honeysuckle now and then wafting in the warm air. Fortunately it was still fairly early, and the day had not yet reached its full heat.

Despite the nagging curiosity about their destination, Leonie enjoyed Morgan's commentary as he showed them about the plantation, and while she was still suspicious of his motives, she had to admit that he had certainly set out to please them.

It was only on their return journey to Le Petit that the first tremor of unease shot through her body. Upon reaching the house, instead of turning into the drive which led to the stables, Morgan kept the horses on the narrow road that ran in front of the house and drove smartly past the estate.

"Where are we going now?" she asked a little sharply.

Morgan grinned at her. "We haven't eaten the food that Mammy packed for us. I know of a particularly nice spot where we can have a picnic." A mocking gleam in his eyes, he murmured, "I'm certain you'll remember it."

Leonie did remember it, and filled with memories she would have given everything not to have, she let Morgan help her down from the gig.

The blue pool of water beckoned just as delightfully as she remembered; the waterfall fell just as cheerfully and the huge, leafy sycamore spread its shade softly on the mat of green clover, just as it had the day Morgan had made love to her. A bright flush of embarrassment staining her cheeks, she glared at him resentfully as he cheerfully laid out the quilt he had brought along and set down the basket of food.

Justin was enchanted with the place, and in no time at all, he was busily exploring under the wild plum trees and peering intently through the blackberry vines, completely oblivious to the adults.

Leonie stood stubbornly near the gig for several minutes. His jacket laid aside and comfortably lounging beneath the tree, his hands behind his dark head, Morgan said provocatively, "I'm hardly likely to attack you with Justin here. And while you're a ravishing piece of femininity, I'm afraid my hunger at the moment is for food . . . and not the other pleasures of the body."

Her eyes flashing retribution, Leonie stalked stiffly over to the gaily colored quilt and angrily plunked herself down as far away from Morgan as she could. His low chuckle of laughter and the gleam in the sapphire-blue eyes did nothing to soothe her temper.

But by the time Justin rejoined them and they had all enjoyed the delicious repast Mammy had packed—golden fried chicken, sharp yellow cheese, crusty bread, a jug of lemonade, and ripe cherries and juicy sweet strawberries, Leonie was too sated and relaxed to start any arguments.

Like a sleepy-eyed kitten she sat curled up near the edge of the quilt, halfheartedly trying to keep awake.

Justin had already given into the temptation and he was sprawled not too far away from Morgan's feet, his small face slightly flushed from the humid heat of the day.

Idly Morgan watched Leonie try to fight off sleep and finally with a lazy laugh, in one swift smooth motion he reached over and pulled her against him. Her head resting on his chest, he said drowsily, "Go to sleep, Leonie—I intend to, and Justin already has."

Surprisingly she did just that—the heat of the day, the full stomach, and the somnolent drone of the insects all made it impossible not to. And that she slept curled next to the strong body of the man she mistrusted most in the world didn't, at the moment, seem to bother her at all.

She woke first, about two hours later, the arm that Morgan had flung over her as he slept pressing across her breasts. Gingerly, trying not to waken him, she edged his arm off her and quickly scooted a little distance away. Wide awake now, she glanced around instantly for Justin, relaxing as her eyes caught sight of him still sleeping soundly near Morgan's feet.

Irresistibly, her gaze traveled to Morgan and a curious feeling of tenderness swept over her as she watched him sleep. How different he looks, she thought tremulously, noting the way a lock of the heavy black hair lay across his brow and the shocking length of the surprisingly feminine dark lashes that shadowed his cheeks. In sleep his face was softer, far more approachable, the suspicion and hardness of those blue eyes hidden beneath his lids and the full mouth not having the grim slant to it she saw so often.

Compulsively, before she even thought of it, she reached out and gently touched the sensual curve of his bottom lip with one finger, a soft, reminiscent smile curving her own mouth. Feeling very brave with him asleep, she allowed her fingers lightly to touch the curve of one lean cheek, liking the feel of his skin under her fingertips. With a longing she was hardly aware of, she stared at him, loving him and hating him, wanting him and yet determined not to let her body rule her mind.

Justin stirred in his sleep, and not wanting him to wake

Morgan, she quickly moved away, quietly hushing Justin when he would have spoken out loud. Whispering she said, "Let monsieur sleep; it was very late when he arrived last night. Shall we explore the pool?"

That suited Justin just fine and like silent conspirators they crept away, leaving Morgan sleeping more peacefully than he had in days. The two of them removed their footwear and Justin waded almost to his knees into the pool; Leonie, mindful of the last time Morgan had found her with her skirts hitched up about her waist, only lifted the hem of her gown slightly and stuck her toes in the cool water.

The hot sun beat down on her uncovered head and, for one wild moment, she wanted to strip off the confining gown and slip naked into the blue depths of the pool, but Morgan's presence stopped her. It didn't, however, stop Justin, and with Leonie's laughing permission he flung off his clothes and like a small golden pagan he frolicked in the water for some time.

It was the sound of Justin's laughter that eventually woke Morgan. For a moment he blinked sleepily up at the branches of the sycamore tree before his eyes caught sight of Leonie and Justin. A small smile lifted the corner of his mouth as he watched Justin splash and paddle in the water.

Leonie too made him smile, the expression on her face making it obvious that under different circumstances, she also would have shed her clothes and taken the same pagan enjoyment of the pool that Justin did. The glimpse of her bare feet beneath the hem of her gown caused his smile to widen and for one wicked moment he considered suggesting to her that they *both* join Justin.

Regretfully, he relinquished the idea and indolently assumed a sitting position. As he idly chewed a blade of grass, the disturbing thought occurred to him that he had never seen his own son play with such natural abandon. Stephanie wouldn't have allowed it, and Morgan frowned at the comparison that was shaping in his mind. Almost angrily he pushed the annoying thoughts aside. Damnit, Leonie *wasn't* his wife, and Justin wasn't his son, so there were no comparisons to make!

He lounged there for some minutes, enjoying the sight of Leonie and Justin, and wondering how she was going to react to his plans for the rest of the day. Even with Justin along to halfway guarantee her good behavior, he rather thought he was going to have his hands full.

Morgan wasn't deliberately using Justin to control Leonie, but he had to admit, he *was* taking advantage of her obvious love for the child. There was no way in hell that she would have consented to come for a ride alone with him, but in front of Justin . . . ah, that was a different matter.

The plan hadn't sprung full blown in his mind, but that morning a glimmer of an idea had occurred to him. He had been in his office riffling through some correspondence when a note from his mother telling him of the ball being held the next evening for Aaron Burr attracted his attention.

He had been disappointed that there was nothing from Jason, even though he knew there had been barely enough time for Jason to have received his letter, but the note from Noelle had aroused his curiosity. What in the devil was the ex-vice-president doing in Natchez? And why in the hell had his mother thought he and Leonie would like to attend a ball in Burr's honor?

Sighing, Morgan had tossed the note aside, Aaron Burr the least of his worries, Leonie and Justin uppermost in his mind. Staring blankly out the French doors, he had admitted to himself that his decision earlier this morning not to fight against the silken chains Leonie was weaving about him wasn't going to be easy to carry out. For one thing, his little wife was going to view every move he made with suspicion, and, a cynical smile crossing his face, he had admitted she had good reason.

Certainly she wasn't going to accept any advances he made . . . and that was when the idea of combining his desire to spend the day with Justin and his equal desire to disarm Justin's mother occurred to him. Why not simply include Leonie in the plans that he had made with the boy? In Justin's presence it was highly unlikely that she would refuse to accompany them.

Pleased with himself, Morgan had left the office and immediately set his plans in motion, just about the time Leonie was hearing of his arrival. He had made a swift trip to Bonheur to have an interesting conversation with mother, a conversation which slightly expanded his original plan.

Noelle, her pretty dark eyes seeking understanding, had said, "Morgan, I was not being critical of your wife nor was I trying to make judgments about her! But if it's escaped your notice that Leonie possesses only three gowns, it hasn't escaped mine. I suggested to her that as the wife of a very rich man there would be nothing wrong with her ordering a few new gowns." Throwing him a resentful look she added, "And I *was* tactful!"

Smiling lightly down into her ruffled features, he had said, soothingly, "I'm certain you were." Then cocking an eyebrow at her, he asked, "Am I to believe that her refusal stopped you from doing anything further?"

A guilty expression flitted across his mother's face. "N-n-no," she got out uncomfortably. "I did go ahead and have Mercy give me Leonie's measurements, and I've had Mrs. Dobson start a limited wardrobe for her." Somewhat defiantly she added, "For the boy and Yvette too!"

"I see. And now I take it you need my help?" Morgan had inquired mockingly.

"Well, yes, you see, several of the gowns are ready to be fitted. . . ." Her voice trailed off.

"And you need me to make certain Leonie is there," Morgan finished for her.

"Oh, yes, Morgan! That would be splendid!"

Giving his mother an old-fashioned look, Morgan had said resignedly, "All right. Somehow, and God knows how, I'll get her to Mrs. Dobson's. When?"

"At three?" she had asked hopefully.

"At three it shall be."

It had seemed rather simple when he had discussed it with his mother, but now he wasn't so certain. And glancing at his watch, the small, gold crucifix dangling from the watchchain, he realized that he didn't have much more time before taking Leonie for her fitting. A fitting he was very certain she was going to object to. But with Justin along . . . . He sighed ruefully, hoping it would work.

Standing up, he slowly walked over to where Leonie was

285

watching Justin, his approach so quiet that Leonie didn't even realize he had left the quilt until he was directly behind her. His warm breath on her ear and his arms gently closing around her waist was the first warning she had that he was no longer safely asleep.

Startled, and not liking the way her heart began to race at his nearness, she muttered sharply, "Let me go, monsieur!"

But Morgan ignored her and nuzzled her ear, murmuring, "Mmmm, I think next time we come here, we should leave Justin at the house, don't you?"

Unbearably conscious of his tall, warm body behind hers and the strength of the arms that were clasped loosely about her waist, Leonie was suddenly tongue-tied, one part of her wanting to melt against him and another part of her angry with the way he played with her emotions, furious with herself for responding to his practiced charm.

Stiffly she finally got out, "I do not appreciate your comments, monsieur. And you are an imbecile if you think what happened here once will ever happen again."

"Is that so?" Morgan replied interestedly, as he loosened his hold on her and turned her around to face him.

Her small face set in stubborn lines, she stared up into his dark, handsome features, disliking the amusement she saw in the blue eyes. "Yes, that is so!" she said with unwonted fierceness. "We agreed that ours was not to be a normal marriage. And I have your signature on just such an agreement, monsieur. . . . Force me and I shall give *that* to the judge also!"

"Ah, yes," Morgan said slowly, a half-smile curving his full mouth. "You did mention that there was another agreement, didn't you? You really must show it to me sometime—my lamentable memory, I'm afraid, has allowed me to forget all about ever signing it."

"Your memory is very convenient, monsieur!" Leonie said through gritted teeth.

Morgan grinned at her. "It is, isn't it?"

Leonie took a deep breath, her hands clenching into small determined fists at her side. "You find it amusing now, monsieur, but when Judge Dangermond orders you to repay me my dowry, I wonder if you shall find it quite so laughable."

Infuriatingly he murmured, "We'll just have to wait and see, won't we, sweetheart."

Leonie might have continued the exchange, but Justin came wading up to them at that moment and in the bustle of getting him dried off and dressed, the opportunity was lost.

Seated once more in the gig, Justin between herself and that abominable creature she was married to, Leonie stared stonily ahead. She relaxed slightly as the house came into view, wanting nothing more than to put a great deal of distance between herself and her husband. *Mon Dieu, but he is impossible,* she thought wrathfully. *He smiles when he should rage and jests about the most serious things!*

When Morgan drove smartly by the house, with not even a break in the stride of the horses, Leonie stiffened in her seat, and sending Morgan a look that could have killed, she asked tautly, "More surprises, monsieur?"

Never taking his eyes off the horses, Morgan replied thoughtfully, "Not precisely. An inevitable event, I think, would more correctly describe the situation."

The green eyes beginning to flash with rising temper, Leonie demanded grimly, "And where does this inevitable event take us?"

"Why, to the dressmaker, of course," Morgan said coolly.

21

An ominous silence seemed to engulf the gig. Even Justin felt it, and turning to look up at his mother, he asked uncertainly, "Is something wrong, maman? Don't you want to go to the dressmaker's with us?"

Leonie took a deep, fortifying breath, fighting desperately to hold on to her flaming temper. With an effort she smiled down into Justin's face and said, with as much lightness as she could muster, "But of course I do, *mon coeur!*" Glaring over at Morgan, she added with an edge to her voice, "I just wish your papa had discussed the matter with me first!"

Morgan smiled at her mockingly. "I would have," he said honestly, "but if you'd known, you'd have found an excuse not to come."

"Why?" Justin asked curiously. "Don't you like the dressmaker?"

Leonie gave him a strained little smile. "Yes, yes, naturally I like the dressmaker. It is just that I had other things I'd planned to do this afternoon."

"What?" Justin innocently persisted, and Leonie had to suppress a decidedly unmaternal urge to shake him.

Angry with herself for growing angry with Justin when it wasn't his fault, she resolutely swallowed the rage against Morgan that rose in her throat. Helplessly, she muttered, "I don't remember exactly."

"Well, then," Justin said sunnily, "you can come with us, *oui?*"

Morgan's strangled snort of laughter was almost Leonie's undoing, but beyond glaring at him, she nodded her head yes in answer to Justin's question, and the remainder of the journey into Natchez was without further incident

. . . but only on the surface. *How dare he!* she thought furiously. *To use Justin as a weapon against me!* Angrily she shot Morgan a look, the palm of her hand itching almost uncontrollably with the desire to connect with his face. *Unscrupulous bastard!* If they had been alone . . .

Mrs. Dobson's proved to be a neat white little cottage near the edge of town. A pristine white picket fence surrounded the small house and beautiful, sweet-smelling yellow roses grew rampant across the front of the fence.

Morgan tethered the horses to the painted white iron hitching post, and keeping his face expressionless, he walked around to Leonie's side of the gig and politely helped her down. Catching a glimpse of the chagrin and thwarted temper that raged in her eyes, his lips twitched. Obviously the little madame didn't like being crossed nor, it appeared, did she care much for his unfair tactics.

Concealing his amusement, he pulled her resisting arm through one of his and murmured teasingly, "Mrs. Dobson is quite nice; you don't have to be frightened of her."

Leonie refused to meet his eyes, her exacerbated temper not helped in the least by Justin's happy acceptance of the situation. Unaware of the currents passing between the adults, he skipped merrily along at Morgan's side.

Feeling like a condemned prisoner, Leonie allowed Morgan to escort her into Mrs. Dobson's parlor. It was a cozy room, cheerful chintz curtains hanging at the windows and an obviously prized blue wool carpet covering the wooden floor. The room smelled of fresh air and beeswax, and the simple oak furniture gleamed with the deep shine that only repeated polishing could give it.

Mrs. Dobson, a plump widow with four daughters to raise, greeted them pleasantly, her expert seamstress' eye running over Leonie's slim figure and Justin's sturdy little body. A pleased smile wreathing her round, kind face, she said delightfully, "I think that several of the items will fit with hardly any alterations. How fortunate!" And seeing that Justin was appraising the room with the look of a young gentleman about to embark upon mischief, she said brightly, "Perhaps we can have Master Justin try on his clothing first?" Pointing to several fashion plates with swatches of material attached to them, she added,

"Your mother-in-law had only ordered certain things that she felt were the most necessary and, if you like, you may look through those plates for additional clothing."

Leonie stiffened and Mrs. Dobson had barely disappeared with Justin in tow before she rounded on Morgan. *"How dare you Slades!* How dare you and your mother go behind my back this way! We do not need your charity, monsieur! Give me my dowry and we shall be gone and you will not have to be embarrassed by our appearance! *Mon Dieu,* but you Slades are arrogant and overbearing!"

Morgan regarded her thoughtfully. If she was acting she was giving a magnificent performance, and almost idly he asked, "Why should the gift of a few gowns for yourself and breeches for the boy distress you? I am a rich man, as you well know, and as you've admitted money is your one reason for being here, why should you object if I choose to spend some of it on you?"

Leonie drew herself up proudly. "We want nothing from you, monsieur, except what is rightfully ours—my dowry!" she spat furiously.

"Why not consider the clothes part of the dowry?" Morgan countered, conscious of both the desire to shake her silly and kiss her senseless.

"Clothes!" Leonie said with loathing. "You think I would waste the money on clothes?" she asked incredulously.

"What would you use the money for?" he demanded bluntly. "Jewels? A larger carriage than all the other ladies possess?"

"There is only one thing that money will be used for," Leonie replied fervently. "Château Saint-André!"

Sardonically Morgan said, "Ah, yes, the ancestral acres. How stupid of me to have forgotten."

Leonie flinched at his words and, turning away from him, she said tonelessly, "You do not believe me, but it is true."

"As true as that marriage certificate you've thrust under my nose?" Morgan inquired cynically.

Her eyes flashing, Leonie spun around to face him. Approaching him, she snapped, "You, sir, are despicable! I wish I had never laid eyes on you!"

His own temper fraying, Morgan grasped one of her

wrists and jerked her up next to him. "You no more than I," he snarled.

She was too tempting that close to him, and throwing caution to the winds, with something between a curse and a groan, his mouth captured hers in a kiss which punished and promised heaven at the same time. It had been unwise to touch her, he realized immediately, to feel her soft lips under his. The intoxicating nearness of that slim body which had haunted his dreams unleashed such a flood of achingly sweet desire that Morgan forgot everything but the woman in his arms.

The effect of that kiss was just as devastating to Leonie. Helplessly she fought to deny the rising tide of desire his touch evoked. Without volition her body pressed itself ardently to his, and when Morgan's arms tightened around her, she gave a small sigh of satisfaction, her lips responding to the hungry demand of his.

As Morgan deepened the kiss her breasts seemed fuller, more sensitive, and she was conscious of the sweet swirl of desire in her loins. Eagerly she returned his kiss, all of her passionate nature aroused; hungry for him, her fingers grasped his dark hair; unconsciously she moved her hips against his groin, excited and pleased to feel proof that he was as aroused as she was.

But even as Leonie gave herself up to the pleasure of his caress, the reality of the fact that she was blindly responding to the man she had the most reason in the world to distrust suddenly burst upon her, and with a choked little cry, she tore herself out of his arms. Putting several feet between them, she looked back at him with self-loathing and disgust. Her breath coming in short little gasps, she said fiercely, "You are not to touch me, monsieur! You promised and I shall not allow it! Touch me again and I will do something that will make you sorry you every laid a finger on me!"

Morgan froze and regarded her stonily as the desire that had swept through him so urgently only a moment ago began to die. His breathing was uneven and there was a glitter in the blue eyes which made Leonie distinctly uneasy. "You little bitch!" he said coldly. "Is it part of the plan to tempt and tease me too? Am I to be brought to my knees by desire for your little golden body? Is that the next step?"

Her expression puzzled and angry at the same time, Leonie snapped hotly, "I do not know what you are talking about, monsieur!"

Morgan gave a mirthless laugh, his lips twisting into an ugly sneer. "Now why do I have trouble believing that?" The blue eyes swept over her contemptuously. "You knew exactly what you were doing when you responded to my kiss. But be careful playing that particular trick, sweetheart. We might not be in such a public place the next time and then, you can be sure, I won't let you take back what you were so generously offering."

Leonie's bosom swelled with furious indignation. Holding on to her temper with an effort, she said tightly, "You will take me back to Le Petit *immediately,* monsieur! I do not want to stay here and certainly I do not want gowns that *you* have bought!"

His own temper hardly better held in than Leonie's, Morgan's face set in a hard line. "No," he said slowly, emphatically. "You're my wife, remember? And as my wife you will dress appropriately."

Leonie lifted her head proudly. "Bah! You care so much for what people will think?"

A grim little smile curved Morgan's mouth. "No, cat-eyes. I don't give a damn what people think, but I think that you do."

"What do you mean?" she demanded with a frown.

Morgan shrugged carelessly. "Just that you hope to use your lack of attire to your own advantage." His voice like steel, he added, "But you're not going to, my dear. You're going to try on the gowns that Mrs. Dobson has ready and we're going to select several more." Leonie's mouth opened in heated protest, but Morgan sent her a freezing look. "And if you don't cooperate," he finished savagely, "I'll take you in the fitting room and strip you myself."

The expression on his face made Leonie swallow nervously. *Mon Dieu, but he would,* she thought helplessly. Knowing when she was beaten, with a nonchalant air that didn't fool him, she said indifferently, "Very well, monsieur, I will do it. If you wish to soothe your conscience this way, it is no concern of mine. . . . And it makes no difference as far as the dowry is concerned. You still owe me the full amount."

A mocking smile on his mouth, Morgan bowed politely. "We'll just have to wait and see about that, won't we?"

Leonie would have liked to continue the argument and she would have been delighted to find fault with everything that Mrs. Dobson had done. Unfortunately, she couldn't; the work was exquisite and Leonie was much too feminine not to appreciate the lovely garments.

Undergarments frothing with lace and ribbons were displayed for her selection, in addition to several nightgowns which made her catch her breath in pleasure. Noelle had commissioned only two ball gowns, one of an ever-changing amber-bronze silk that made Leonie feel like a queen, and another of a beautiful hue of moss green satin, that intensified the color of Leonie's eyes. Several day gowns had been selected and, while there were still many which were incomplete, six of the gowns could be made ready by the next day, Mrs. Dobson said cheerfully. The amber-bronze ball gown needed only an adjustment to the hem and then it too, would be sent along with the others to Le Petit. Looking at the moss-green gown, Mrs. Dobson remarked regretfully, "I'm afraid it'll take a few days longer for this one. Even as fast as my girls ply their needles, it will be next Wednesday before I can have it delivered. Will that be all right?"

When Leonie didn't answer, her gaze held spellbound by the gorgeous array of clothing, Morgan answered dryly, "I think that'll be just fine."

Leonie tried to resist the appeal of the beautiful things laid before her, but she was only human. Like a starving waif at a feast, she sat and stared with hungry eyes as the lovely garments were shown to her, almost dazedly agreeing with every suggestion Mrs. Dobson made. Several more gowns were selected from the fashion plates and swatches of material. Nearly numb with pleasure, Leonie could only nod her head in stunned accord with the various trims, laces, and embellishments which Mrs. Dobson recommended as finishing touches to the gowns. The question of shoes and slippers was discussed, Mrs. Dobson cheerfully measuring Leonie's small foot and saying that she would see that several pairs of footwear were purchased and sent along.

It was only when she tried on the different gowns and, under Mrs. Dobson's friendly eyes, had been forced to parade in front of Morgan that Leonie's enjoyment faded. Justin's presence helped and, though he got rather bored, his enthusiasm for the amber-bronze ball gown was almost as great as Leonie's.

"Oh, maman!" he cried rapturously. "You are very beautiful, *oui?*" Turning to look up at Morgan he demanded, "She is, yes, papa?"

A peculiar expression in his eyes, his gaze never leaving Leonie's face, Morgan said huskily, "Yes, she is. Incredibly lovely."

Morgan was not just being polite; Leonie *was* incredibly lovely as she stood there before them. Her shoulders rose beguilingly from above the low-cut bodice, and the excellent fit of the gown cupped her small breasts lovingly. A high waistline, just beneath the bosom, hid her slender waist, but the fashionably slim skirt cunningly, yet discreetly, revealed the gentle swell of her hips. There was an added glow to her skin, the amber-bronze color intensifying the golden flecks in her eyes, even making the tawny hair shine like warmed honey as it tumbled about her shoulders.

Staring at her, Morgan was aware of his quickened breathing, but even more than that, he was aware of the sharp stab of pain in the region of his heart. She was so damned lovely, and he wanted her desperately . . . regardless of the game she was playing.

Leonie's face was the picture of bemused pleasure as she reverently touched the skirt. Her intense delight in wearing such a beautiful gown pushed Morgan's hateful presence from her mind, and watching her, seeing her enjoyment of the gown, Morgan felt a queer tenderness sweep through his body. He'd buy her hundreds of gowns just to keep that look on her face, he vowed, then laughed with silent mockery at himself.

And yet . . . The look on her face troubled him and he suddenly had the unsettling thought that she had never before in her life possessed anything quite as lovely. Perhaps those old gowns she and Yvette wore *were* the only gowns they had, he mused slowly. Then, angry with himself for allowing himself to be moved by what must be a clever act, he glanced away and said lightly to Mrs. Dobson, "Your work is to be complimented. And if the other gowns and fripperies are of this quality, I'm certain my wife will be most pleased."

Leonie was silent during the journey to the house and even Justin seemed disinclined to chatter away with his usual ebullience. Morgan was busy with his own thoughts and consequently there was little conversation as they drove home.

Once they reached the house, they went their separate ways. Morgan took the gig to the stables; Justin scampered off happily in search of his dinner, and Leonie sought out the quiet sanctuary of the summerhouse to sort out her thoughts.

Curled up in one of the woven-cane chairs of the summerhouse, she stared blankly through the wisteria-draped lattices, wondering at Morgan's inexplicable behavior. *He has changed again,* she thought with angry perplexity. *He was so hard and ugly to me before he left to visit Thousand Oaks and now* . . . Her little face was wistful. *And now he is being so charming . . . so . . . so . . . kind.* She frowned at that idea, her fierce pride wanting no *kindness* from Monsieur Slade.

Moodily she broke off a clump of the purple wisteria and unconsciously began to strip off the tiny clusters of flowers. Why hadn't he been angry about her visit to Judge Dangermond? she wondered again uneasily. And why, dear God, she suddenly thought erratically, do I find him so attractive?

She knew the answer to that particular question and she didn't like it one bit! *Mon Dieu, but I will not be in love with him!*

But telling herself not to be in love with him was easier than actually doing it, and Leonie was grimly aware of that fact. *I am a fool,* she finally decided. *I have let my emotions become involved in what was and is purely a business transaction. I shall not,* she vowed tightly, *make that mistake in my future dealings with Monsieur Slade!*

Feeling more confident within herself than she had in days, Leonie left the summerhouse and walked slowly toward the house, her thoughts busy with plans for the straightforward, practical, businesslike manner she would now display toward Monsieur Slade. *I shall treat him with cool, polite disdain,* she concluded firmly. *Certainly I shall not allow him to maneuver me as he did today.*

Reaching her rooms, after a visit to the nursery where Justin had been installed in regal splendor, Leonie ordered a bath, and it was while she was emerged in the warm frothy water that she decided there would be no more of this polite dining together and the semblance of a happy marriage. *Non!* she would no longer take part in this ridiculous facade.

Rising somewhat abruptly from the rose-scented water, she brushed aside Mercy's offer of help and said quietly, "I will not need you further tonight. I have decided to remain in my rooms for the evening. Please have Mammy prepare a tray for me and have one of the servants bring it up in an hour."

Mercy's black face was puzzled, but recognizing the stubborn expression, she shrugged her shoulders and did as she was told.

When Morgan entered the dining room that evening he was unpleasantly surprised to find Yvette, Robert, and Dominic the only occupants besides the servants. Cocking an eyebrow he asked, "Is Leonie delayed?"

Yvette shot him a nervous glance and said in her soft voice, "Leonie will not be joining us this evening. She, she—" Yvette stopped and then added helplessly, "she said she was indisposed when I stopped in to see her just before I came downstairs."

"I see," Morgan said in a hard tone. "Well then, as my wife will not be gracing us with her lovely presence, shall we all be seated?" And looking at his brothers he remarked dryly, "You really must tell me sometime, how it is that I find you at *my* house and table far more than I do at your own?"

Robert blushed, and cleared his throat uncomfortably, but Dominic merely grinned and murmured audaciously, "Morgan, don't you know? We've *missed* you! How could you think it was anything else but a natural desire for your company?"

Morgan snorted, but there was a gleam of mocking amusement in the blue eyes.

There was no amusement in his eyes a few hours later though, as he stood in front of the window in his bedroom and glared down into the darkness. What sort of game was she playing now? he wondered with helpless frustration.

He'd known she would be angry with the way he had blatantly used her affection for Justin to gain his own way, but there had been times during the day when he had thought she had enjoyed herself. And even despite the acrimonious exchange between them at Mrs. Dobson's, and Leonie's obvious dislike of being forced to accept the clothing, during their ride home together he hadn't felt that she had been unduly infuriated—subdued was more like it. Or calculating . . . ?

Furiously he swung away from the window, unwilling to let all the ugly suspicions about her destroy the pleasure this day had given him. No, he would not begin anew the battle within himself. And yet, *why* hadn't she joined them for dinner? Why had she kept herself aloof from this evening?

A frown beginning to pucker his brow, he absently lit a thin, aromatic cheroot, the wispy cloud of blue smoke circling his dark head. Perhaps she really was indisposed.

Impatiently stubbing out the cheroot, thoughtfully he eyed the set of double doors that connected his room with hers. Doors that he had never opened. But if she were ill . . .

Telling himself repeatedly that his only reason for entering her rooms at this hour of the night was to assure himself of her well-being, Morgan walked slowly over to the doors and opened them.

Almost total blackness met his gaze. The slim sliver of the new moon barely gave enough light to illuminate the dark, looming shapes of the furniture. Quietly he walked further into the room, his eyes rapidly adjusting to the darkness.

Despite the newness of the moon, a thin shaft of silver light streamed through the pair of French doors which led to the veranda and fell across the silk-swathed bed, the ruby color of the silk hardly discernible. Morgan's eyes were drawn irresistibly to the place where Leonie lay sleeping, and like a man in a trance he silently approached the bed.

Standing there at the side of her bed, he stared at the sweet picture she made, the slight illumination from the moon caressing her delicate features.

Her face was turned into the pillow, the tawny hair flowing like living gold down her back; the moonlight etched the lovely profile, the high forehead, the straight little nose, and the impudent mouth. The old cotton shift she had worn to bed left her arms bare, and in her sleep it had slipped to uncover one slim shoulder and revealed the slight swell of her small breast.

Staring at her, wanting her, Morgan was aware of some emotion akin to pain that slashed through him. Why, oh God, did she have to come into his life? And why having come into his life, did she have to be such a lovely, bewitching little liar?

He started to turn away, but Leonie, perhaps sensing a presence, tossed restlessly in her sleep and made a small sound of distress. Morgan's reaction was instinctive and lightly he touched her and said softly, "Hush, sweetheart, I won't hurt you."

The sound of his voice as well as his touch on her shoulder woke Leonie instantly and with wide startled eyes, she gazed up at the shadowy figure bending over her. Still half-asleep she didn't recognize Morgan and for one terrifying second she was reminded of the night she had lost her virginity. With a violent movement, her balled fist struck out viciously and connected with Morgan's mouth, splitting his lip.

"Jesus Christ!" he swore painfully under his breath, his hands automatically capturing her flailing arms before

298

she could inflict more damage. "Calm down, tigress!" he muttered as Leonie, fought blindly to escape.

Suddenly, realizing who it was, she stilled instantly in his hands and uncertainly inquired, "Monsieur? Is that you?"

Morgan laughed ruefully. "Yes, cat-eyes, I'm afraid it is."

"What are you doing here?" she demanded and then a note of apprehension in her voice she asked, "Justin? Is something wrong with Justin?"

Morgan shook his head in the darkness, and then realizing she couldn't see the motion he said quickly, "No, he's fine."

Aware of the warmth of his hands on her arms and the way his nearness was affecting her, Leonie hastily shrugged out of his slackened hold. "If nothing is wrong with Justin, why are you here?" she asked tartly, wishing her heart wasn't beating with such an erratic rhythm.

Wryly Morgan admitted, "I came to see if you were ill. When you didn't join us for dinner I was . . . concerned."

"Were you?" Leonie asked incredulously, never once having considered that possibility.

"Mmmm," Morgan replied absently. "Do you have a lamp nearby?" he asked. "I dislike talking to you in the dark."

Momentarily forgetting the animosity between them, Leonie scrambled across the bed and reached for the tall candle beside her bed. It took only a moment to light it, and then turning back to Morgan and seeing for the first time the damage she had inflicted upon him, she cried softly, "Oh, monsieur! Your lip! It is all bloody!"

"I rather thought it would be," Morgan said resignedly, reaching up to touch it somewhat gingerly. "Remind me," he murmured ruefully, "not to awake you so suddenly in the future. It could become quite embarrassing explaining how I came by my wounds."

Feeling guilty for having hurt him when he was only being considerate, Leonie offered anxiously, "Let me cleanse it for you." And before Morgan could protest, she was out of bed to get water from the pitcher that sat on the

299

marble-topped washstand. Grabbing the towel that lay nearby, she hurried back to him.

Kneeling on the bed, the bowl of water nestled precariously on her pillow, oblivious at first to anything but Morgan's cut lip, she concentrated on gently wiping away the smear of blood.

Morgan was very aware of other things besides his cut lip. Her body was only inches from his, and he was quite conscious of the curves which the worn cotton shift did nothing to hide. A faint intoxicating scent of rosewater teased his nostrils and, staring at the way she pursed her mouth as she went about her task, he could feel his body stirring with desire.

It was only as Leonie sat back on her haunches and surveyed her work that she became conscious of the intimacy of the situation. The candlelight shed a warm glow over the bed, and Morgan was overpoweringly attractive as he stood in front of her, the dark blue of the brocaded robe deepening the color of his eyes. Her gaze was drawn irresistibly to the naked flesh that showed above where the robe was belted making her tinglingly aware of the fact that underneath the robe Morgan was naked, and her own state of undress suddenly dawned on her.

Hastily she dropped her eyes, and with a jerky movement, she put the bowl and towel on the table near the bed. Trying desperately to ignore the hungry heat that was clawing up through her stomach, she said brightly, "Well, I think that takes care of everything. Good night, monsieur."

Morgan stared at her, aware of his blood rising hot and thick in his loins. His voice suddenly husky, he muttered, "I want to make love to you."

Leonie swallowed nervously, her entire body responding wildly to his words. She tried to rouse the anger she was certain she should feel, and she tried to recall all the reasons why she should hurl his words back into his face and order him from her room. But the words would not come, and she could only stare at him dumbly, wanting with painful fierceness to have him take her into his arms.

They stared at one another a long time, neither moving until Leonie, dredging up a grim determination she hadn't

300

known she possessed, shook her head and said in a low tone, "No, monsieur. I do not want you to make love to me."

Morgan didn't move, although his eyes narrowed. In a soft unhurried voice that sent a thrill of anticipation and anger through her, he finally said, "I'm afraid, my dear wife, you misunderstood me. I didn't ask your permission to make love to you . . . I told you what I wanted to do. What I am *going* to do."

22

An electrifying silence met Morgan's words. With a sparkle of temper in the sea-green eyes, Leonie stiffened and spat, *"Non!* I will not have it!"

"Won't you, cat-eyes?" Morgan inquired with a caressing note in his voice as he reached for her.

Conscious of a conflicting mixture of fury and pleasure, Leonie felt his hands capture her slim shoulders despite her wild struggles to escape him. Effortlessly she was dragged up next to his hard body and with a feeling of half-anger, half-despair, she was aware of a sudden flood of desire as his mouth caught hers in a hungry kiss.

Determined to resist his advances, forcing herself to remember that just this afternoon she had vowed not to let this sort of thing happen again, she made a valiant attempt to withstand his unfair, almost overpowering attack on her senses. Desperately she tried to ignore the treacherous leap of her pulse at his touch, but Morgan's hands were too knowledgeable and his lips too persuasive. Gently, inexorably, he drew a response from her traitorous body. He had awakened her to passion, shown her the joy his caressing touch could give, and she was defenseless against the hungry dictates of her own flesh. As his kiss deepened, his arms crushing her next to him, shamefully Leonie admitted that she wanted him, wanted him to make love to her again, wanted once more to know the rapture of his intoxicating lovemaking.

Morgan was hazily aware of her resistance, but he was already too aroused, his body too full of hungry need to stop his mouth from searching hers, or his hands from urgently exploring her soft, warm body. Perhaps, if Leonie had continued to resist, he might have been able to control

302

the demands of desire that clawed through him, but the same emotions that ate at him were also devouring Leonie and as he continued to kiss her, long, drugging, demanding kisses, she lost the fight with herself.

His lips were warm and compelling as they moved across hers; the touch of his hand on her breast was nearly unbearable and with a soft moan of helpless pleasure she stopped fighting the yearnings of her ardent young body and melted against him. Urgently her arms fastened around his neck and uncontrollably her body arched up next to his, wanting . . . Oh, God, wanting him so very much. It didn't matter any more that she should distrust him, it didn't even matter that he was a master of duplicity, all that mattered was this moment, this moment, when his lips were fervently exploring hers and his tall, hard body was crushed against hers.

Leonie's sweet response destroyed any coherent thought Morgan had, and almost savagely he searched her lips, his tongue erotically penetrating the inner sweetness of her mouth. With a brutal tenderness, his hands roamed over her slender body, kneading her shoulders, caressing her back and cupping her buttocks to pull her even closer to him. He wanted her with a desperate intensity that only increased as they strained together, their bodies locked together in a fiercely passionate embrace.

Desire ruling her body, Leonie's hesitating touches grew bolder. Compelled by an ageless need, she pushed aside his robe and stroked his naked chest, his skin feeling warm and rough under her hands. Slowly, savoringly, she explored his upper torso, her fingers lightly traveling over him, lingering on his muscled chest. To her delight she felt his nipples harden and throb beneath her touch and eager to explore further, her fingers undid the sash of his robe and slipped lower to tangle in the thick mat of black curly hair of his groin.

Morgan sucked in his breath painfully, her caresses nearly driving him mad. Needing desperately to touch her as she was touching him, his hand fastened on the cotton shift and with one swift motion he pulled it off her. A second later, he had thrown aside his confining robe and with a low growl of satisfaction he jerked her slim body next to his.

Leonie was still kneeling on the bed and with Morgan standing directly in front of her, their bodies fitted perfectly together from head to thigh. The tight ache of desire that was throbbing in her loins dominated her entire being. She trembled at the exquisite sensation of being held naked against him, her breasts pressed against the soft hair of his chest, and her hips and thighs molded lovingly to Morgan's warm, hard body.

Her arms hung helplessly at her sides. Morgan's hands held her shoulders as he kissed her again, a long intoxicating kiss that Leonie wanted never to end; She sighed with disappointment when he at last lifted his mouth from hers. Immediately his lips began a fiery exploration of her face and shoulders, as he dropped light passionate kisses on the lids of her eyes, the lobe of her ear and the sensitive area where her neck joined her shoulder. He lingered there a moment, his tongue caressing the silken flesh before his lips dropped to the base of her throat and he gently kissed the spot where her pulse beat madly beneath the skin.

Teasingly, the feel of his mouth like a soft flame across her flesh, his head dropped lower, and with a sharp stab of pleasure she felt his lips close hungrily around the taut nipple of one breast. Unashamedly she arched her body up against his mouth, further aroused by the way he played with her breast, his teeth gently rubbing across the tip and his tongue warmly curling around the nipple. As his mouth explored first one breast and then the other, Leonie swayed breathlessly in his hold, wanting to put her arms around him, wanting to touch him, but his hands held her prisoner.

Leonie's entire body was on fire, her breasts were aching with the tautness of her nipples; her lips were desperate for the touch of his, and her loins throbbed and yearned for his possession. Almost frantically, she pressed herself to his searching mouth, unaware of her own soft moans of pleasure.

Her small sounds excited him, and he could feel his body responding to her sweet nearness. His breathing quickened and he was aware of an almost painful need to bury himself deep within her, to experience again the overwhelming exultation of making love to her. And yet he held back, denied the urgings of his body, wanting to make her as wild for him as he was for her.

He lifted his head and looked at her, observing with satisfaction and growing hunger the flush of desire that shaded her high cheekbones, and the passion-dazed expression of her half-closed green eyes. With an effort he moved slightly away from her, allowing himself to savor the sight of her lovely body as she knelt on the bed before him.

Her small breasts jutted out impudently from her chest, the coral nipples rigid with passion, and Morgan knew that soon he must taste their sweetness again . . . but not now. Caressingly his eyes dropped to the flat stomach; unable to help himself, he reached out and lightly ran his hand down the smooth expanse of taut, golden flesh, his fingers stopping just above the triangle of tight blond curls.

At his touch Leonie shivered, the pulse in her throat beating even faster, the tingling sensation between her thighs nearly unbearable. Compelled by her own need to explore him, she lifted the arm he had just freed and lingeringly, wonderingly let her hand drift through the mat of fine black hair on his chest.

Morgan stiffened at the feel of her small hand against his skin and compulsively his own hand began his own exploration, seeking the delicate area between her thighs, gently penetrating her with his finger. She was so soft, so warm, so desirable that with a groan of impatience his mouth captured hers and he pushed her onto her back.

They fell together, Morgan half lying on her as he kissed her with all the passion that was surging through his body. Only vaguely aware of the comfort of the bed, he continued to touch and tease the satiny flesh between her legs until Leonie was oblivious to everything but Morgan, his hard mouth on hers, the warmth of his body as he lay next to her and the intense pleasure his hands and mouth were giving her.

Without restraint she offered herself to him, her arms closing hungrily about his shoulders, her hands transmit-

ting by their frantic movements the excitement and pleasure building within her. All her innate sensuality
aroused, she returned his passionate kisses, her tongue a
small flick of fire darting into his mouth and driving him
insane with the fierce desire to possess her again.

No words were spoken; each body responded instinctively to the other's passion. The words, the confessions of
love they would not say aloud, were clearly revealed in
every kiss, every caress they exchanged.

The bed curtains formed a silken ruby cocoon about
them; the flickering candlelight played over their naked
bodies, gilding Leonie's fair skin and revealing the
bronzed darkness of Morgan's muscled length as they lay
together, each one totally absorbed by the other. There
was a sinuous grace about their movements, the yearning
arching of Leonie's hips, the almost languid way Morgan's
head moved as his lips traveled down to her breasts.

It was a sweet agony not to take her, and as much for her
pleasure as his Morgan, deliberately delayed the joining of
their bodies, his mouth moving erotically down her rib-
cage, leaving a path of burning kisses. Her flesh was warm
and silken beneath his questing lips and he was drunk
with the taste and scent of her as his mouth slid lower
across her body.

Slowly, sensuously, Morgan's tongue traced an exquisitely nerve-shattering path down her stomach, but when
he would have gone lower, Leonie's shocked protest
stopped him.

"Ah, monsieur, no!" she cried breathlessly, desperately
fighting back the almost overpowering desire to let him do
what he would with her. She was thoroughly aroused,
every fiber of her being searingly aware of him, every part
of her wanting him—and yet she was terrified of the new
passions he might evoke.

Reluctantly Morgan raised his head and looked at her,
his eyes nearly black with the passion that flamed through
his veins. His voice thick, almost unrecognizable, he muttered, "I want you . . . all of you, Leonie."

Leonie gave a frightened shake of her head and with a
groan of frustration, Morgan moved away and propping
himself up on one elbow, his face only inches above hers,

he stared down at her. Hungrily his eyes moved over her features and softly he said, "You're beautiful, cat-eyes, beautiful . . . *every*where." Gently his hand moved down her stomach and slipped between her thighs. "Even there," he murmured huskily as he bent to kiss her lips.

His words were as potent as the caresses he was lavishing on her slender body, but when his head moved lower a few minutes later, Leonie's body stiffened in protest and with a defeated sigh, he stopped her further initiation. A crooked smile curving his mouth he said softly, "Tonight you win, but next time . . ."

Her eyes a luminous green in the candlelight, Leonie stared dumbly up at him, her mouth half-parted to argue further, but Morgan suddenly bent down and kissed her deeply, one hand tangling in the mass of tawny hair that was spread out across the bed. Like a man with a desperate hunger to satisfy, his tongue filled her mouth as if seeking sustenance from the honeyed warmth he found there.

Once again, his hand traveled down her body and this time when his fingers explored the silken softness between her thighs, he didn't stop his sensual movements until Leonie was twisting mindlessly under his caresses, small whimpering sounds of pleasure coming from the back of her throat. His own body pushed to the limit, he moved swiftly then, slipping between her legs, his knees nudging apart her thighs. With a low groan of fierce satisfaction he slowly entered her, trembling from the pleasure he experienced as he pushed his swollen, rigid length deeply into her welcoming warm softness.

They lay there motionless a second, their bodies locked together, Morgan embedded within her; Leonie was dazed at the size of him. He filled her completely, and with a surge of love and pleasure she felt her body stretching to accommodate his exciting intrusion. Hungrily her arms closed around him, her hands feverishly running over the muscled back, down to his hard buttocks, loving the feel of him.

For Morgan it was an incredibly sweet torture to lay there, feeling her fingers sliding over his skin, but overwhelmingly aware of his throbbing manhood buried within the tight, silken prison of her flesh, he could not tolerate her unknowingly provocative touches for very long and, a second later, he began to move. Wanting desperately to prolong the pleasure, he made love to her gently, his kisses intoxicatingly tender as his tongue probed her mouth, even as his body thrust into hers.

Leonie also wanted this moment to last, didn't want this sweet intimacy to end, but the same demanding dictates that were driving Morgan drove her too. As he continued to move upon her, her hips rose eagerly to meet him and her hands increased their exploration of his body, her fingers small streaks of fire as they moved over his skin.

The tempo increased, their bodies meeting and parting with a growing wildness and Morgan buried his mouth in her neck, groaning thickly, "Oh, Jesus, Leonie, you're so warm . . . so sweet. I . . ."

Whatever he had been about to say was lost, for Leonie's body quivered and knowing what was happening to her, he was suddenly aware that his own body was also reaching the pinnacle of pleasure. Urgently, his movements now nearly frenzied, he drove into her, wanting the release he knew was only a second away.

Leonie had hardly heard his words, for the tight bubble of exquisite pleasure that had been building within her suddenly exploded into a surge of wild sensation that shook her body. Stunned by the extent of the pleasure that raced through her body, she was only vaguely aware of Morgan's body slamming into hers, of the jump and shudder he gave, as he, too, knew fulfillment.

Even when the forces that had driven him had lessened, Morgan found it impossible to withdraw from her. Unwilling to leave her, their bodies still entwined, he continued to kiss her gently, his hands tangling in the tawny hair, holding her head still.

For Leonie it was a bittersweet moment. With the passion he had so unfairly aroused slowly dying, harsh reality began to seep into her thoughts and she was unhappily aware of the fact that while she might love him, and that while this had been an act of love for her, she was certain that for him it had been nothing more than a lustful mating.

She wronged Morgan in thinking that, but she wasn't to

308

know it. Nor was she to know that when he finally eased
his body off hers, and gathered her into his arms, that he
had finally admitted to himself that he loved her. It was
neither an easy nor a pleasant admission, but he was honest enough to realize that every action he had undertaken
since Leonie had burst into his life was a result of the fact
that she had bewitched him the moment he had laid eyes
upon her.

The knowledge that he had against all reason fallen in
love with her was not welcome, and its impact was all the
more potent because it came at a time when he was not
blinded by desire for her—his body was satiated as it had
not been in a long, long time . . . not since the blissful
early days of his marriage to Stephanie.

Darkly Morgan smiled to himself. It seemed he was des-
tined to love women who practiced deceit as easily as they
drew breath.

At least, this time, he told himself grimly, I'll be prepared for treachery. Never will another woman deceive me
as Stephanie did! *Never!* Unconsciously his arms tightened
around Leonie and his lips sought her in a savage kiss that
caught her by surprise.

Her soft lips parted easily and with none of the tenderness or gentleness he had shown previously, his mouth
ravaged hers, almost as if he wanted to hurt her. Leonie
stiffened in his arms, her small hands pushing at his
shoulders as she tried to twist her lips away from his.

Fighting him in earnest, deriving no pleasure from this
unexpected assault, she managed to free her mouth and
snap, "Monsieur! Stop it! I tell you, *stop* it!"

Oddly enough it was the word *monsieur* that banished
the sudden mood that had overtaken him, and with a startling shift in temperment, his attractive grin tugging at
the corner of his mouth, he asked in a mocking voice,
"Don't you think, sweetheart, that it's time you stopped
calling me *monsieur? Monsieur* is so formal. . . ." Gently
he cupped one breast, his tongue curling teasingly around
the small nipple which instantly went rigid. Lifting his
dark head, the blue eyes staring into hers, he finished
huskily, "And formal we certainly have not been!"

Leonie blushed at the expression in his eyes, as well

as from embarrassment at how effortlessly her body responded to his caresses, and tried to wiggle away from him.

"Oh, no, you don't," Morgan said mildly, pulling her back into his arms. His lips only inches from hers, he commanded softly, "Say my name, Leonie. Say *Morgan.*"

Stubbornly, Leonie resisted, needing desperately to keep the word *monsieur* as some sort of frail barrier between them.

"Say it!" he repeated softly, his lips unfairly beginning a trail of fire down her neck. And when she maintained her silence, Morgan laughed gently and his head bent lower, his mouth moving slowly towards her breast, even as his hand deliberately swept down across her stomach.

Frantically Leonie grabbed at his questing hand and stammered breathlessly, "M-M-Morgan."

He liked the sound of his name on her lips, unaccountably pleased at the soft inflection her French accent gave it. Freeing his hand from hers, he continued his provocative exploration of her body and a glint of devilment in the blue eyes, he murmured, "Say, *darling* Morgan."

Stormy sea-green eyes glared up into his and Leonie's soft mouth tightened in rebellion. "No!" she got out between clenched teeth, trying desperately to ignore the sensations his warm hand was creating as he gently kneaded her flat stomach.

Morgan cocked an eyebrow at her. "No?" he asked with feigned astonishment. "Pity. We'll just have to see if I can't change your mind, won't we?"

Giving her no chance to answer, his mouth caught hers in a long, sweetly punishing kiss, his hand gently caressing her breasts. He'd only meant to tease her further, but the feel of that soft mouth beneath his and the fullness of her breast in his hand was too much for him. With a groan, he deepened the kiss, his hands moving now with an increasingly feverishness over her skin. His mouth against her lips he muttered thickly, "Say it, damn you, say it!"

The blood rushing madly through her veins, her body already beginning to arch up to meet his seeking hands, Leonie finally capitulated and whispered, half-caressingly, half-angrily, *"Darling* Morgan."

But she had waited too long and Morgan, his body aflame to know again the pleasure only she could give him, was no longer in a teasing mood. He needed to take her again and in the moments that followed; he made love to her with a fierce urgency that left Leonie both exquisitely fulfilled and shattered. Her mouth felt bruised and her body ached from his hungry possession, and yet, despite the almost violent way he had taken her, there had been an odd sensation of tenderness about his lovemaking.

There was no conversation between them when Morgan at last withdrew from her body, but his hands were still roaming over her heated flesh, and his mouth pressed a warm path of light kisses from her temple to the corner of her lips. He seemed unable to stop touching her, but the wild emotion that had driven him moments before was gone, and Leonie found herself enjoying far too much this gentle aftermath of his passion.

She was exhausted, as much from Morgan's lovemaking as the unending struggle with her own emotions, and despite the strong feeling that she should argue with him, that she should berate him for this further breeching of the agreement between them, she discovered that her body was filled with a delicious, almost overpowering languor. To her intense shame, she admitted the only thing she wanted to do at the moment was sleep . . . sleep with her naked body curled against Morgan's hard form. Which was precisely what she did a few minutes later.

Sleep did not come as easily to Morgan. For a long time after Leonie's even breathing told him she had fallen asleep, he lay there with her head resting on his shoulder and stared up at the ruby silk canopy. His body was at rest, but his brain was working at a frantic pace, and his thoughts were not pleasant.

He might have admitted to himself that he had been unwise enough to fall in love with Leonie Saint-André, but it was a bitter, *bitter* admission. Certainly, it gave him no pleasure, and the knowledge that there could very well be a *real* husband lurking in her background displeased him even more. And there was the question of the future. . . .

311

What the hell was he supposed to do now? Fall down on his knees and beg her to love him? To marry him? Morgan snorted contemptuously. *That* was goddamned unlikely!

But what was he going to do? With a less than gentle movement, he shifted Leonie away from him and propping himself up on one elbow, he stared down at her sleeping features. How sweet and innocent she looked, he thought furiously. Angrily aware of the wave of tenderness that swept through his body as he watched her, he tore his gaze away and left the bed.

Snatching up his robe where it had fallen earlier, he shrugged into it and sparing one last look at Leonie, he left the room in a black, hostile mood. *Why*, he wondered grimly, *is it my fate to fall in love with deceitful women?*

The question remained unanswered the remainder of the long night and when Morgan did finally fall asleep, he slept only fitfully, images of Leonie and Stephanie drifting in and out of his dreams. Even more disturbing was the return of the nightmare he hadn't experienced in years—he was filled with fear and he was riding desperately up the Natchez Trace, knowing that his son's life was hanging in balance. And as always in his recent nightmares, he approached them and to his horror and pain, when he moved the still forms to discover their identities, the woman had Leonie's sweet face and the dead child lying at her side was Justin.

A moan of anguished denial broke from him and Morgan woke up to find himself safely in his own bed, his body bathed in perspiration, his heart beating as if it were going to burst from his breast. Knowing it was foolish, and yet unable to deny the impulse he slid from the bed and walked quickly into Leonie's rooms, a small sigh of relief escaping as he stared at her sleeping form. Still driven by the reality of the dream, he left her room and quickly found his way to the nursery, where Justin lay sleeping in childish abandon.

With a hand that shook slightly, Morgan reached out and touched the dark, tousled curls, aware that Justin had come to mean a great deal to him.

The nightmare having faded, Morgan walked slowly back to his own rooms and this time when he slept, he slept

312

dreamlessly, deeply, for the first time in weeks at peace with himself.

If Morgan had momentarily found peace within himself, the opposite was true for Leonie. Waking with soft, yellow rays of sunlight spilling into her room, she was both pleased and inordinately disappointed to find herself alone in the big bed. Gently her hand touched the snowy pillow where Morgan's head had rested and then angry with herself for giving in to a stupid rush of love for him, she jerked her hand away.

Sitting bolt upright in bed, she rang for Mercy, pulling on the velvet bellrope with unnecessary violence. When Mercy arrived a few minutes later, her mood was not helped by the knowing glance Mercy gave the bed, the tangled sheets, as well as Leonie's naked state and the torn nightshift which clearly revealed that *something* had transpired during the night.

A sly smile curving her full pink mouth, Mercy murmured, "And did Miz Leonie sleep well last night?"

Leonie glared at her and muttered, "I want a bath, Mercy . . . and no prattling from you."

Unruffled by Leonie's manner, Mercy chuckled and disappeared. Knowing the gossip Mercy would gaily spread as she oversaw the preparation for the bath, Leonie could have sworn outloud with frustration and embarrassment.

But there was nothing she could do about it and almost viciously, she grabbed the torn shift and bundled it into an unrecognizable knot. Feeling slightly better, she waited for her bath, wondering what the day would bring and, more importantly, how she would react when she saw her detestable husband.

That night had effectively destroyed whatever defenses she had been able to erect against him. Frightened of becoming his plaything and yet loving him, Leonie viewed the future with both terror and anticipation. Thinking of last night, remembering the touch of his hands on her body and the drugging sensuality of his kisses, she sighed with a mixture of pleasure and shame. *I must not let that happen again,* she decided unhappily.

Mercy's return with the news that her bath was ready temporarily banished Leonie's troubled thoughts. Slipping into the brass tub of hot, soapy water, she forced herself not to think of last night. And yet when Mercy would have added some rosewater to the bath, Leonie said sharply, *"Non!* Not *that* one." Realizing that Mercy was staring at her in astonishment, she added hurriedly, "I think I would prefer lavender, it is less overpowering, don't you think?"

Mercy shrugged her plump shoulders and did as she was told. Uh-huh. Miss Leonie was in a most *peculiar* mood this morning!

Avoiding the quizzical expression in Mercy's gaze, Leonie silently finished her bath. Rising from the water, she was equally silent as Mercy handed her a fluffy white towel and began to briskly rub her dry.

It was only when Mercy resignedly handed her the old yellow linen gown that Leonie spoke. Her voice filled with bitterness, she muttered, "At least *you'll* be happy—Monsieur has ordered several new gowns for me. They will be arriving some time today and tonight, for once, you shall have a choice when it comes to selecting what I shall wear for the evening."

Mercy's round, black face was instantly wreathed in smiles, but Leonie did not share her pleasure in the new clothing and after dragging on the old yellow gown and having her hair brushed, she left the room for the breakfast parlor in a belligerent mood. Her temper wasn't helped by the unwelcome knowledge that she had made no *real* effort to stop Monsieur Slade from having his way with her the night before.

And I will call him monsieur! she thought with a tightening of the soft mouth, recalling with shame the way he had forced her to say his name. *He is an unfeeling monster,* she decided grimly. Morgan had ruffled her fierce little pride badly and she was determined to be as obstinate and stubborn as possible. He is *not* going to charm *me!*

Sailing into the breakfast parlor ready to do battle, she suffered a check when she discovered the room was empty. A short conversation with the butler elicited the information that Monsieur Slade seldom ate breakfast, preferring a tray sent to his room.

"And Mademoiselle Yvette?"

314

"I believe that the mademoiselle is indisposed this morning." the butler returned calmly.

Instantly concerned, Morgan's wicked tactics flying from her mind, she swept from the room and hurried up the stairs in search of Yvette. Entering Yvette's room a few seconds later, she was alarmed to find that young lady still abed.

Crossing the charming room with its green and yellow decor, she swiftly approached the bed. *"Ma petite!* What is this I hear, that you do not feel well?" Leonie inquired anxiously.

Propped up with several plump pillows, her face paler than usual, Yvette smiled wanely at Leonie. "It is nothing. I think perhaps something that I ate last night disagreed with me. I will be better tomorrow, you'll see."

Laying her hand across one of Yvette's, Leonie peered closely at Yvette's features. "You are not lying to me?" she asked suspiciously, well aware that Yvette was perfectly capable of doing just that if she thought it would keep her from worrying.

Yvette smiled weakly. A faint sparkle in the beautiful brown eyes, she murmured, "No, I am not lying." And when Leonie still looked unconvinced, she added, "Truly, Leonie! I am just a trifle indisposed. Tomorrow I shall be up and about. Do not worry so."

It was easier for Yvette to say it than it was for Leonie to do it, but after several minutes more conversation with Yvette, Leonie was finally convinced that there was nothing seriously wrong with her half-sister. Sitting casually on the edge of Yvette's bed, Leonie stayed for quite some time. She told her of the new clothing that would be arriving and suggested that tomorrow Yvette might like to select several things for herself.

Yvette looked hesitant and Leonie scowled at her fiercely. "You will share these things, Yvette! I do not want to hear any nonsense from you about how monsieur is my husband and that he doesn't need to provide for you, too."

There was a note in Leonie's voice that made Yvette glance at her intently. "You did not want him to buy you anything, did you?" she asked shrewdly.

315

Leonie avoided answering. "Bah! It doesn't make any difference what *I* want."

Her lovely face worried, Yvette leaned forward. "Leonie," she began slowly, "I haven't wanted to intrude, but I can't help wondering if you are happy here. You have been acting very strangely. Are you sorry that you came to find Monsieur Slade?"

With difficulty Leonie choked back a bitter answer and made some light reply. But later after she left Yvette's room the question came back to haunt her. Was she sorry she had found Morgan Slade? She knew the answer to that question in her heart, and miserably she admitted that no matter what happened in the future, she wouldn't have missed knowing Morgan Slade for anything in the world.

23

The clothes arrived that afternoon, and watching Mercy blissfully shake out and admire the delicate chemises, lacy nightgowns, and silky peignoirs, Leonie was hard pressed to remain indifferent to the lovely things scattered across the room. At least a half dozen fashionable gowns were spread across the bed; the elegant amber-bronze ball gown had been reverently laid on a chair. There were several other articles of feminine apparel which had been included, but it was the filmy undergarments and nightwear which held the black woman's attention, and Leonie could have boxed Mercy's ears for the sly glances she sent her way.

"My, my," Mercy exclaimed for the tenth time, "ain't we goin' to be fine! Uh-huh. Yes, indeedy, we is goin' to be *fine!*"

Leonie shrugged her shoulders and said tartly, "We is not going to be *anything* if you don't start putting some of this away!"

Mercy shot her a look. "Somethin' sure is bitin' you, Miss Leonie."

Aware that her resentment had nothing to do with Mercy, Leonie forced a smile and said lightly, "Oh, stop chattering and put those things away."

"What? Before I've had a chance to inspect them?" Morgan asked from the connecting doorway.

At the sound of his voice Leonie spun on her heels to face him, her heart beginning to pound frantically. She had not seen him all day and if she hadn't known better she would have thought he was avoiding her. Not only had he not joined her in the breakfast parlor, he had sent word that he

317

would also not be in for lunch, requesting a tray in his office.

Leonie had debated the wisdom of bearding him there, but remembering the last time she had entered his office, she had decided against it. Consequently, she had spent a frustrating day, bottling up all the hot, angry words she longed to hurl at him. It hadn't helped to know that all she had to do was walk across the expanse of lawn that separated his office from the house to face him. Angry with herself for being a coward and furious with him for placing her in that position, her simmering temper was not the least bit soothed by her heart's reaction to his unexpected presence. He was so handsome in his bottle-green jacket and buff breeches. A crooked smile was curving his mouth and there was a mocking gleam in the blue eyes, almost as if he were aware of the frustration that had eaten at her all day and was laughing at her.

Leonie took a deep breath as her hands unconsciously clenched into fists. With as much calm as she could muster, she said to Mercy, "Please leave us, Mercy. I wish to speak alone with Monsieur Slade."

Morgan's eyes narrowed at the word *monsieur*. Walking slowly into the room, he agreed, saying, "Yes, *do* leave us, Mercy. I must teach my wife the proper way to say my name."

Leonie flushed hotly and Mercy, a speculative glint in her eyes, laid down the frothy confection of lace she had been holding and left the room.

Alone, facing him, Leonie discovered that the abuses she had yearned to heap upon his head were scattering before the reality of his powerful presence. *He has become so dear to me,* she thought painfully; *I love him and yet I must not! He is a blackguard, a man without honor who is not to be trusted and yet . . .*

Fighting the urgings of her heart, she was finally able to revive the rage she had kept tamped down, and glaring up at him, she said stiffly, "Monsieur, we must talk! This situation is intolerable and I will not allow it to continue."

"My sentiments precisely," Morgan returned imperturbably, as he flicked a finger through the pile of filmy garments Mercy had left on a small velvet sofa.

The wind unexpectedly taken out of her sails, Leonie gaped at him, and then quickly recovering herself, she asked suspiciously, "What do you mean by that? Are you going to repay my dowry?"

Morgan regarded her thoughtfully. As if choosing his words with care, he said slowly, "I might. It depends on what you're willing to give in return."

A frown creased her forehead. "I don't understand. I already *have* given you what was required—my hand in marriage."

"But suppose," Morgan asked quietly, "I wanted you and Justin to stay with me?"

Her heart knocking painfully against her ribs, an odd fluttering sensation in the pit of her stomach, Leonie regarded him dumbly. She longed to shout out a joyous, unreserved yes, but caution held her back. Was this another trick? Was he only attempting to disarm her in order to gain some advantage?

Leonie's distrust was not without foundation. The men in her life had done nothing to make her trust the male of the species. And Morgan's recent actions had done nothing to change her opinion. Why now should she consider for one moment the possibility of staying with him?

Quite simply because her heart was blind to all reason. She loved this bewildering man, and more than anything she did indeed wish to be his wife. But her practical nature and her sensible mind were in direct and violent conflict with the demands of her wayward heart.

Almost despairingly she got out, "Monsieur, I must have time to think. You have asked me no easy question and before I give you an answer, it is imperative that I consider many things."

It was not the reply that he wanted and with a sinking heart she watched the way his face changed, the shuttered expression that came down over his proud features, and the cold glitter that entered the dark blue eyes.

"I see," he said coolly, furious and yet almost relieved at her cautious fencing. He hadn't meant to even mention a permanent arrangement, and if he was furious at Leonie for her reluctance to commit herself, he was equally furious at his own lack of control. *Fool!* he berated himself silently. *Did you really think that last night changed anything? My God, how could you have been so stupid as to let the passions of the flesh blind you to reality?* A bitter smile on his mouth, he made a bleak promise not to make that mistake again. *And if it is love I feel for her,* he thought viciously, *I'll damn well* kill it!

All day long he had fought that particular battle within himself, fighting savagely against the attraction he felt for her, trying to convince himself that he did *not* love her, that the admission he had made to himself last night had been some wild aberration brought on by the pleasure of her body. But when he had entered her room and had seen her, all his calm resolve had gone flying and he had spoken without thinking. Something that won't happen in the future, he decided grimly, his pride as well as his heart smarting under her rebuff. And the thought occurred to him again that perhaps there was a *real* husband lurking in the background. He found the idea nearly unbearable, and conscious of an ugly jealousy, he turned away from her and walked over to the chair where the amber-bronze gown lay in regal splendor.

"You'll wear this tonight when we attend the ball for Burr?" he asked, deliberately changing the subject.

"Ball? What ball?" Leonie inquired with puzzlement, her emotions thrown into complete confusion by his abrupt change of topic.

Morgan cocked an eyebrow at her, and then realizing that he hadn't mentioned the fact that his mother had accepted the invitation for them, he smiled faintly and said mockingly, "My lamentable memory again, I'm afraid. There is a ball being held tonight to honor Aaron Burr, our ex-vice-president, and we are expected to attend."

"Oh, but—" Leonie began to protest.

Morgan stopped her by interrupting and saying harshly, "We *will* attend, my dear, and I will accept no excuses." A sardonic expression on his face, he added, "I think it is time we made our first public appearance and put an end to the wagging tongues, don't you?"

Her features stormy, Leonie returned swiftly, "Bah! What do I care about wagging tongues?"

Morgan strode over to her and said in a dangerous tone,

"You may not, but my family has had to put up with a great deal of scandal they could have well done without. Our argument aside, I believe you owe it to them to make some amends. Attending this ball will do much to stop speculation, and Leonie," he finished with a hard glint in the blue eyes, "we *are* going to the ball tonight."

Rebellion sparkling in her eyes, Leonie debated the wisdom of defying him, but something about the set of his jaw made her decide that this was not the time to declare war. With a meekness that was a direct variance with the expression on her face, she capitulated. Shrugging a shoulder, she turned away from him and said insouciantly, "Oh, very well, monsieur, I will go to your silly ball. And I will behave very prettily. Does that satisfy you?"

A sudden hint of laughter in his voice he reached out and spun her around. "Cat-eyes, I thought last night you had learned my name. Don't tell me you've forgotten how to say it so soon . . . or is it you would like another lesson?"

Leonie spluttered an angry reply, but Morgan's mouth effectively stopped further speech as his lips came down hard on hers. He kissed her thoroughly and only when Leonie was limp in his arms did he lift his mouth from hers. He looked down into her bemused face and murmured, "Does that make you remember? Can you say *Morgan*, or must I give you further lessons?"

The sea-green eyes spitting golden flecks, Leonie glowered up at him, but aware of what would follow if she continued to defy him, she muttered, "I have not forgotten, mon—M-M-Morgan."

Morgan sighed. "Pity," he said regretfully. "You are such a delightful pupil."

Leonie blushed and Morgan laughed aloud. Flicking a careless finger down her hot cheek, he said cooly, "There are things I must do before this evening, so for the time being, my prickly little cat, I shall leave you to preen amongst your spoils." Before Leonie could think of a scathing reply, he turned and left the room.

Furious with her own helplessness, Leonie stamped her foot in rage, wondering if she dared to ignore his command to attend the ball. Remembering the hard blue eyes and unyielding chin she decided against it—the uneasy feeling that it would be foolish indeed to ignore what he had said was too persistent.

Consequently, trying very hard to remain unmoved and indifferent to the excitement that was coursing through her veins at the idea of attending her first ball, she docilely permitted Mercy to have full rein. And when the grinning black woman finally stepped back and turned Leonie in the direction of the tall mirror at one end of the room, Leonie's breath caught in her throat.

Is that really me? she wondered, staring open mouthed at the slender, fashionably attired young woman who stared back at her. Mercy had done her work well; the tawny curls had been piled high on Leonie's small head, and several tiny ringlets had been coaxed down to caress her ears and cheeks. A very light dusting of pearl white powder across her face and bosom had given her an ethereal look, but no artifice was needed to add color to her soft coral mouth or to intensify the depths of the green eyes. The exquisitely fashioned gown was as beautiful as she remembered it, and it gave her an air of elegance with its slim, classical lines, the ever-changing amber and bronze hues of the silk a perfect foil for Leonie's coloring. From beneath the narrow skirt, a neatly turned ankle could be glimpsed above delightful amber satin slippers; Leonie was aware that she had never been so richly dressed in her entire life.

Next to her skin, she could feel the fine lace-trimmed lawn chemise and petticoat and the softness of her silken stockings. It was a delicious feeling and she felt slightly sinful for enjoying it. Even the perfume she wore tonight had a wickedly intoxicating scent to it; a faint scent of gardenia lingered in the air wherever she moved.

It was difficult not to be excited and pleased with herself, and though Leonie fought a valiant battle, she lost. A happy smile on her face, she nearly skipped down the hall to Yvette's room to share her pleasure.

"Yvette," she cried gaily as she danced into the room. "Look at me! What do you think?" With an endearing innocence she added "I am very grand, *n'est-ce pas?*"

Yvette, feeling much better, eagerly agreed. "Oh, Leonie, how beautiful you are! You will be the belle of the ball, *oui?*"

Remembering that she was not supposed to enjoy herself, Leonie grimaced, "Bah! What do I care?" And sitting down on the edge of Yvette's bed she suddenly asked anxiously, "You do not mind that I am going out and leaving you here?"

Yvette smiled gently. "No, I do not mind. After all, it is you who are married to Monsieur Slade. I am merely your companion."

Leonie scowled fiercely. "You will not say such things! You will have just as many beautiful gowns, too. You will see! I promise that it will be true!"

Yvette giggled and murmured, "Leonie, *ma petite*, I never doubted it." And struck by a sudden thought she asked, "Has Justin seen you yet?"

"No, but I am on my way to him now. Do you think he will like me this way?"

"I'm certain he will," Yvette said warmly.

Justin was enchanted with Leonie's appearance, but it was the scent of gardenia that he liked best. Burying his little face in her neck, he prattled happily, "Ah, maman, you smell like a flower. A very pretty one, *oui?*"

Leonie gave a gurgle of laughter. "But of course, *mon coeur!* I am your maman, am I not?"

She did not stay long with Justin, but having kissed him good night and having given the nursemaid instructions for the evening, she made her way to the main parlor. Entering it, some of her happiness evaporated. After all, nothing had *really* changed between her and Monsieur Slade. But, she could not restrain her pleasure and excitement.

She knew the reason for her elated mood, but she stubbornly persisted in pretending otherwise. *It is merely the thought of going to my first ball and the enjoyment of having fashionable clothes,* she told herself time and time again. But her heart knew the real reason and though she had tried to push Morgan's question out of her mind all afternoon and evening, it came back to haunt her.

Appearances would lead one to believe that he wanted a real marriage, and it was all Leonie could do not to throw common sense to the winds and fling herself into his arms shouting, yes, yes, *yes* when he walked into the parlor a few minutes later. But uncertainty—he had shown himself to be as changeable as the winds—held her back.

In his evening clothes, he was very formidable, his dark, lean good looks intensified by the white ruffled shirt and the low-cut black kerseymere waistcoat he wore. Black breeches with black silk stockings encased his muscular legs and the double-breasted coat of black velvet fit his broad shoulders superbly.

Watching him covertly as he walked across the room with that lithe, loose-limbed stride of his, she was reminded vividly of an elegant, extremely dangerous black panther. The air of aloofness about him did nothing to dispel the image Leonie had conjured up, and she was caught by surprise when he suddenly sent her a slow, heart-stopping smile.

His voice husky, he said, "You're very beautiful this evening, cat-eyes. More beautiful than I ever realized before."

Embarrassed and suddenly shy, Leonie gazed everywhere but at him and replied in a gruff little voice, "You are very handsome too, monsieur." Her eyes flying to his, she amended hastily, "I m-m-mean, M-Morgan."

He grinned at her. "Very nicely done. And because I do not want you to think me a miserly sort of fellow, I went into Natchez this afternoon and visited a jeweler." A teasing note in his voice he added, "Would you like to see what I bought?"

She nodded, thoroughly mesmerized by this appealing side to his personality, and her eyes widened, when he opened a slim leather case and presented it to her. On a bed of white satin was a lovely topaz pendant and matching earrings.

Almost off handedly, Morgan said, "I thought they would go well with your gown. Do you like them?"

Reverently Leonie stared at the glittering jewels. She had never possessed, never thought to possess anything like them and she was momentarily dumbstruck. "They're beautiful!" she breathed a few moments later. Morgan grinned, pleased that she was so taken with his gift.

Lifting the pendant from its bed of satin, he fastened it around her neck and then stood back to admire it. "Just as

324

I thought, the perfect compliment to a lovely gown . . . and a lovely lady."

Still slightly stunned by this unexpected gift, Leonie reached up to touch the pendant with a caressing hand. "I have never seen anything quite so exquisite," she murmured almost to herself.

If this is a performance, it's a good one, Morgan thought cynically as he watched her through narrowed eyes. Tonight his armor was well in place and though he could act lightly, there was no lightness within him, only bleak derision at his own vacillation. One moment he was certain he loved her, and the next he was quite positive that she was a scheming, lying little bitch. The gift of the jewels betrayed his erratic state of mind—he hadn't meant to buy them, and definitely Leonie's pleasure had been the last thing he had been thinking about when he had left her earlier in the day, but when he had seen them, he hadn't been able to resist the impulse. But if he had given into that particular impulse, he had then convinced himself that it was only for his own twisted, sardonic amusement that he had done so. And continuing his role of cool detachment, he murmured easily, "I'm happy that my gift pleased you. Perhaps, in the future, I can find a brooch that will match it, and if you like, I will buy it for you too."

Even more startled, for the man she had married in New Orleans had never struck her as being particularly generous, Leonie stared up at him with perplexity. "No. I do not need you to buy me things. I should not accept either these lovely clothes or these beautiful jewels."

The conflict within her was easy to see, one part of her wanting to keep everything he had given her and another rebelling against anything that remotely smacked of charity. Morgan frowned, his armor cracking just a little. *She never stays the same,* he thought with angry frustration, wanting to kiss her and shake her at the same time. But she was so adorable, so sweetly determined to do the right thing as she stood before him, that helplessly Morgan felt his cold anger melting. Unable to help himself, he shook his head at his own contradictory emotions and reached for her. Holding her loosely by the shoulders, and looking

325

down into her face, he said slowly, "May we put aside our differences for this evening?"

Wariness as well as uncertainty was obvious in her sea-green eyes, but after a long searching moment, she nodded her head. And determined that he not take advantage, she added, "For tonight only."

Morgan smiled derisively, "For tonight only, cat-eyes! Now we had best be on our way, or we shall be the last to arrive."

The ball for Aaron Burr was being held at Concord, Stephen Minor's estate. Minor, an ex-governor of Natchez, was a wealthy and powerful man, and Morgan knew that the place would be thronged with influential men of the district and their families.

He wasn't wrong. The house was ablaze with light when Morgan and Leonie arrived. Candlelight from several crystal chandeliers spilled out over the wide veranda and from the open windows and doors could be heard the sound of many voices, the softly pitched laughter of women and the deeper tones of the men.

Despite her fine clothes and outward appearance of elegance, inside Leonie was trembling. There was no doubt that tonight she would meet many of the people who had attended the ball meant to announce Morgan's betrothal to Melinda Marshall, and she was not unnaturally nervous. It was her first venture into polite society and, to a young woman more at home scampering about a run-down plantation in her bare feet than in the lofty precincts she now found herself, it was a daunting experience.

Morgan must have had some idea of her trepidation, because as they entered the magnificent ballroom, he squeezed the small hand that rested on his forearm and murmured, "No one will bite you, cat-eyes! And if anyone causes you the least bit of apprehension"—his eyes suddenly hardened—"don't worry, *I'll* deal with them."

Leonie might still harbor a faint resentment against the Slade family in general, but the way they closed ranks around her this evening, never allowing her to be alone for one moment with curious, sometimes spiteful strangers, did much to endear them to her. The entire family, with the exception of the twins, were in attendance, and if Noelle was unexpectedly absorbed in conversation with her many friends and Leonie was swept away by the crowd, she instantly found Morgan, Matthew, Robert, or Dominic at her side. The Slade family formed a formidable ring of protection about her, and consequently she found herself relaxing, actually enjoying her first ball. Morgan's tall presence was never far from her, and her father-in-law's pride in his new daughter-in-law was almost palpable as he danced her around the crowded ballroom. As for Robert and Dominic, they kept her amused with wickedly accurate appraisals of various people she met. Dominic did most of the talking, but Robert added his own witty comments now and then.

The meeting between her and Noelle had occurred just as they entered the room, and at first Leonie was stiff, her pride still wounded from the way Noelle had gone behind her back in the matter of clothes. But Noelle, a twinkle in her dark eyes, had instantly banished any ill feeling between them when she said, *"Petite,* am I forgiven? It was horrid of me and if you never speak to me again, I shall understand. But you are so lovely and I could not bear to see such gorgeous charms hidden away—you are not still angry with me?"

What could Leonie say? During the remainder of the evening she had been grateful for her mother-in-law's lively presence, as Noelle dragged her willy-nilly into the throng and began to introduce her to people.

Actually, a better opportunity to introduce Leonie to Natchez society couldn't have been chosen. Tonight the scandal of Morgan's marriage was the last thing on anybody's mind. Burr was the name on everybody's lips, Aaron Burr, the man of the hour.

No matter which group Morgan and Leonie joined, within moments the topic of the conversation was Burr. Burr was a devil. Burr was an angel. A patriot. A traitor. A victim. A murderer. By the time the great man himself appeared, Morgan was more than just a little curious to meet him. And even more curious about this odd trip of his down the Mississippi.

Having lived such a nomadic life, Morgan had missed most of the controversy surrounding Aaron Burr during the past several years. But Matthew along with Robert and Dominic had been more than happy to inform Morgan of some of the facts and speculations concerning the ex-vice-president. It was, Matthew had said, President Jefferson's suspicion that Burr had attempted to sway the election of 1800 against him, and in his own favor, that had led to Burr's downfall in Jefferson's Democratic party. The election of 1800 had been close—the tally of the electorate resulting in a tie between Burr and Jefferson. Vote after vote was taken, but the tie remained and there was a great deal of speculation that Burr had made a deal with the opposing Federalist party and was actively seeking to take the election away from Jefferson. And this when it had been clearly understood within his own Democratic Party that he was to be Vice-President and not President.

In the end it was the House of Representatives who decided the issue, voting by the slim margin of one vote for Thomas Jefferson. Understandably, Jefferson's distrust of his Vice-President remained, and for his second term of office he had chosen George Clinton as his running mate, signaling loudly and bluntly that Burr was out of favor.

But it wasn't only the election of 1800 that was against Burr. Colonel Burr, as he was called, was a man whom whispers seemed to follow—there was always a hint of scandal, of questionable ethics, of things better left unsaid. His reputation as a womanizer was well-known, although no one doubted the depth of his feelings for his only daughter, Theodosia. He was no stranger to the dueling field, facing Alexander Hamilton's brother-in-law in 1799 when that gentleman accused him of bribery, and just last year, in July of 1804, he had killed Alexander Hamilton himself in a duel when Hamilton questioned some of Burr's ethics.

More than any one thing, it was, perhaps, the killing of Hamilton, "saint of the Federalists," that had brought about his political ruin. Despite the fact that the duel had been fought correctly, Burr had found himself facing the prospect of having a murder warrant sworn out for his arrest. Some said it was because Jefferson was hounding him, others suspected the enraged Federalists of wanting his blood. At any rate, Burr was decidedly unpopular in the East at the moment. He was still under indictment in New York and New Jersey and as for his political future . . .

But if he was not in favor in Washington, the same could not be said west of the Appalachians. Everywhere Burr went on this peculiar southern journey to New Orleans, he was greeted as a conquering hero. Crowds turned out to meet him; parades and balls and parties were arranged to entertain him; everywhere, everybody wanted to meet with the charming, enigmatic, dapper man.

Burr had stayed with General Andrew Jackson when he passed through Nashville, but Morgan found it particularly interesting that he had also held a meeting at Fort Massac on the Ohio River with General James Wilkinson before traveling on to Natchez. Now why, Morgan wondered, should Wilkinson, who owes his position and power as *the* senior officer of the military to Jefferson, entertain a man known to be out of favor with Jefferson? A most curious circumstance, he decided thoughtfully, especially in view of Wilkinson's penchant for intrigue.

24

Morgan did not exactly wish to be introduced to Aaron Burr, but it was an honor he didn't avoid either . . . particularly since his curiosity had been aroused about Burr's meeting with Wilkinson. Certainly there were many present who had come expressly for the purpose of forming an acquaintance with Aaron Burr, and watching the excited surge of the crowd as Burr made his languid way through the throng, Morgan was amused. Lazily viewing the clamor about the small party that accompanied Burr as he moved about the huge ballroom, Morgan smiled cynically, momentarily entertained by the furor.

Burr was not an imposing figure—standing only six inches above five feet, and of a slim, wiry build, he didn't appear to be the type of man whose mere presence would arouse such a feverish commotion. Just fifty years old, Aaron Burr was a dark man with thin, almost horizontal eyebrows above well-shaped hazel eyes. Often called a dandy, he was elegantly attired in a white ruffled shirt and black satin breeches, a coat of dark gray velvet fitting snugly over his slender shoulders. His allure was undeniable, but sardonically watching the effortless grace with which he bowed and exchanged greetings with those fawning around him, Morgan wondered that others didn't question such facile charm.

Most people had already been introduced to Burr so the initial excitement of his presence had begun to die down when Morgan found himself face to face with him. Leonie was at his side, her little hand unconsciously clasping his forearm with unnecessary pressure as they approached Aaron Burr.

330

Once again, Morgan's hand covered hers in a reassuring touch and he murmured, "Chin up, sweetheart. He's only a man."

Leonie shot him an indignant look, "I am not nervous!" she hissed under her breath. "I'm excited!"

At the moment, there were only two small groups near Burr. The group that interested Morgan consisted of Noelle, Matthew, and Robert, as well as their host, Stephen Minor, and Colonel Osmun. Morgan was well acquainted with Stephen Minor—Matthew and Stephen were old friends and Morgan's friend Philip Nolan had been Stephen's brother-in-law. Osmun he knew only slightly, but the man's firm handshake and bluff, hearty personality were hard to resist.

"Pleasure to meet you again, Slade," Osmun replied pleasantly to Matthew's introduction. And turning to Leonie, he said gallantly, "So this is the beautiful sister-in-law I have heard Robert singing the praises of all evening. My dear, I am enchanted." Throwing Morgan a teasing look, he added, "If I were you, sir, and I had a brother like Robert, I'm afraid I'd be a mite jealous."

Morgan laughed and made some light remark, just as Burr, who had been talking with several gentlemen to their right, suddenly entered the conversation. Swinging around to face Morgan and the others, he smiled urbanely and murmured, "And if I were married to someone as lovely as young Mrs. Slade, I *know* I would be jealous!"

Burr's unusual eyes seemed to caress Leonie's sweet features and to Morgan's amusement she blushed. But as Burr's reputation for being a devil with the ladies had preceded him, Morgan sent him a level glance and said lazily, "But, gentlemen, let me assure you, I *am* jealous! And as capable as the next man of defending my honor." Putting a possessive arm around Leonie's slender waist, he finished blandly. "Fortunately, my wife is the epitome of virtue and I am content to know that she would never give me reason to doubt her."

That Burr received Morgan's message was clear from the elegant shrug of his narrow shoulders and the mournful glance he sent Leonie. "Ah, madame, I fear your hus-

331

band is a jealous brute! It is very apparent that he will tolerate not even the mildest dalliance."

Unused to this sort of sophisticated banter and slightly shocked at Burr's open admiration of her, she blurted out, "Oh, but, Monsieur Burr, I would never be unfaithful to my husband!"

There was a burst of delighted laughter, and Leonie flushed with embarrassment, but Morgan bent down and touched his lips lightly to her temple. "Well done, my dear. Well done!"

As the laughter died down, the introductions were finished and for a few minutes there was a spate of polite conversation before Morgan was able to escape, leaving Leonie under his mother's protective eye.

Needing a respite from the heat and press of the crowd, Morgan strolled outside to the veranda to enjoy a cigar and get a breath of fresh air. He hadn't been there long when Stephen Minor joined him and for a few minutes they smoked in companionable silence, until Minor said, "And what do you think of little Burr?"

Morgan shrugged. "I don't think about him a great deal, but I confess I do wonder about what he is up to. Especially knowing that he just spent a few days with our good general at Fort Massac."

"Ah, yes, our dear friend, General Wilkinson," Stephen said blandly, throwing Morgan a teasing look.

Morgan grinned back at him and murmured, "Is there anybody you cannot charm?"

Stephen regarded the tip of his cigar and said thoughtfully, "I don't think so. . . . At least I haven't met anyone . . . yet."

It was no idle boast Minor made. He had come from Pennsylvania as a youth and had managed to carve out a powerful and respected niche for himself in Natchez. He had prospered under the Spanish rule and it was a mark of his adroitness that when Natchez passed into American hands, Stephen Minor had been its first American governor.

In his late forties, he was still a handsome man, although the thick dark hair had begun to recede near his temples. He was likely to laugh when others cursed and inclined to stay calm in the face of adversity that would make another blind with rage.

Morgan liked him; an easy relationship existed between them. They were not close friends, but each respected the other, and consequently, Morgan was not guarded in his conversation.

Jerking his head in the direction of the ballroom, Morgan asked, "Do you believe his tale of settling on those lands near the Washita River in the northern part of the Orleans Territory?

"The de Bastrop tract?"

"I suppose that's the one, unless you know of another four hundred thousand acres he's laid claim to," Morgan returned dryly.

Stephen smiled faintly. "Point taken." The two men talked for some minutes about Burr, speculating about his trip, but soon the conversation turned to more personal matters as Stephen remarked casually, "I must congratulate you on your bride. She is delightful . . . not at all what I expected."

Morgan made a face. "Has there been a great deal of talk?"

"A great deal," Stephen agreed coolly, "but I think after tonight, it will die down. Certainly your wife can be assured of the support of my wife and me. That alone should still the majority of the wagging tongues . . . even Melinda's."

Morgan looked surprised. "In view of what happened I would have thought that she would be the *last* one to talk about it! Unfortunately, it was, I'm certain, a humiliating experience for her and one she wouldn't particularly like bandied about."

"One never knows with the Melindas of the world. But I shouldn't worry—she already has her sights set on someone else."

"Anybody I know?"

Stephen's forehead creased into a slight frown. "I don't think you do know him." And looking intently through the open doors into the ballroom, he suddenly said, "That's the fellow—the tall young man in blue talking with your brother."

Morgan quickly found Dominic and with interest he noted the handsome dark-haired man about the same age at his side. "Who is he?"

"Adam St. Clair. He's English. Came here a few years ago. Has a very nice place on the bluff, Belle Vista, and owns quite a bit of acreage across the river. Nice boy. His sister lived with him for a while—but after her son was born, she left Belle Vista to join her husband. She left just last year, I believe." Suddenly struck by a thought, Stephen turned to look at Morgan. "By God, I just realized! Catherine, Adam's sister, is married to your friend, Jason!"

Morgan appeared thunderstruck. "Jason's married?" he finally got out. "And has a son?"

Stephen nodded. "Yes—and if you two were better correspondents you would have known about it! At any rate young Adam is Jason's brother-in-law, and I don't think your friend could have a nicer one."

Morgan nodded in the direction of Adam and Dominic. "And Dominic and Adam are friends?"

"Hmm, yes, quite good ones, as you'll soon discover for yourself, now that you have decided to rejoin polite society."

Morgan pulled a face. "Well, I'll tell you one thing, I certainly don't envy young St. Clair's position—not with Melinda in pursuit! Which was," Morgan added with a rueful smile, *"most* ungentlemanly of me to say."

Stephen laughed. "Very ungentlemanly . . . but perhaps appropriate under the circumstances."

The two men conversed for several more minutes and then finally Stephen said regretfully, "As I am the host of this affair, I suppose I should mingle with my guests. It has been a pleasure renewing our acquaintance, Morgan, and I look forward to seeing more of you now that you have decided to settle down."

Uneasily aware that his future might not be as secure and serene as envisioned by Minor, Morgan replied dryly, "I wouldn't count too heavily on my apparent fondness for home and hearth, Stephen—I've been searching after ad-

334

venture for so many years now, that I don't know if I could remain happy in one place for very long."

Stephen pursed his lips and shook his head. "Brett Dangermond said practically the same thing earlier this evening. You young bucks, never satisfied. Always looking for excitement. I'll tell you what I told him: Remember Philip Nolan—*he* went searching for adventure once too often!"

His attention caught by the name of Dangermond, Morgan asked eagerly, "Brett? Brett Dangermond is here tonight?" And at Stephen's nod he said slowly, "By God, I haven't seen him in years!"

Stephen laughed. "If the pair of you would remain in one place long enough, you might be able to spend time with each other. I don't know which of you is worse—both of you always harrying off after this or that!" Giving Morgan a stern look, he finished, "At least *you* have a wife now, which should slow you down a bit!"

Morgan only grinned and watched as Stephen walked into the ballroom to rejoin his guests. For a moment Morgan stood there considering entering the crush in search of his friend, Brett, but then dismissed it. If Brett were around they'd meet up sooner or later.

Having finished his cigar he absently reached inside his coat for another one, telling himself that just as soon as he smoked it, he would go inside in search of Leonie. Hopefully she would be ready to go home; he'd had enough of society for the night.

It didn't take him long to find her, and as the hour was approaching two o'clock in the morning and the many glasses of champagne she had been served had given her a headache, she was more than happy to leave. It had been an exciting evening for her, but at the moment all she longed for was her bed.

The ride back to Le Petit was accomplished in almost total silence; they had exchanged but a few comments about the ball before sleep overpowered Leonie. Stifling a mighty yawn, she had curled up against the cushioned seat of the gig and before Morgan had driven a quarter of a mile, she was sound asleep.

335

Reaching Le Petit, Morgan drove directly to the stables, and after handing the reins to a drowsy Abraham, he effortlessly plucked the sleeping Leonie from the gig. She fitted his arms nicely, he thought with a swift rush of tenderness as he carried her to the house. Her head was resting naturally against his shoulder, her slim body curving gently next to his and he suddenly wished that she was always as sweetly yielding as she was at this moment.

Silently he entered the house and made his way to her rooms. Knowing she would probably object vehemently if he attempted to make love to her, and not wishing to disrupt the uneasy harmony between them, he laid her on her bed to await the tender ministrations of Mercy.

He found Litchfield waiting for him, and shrugging out of his black velvet jacket, he said with a yawn, "I really didn't expect you to still be up."

Litchfield sent him an affronted look. "As if I would dare go to sleep before your return. Especially," he added, "when I know you would want to be informed immediately of the arrival of a letter from Jason Savage."

Sleep suddenly forgotten, Morgan spun around. "Well, for God's sake, where is it?"

Smiling loftily, Litchfield walked slowly over to a nearby table and picking up a small silver tray, presented it to Morgan.

Morgan made a face at him and snatched up the letter.

The two men had not written to one another in some time, and so briefly, Jason brought Morgan up to date—most of what he wrote, Morgan had just learned. Jason touched lightly on his marriage to Catherine Tremayne, the fact that he was now the proud father of a son, Nicholas, and that he had made Terre du Coeur, one of the many properties owned by the family in the northern part of the Territory of Orleans, his home.

It is sheer luck, Jason wrote, that you found me in New Orleans.

My grandfather suffered a seizure some weeks ago and I have been staying here only because of that. Catherine is expecting our second child at the end of

August and I mean to leave here just as soon as possible. I was not present when Nicholas was born but I damn well intend to be there for the birth of my second child!

I have done as you asked and inquired after information concernine Leonie Saint-André.

Morgan, my friend, you are not going to like what I have discovered.

I don't know if your Leonie is the same one I have learned about, but they sound very much the same. For your information, such a young woman does exist; Claude Saint-André was her grandfather as she says, and he did die in the fall of 1799. She lived, also as she says, at the family plantation, Château Saint-André, some miles below New Orleans.

I have talked with the priest, Père Antoine, who performed the ceremony of marriage, but he could throw little light on the subject. I looked over the records and saw the entry where one Morgan Slade, bachelor, from Natchez, Mississippi Territory, did indeed marry Leonie Saint-André in July of 1799.

Claude Saint-André was well thought of, if pitied at the end of his life. Apparently it was only after the death of his son some years ago that he began to waste what was a considerable fortune. Many people I spoke to expressed dismay at the state of finances that faced your Leonie when he died. Evidently, simply by pure guts and pluck she was able to keep the plantation going for several years, and it was only when old Etienne de la Fontaine died and his son Maurice took over that she was forced to leave.

I feel I should mention that there are those who imply that Maurice would have been quite happy to have simply ignored the debt, if Leonie had been more receptive to his person. And in view of her supposedly married state it is quite clear that his intentions were entirely *dis*honorable.

I don't know what else to tell you. Everything I have discovered appears to agree with what you wrote me. Certainly I haven't been able to find any facts to the contrary. Are you positive you *didn't* marry her? I was, of course, only jesting, *mon ami.*

As for there being another man involved, other than my comments about Maurice de la Fontaine, I have discovered nothing. She seems to have lived an extremely secluded existence at Château Saint-André, venturing into New Orleans only once or twice a year, and no one that I spoke to ever heard of any man in her life . . . except for her husband. That doesn't mean that there isn't a man involved, only that I can find no hint of one. I might also mention that there are those people, a few, who seriously doubt she was ever married—who believe that the marriage to Morgan Slade was all fabricated to give her son a name and respectability. They thought it strange that her husband was never in residence and that Leonie and her husband had actually never been seen together or appeared to spend *any* time with each other. It *is* peculiar, I must admit.

Jason's letter didn't contain much more, just a few added odds and ends that he had discovered about Leonie and her background and thoughtfully Morgan laid it aside. He found himself disappointed and yet not surprised by what Jason had written. It wasn't likely that someone embarking on a scheme of this type would totally fabricate everything, but he had hoped that Jason would have been able to ferret out at least one discrepancy that would have given him something to go on.

The news that Jason could find no hint of another man pleased him and at the same time troubled him. He was so certain that there was another man, that Leonie was not doing this just on her own. *Because you want someone to blame for her actions?* he asked himself jeeringly. *Or because you really do feel that there is another man in her life?*

Obviously at one time or another there *had* been a man in her life—Justin hadn't been found in a cane field!

Realizing that Litchfield was still in the room, Morgan said lightly, "Jason has nothing new to impart; his letter confirms most of what Leonie claims."

"What do you intend to do now, sir? Pay her the money?"

"I've considered it," Morgan admitted slowly, "if for no other reason than to discover the next step in the farce!"

"Mayhap you should pretend to fall in with the idea," Litchfield offered.

"Hmm. Perhaps, but somehow I doubt the little witch would believe me if I told her I was going to accede to her demands. I've expressed myself too forcibly in the past on that subject to now suddenly do a *volte-face.*"

"Then what?"

"I don't know. I'll be *damned* if I know what to do now. She's brought me to a standstill, I'm afraid . . . at least for the moment." Throwing Litchfield a crooked smile, he added, "At any rate nothing will be decided this evening, so you might as well seek out your own bed—I am quite competent, I'm certain, in preparing myself for bed."

For several moments Morgan stood in the center of his room staring at nothing, his brain busy mulling over Jason's letter and its effect on the current situation. Certainly it resolved nothing, and if anything he felt more helpless and confused than he had before.

With frustrated anger he stared at the letter. I *know* I didn't marry her—even if Jason hasn't been able to find anything wrong with her story. *I did not marry her!*

And yet faced with mounting evidence to the contrary, Morgan actually began to doubt himself. *Had* he gotten blind drunk one night and married her? Was *she* telling the truth? Perhaps he couldn't remember what had happened because he had been too drunk to even know what he had been doing? It was the only explanation that came to him and he found it curiously dissatisfying. He had never been *that* drunk in his life! Or had he?

Shaking the disconcerting thoughts from his mind, he shrugged out of the black velvet jacket. *I didn't marry her,* he told himself vehemently. *I would have remembered . . . I would have remembered her. I didn't sign that damn dowry agreement either! I wouldn't have— why the hell would I need her money? And as for any*

*other agreement she might claim I signed I know damn
well that I didn't.*

Suddenly deciding that he wanted very much to see the
other document which Leonie had mentioned on at least
one occasion, he spun on his heels and strode purposefully
into her rooms.

Leonie hadn't yet retired. She had been drowsy when
Morgan had left her, but by the time Mercy had undressed
her and had made her slip into a gorgeous negligee of yellow silk and lace, she was wide awake. Her hair still had to
be undone and brushed, and as Mercy briskly wielded the
tortoise-shell brush through the thick tawny mane, Leonie
glanced idly around the room.

With a faint frown furrowing her forehead she noticed a
pile of clothing heaped on one of the chairs. Recognizing
her own yellow gown on top of the clothes, she asked
sharply, "What are you going to do with those?" indicating
the pile of clothes with her hand.

Never missing a stroke, Mercy said calmly, "They's
goin' to be burnt. Monsieur's field hands is better dressed
than you was, missy! Now you got all them new, fine
things, ain't no reason to keep those."

For a second Leonie looked stubborn, and then realizing
it was silly to continue to so adamantly resist the situation, she hunched a shoulder and said grumpily, "I suppose you're right. Is that everything?"

"Oh, no, ma'am, I'll leave the lavender gown and rose
one with the new things—they's still nice."

Leonie's aversion to her wedding gown was too deeply
rooted to be easily overcome and her mouth tightened at
the unwelcome news that Mercy had kept it with the new
clothes. Unable to explain it herself, but wanting the garment out of her life, she snapped, "Not the rose one—it
goes with the others." And before Mercy could reply, Leonie jumped up and marched over to the big wardrobe and
flinging open the doors, rummaged around until she found
the offending garment. With a great deal of satisfaction, as
if by destroying it she could obliterate the confusion within
herself that her marriage to Morgan Slade caused, she
threw it down on the other clothes and said grimly, "Burn
it too. I never want to see it again!"

340

It was at this point that Morgan strode into the room and hearing her words, he not unnaturally asked, "Burn what, and why don't you ever want to see it again?"

Leonie turned to look at him, her earlier charity with him suddenly vanishing as she reminded herself almost despairingly that he was not to be trusted—even if earlier he had seemed to want to make their marriage real. Lifting up the rose satin gown, a hard light in her eyes she demanded, "You don't recognize the gown, monsieur?" And at Morgan's mystified expression and the negative shake of his dark head, she said with soft irony, "Ah, but of course, you don't! You don't even remember our wedding at times, so how could I expect you to remember my wedding gown? How stupid of me!"

Morgan's eyes narrowed but glancing across at the open mouthed Mercy, he said cooly, "You may leave, Mercy. Your mistress will have no further need of you tonight."

Leonie promptly countermanded the order. *"Non!* You will stay; I am not finished with you for the night."

Mercy shot a nervous look over at Morgan's unrevealing features and then back to Leonie's angry face. Deciding she would rather have to put up with a tantrum from Leonie than the unknown from Monsieur Slade, Mercy dropped a quick curtsy and scooted from the room.

Infuriated by Mercy's defection, Leonie rounded on Morgan. "How dare you order my servants about! I will tell them what I want them to do—not *you!"*

"You'd rather she stay and be a witness to the argument I'm certain is about to take place?" Morgan retorted caustically, walking further into the room.

Her hands unconsciously tightening on the rose gown, Leonie felt a shaft of frustration surge through her veins. Was he never wrong? she wondered viciously. Aloud, she said, "Bah! I'm surprised you show such restraint, monsieur. Or did you do it simply to humiliate me in front of her?"

His lean jaw clenching, refusing to be drawn, he replied evenly, "What an odd assessment of my character you've made. Someday you really must tell me what I have done

341

to make you think I would enjoy humiliating you under any circumstances."

Leonie flushed; on the defensive and not liking it at all, she asked pointedly, "What do you want? Why are you here now?"

For just a second Morgan let his eyes roam appreciatively over her silk-clad body, the soft yellow negligee clinging revealingly to her slender form. "I could say that I came to make love to you . . ." he said slowly and when Leonie stiffened and backed slightly away from him, he sighed and added, "but that isn't the case. I wanted to see that agreement you claimed I signed. The one that supposedly waivers my rights to the marriage bed."

Disappointed and yet relieved that he hadn't come to subject her to his devastating lovemaking, Leonie dropped the rose satin gown and brushing past Morgan she walked stiffly over to a small table near her bed. Opening the drawer she extracted a paper and handed it to him, suddenly uncertain how she would feel if he said he intended to abide by the agreement.

A curiously tense silence filled the room as Morgan read the document. It stated quite simply that the marriage between Leonie Saint-André and Morgan Slade entered into on July 26, 1799 was to be a marriage of convenience. Morgan Slade agreed that the marriage was to be in name only, that he would not now or in the future make any attempt to exert his conjugal rights. For a long time, Morgan stared at the bold, scrawling signature. It was his—even he could recognize that—or rather an extremely clever forgery.

Glancing over at Leonie with cold, hard eyes, he bit out, "I might have been able to convince myself that maybe I did get drunk one night and married you—but there is no way in hell that I would have signed such a document." Not giving Leonie time to reply, he walked over to where the rose satin gown lay in a bright heap on the floor. Picking it up, he said harshly, "Put it on. I want to see how you looked. I want to see if seeing you as you were when you claimed we married jars my memory."

"Monsieur, this is ridiculous!" Leonie burst out angrily. "I do not understand what you are saying. What do you mean that I *claim* we are married? We *are*, monsieur—I have all the documents to prove it!"

"So you've said all along, cat-eyes, but there's just one thing wrong," Morgan said in a dangerous tone, *"I didn't marry you!* And I'm tired of this game we have been playing the past few weeks—it's time things were settled between us. Now put on the damned gown or I'll strip you and put it on you myself."

Leonie stood resolute for a moment, but seeing the determined glitter in Morgan's eyes, she stalked over to the gown and picked it up. Giving Morgan a scathing look, she said tightly, "Will you leave so that I may dress in privacy? I do not want your lascivious eyes on me."

Morgan smiled grimly. "If you don't hurry, you're going to have more than just my eyes on you. It wouldn't take much for me to decide that making love to you is a more enjoyable way to pass the time."

Leonie's bosom swelled with indignation and fury, and throwing Morgan a look that would have annihilated a lesser man, she turned her back to him and struggled into the rose satin gown, not bothering to remove her negligee. It didn't matter, the negligee acted as a chemise and with the sea-green eyes spitting gold flecks of fury she spun around to face him.

"There, monsieur, does this satisfy you?" she snapped hotly, angry with herself for obeying him.

He stared silently at her for several seconds, noting the way the rose satin gown fit her slender body, the small breasts pushing eagerly against the smooth material, the straight, narrow skirt falling neatly to her feet and the color enhancing her complexion and tawny hair. *I would have remembered her,* he thought slowly, painfully. *I wouldn't have forgotten her if I had ever seen her.* His eyes dropped to the document still in his hands, and almost idly he asked, "If I signed this damned thing, would you please tell me, how it comes about that I am the father of a son?"

Leonie hadn't been prepared for that question. She had feared that sooner or later he would ask it, but somehow she had thought she would be better prepared when he did ask. Caught by surprise, she blenched and the expression

343

of mingled fright and guilt that flickered in the golden-green eyes was obvious even to Morgan.

Like a beast of prey leaping for the kill, he was across the room instantly and grasping one shoulder, he jerked her up next to him. "He's not my son, is he?" he ground out, all the pain and disillusionment, as well as the fury, he would have felt had she really been his wife and betrayed him coursing through his body.

Leonie's mouth and lips were dry with fear. Not fear for herself, but fear for what he might do to Justin. Almost beseechingly she began, "Monsieur, you must listen to me! I never meant to—"

Morgan shook her like a dog with a rat, and cut her off with, "You meant to what? Foster a bastard on me? Is that what you were going to say?"

At the word *bastard*, Leonie's fear fled, and with a blind fury she lashed out at Morgan's dark face, her small hand catching him a stunning blow at the side of his head. "You will not call Justin names!" she spat with rage. "You leave your filthy tongue off my son or I will kill you!"

His ears ringing from the force of her blow, Morgan shook his head as if to clear it, and savagely aware that he had allowed his emotions to rule him, that he had no right or reason to feel as he did, he released her and stepped away from her. The blue eyes hard and unfriendly, he said stiffly, "I shouldn't have called the boy that. I apologize. The argument is between us, and he shouldn't be made a part of this ugliness."

Openmouthed Leonie stared at him, unable to believe that he had apologized or that he wasn't going to toss her and Justin out into the night. Swallowing painfully, she admitted in a low tone, "I should never have told everyone he was your son, monsieur, but," the great green eyes lifted pleadingly to his, "I could not have people call him names, to laugh and jeer and call him a bastard. *I could not!* Not for myself, you understand, but for Justin."

Morgan saw very well, and he was angrily conscious of an unwanted feeling of tenderness welling up inside of him for her. Fighting off the almost overpowering urge to take her into his arms and croon passionate promises of protection and comfort into her ears, he replied coolly, "We'll leave your son out of this for the time being, but I would like to know who his father really is. Perhaps you wouldn't mind telling me—after all, if I'm to take responsibility for him, I think it is only fair that I know his background, don't you?"

Leonie looked away, her face flaming with shame. How could she tell him that she didn't know? How could she baldly come out with the news that Justin's father had been a stranger to her? A stranger who had raped her and carelessly taken her virginity? A stranger, she could tell him nothing about? She tried, but the words stuck in her throat and finally she got out in a low, mortified whisper. "Monsieur, I cannot tell . . . please do not ask me this."

A less sensitive man than Morgan would have been aware of her distress and embarrassment, and he said in a flat voice, unwilling to prolong what was obviously painful to her, "Very well, we'll leave that for now too. But I'm not moving from this room until several things are settled between us."

"What do you mean?" Leonie asked, so relieved at the moment that he was not going to pursue the painful subject of Justin's father, that she wasn't even angry . . . yet.

"Just this, cat-eyes—I didn't marry you, of that I'm positive. Neither did I sign any dowry agreement, nor that preposterous agreement concerning my rights to the marriage bed." His eyes blue chips of ice, he added, "If I'd seen you and married you, I would have brought you back to Bonheur with me—I would never have left you in New Orleans and certainly I would never have allowed you to present me with another man's son!"

"I don't understand," Leonie said slowly. "Are you going to pretend now that we never married? Is that how you hope to avoid paying the dowry back—by claiming that *I* am the one who is lying?"

Morgan smothered a curse under his breath and once again grasping Leonie's shoulders he shook her with a sort of frustrated gentleness. "You're a stubborn fighter, I'll give you that," he said harshly. "But the time for fighting is over, sweetheart. I'm through playing this game and tonight you're going to tell me the truth if I have to beat it out of you."

"But I am telling the truth!" Leonie cried angrily, her hands pushing frantically against his chest, trying to free herself.

But Morgan's hold only increased and in a surprisingly level tone of voice he said, "I made a mistake in acknowledging you and I'll admit it. It is something I should never have done, but if you think I'm going to let this situation drag on until you have firmly entrenched yourself with my family and friends you are very much mistaken."

Bewildered, confused by what he was saying, but angry too, Leonie continued to fight against him. Was he mad? she wondered. Only this afternoon he had implied he wished to make their marriage real, and yet now he was claiming he had never married her. Why had he suddenly changed?

Even Morgan couldn't have answered that question. He only knew that the situation had become intolerable. He could not and *would not* allow this mendacious state of affairs to continue any longer. And knowing he shouldn't have allowed things to reach this point didn't make his decision any easier. Whether it was Jason's letter or the certain knowledge that he hadn't married her that had crystallized that thought in his mind he didn't know; he only knew that he was not going to exist between heaven and hell as he had these past weeks.

Pulling Leonie's struggling body closer to his, he demanded grimly, "Are you going to tell me the truth? Are you going to admit that you've lied all along? I promise I'll not harm you or the boy, but for God's sake, have done with this travesty. My patience has run out, Leonie, and I think I should warn you that I am a dangerous man when provoked and God knows you have provoked me deeply enough!"

"Monsieur, I think you are insane!" Leonie said furiously. "You accuse *me* of lying, when you are the one who is lying!" Glowering up at him, she spat, "Everything I have said can be proved. Ask anyone in New Orleans and they will tell you that *Saint-Andrés do not lie!* The record of our marriage is there and yet you dare to say *I* lie! It is

346

you who are lying, monsieur! You who are not telling the truth!"

Morgan had to admire her acting ability, but it also infuriated him and in a goaded tone he snarled, "Very well, cat-eyes, we'll go to New Orleans! It's there that this bloody farce started and it's there that it is damned well going to end!"

PART FOUR

SHADOWS FROM THE PAST

The love of my life came not
  As love unto others is cast;
For mine was a secret wound—
  But the wound grew a pearl, at last.

"The Deep-Sea Pearl"
Edith Matilda Thomas

25

The first day in New Orleans passed swiftly for Leonie—as had the days before she and Morgan had left Le Petit. Having decided to come to New Orleans, Morgan had moved quickly. Within forty eight hours of his astonishing announcement, they were on a flatboat sailing down the Mississippi.

Mercy and Saul had accompanied them, as had Litchfield, but Morgan had been grimly adamant about Justin's presence. His eyes hard and cold he had stated flatly, "No. Your son isn't going to come with us! He'll be perfectly content here while we are gone. And considering the situation between us, I would have thought you might think it best that he not be subjected to any unpleasantness that arises between us."

Despite grave misgivings and a mother's natural reluctance to leave her child behind, Leonie had uneasily capitulated. Justin *would* be better off at Le Petit, she decided unhappily.

Since their argument Morgan had become very cool and aloof, as if he had retreated behind an impenetrable barrier. He was polite, very, but it was an icy politeness that froze Leonie in her tracks.

At first anger had carried her through the tense time that had followed his decision to go to New Orleans, but now her predominant feeling was confusion. Leonie was confused not only by his abrupt change in manner, but also by the ugly accusations he had hurled at her. He acted as though she had tried to trick him and there was such a note of sincere fury in his voice that Leonie was utterly bewildered. The thought had occurred to her more than once that perhaps he suffered from an occasional loss of mem-

351

ory. What else could explain his erratic behavior? One moment he appeared to want their marriage to be real and the next he stated quite forthrightly that she was a liar and an extortionist. What was one to think? Her heart wanted desperately to believe that there was a logical explanation for his wild accusations and vacillations, but her practical head came to the unhappy conclusion that he was acting, acting the part of one wronged in order to discredit and disarm her. It was, she decided angrily, simply another ploy of his not to pay the dowry.

And thinking that, she retreated behind her own wall of icy reserve, just as eager as Morgan to leave for New Orleans, to prove at last that she was no easy prey. *Mon Dieu, but I shall show him!* she vowed fiercely.

More gowns had arrived from Mrs. Dobson's before they had left Natchez. With the clothes had also come all sorts of things Leonie hadn't even thought of—satin slippers, kid boots, lacy shawls, bonnets, soaps, perfumes, pearl combs, and various other things necessary for a young matron. Noelle provided trunks and valises and Leonie had departed with a fashionable and extensive wardrobe.

Upon their arrival in New Orleans, Morgan had found a suite of rooms at a very pleasant inn south of the city. He had barely allowed Leonie to wash the travel stains from her face and change into a less crumpled gown before he had whisked her back into the city.

Having shipped a team of thoroughbreds and his curricle on the same flatboat that had brought them to New Orleans, transportation had proved no obstacle. Somewhat abruptly he had helped Leonie into the vehicle, and moments later they were headed toward the St. Louis Cathedral on Chartres Street.

It was a silent ride. Leonie stared pensively at the mud-clouded waters of the Mississippi as they rode along the river road. She missed Justin almost unbearably, and wished that he were with her. *What is he doing at this moment?* she wondered. *Is he happy with Yvette and the others?* She hoped fervently that he wasn't missing her as much as she was missing him. *Mon Dieu, but life can be very hard at times,* she thought unhappily, wishing the anger that had kept her spirits up during the first few days of their journey would return.

Anger was such a comforting emotion, she mused. It could carry one through all manner of events without allowing more disturbing or painful emotions to intrude. The problem was though, that anger—at least her anger against Morgan—could never be sustained for any length of time. After a day or two stronger emotions began to erode her anger, leaving her vulnerable and unprotected from the promptings of her own stubborn heart. Almost resentfully she shot Morgan a look from underneath her long, curling lashes. *Why does he have to hold this power over me?* she asked herself crossly, not liking the way her senses responded to his presence, the way her heartbeat quickened whenever he was near, or the way her arms ached to embrace him.

Leonie sighed again. *His attraction is extremely potent,* she admitted gloomily, *but I would be a great fool if I even seriously considered following anything but my original plan.* Her full mouth tightened. *I must be strong, and no matter how much it hurts, no matter how painful it will be—for both Justin and myself—just as soon as I can make him pay me the dowry, we must escape from his spell.*

But can you bring yourself to leave him? Leonie wondered painfully. Slyly her mind taunted her: *Why would you willingly cling to a man who has proved himself to be so dishonorable?* She knew the answer to that question and convulsively she swallowed. *I love him and I am a great fool!* she thought disgustedly, her emotions in a tangled agony.

Morgan's emotions were not in much better condition. At the moment he was cursing himself for having embarked upon this journey, grimly aware that the old adage of letting sleeping dogs lie had much to recommend it.

You bullheaded ass, he thought furiously, *you had to have this settled, didn't you? You had to force the issue—instead of wooing her and thanking God every day that she had come into your life . . . and* damn *the reasons!*

It was the same futile argument he'd had with himself ever since he had determined upon this trip to New Orleans; time had not lessened the bitter frustration that ate

353

at him. He wanted the truth and yet he feared it, which didn't help his lacerated emotions at all. With a feeling of dull rage he realized that nothing was ever going to be the same again. The little witch at his side had made certain of that, he thought viciously. She had woven her spell too well for him to ever escape and he was furiously aware of it.

In an unfriendly silence they reached the St. Louis Cathedral. After tying the reins to an iron hitching post, he walked around the curricle and, in the same unfriendly silence, helped Leonie down.

Together they walked into the cathedral, its Spanish influence obvious from the round towers set on either side of the building and the Moorish arched windows and doorways. It was cool and quiet inside.

Leonie was aware of an odd feeling as she walked down the aisle with Morgan at her side. She had married this man here almost six years ago, and it was here that her infant son had been baptized. *Grand-père* had been standing there, near the altar, as she and Morgan had repeated their vows and she remembered with surprise all the resentment and anger she had felt against both her grandfather and the man at her side. *How long ago it all seems,* she thought slowly, *as if it happened to someone else in another lifetime.*

Justin's baptism was a bittersweet memory. She could remember the comforting warmth of his little body and the great squall of outrage he had given when Père Antoine had poured the holy water on his little head. How lonely and frightened she had been that day! *Grand-père* was dead, she had no money, the servants and Yvette were completely dependent upon her, and the small, squirming baby in her arms was her sole responsibility. At seventeen how bleak and terrifying the world had seemed, and unconsciously she shivered.

Morgan felt the slight movement and thinking it was nervousness, his hand tightened slightly around her elbow. Bending his head a little, he whispered, "I'm not going to strangle you, cat-eyes . . . no matter what we find out."

Leonie sent him a scornful look. "Monsieur, I have nothing to hide! I have been telling the truth and you will discover nothing here that will come as a surprise to me!"

Morgan's brow rose cynically. A mocking smile lifting the corner of his mouth, he murmured, "Somehow that's exactly what I suspected you would say. Under the circumstances you are to be commended for your brave stance."

"Ah, bah! You do not make sense, monsieur! None of this makes any sense! What do you hope to prove by your poking and prying? That I am lying?" Leonie gave a low, angry laugh. "You are much mistaken, monsieur, if you think you can discredit me. The truth *will* prevail!"

"Which is *precisely* what I want," Morgan said sharply, the blue eyes hard as they rested on her flushed features.

A decidedly unladylike snort came from Leonie, but whatever else she would have said was stilled by the sight of the gaunt figure walking out the vestibule near the altar. Throwing Morgan a strangely entreating glance, she shook off his hand and muttered, "Monsieur, please do not be rude to me in front of Père Antoine. He would not understand how it is with us."

Feeling like the villian in the piece and not liking it, Morgan barely had time to murmur, "I have no intention of making our differences public," before the priest walked up to them.

Père Antoine's brown eyes widened with pleasure as they rested on Leonie's face and with obvious warmth he said, "Leonie, my dear! What a most pleasant surprise to see you here." Taking her hand in his he smiled down at her and continued, "But how is this? I had heard that you had left Saint-André and meant to live in Natchez with your husband? What has brought you back to New Orleans?"

Almost shyly Leonie indicated Morgan and answered nervously, "M-my h-husband, Père Antoine, He wished to visit the cathedral to view our marriage records."

One thin black brow rising quizzically, Père Antoine turned to look at Morgan. "How curious! A Jason Savage was here recently and he, too, wanted exactly the same thing. Have you some doubts about the validity of your marriage? It was most proper I assure you—if you remember, I performed the ceremony myself."

355

Staring intently into the lined, serene face Morgan asked bluntly, "And was I the man you married her to?"

Père Antoine was clearly taken aback. "But of course, monsieur! I have known Leonie all her life and while I had never met you before the wedding, I remember what a lovely couple you made. I also remember how happy I was that Leonie's future was finally assured, and how fortunate she was to have such a handsome young husband."

Conscious of a sinking feeling in the pit of his stomach, Morgan forced himself to press further. "Are you quite certain that I am that man? You have no doubts?"

Affronted and yet puzzled, Père Antoine's eyes traveled slowly over Morgan's grim features. "I believe so," he finally said. "As I told Monsieur Savage, and as I told you just a moment ago, I only met you the one time, and while I might not have remembered you exactly if we had passed on the street, seeing you here in the cathedral with Leonie at your side brings it all back to me." His brown eyes boring into Morgan's blue eyes, he said softly, "Monsieur, I do not know what the problem is, but be assured that I recognize you as the man I married to Leonie . . . unless, of course, you have a twin whose name is also Morgan Slade."

Morgan's face went white and in that second, like a bullet striking him between the eyes, the answer to the entire mystery exploded in his brain. The disquieting feeling that there was something vital about that trip to New Orleans in 1799 that he should have remembered, the missing piece of the puzzle that had eluded him, and the certainty that there was another man involved, all those baffling fragments added up just one thing.

"Ashley!" Morgan snarled with such suppressed venom that Père Antoine took a step backwards and Leonie stared at Morgan with openmouthed astonishment.

Hardly aware of the two of them, Morgan's hands unconsciously clenched into fists. With silent virulence he cursed himself as he remembered times in the past that Ashley had taken advantage of their extraordinary resemblance, and had impersonated him and forged his signature as well. *I should have remembered as soon as I saw those damned documents!* he thought with helpless rage.

356

The episode of the forged gaming vowels, and the seduction of the tavern wench came flooding back to Morgan. "How could I have been so blind? So God damned *blind!*" His voice exploded and echoed in the silent cathedral.

"Young man! I think you forget that this is God's house! You will not profane His name here!" Père Antoine said sharply.

Blankly Morgan stared at him, and then with an effort he shook himself free of the ugly thoughts that were raging in his brain. Guiltily aware that he had offended the priest, he said honestly, "Forgive me, Father! Your words gave me a shock." And feeling some further explanation was necessary for his peculiar behavior he added, "You made me remember something that I should never have forgotten . . . but that was no excuse for my profanity. I am sorry if I gave offense and can only beg your forgiveness."

Slightly mollified, Père Antoine replied, "Of course, my son. And I am happy I could help you. I trust that I have answered all of your questions?"

There were many questions rioting through Morgan's brain, but Père Antoine could answer none of them. It was apparent that Leonie had not lied about the marriage and obvious too that the priest knew her well—at least *she* was no impostor! Had she known what Ashley was up to? And been a willing party to the farce? He rather thought not, but it was an avenue that needed exploring before he made any decisions. Conscious of the priest waiting politely for his answer, Morgan nodded. "Yes, you have, Father. . . . I cannot tell you how important this conversation has been to me."

Turning to the confused Leonie, Morgan gently grasped her upper arm and said lightly, "We won't take up any more of your time, Father. I think we had best be off now, don't you agree, my dear?"

Leonie nodded dumbly, left totally at sea by his sudden transformation. *Mon Dieu,* would she ever understand him?

Père Antoine regarded them for a long moment and then asked suddenly, "Monsieur Slade, is it possible that you suffer from a loss of memory? Is that why you have asked

357

these most peculiar questions? Why you had Monsieur Savage examine the marriage registry?"

"That's it exactly!" Morgan replied quickly, as he seized blindly upon the excuse offered for his odd behavior. Swiftly embellishing the theme, he prevaricated, "It is an old dueling wound, you understand? And sometimes certain events are hazy to me."

"Somewhat unnerving for your family and friends, I would suspect," Père Antoine said dryly.

"I fear it is!" Morgan answered quite cheerfully. Glancing at Leonie's perplexed features, he added coolly, "My wife has found it a great trial these past weeks, but I think now, after this enlightening conversation, that things will be much easier between us."

Wanting time to think, Morgan almost dragged Leonie out of the cathedral. Furious with himself for not realizing sooner what had happened, his brain was wildly sorting out the implications of what he had learned. *If only,* he thought viciously, *I had remembered receiving the news of Ashley's presence in New Orleans, that would have explained a great deal!*

Morgan hadn't completely organized his racing thoughts, but he knew for damn certain now that Ashley had been impersonating him to his own advantage. And as the minutes passed, and he hurriedly reviewed all he knew about the situation, he was inclined to believe that Leonie had also been Ashley's victim. The cold cynic in him objected on principle to such weak proof of Leonie's innocence, but his heart would have none of it—she *had* to be innocent!

As he drove the horses through the narrow streets, Leonie was quiet for several moments. Finally she asked, "Is it true, monsieur? Is that wound the reason you have acted so strangely?"

For a second Morgan's mind went blank. Unwilling to try to explain what he thought had happened—and still somewhat suspicious of her possible involvement in the scheme—he replied, "Yes. But I have never let my family know the full extent of my injury. It would trouble my parents too much, I fear, so it has been not much discussed in the family. I should have told you about it earlier."

358

Still suspicious, Leonie stared at him, trying very hard to ignore the attraction between them. "You are telling me the truth? You are not lying? This is not just another way to avoid repaying my dowry?"

Morgan took a deep breath, torn between the desire to curse and laugh at the same time. Cynicism aside, he wanted nothing more than to kiss her soundly and tell her the truth, but this was not a propitious time. She was far more likely to box his ears than to respond passionately to his embrace. He was certain that given the tense situation between them, if she *were* innocent and he attempted to explain about Ashley, she would be convinced that it was only another delaying tactic. But wanting to reassure her, he said quietly, "This is not a trick. Leonie." Ruthlessly throttling the suspicion of lingering doubt, his face suddenly hard, he continued with a harsh note in his voice, "As for your dowry, I'll start making arrangements for it to be paid to you, just as soon as I can see my business agent here. By the end of the week you should have your damned money!"

Instead of the triumph she had expected to feel at these words, Leonie found herself strangely bereft, as if her protective armor had been stripped from her. She tried to tell herself that she *was* overjoyed at his unexpected capitulation, but her apparent victory filled her with an aching hollowness. Once Morgan had repaid the money, there would be no reason for them to continue their marriage. *No reason at all,* Leonie thought painfully, angrily squeezing back sudden, hot tears. The agreement they had signed before their marriage had made that *quite* clear.

The news of his old dueling wound did much to explain his erratic behavior and she felt her heart fill with sympathy for him. It must have been extremely galling for him, she decided miserably, to have accepted her accusations of treachery and her assertion that she was his wife, when he couldn't even remember marrying her! No wonder he had been cruel at times! He must have thought she was an unprincipled jade!

Curiously, she asked, "Does the wound trouble you overmuch, monsieur? I mean, does your memory come and go?"

Uncomfortably, Morgan muttered, "Er, no, it doesn't.

Our marriage seems to be the only major event I have ever forgotten."

Leonie frowned. "But you *do* remember it now?" she asked suspiciously.

Morgan debated again the wisdom of more lies and decided against it. Sooner or later he was going to have some unpleasant explaining to do and the more truth he told now, the better off he was going to be then. He definitely didn't relish the prospect of telling Leonie about Ashley, especially since she was so understandably mistrustful of him, but he disliked even more the idea of pretending knowledge he didn't have. Unable to look at her, he said only, "No . . . not exactly."

Leonie threw him a speculative glance, the lingering distrust obvious in the green eyes. "But when you spoke to Père Antoine, you implied you remembered everything!"

Morgan swore softly under his breath and replied sharply, "I know that the marriage took place . . . but I don't know the events that led up to it." Looking across at her, he asked surprisingly, "Would you mind telling me how the marriage came about? I'm afraid the times you have spoken of it in the past, I didn't pay much attention." Giving her a lopsided grin, he added honestly, "I was too busy telling myself what a convincing little liar you were."

Uncertain whether to take umbrage at his words or not, Leonie regarded him thoughtfully for a moment. Coming to the reluctant conclusion that if he *hadn't* remembered the marriage that he deserved some explanation, she told him how her grandfather had decided it was time for her to marry.

"It was only after he died," she said sadly, "that I learned from our physician that *grand-père* had known he didn't have long to live. *That* was why he was in such a hurry to marry me off." Smiling tentatively at Morgan, she went on, "I was furious when he first told me about the marriage! And I wasn't precisely happy when he mentioned *you* either! He told me that he had met you at the governor's house and that it was all decided . . . everything, that is, but the dowry."

She stopped, remembering how she had felt the morning Claude had told her about meeting Morgan Slade, and then remembering too what had happened to her that night at the governor's residence, she trembled. Morgan noted the movement and aware of just how bestial Ashley could be, he lightly touched her arm. His blue eyes fixed intently on her, he said softly, "Was I such a boor, sweetheart? I assure you, I didn't mean to be."

Leonie looked at him, the puzzlement she was experiencing clear in her eyes. "I did not like you, monsieur," she admitted painfully. "I did not think it fair that you should have the dowry that would have meant so much to Saint-André . . . that still means so much to Saint-André." Her eyes sparkling with remembered anger, she burst out unexpectedly, "And you were dishonorable even on our wedding night! You tried to force your attentions on me!"

A surge of swift fury against Ashley shook him, and jealousy flaming through him, his face suddenly savage, Morgan ground out, "And did I succeed?"

Leonie smiled angelically. "No, monsieur, you did not! I held you off with *grand-père's* dueling pistol. You were very angry." Staring at him, she inquired earnestly, "You do not remember it?"

His fury dying, and conscious of a feeling of relief, of a swift, almost painful stab of joy at his belief in her innocence grew, Morgan shook his head. Glad that there was something he could tell the truth about, he answered her question carefully, "No, I'm afraid I don't remember a bit of it."

Conversation languished after that, and though they rode back to the inn in silence, it was not the same unfriendly silence that had accompanied them on their outward journey.

While the dueling wound explained most of his actions to Leonie, it did nothing to explain her bewildering dismay at the news that he would at last pay her the dowry. She had yearned for the money so desperately, for so long that it was only now that she realized she would gladly, joyously, forget the debt had ever existed, if only Morgan would tell her he loved her and wanted her as his wife. Which was highly unlikely, she admitted miserably. He had never wanted a wife in the first place, so why would he

361

change his mind simply because he realized now that the marriage had indeed taken place?

Morgan was involved with his own thoughts and he didn't notice her introspection as they neared the inn. He had attempted to think through all the implications of Ashley's actions upon the current situation, but the fierce elation he had felt when he could finally acknowledge Leonie's innocence had effectively distracted him. She had been telling the truth, as she knew it, right from the beginning, he mused with a growing sense of delight. Over and over again that thought was reverberating through his brain and he was aware of an insane urge to laugh, to shout, to share his burgeoning happiness with the world.

But then a wave of bitter remorse flooded his body as he remembered all the ugly and arrogant accusations he had thrown at her. *What a bloody fool I've been,* he reflected bleakly. *How could I have been so deaf to her honest appeals? So determined not to believe her, when the truth had been right there before me all the time? My God! How could I have forgotten Ashley's trip to America? And now, how to undo the damage?*

There were, as Morgan was well aware, no easy answers. And even when Leonie knew the truth and realized that he had been laboring under as great a misapprehension as she had been, could she find it in her heart to forgive him? Could she learn to love him? His mouth twisted in bitter regret—he'd certainly given her no reason to love him!

26

A few minutes later, Morgan helped Leonie down from the curricle and escorted her inside the inn to their rooms. The long, two-storied building had once been a private residence. Shiny black shutters hung at the narrow windows; a wide, shady gallery ran across the front of the house, and the plastered brick exterior was an unsullied white from regular coatings of whitewash.

Morgan and Leonie's rooms were on the second floor and had originally been the master suite. The two respectable-sized bedrooms were separated by what the innkeeper extravagantly referred to as a private sitting room. Judging by its tiny, cramped interior Morgan suspected that it had once been a dressing room.

The sitting room was an added comfort not often found in inns and Morgan was satisfied with it. Turning to Leonie though, he asked, "I hope this meets with your approval."

Leonie glanced blankly at the room, too lost in her own unhappy thoughts to pay much attention to her surroundings. She nodded her head and said politely, "Oh, yes. It is quite pleasant." *Such stilted words,* she mused wretchedly to herself. *Such a correct reply, when all I want to do is cry aloud that I love you and where we are matters little . . . if you love me.*

Morgan noted the hint of unhappiness about her and mistaking its cause, he asked abruptly, "Are you missing Justin terribly? Is that why you look so forlorn?"

Distressed that her misery was so plain, she forced a smile to her lips and answered with partial honesty, "I do miss him most awfully. Will we be here for any great length?"

363

It wasn't a question that Morgan could answer easily. Still off balance from the discovery that Ashley had impersonated him—with such complicated results—he hadn't had time yet to think things out. There were so many facets to consider, and beyond his certainty of Leonie's innocence, he had explored none. Frowning a little, he admitted, "I don't know. But I would suspect that it will be some weeks before we return to—" he stopped, his frown increasing, as he found himself viewing a return to Le Petit with an odd reluctance. There was nothing specific that he could put his finger on, but he imagined it was simply that the house had served its purpose as far as he was concerned. Beyond the ill-judged step of becoming engaged to Melinda, he had never thought to tie himself to Natchez and the Bonheur plantation; he had considered living at Le Petit with Leonie merely as a means to an end. Certainly he had never planned for them to live out their lives there. As for Thousand Oaks . . . He grimaced. No. Thousand Oaks belonged to the past and any pleasure it may have once given him was as dead as his love for Stephanie.

A thoughtful expression on his lean face, he looked across at Leonie and asked carefully, "Have you any particular place you would like to live?"

Her heart sank like a lump of lead to her toes, as any hope that he might want to make their marriage work fled. Obviously he meant to send her away as soon as he repaid the dowry. Perhaps sooner, if he could arrange it, she thought miserably. Valiantly gathering her flagging spirits and ignoring the agonizing ache in the region of her heart, she smiled and said staunchly, "It was always my intention to live at Château Saint-André."

For a long, reflective moment, Morgan turned the idea around in his head. Everything he had learned of the Château Saint-André was discouraging, but then, it had once been a productive, profitable plantation . . . and it could be again. Especially, he decided slowly, if he could regain the lost acreage. If he were to invest his own money in it there was no reason why it couldn't provide them with a pleasant living. Besides which, he admitted ruefully, he rather doubted his stubborn beloved would settle for anyplace else. He said calmly, "Very well, if that's what you want."

Her chin set at a proud angle, Leonie replied stiffly, "It is, monsieur. If you will remember, it was to save Saint-André that I came to Natchez in the first place."

Morgan made a face. "So it was," he admitted wryly. "Well, since that has been decided," he continued slowly, "I see no reason not to send for Justin and the others. It will take them some time to pack and ready for the journey and by the time they arrive here we should have things settled."

Leonie nodded numbly, wondering if people really did die of broken hearts. Certainly hers was cracking into tiny pieces with every calm, indifferent word Morgan spoke. *How easily he disposes of everything,* she thought painfully. *As if we were unwanted baggage that he is pushing out of his life. But did you expect anything else?* she demanded of herself angrily. *You knew he never wanted to marry you! So why should you be so surprised now that he wants you out of his life? Because,* her heart replied wistfully, *there were times when he looked at me or held me in his arms and—and because I love him most dreadfully. Ah, bah!* she suddenly scolded herself disgustedly. *You are a simpleton, Leonie, a gooseheaded simpleton, if you do love him!*

To Morgan, she merely asked, "Will you send the message to Le Petit, or shall I?"

"I'll do it," he said easily. "There will be several other things that must be taken care of too, so if you don't mind, I'll send Saul with the letter rather than entrusting it to the mail."

"As you wish," Leonie returned coolly, her fingers digging into the palms of her hands as she fought to control the ridiculous urge to burst into tears.

Leonie's unusually subdued mood hadn't escaped Morgan, that and the fact that she seemed to be angry and yet oddly forlorn at the same time. That she had reason to be angry he couldn't deny—from her point of view she had been treated abominably and he was uncomfortably aware that it was going to be no easy task convincing her of his own innocence . . . or gaining her trust. A feeling of impotent rage swept through him when he thought of Ashley, and bleakly he looked across at Leonie, cursing the trick that fate had played against them. But conscious of the need for time, and hoping to erase the slight, unhappy droop to her lovely mouth, he said with forced cheerfulness, "I'll see to it immediately and in no time at all Justin will be scampering underfoot." Glancing at his watch, he murmured, "And as there are several things I mean to see about this afternoon, if you do not mind, I shall leave you on your own for a few hours."

Leonie shook her head, almost glad to see him leave. She needed a respite from the bittersweet pleasure of his company . . . and time to consider a future that did not have Morgan Slade in it.

Bidding Leonie a brief good-bye, Morgan quickly left the room and went in search of Litchfield. Finding his man-servant unpacking the few valises they had brought with them, Morgan swiftly informed Litchfield of what had transpired.

His face perfectly composed and showing no surprise at all, Litchfield replied sedately, "Of course, Ashley. How stupid of us not to have thought of him." Throwing Morgan a questioning glance, he asked, "Have you told the madame?"

Sardonically, Morgan remarked, "And have her think I'm mad? Do you honestly think she'd believe me, if I said, 'Oh, by the way, it wasn't me you married, only my cousin masqerading as me?' " His face twisting wryly, he added, "And considering everything, I can't say that I would blame her!"

"Yes, I do see the problem," Litchfield admitted slowly, carefully hanging up a white linen shirt in the tall mahogany wardrobe. Glancing back at Morgan, who had discovered quill and ink and was beginning to compose a letter to Dominic, Litchfield said, "If Ashley married her using *your* name, and forging *your* signature, is she *your* wife? Or his?"

"Mine!" Morgan shot back before he had time to really consider Litchfield's question. Then he muttered, "I think. I don't know. But," he added, an implacable note in his

366

voice, "it doesn't make any difference. Leonie *will* be my wife."

A few minutes later, the letter to Dominic safely on its way to Le Petit, Morgan was once again driving the curricle into the city. Though he had planned to drive back into the city before Litchfield had raised the disturbing question of Leonie's *real* husband, the need to know that answer made the trip even more imperative.

His first stop was the Beauvais townhouse where he learned to his disappointment that Jason had left the city not two days before, heading for Terre du Coeur. His inquiries about Armand's health brought forth the happy news that the old man was on the mend at the Beauvais plantation and that it was hoped he would return to town once he had regained his strength.

Leaving the townhouse, Morgan drove to the offices of Ramey, Ramey, and Jardin, the firm that had always handled the Slade legal affairs in New Orleans. Over several glasses of fine brandy, Morgan told Monsieur Leon Ramey the tale of Ashley's impersonation. At the end of the story, Morgan stared intently into his brandy and asked quietly, "So, now that you know what happened, what I am almost positive happened . . . tell me, is Leonie my wife, or not?"

It was silent in the room for several seconds as the older man sat in his overstuffed leather chair and seemed to contemplate the air in front of him. Finally, looking at Morgan's tense features, he said abruptly, "He may have impersonated you, he may even have married her under your name, tricked the girl and her grandfather to gain the money, but . . . it is *Ashley* Slade who is legally her husband."

A shaft of paralyzing pain shot through Morgan's body, and a shout of angry, agonized denial rose up in his throat, but coldly, ruthlessly he throttled it. Grimly hanging onto his helpless rage, he asked carefully, "Can the marriage be annulled? To my knowledge it has never been consummated." Some of his fury bursting through, he snarled, "She's never even seen the bastard in the past six years!"

Monsieur Ramey was impervious to Morgan's rage, and calmly he considered the problem. Glancing at Morgan, he

367

asked abruptly, "What of the child? Are you certain the marriage was not consummated?"

His jaw set in a harsh, uncompromising line, Morgan gritted out, "Yes, I'm certain—she told me so herself. She will not talk about the child's father, but if he was"—the name gagged him—"Ashley's, she'd have no reason to deny it. Quite the contrary!"

Monsieur Ramey settled back in his chair, looking thoughtful. "The child," he said eventually, "does complicate things, but I think we can resolve that particular problem. But to return to your original question—I believe, considering the circumstances," he murmured slowly, "that an annulment could be obtained . . . but it will take time. And there will be no way to conceal the infamy of your cousin's actions. The woman would be the one to suffer—could you bear to have her name on everyone's lips?" At the expression on Morgan's face, Monsieur Ramey held up an admonishing finger, "No, *mon ami*, no matter how many duels you fought, you would not be able to stop the gossip."

Tightly Morgan asked, "What do you suggest?"

Monsieur Ramey pursed his lips. "For the moment I would suggest you continue as you are. Tell her the truth if you wish, but I would not let the truth go any further. It is possible that if we keep the truth amongst ourselves and everyone acts with discretion, that we might brush through this most awkward situation with a minimum of distress for everyone. With your permission, I shall speak to Père Antoine, to find out what he can do to start proceedings within the church. If we are fortunate, he may be the only other person besides ourselves in New Orleans to know of this travesty."

Morgan nodded his head, aware of the calm good sense in Monsieur Ramey's words. But it did nothing to still the ugly fury that raged within his breast. Ashley was *not* going to have Leonie! He'd kill him first . . . slowly and with pleasure.

They conversed for some time longer, but finally Morgan prepared to depart. He shook Monsieur Ramey's hand and said, "I'll leave it to you. If you need me, a messenger will find me at Mrs. Brosse's Inn or Château Saint-André."

Morgan next sought out the Slade business agent. As New Orleans was the port of departure for most of Bonheur's goods, the Slade family had extensive business and social connections in the city. The gentleman Morgan went to see, like Monsieur Ramey, had dealt with the family for many years.

Monsieur LeFort, a dour, pragmatic man approaching middle age, had thought that nothing the heir to the Slade estates could ever do would surprise him. After all, what could one expect of a gentleman who willingly lived with savages for two years? But when Morgan blandly stated that he wanted a rather large sum of gold put into an account for the sole use of his wife, Monsieur LeFort's round blue eyes nearly started from his head. "But—but, Monsieur Slade! Isn't that a trifle excessive? I certainly do not venture to tell you how to spend your money, but do you think it wise to allow a woman to handle so large a sum?"

Morgan smiled ruefully, thinking of the years that Leonie had thriftily kept her little family living on a mere pittance. "Monsieur," he said dryly, "believe me when I say that the young lady is more than capable of handling her own affairs."

Monsieur LeFort shrugged his narrow shoulders. "Very well, monsieur. And will there be anything else?"

Morgan was silent for several minutes, wondering at the wisdom of the step he was about to take. He was aware that he could simply allow Leonie to use what she assumed was her dowry to pay off her debt to Maurice de la Fontaine, but something within him balked at that idea. God knows what the little minx could have accomplished with the money, he thought dryly, if her grandfather had not insisted that it be squandered in buying a husband . . . especially a husband like Ashley! For a moment he looked grim. If only the old man hadn't made the mistake of approaching the wrong Slade!

Feeling an overwhelming need to make some sort of restitution, to do something that would make Leonie see that all men were not unscrupulous bastards, Morgan finally said, "There is a gentleman by the name of Maurice de la Fontaine who holds a note on my wife's home, the Château

369

Saint-André." The long mouth tightened slightly and he went on, "I should say rather, he holds a note against what remains of the plantation, after the bulk of the acreage had been sold. At any rate, I want you to pay off the debt in full immediately."

Thinking of all the money that was going to be leaving his wise management, Monsieur LeFort fidgeted with some papers on his desk. "That is in *addition* to the money you want deposited in your wife's account?"

Morgan almost grinned, aware of Monsieur LeFort's frugality. "Yes," he answered cheerfully. A mocking gleam in the blue eyes, he asked dulcetly, "I *do* have enough money, don't I?"

Monsieur LeFort sent him a speaking glance. Aware that he was being mocked, he said stiffly, "There is no lack of funds, monsieur, as you must know!"

"Then there shouldn't be any trouble for you to arrange everything, should there?"

Monsieur LeFort nodded his head curtly. "It will be done within a matter of hours."

Morgan cocked an eyebrow at him. "That soon?" he asked skeptically.

Monsieur LeFort allowed a superior smile to cross his thin features. "Claude Saint-André was my client as well as the de la Fontaine family. Maurice de la Fontaine was in here at the beginning of the month speaking to me about the Saint-André note—he wanted a quick sale, but until now, I have been unable to find a buyer. He will be quite pleased that I have arranged the matter so satisfactorily."

"I see," Morgan said slowly. "It appears that de la Fontaine was *not* going to wait for his money, after all."

"Pardon, monsieur? I'm afraid I don't understand."

"Apparently, de la Fontaine had told my wife that he would give her an additional thirty days to redeem the property. She thought she had until the first of July to come up with the money."

Monsieur LeFort appeared uncomfortable. Reluctantly, he said, "Monsieur Maurice is not the gentleman his father was."

Privately Morgan thought that was an understatement, but he let it go, even though he filed the information away for future reference. "It makes little difference," he said crisply. "The important thing is that I have that note just as soon as possible."

Monsieur LeFort nodded his head. "It will be in your hand by tomorrow afternoon. I am aware that Monsieur de la Fontaine is in the city and one of my assistants will inform him of our transaction immediately. In the morning all I will need is his signature clearing the debt." Hopefully, he asked, "And will that be all for you today, monsieur?"

Morgan slowly shook his head, his lips twitching a little as he pictured the gloom that was about to descend upon Monsieur LeFort's face. And when he informed LeFort what it was he wanted, the business agent's face was gloomy indeed.

A few minutes later a smiling Morgan strode out of Monsieur LeFort's office, but the smile faded as he settled himself into the curricle and began to drive away from the city toward the inn. Despite the plans that he had set in motion, nothing had really changed. Leonie was still Ashley's wife, and Morgan was dismally aware of the fact that if he tried to explain the tangle, she wouldn't believe him. He had trouble believing the situation himself.

If only I had remembered Ashley's trip to New Orleans sooner, he berated himself for the hundredth time. *Then at least we wouldn't be so firmly enmeshed in this silly charade. And Leonie wouldn't be so mistrustful of me,* he thought regretfully. *All it would have taken,* he mused reflectively, *was just the mention of Ashley's name and everyone in the family would have realized what had occurred.* The outcome would have been the same: The entire family, himself included, would have been united behind Leonie and against Ashley. But more importantly, the mistrust and suspicion that had underlined his every move with Leonie would never have existed.

Thinking of how much simpler his relationship with Leonie could have been, Morgan sighed. But then his lips curved in a reminiscent smile. No, he couldn't say that he *entirely* regretted what had transpired in Natchez, the

371

memory of Leonie in his arms crossing his mind. But even without their living together at Le Petit, he knew he still would have fallen in love with her. *I could have courted her properly,* he thought slowly, *wooed her as she deserves, instead of treating her like the little scheming devil I assumed she was.* His mouth twisted. *Damn Ashley!* he cursed silently. *Damn, damn him.*

At the moment, Ashley was cursing too, but his cursing had to do with the cramped quarters that had been assigned to him on the ship. At first they hadn't seemed too bad, but after almost a month at sea, and the prospect of another two weeks, his complacency was rapidly disappearing. Even dwelling on the fortune that would be his once he found his wife and returned to Europe no longer had the power to cheer him. Cursing the weather, the sea, the ship, and the necessity for the trip, he stared moodily at the choppy blue-green waters.

I just hope I can find the little bitch without too much trouble, he thought sourly. *It'll be my damned luck that she's run away with some itinerant peddler.* But then again, he mused idly, it was possible she was still clinging to the old plantation, in the hope that he would honor their bargain and return the dowry. For a second an unkind grin split his face. *Stupid bitch!* To think, she had tried to get the better of Ashley Slade. His good humor restored, for a moment he considered the remote possibility that she had finally managed to meet the real Morgan Slade. Picturing the confusion and dismay such an event would have caused, he laughed out loud. If it wasn't imperative for his own bright future to take his rightful place as her husband, Ashley rather thought he would have arranged just such a confrontation. It would have been one way of taking a small measure of revenge against Morgan. *By God, but it would be a joy to watch,* he chuckled wickedly to himself.

Morgan found no joy in his present predicament, and Leonie's withdrawn, almost aloof manner that evening did nothing to help his frustated impotence. A dozen times, he nearly broached the subject, but Leonie's attitude, stilled the words on his lips. Not that he blamed her—his own actions since they had met had not been precisely charming, he thought with a grimace, as he prepared for bed that night. *Tomorrow,* he promised himself determinedly, *tomorrow will be different. Tomorrow I begin as I should have in the first place.*

Leonie's view for the next day was not particularly hopeful. It was true Morgan had been very kind at dinner, but protecting herself from the further pain of the approaching separation, she would not let herself respond to his attempts at gallantry or conversation. She wanted it over with. If he was going to leave her, she did not wish to be subjected to a lingering, painful farewell. *Just leave me!* she thought fiercely, as she lay in bed that night. *Just leave me and let me get on with my own life.*

In the morning she woke with a feeling of exhaustion and depression. It was an effort to dress, and all she longed for was privacy where she could release all the bitter, unhappy tears that clogged her throat. But Leonie was a fighter, so she forced a pleasant smile, and went to meet Morgan for breakfast.

It was a delightful morning. The sky was a bright, cloudless blue; there was no hint of the enervating mugginess that would permeate the air later.

Even the setting for their breakfast was delightful. During the summer Mrs. Brosse preferred to serve her guests their morning meal on a small patio at the side of the inn. The iron tables and chairs were placed under the welcoming shade of a huge oak tree. Vivid flowers bloomed everywhere; purple bougainvillea cascaded down near one corner of the house, pink camellias grew nearby, and scarlet geraniums danced in the slight breeze that broke the stillness of the air.

But Leonie had no heart to take enjoyment from either the day or her surroundings; her only thought was to see Morgan and make clear that once he had seen to the business of repaying her dowry, that there was no reason for him to have any further involvement in the affairs of the Saint-Andrés. She had managed alone before he had so high-handedly taken over her life, and she would manage again.

Consequently, just as soon as she had been seated and morning greetings had been exchanged, ignoring the stabbing pain in her heart, she said staunchly, "Monsieur, I think it is time for some plain speaking between us." At Morgan's quizzical look, she continued doggedly, "Now that you know I was not lying about the marriage, and that you really do owe me the dowry . . . as . . . as soon as you have seen your banker about paying me back my money, I see no reason for us to continue to intrude in each other's lives."

For a long moment Morgan contemplated her, one part of him taking pleasure in the pretty picture she presented in a stylish gown of pale apricot muslin. But while he could take enjoyment from looking at her, another part of him was puzzled and angry that she could speak so coolly of a parting. With a hint of hardness in his voice, he parried, "Is there some great urgency that makes it so important that we discuss the matter immediately? I'm in no hurry to make *any* decision that will disrupt our present situation."

His tone confused her, as well as the look in the blue eyes. Yesterday she had thought he could hardly wait to get away from her, and yet today . . . Bewildered, she blurted out, "But yesterday . . . yesterday you made it quite clear you wanted only to be rid of me."

Startled, Morgan stared at her. "I did?" he said perplexedly. Unable to recall having said anything that even hinted at a parting, he reached across the table to catch hold of her hand and said earnestly, "God knows what I said yesterday, Leonie! But this is today and today I want us to make a new beginning." His voice softening, an expression in the dark blue eyes that caused her heart to lurch in her breast, he murmured, "I know that things have not been pleasant between us, but would you agree to a cessation of hostilities, cat-eyes? A time for us to let the past die, and the future to unfold?" A rueful smile lifting one corner of his full mouth, he stated bluntly, "I'm asking for a truce, Leonie. Will you be very magnanimous and give it to me?"

Indecisively she regarded him, ripped apart by the fierce struggle that was raging within her—her heart joyfully

374

agreeing, her practical little brain violently rejecting his request outright. But her heart won the battle—as it always would—almost shyly, she nodded her head, saying softly, *"Oui,* monsieur, we shall try your truce and see what it brings."

27

The truce started out well. With Morgan's impending departure no longer looming ominiously on her horizon, and the very faintest of possibilities that they might make their marriage work in the offing, Leonie suddenly found the day wonderful.

As for Morgan, the knowledge that Leonie was willing to give him an opportunity to establish himself in her life, gave him hope that perhaps he could risk telling her about Ashley. *But not yet,* he vowed grimly, watching the small smile that hovered about Leonie's mouth as she sipped her coffee, *not yet . . . I want nothing to change that sweet expression on her face. Nothing to make her look at me with distrust and suspicion. And nothing will,* he promised fiercely. *Nothing.*

They spent a delightful day together, wandering aimlessly through New Orleans, browsing happily in the shops and viewing the goods of the street vendors. A picnic lunch of fried oysters and crusty French bread was eaten in perfect harmony on a grassy spot near the river, and they leisurely watched the cloudy waters of the Mississippi River as it flowed towards the sea. Munching blissfully on a praline, Leonie leaned back against a moss-covered oak tree and thought she had never been so happy. For the first time in her life, she actually viewed the future as something that *might* be enjoyed—instead of a desperate battle that had to be fought.

For Morgan the day was a mixed blessing. He was becoming more enchanted by Leonie with every passing moment, but he was also bleakly aware that it wasn't the wisest thing he had ever done in his life. He had no guarantee that the lady cared overmuch for him or that she would view his suit with favor. . . . Especially when she finds out about Ashley, he reminded himself unpleasantly. The galling knowledge that Leonie really wasn't his wife, that legally, if not rightfully, she belonged to Ashley loomed continually like a sinister black thundercloud on his horizon.

But despite the obstacles the future might bring, he was able to take a great deal of pleasure from the day. And by the time he dropped a strangely chaste kiss on Leonie's surprised mouth when they parted for the night, he was looking forward to the morrow with a sensation of indomitable optimism.

He hadn't wanted to seek out his own lonely bed, but now that he knew of her innocence, an innate streak of honor kept him from forcing his attentions upon her. Besides, he told himself savagely, she *was* Ashley's wife!

The next morning was as beautiful and warm as the previous day. Once again they ate breakfast on the small patio. This time though, when Leonie joined Morgan, her eyes were sparkling. *"Bonjour,* monsieur," she greeted him brightly.

Morgan glanced at her appreciatively, liking the way her white muslin gown contrasted attractively with her golden skin and tawny hair. Dropping a light kiss on her temple, he murmured, "And good morning to you, sweetheart." An imp of mischief dancing in his blue eyes, he teased, "I trust you slept well, in that strange bed. A pity I didn't join you. . . ."

Leonie blushed and wished she were brave enough to return his challenge, but as it was, she ignored his question and instead asked one of her own. "What do you intend to do today, monsieur?"

Looking thoughtful, mindful of the fact that if all had gone well, he should be in possession of the note against Château Saint-André in a matter of hours, Morgan answered slowly, "I have to drive into town, sometime this morning, but other than that my time is at your disposal. Is there something you would like to do?"

Leonie nodded her head. *"Oui,* monsieur. I should very much like to drive to Château Saint-André." A slightly anxious expression on the lively features, she added, "It is

377

almost four hours from here, but if we were to leave fairly early . . ."

"I don't see any problem," Morgan replied easily. "As soon as I finish my coffee, I'll drive into town and take care of my business. If you will have our hostess pack a lunch, we could leave within the hour."

Less than twenty minutes later, Morgan was again seated in Monsieur LeFort's office. After explaining the reason for his unfashionably early arrival, Morgan asked, "Were you able to talk with de la Fontaine? And has he signed over the note?"

Monsieur LeFort smiled sourly. *"Oui,* monsieur. It was simpler than I thought." And at Morgan's look of inquiry, he added, "De la Fontaine has a passion for gambling, but I am sorry to say that he is a *very* bad gambler. When my messenger found him and gave him the news that the note would be paid in full, he came instantly to my office."

Morgan shrugged. De la Fontaine's plight aroused no sympathy. Quite the reverse. "You have the note?"

"Oui, monsieur. Here it is. Your wife should be pleased."

Morgan glanced at it, a wry smile curving his mouth. "I hope so." He knew LeFort would be unable to understand that his wife would likely berate him for taking a hand in her affairs. Morgan said only "I must commend you for the swiftness of execution in this matter. I hope that you will have the same luck in the other matters."

Monsieur LeFort looked smug. "The money you asked to have transfered into her name will be taken care of this morning. As for the other matter, I have already contacted the current owner of the lands, and he wishes to sell . . . especially at the price you have offered."

The rest of the conversation moved swiftly and Morgan left LeFort's office, the note that Leonie had wanted so desperately safely tucked in his waistcoat pocket.

Morgan drove the curricle back to Madame Brosse's where Leonie was waiting for him, a small reed basket at her side. Five minutes later, they were on their way to Château Saint-André.

As the horses trotted swiftly along the winding, dusty road that followed the meanderings of the river, Leonie looked across at Morgan and asked shyly, "Did you complete your business, monsieur?"

Morgan nodded his head, his eyes on his horses as they swept narrowly by a large, slow-moving farm wagon. "Yes, as a matter of fact I did." The wagon passed, he glanced down at her and murmured, "And you should be gratified with the results."

Because suspicion died hard, especially in view of Morgan's past behavior, Leonie asked cautiously. "Why? Was your business about my dowry?"

Morgan grinned. "That, too, was taken care of. As a matter of fact, by this time tomorrow, it is very possible that I shall be handing you your dowry, or at the very least, the legal documents that transfer the money from my account to one in your name alone."

An expression of mingled delight and wariness crossed her face. "Truly?"

"Truly," he said gently. "Monsieur LeFort assured me that by tomorrow he will have taken care of everything."

Momentarily diverted, Leonie asked with surprise, "Monsieur Emeri LeFort? He is your business agent?"

Morgan nodded.

"How strange! Did you know that he was also my *grand-père's* man of business?"

"I didn't until yesterday when he informed me of that fact." Morgan answered easily.

Leonie shook her head in amazement. "It is a very small world, isn't it, monsieur?" she said at last.

There was a light reply from Morgan and for several seconds they rode in silence, Leonie swamped by a bewildering variety of emotions. The news that Morgan was finally repaying her dowry filled her with excitement and joy; at last she could pay off the note that Maurice de la Fontaine held against the Château Saint-André! Her hope of saving it for Justin would be realized, she thought exultantly. Yet interspersed with this elation was a pang of sudden doubt and confusion. Was saving the plantation the wisest course? Once, and not too long ago, she had decided that if Morgan had wanted to make their marriage real that the dowry could be used to secure Justin's inheritance, but now she was unexpectedly assailed with uncertainty.

Unconsciously biting her lower lip, she calculated the amount of money that would remain after the note had been paid. It would be a mere pittance, barely enough to support her little family. *I have been deluding myself,* she finally concluded disgustedly. *Using the money to save the plantation would be foolish, and Justin certainly would not thank her for it when he became a man. But if he loved the land as much as she did?* She sighed. How could one decide that about a five-year-old boy?

There was another aspect to the situation that she had not considered, she suddenly realized. Despite the fact that Morgan was being extremely charming at the moment, and while she surreptitiously had her fingers crossed for the future, there was no guarantee that he wouldn't do as he had done in the past and make another one of those lightninglike changes. Uncertainly she looked at him. *I love him so much,* she thought despairingly, *and yet I do not understand him, nor do I quite trust him. Perhaps,* she mused unhappily, *there will be no need to make a decision about the dowry—our truce may not last. . . .*

Leonie's silence hadn't gone unnoticed by Morgan, nor had his news pleased her as much as he had thought it would. Frowning slightly, he asked abruptly, "Don't you believe me about the dowry? God knows, I haven't given you much reason to trust me, Leonie, but I swear to you, you shall have the money tomorrow."

As that particular disagreeable notion hadn't occurred to her, she was able to say quite truthfully, "Oh, no, monsieur! I mean, oh, yes, I do believe you! At least," she added with a sudden mischievous smile, "I haven't *yet* considered the possibility that you might be lying."

A rueful grin curved Morgan's mouth. "I'm not lying, cat-eyes. But if you do believe me, why do you seem so unhappy? I thought you wanted the dowry above everything."

"I did! I do!" she began vehemently and then stopped helplessly. Staring blindly at the verdant undergrowth that lined the meandering road, she said reluctantly, "Before I went to Natchez everything seemed so simple. I

needed my dowry to save Château Saint-André, and I was
going to get it from you, no matter what! I would pay off
Monsieur de la Fontaine, and then Justin and I, and the
others, if they wished, would have lived our lives as we always had." Almost resentfully, she added, "But *nothing*
worked out the way I had it planned!"

"Is that so very bad?" Morgan murmured gently.

Her troubled gaze swung back to him, the golden-green
eyes studying his lean features intently. "I don't know,"
she admitted slowly.

"Suppose you don't worry about it this afternoon,
hmm?" he suggested mildly. "We will put our troubles
aside and enjoy each other's company, taking the hours as
they come."

Imperceptibly, Leonie nodded her tawny head. Morgan
was right. She didn't have to decide anything today—she
was on her way to her beloved Château with the man she
adored, and she would think of nothing else but the joy
that was hers at this moment.

It was almost two o'clock when Morgan finally turned
the horses off the main road and headed them down the
bumpy, overgrown lane that led to the Château. The closer
they had come to the plantation, the more obvious had
been Leonie's growing impatience to see her home again.
With childlike glee she had eagerly pointed out familiar
sights—the homes of neighbors, barely seen through the
moss-hung oaks and underbrush, the small bayou where
she went fishing, and protruding out into the muddy
waters of the Mississippi the sagging, rotting landing
docks of Saint-André.

She made no excuses, neither for the disreputable condition of the wooden docks, nor the wretched state of the road
that would bring them to the house. Instead there was an
odd air of haughtiness about her, as if she dared Morgan to
make even one critical remark. Not that he would have
been so foolish, he thought with tender amusement observing the pleasure and pride with which she revealed the
faded charms of the plantation.

Having cast an experienced eye at the landing docks, he
came to the instant conclusion that the most practical solution would be to dismantle them entirely and have new

docks built. As for the lane to the plantation, he grimaced as the wheels of his well-sprung curricle hit a large pothole. *Tomorrow morning,* he promised himself firmly, *I shall hire a crew to come out and get started on repair work.*

It was only as they came closer to the house itself that Leonie displayed any sort of nervousness. Shooting Morgan a curious look of mingled embarrassment and fierceness, she said abruptly, "The house has not had any money spent on it in at least twenty years, monsieur. Please remember that when you see it." That was as close to a defensive remark about her home that she would ever come. But unconsciously her fingers dug painfully into the palms of her hands, and she deliberately steeled herself for Morgan's reaction to his first sight of the Château.

The lane ended abruptly and there drowsing in the hot, yellow sunlight was the Château Saint-André. Leonie's heart leaped at the sight of the house and she felt a sudden rush of tears. Despite its faded elegance, to Leonie it was the most beautiful house in the world. She reveled in its remembered charms—the tall double doors with the attractive fanlights above them, the steep, dormered, hipped roof, the intricately designed balusters and the glorious sweep of the horseshoe-shaped staircase. It didn't matter that some shutters dangled lopsidedly at the doors, or that the paint was peeling, the gutters sagging, or that weeds choked the grounds—it was home and she had fought for it too long, had loved it too intensely, to be deterred by such mundane things. With an agonizing knife-thrust of pain, she wondered how she had even for one moment considered *not* saving it. Then she swallowed convulsively. If she had to choose between the house or Morgan, she knew that there would never be any real choice. She loved Château Saint-André but Morgan was her life; without him *nothing* would matter.

Effortlessly Morgan pulled the horses to a stop near the house and thoughtfully stared at the building. Taking in the blistered paint, the sagging staircase, the missing gaps in the balusters, the shutters that hung haphazardly at the long double doors and the general air of decay, he very nearly turned the horses around and drove them at a breakneck pace back to New Orleans.

But realizing that to do so would seriously jeopardize his standing with the proud little creature at his side, he took another look—a long, careful look—and it was then that the house began to cast its spell over him. For the first time Morgan saw the charm in the building, the elegant sweep of the horseshoe-shaped staircase, the fine workmanship of the slender wooden colonnettes that encircled the upper story, and the delicate grace of its construction. It must have been absolutely breathtaking at one time, he admitted slowly to himself, aware of a sharp pang of regret that it should have been allowed to reach its present state of decay. Consideringly, his gaze swept to the matching pair of collanaded *garçonnières* that flanked the main house, noting how their equally moldering state could not obscure the elegant lines. The smaller buildings duplicated the design of the house, and viewing the attractive setting of the buildings, the massive, spreading moss-draped oaks, the towering cedars and magnificently flowering magnolia trees, Morgan decided that the site held definite possibilities.

Staring intently at the house and its lush, beautiful background, he was suddenly aware of an odd sense of homecoming, as if all his restless wanderings had been leading him to this one place . . . to this one woman. Such a powerful sensation of rightness, of inevitability swept over him that he was startled by its depth and intensity. The house pulled at some buried part of him, wakening him to dreams he had thought long dead . . . perhaps, even to happiness.

The silence seemed to go on forever, and finally, unable to bear the suspense much longer, Leonie risked a look at his face, and demanded almost fiercely, "Well? What do you think of it?"

His head full of half-forgotten dreams, for a second Morgan stared at her blankly, and then said huskily, "I think it is perfect. Or, rather, it will be."

A smile of pure delight crossed Leonie's expressive features. "Truly, monsieur?" she breathed eagerly.

A mocking gleam in the dark blue eyes, his gaze on her mouth, he murmured softly, "I thought we had decided my name was Morgan?"

383

Leonie blushed, but she would not be sidetracked. "It is beautiful, isn't it?"

His eyes never leaving her face, he agreed, *"Very* beautiful."

Suddenly shy with him, she glanced hastily away from the look in his eyes, and scrambled out of the curricle. "Come, I will show you everything."

After securing the horses, Morgan followed her as she darted excitedly to one place and then another. "See, here is the barn!" And then rushing off in another direction, she cried, "And there is the stables. And over there is where our garden was. And over here is . . ."

By unspoken consent they saved the house for last. Gingerly climbing the creaking horseshoe staircase, Morgan remarked unwisely, "It's a wonder you haven't broken your neck on this damned thing."

Like a tigress defending her young Leonie instantly turned on him. "You shall not find fault with the house! If you had paid me my dowry, it would not have gotten this bad." Her eyes flashing with gold flecks, she muttered, "It is all your fault!"

"But you're going to forgive me, aren't you?" he asked teasingly, a gently derisive smile twitching at the corner of his mouth.

Leonie gave a saucy toss of her bright hair. "I might," she returned tartly. "And then again . . ."

There was an easy air between them, and Leonie was conscious of a great bubble of joy that seemed permanently lodged in her chest. She had never thought there would come a day when Morgan Slade would step foot in Château Saint-André, or that she would be happy to have him at her side . . . or even more amazingly that she would dare to tease him. But today nothing seemed out of her reach . . . not even his love.

Covertly watching him as he studied the house, she felt her chest swell with love and wondered at the strange workings of fate. Less than six weeks ago his name had been anathema to her, and now, against all reason, she loved him, wanted above all things to share the rest of her life with him. *Mon Dieu, but my heart has much to answer for,* she thought with a rueful smile.

When Leonie and the others had left Saint-André, the house had been boarded up, but Morgan found a door that had not been properly barricaded and in a few minutes he had forced it open. Grinning at Leonie, he said, "I trust you do not intend to accuse me of housebreaking?"

Laughing, she shook her head and happily danced ahead of him into the house. They did not linger inside. After being closed up for almost two months, the house had an unpleasant musty smell and there was a depressing, forlorn look to the empty, echoing rooms. But the tour gave Morgan a fair idea of the floor plan of the living quarters on the upper floor and the condition of the interior of the house. Walking out onto the shaded gallery, he asked thoughtfully, "What's on the ground floor? The plantation office and such?"

"*Oui,* monsieur." Leonie pulled a face. "And what few things we had to store. Monsieur de la Fontaine said he would let me keep some of the larger pieces of furniture and what odds and ends that we could not take with us in there until I redeemed the house or until it was sold . . . whichever happened first."

Morgan's mouth tightened. "That was generous of him."

Leonie glanced at him, a little uneasy at the note in his voice. "It doesn't matter anymore," she finally said. "With my dowry back, I shall be able to deal with him."

Morgan moved closer to her and tipping her chin up lightly, he stared down into her face. "You don't have to, sweetheart. I'll take care of de la Fontaine."

"Oh, but—" she began to argue, and then stopped abruptly as Morgan gently covered her mouth with his hand. Staring down into her face, he said roughly, "You're not alone anymore, Leonie. You don't have to fight *every* battle yourself. Let me settle with de la Fontaine. I don't mean to belittle your efforts, but I think," he added grimly, "that I can settle all accounts with de la Fontaine far more effectively than you can." A gleam in his blue eyes, he ended with, "He won't try to seduce *me!*"

Her eyes widening, she jerked her head away and demanded sharply, "How do you know that he tried to seduce me, monsieur?"

Silently cursing his slip, Morgan shrugged his broad shoulders. "Monsieur LeFort mentioned that de la Fontaine is not the gentleman his father was."

"It seems to me you have been doing a lot of snooping! How dare you, Morgan Slade!"

Becoming angry himself, he snapped back, "If you'll remember, until yesterday, I didn't know about the damned marriage! And not knowing about it, I had every reason to believe that you were a conniving cheat out for my money. I'm certain you'll agree it was only logical to find out as much about you as possible."

Some of her quick fury dying, Leonie regarded him indecisively. She was still affronted with his actions, but her sense of fair play made her aware of the reasons behind what he had done. She confessed honestly to herself that, if their positions had been reversed, she would have done the same. Reluctantly, she muttered, "Perhaps you were right, but it still isn't a very pleasant feeling to know that strangers are poking into one's past."

Watching her closely, Morgan asked carefully, "Is there something in your past that won't bear close scrutiny?"

Puzzled, Leonie glanced at him. "What do you mean?"

His eyes locking on hers he said bluntly, "If I didn't consummate the marriage six years ago, would you please explain to me how it comes about that you arrived in Natchez with a child? A child that you claimed, at first, was mine?"

28

Leonie froze. Turning her pale face away, she said stiffly, "I do not want to talk about it."

Morgan regarded her keenly for a taut moment. He wasn't prying maliciously, but the more he knew, the more effectively he could forestall an unholy scandal from breaking over her innocent head. He particularly disliked his own role at the moment—he wasn't her husband as she thought, and yet he was making no attempt to enlighten her. *I am as bad as Ashley,* he thought. But he dared not tell her the truth, and in order to free them all from the damnable coil Ashley had created he needed all the information he could gain—even if it pained her and was gotten under misleading circumstances.

He almost let the subject drop, but he couldn't; finally he replied quietly, "That's what you said the last time. And as I was laboring under the mistaken impression that you were telling nothing but lies in the first place, I let it go. But I can't any longer—you bear my name, and because of that, I am legally responsible for Justin. I think that entitles me to know his parentage, don't you?" His conscience writhed at the half-lies he was telling, but it had to be done, he reminded himself bleakly. And he *did* wonder about Justin's parentage.

Not looking at him, Leonie gripped the railing of the gallery so tightly that her knuckles showed white. Morgan's request wasn't unjustified, she admitted miserably to herself. He *had* acknowledged Justin, and if he was going to allow her subterfuge to continue, then it was only fair that she answer his question.

She closed her eyes in anguish. It had been her secret for so long, her shame and degradation suffered alone in si-

387

lence, that she didn't even know if she *could* tell anyone of
it. And with things still unsettled between them, still uncertain of his true feelings, she found it even more difficult.

Morgan watched her intently for several seconds, aware
with an angry sort of compassion of her embarrassment
and bitter reluctance to speak of what had obviously been
an ugly episode in her life. That she would not talk of it,
told him much. Unable to bear the sight of her unhappy
face any longer, he asked roughly, "Was it Maurice? Did
he rape you?"

Astonishment caused Leonie to whirl and stare at him
openmouthed. Her eyes widening with amazement, she finally got out incredulously, "Maurice? Maurice de la Fontaine?"

That he had guessed badly was very apparent and almost savagely he replied, "He seems to have been the only
man in your life. And as I have gathered Justin's conception is not a pleasant memory for you . . . it was only natural that I should think of rape . . . and Maurice."

Leonie gave a half-hysterical little laugh, and the sea-
green eyes shimmering with suppressed tears, she said
wretchedly, "How very perceptive of you, monsieur! It was
rape, you were right about that, but not that it was Maurice. *Never* Maurice!" She turned her head away in pain,
and her throat clogged with remembered shame. But the
words came tumbling out, as if the admission of rape had
destroyed the restraint she had placed on herself six years
ago. "I was somewhere I shouldn't have been, and . . . and
a man, a stranger, m-mistook me for something I wasn't."
Her voice raw with agony, she spat out, "He raped me,
monsieur! He was too big and powerful for me and I could
not stop him! And, and w-w-when it was over I fled." Bitterly she added, "And so now you know—Justin's father
could be anyone!" The threatened tears suddenly spilling
down her cheeks, she added defiantly, "And—and if you're
ashamed of us, disgusted with me, if you don't want Justin
tin and me as part of your life, well then, it will be *your* loss!"

The expression in his hard blue eyes difficult to understand, Morgan stared at her for a moment, and then gently
but firmly he pulled her unresistingly into his strong

arms. Her cheek crushed up against the smooth cloth of his jacket, she felt his hand moving with incredible gentleness over her hair. "Shush, little firebrand," he murmured into the tawny curls that tickled his chin. "Did you really think you *could* disgust me?" he asked unsteadily. Not giving her a chance to answer, he added softly, "I consider it an honor to have you and Justin in my life." Tipping her head up with warm fingers, the blue eyes searched her tear-wet face. "Leonie . . ." He stopped uncertain what to say, but wanting to say something to ease her pain, to lessen her shame. "It all happened a long time ago—there is no need to punish yourself for something that you couldn't help. You have a fine son . . . no matter who his father is. And if you'll allow me, I'd like to take the place of his unknown father—I would be proud to call Justin my own."

For a long time they simply stood there staring at each other, each a little hesitant, each a little wary of the other's reaction. And yet as the seconds passed and Leonie saw no sign of the revulsion and condemnation she was positive he would feel, the icy ball of pain that had been lodged in her chest gradually melted. With eyes full of wonderment, she look at his lean face. "You don't mind?" she got out eventually.

Morgan's mouth twisted. "Of course, I mind!" Something cold and deadly entering the blue eyes, he said harshly, "I'd like to kill the bastard! And if I ever find out who it was, I'm very likely to do just that!"

Her tears drying, a curious lightness spreading through her entire body, the huge, leaden weight of shame she had carried for so long suddenly lifting from her heart, she reached up and with shy fingers gently traced the outline of his wide mouth. In a voice that only shook slightly, she murmured, "You are so kind. So much kinder than I ever dreamed. I am grateful to you, monsieur . . . so *very* grateful!"

Morgan jerked as if stung, and in an unfriendly tone of voice, he snapped, "I don't need, nor do I *want* your gratitude, damnit!"

Bewildered, she stared back at him. "But I *am* grateful. You could have been cruel to Justin, but you weren't. You have been exceedingly kind to him . . . even to me, and I would think it spiteful and mean of me not to tell you of my gratitude, not to express my thankfulness for the way you have treated Justin."

"Very well, you expressed it," Morgan said ungraciously. "So let's just forget about it, shall we?" He didn't mean to be so curt, but as gratitude was the *last* thing he wanted from Leonie, her words had given him an uncomfortable shock. Perhaps it was *only* gratitude that had made her accept his offer of a truce, he thought sourly. Only gratitude that kept her by his side? It was a painful assumption on his part, but one that couldn't be ignored. And remembering the note that burned in his vest pocket, he wondered if paying off de la Fontaine had been the wisest thing to do under the circumstances. Might that make her feel even more indebted to him? He wanted her love, not her damned gratitude!

Frustration with the situation and fury at Ashley's imposture eating at him like acid, he turned away and muttered, "I think we've said enough about the entire affair." And changing the subject abruptly, he asked, "Will you show me the boundaries of the plantation?"

Confused by his attitude and dismayed at the coolness that had fallen between them, a subdued Leonie began to point out the various landmarks that set the bounds of the property. There was silence as they tramped over the land, Morgan politely helping her over any obstacles that lay in their path—a fallen cedar tree, the boggy remains of a bayou, sagging fences that lined the property.

Standing near the edge of a dark, sluggish-moving bayou, Morgan looked over in the opposite direction over towards a hardly discernible Mississippi River. "This is the rear boundary? You own from here to the river?"

Leonie nodded her head, her eyes straying wistfully to the luxuriant, rich acres that lay on the other side of the bayou. "We used to own the land that surrounds the Château, but all that was sold when *grand-père* died." She sighed. "Without the land, the plantation can barely support itself."

"Mmm, you're right about that," Morgan answered vaguely, his fingers gingerly touching the frond of a prickly Spanish dagger plant that grew nearby. Idly his gaze rested on the tasseled tops of the sugar cane that was growing in the fields on the other side of the bayou. He had to tell her he had paid the note, and despite having had second thoughts about the wisdom of what he had done, he knew he couldn't have done otherwise. From gratitude could grow love, he reminded himself savagely, knowing he would hate for his love to come to him because of gratitude. But what else could he have done? he asked himself bitterly. Watch her pay out every penny of that damned dowry on the Château, when he could do it and not even miss the money? She had suffered enough because of Ashley and he could not, *would* not, stand by and watch her lose the independence the dowry would give her. It was hers to use for the little elegancies she might desire, for the many things that are dear to a woman's heart . . . for all the lovely personal things she had never known—not to provide a roof over their heads! *That,* he vowed grimly, was *his* concern!

Knowing he could not put off the moment indefinitely, he reached into his vest pocket and extracted the signed note. Almost offhandedly, he said, "I have something for you." A wry smile tugging at the corners of his full mouth, he murmured lightly, "You might consider it a token of my esteem."

Despite his casual behavior Leonie was conscious of an odd tension about him. Puzzled, she reached for the paper he held in his hand. The document crackled loudly in the uneasy silence that had fallen between them. A slight frown marred her smooth forehead as she glanced at the paper, her eyes widening with shock. A dazed, confused look on her face, she muttered, "But how is this? *Mon Dieu,* how did you get this?"

Studiously keeping his face expressionless, Morgan said carelessly, "I think it should be obvious. I saw Monsieur LeFort and arranged for the note to be paid off."

Her frown increased as she stared first at him, then at the paper. Not quite understanding, she finally asked, "Do you mean that instead of paying me the dowry, you have paid off the note?"

Aware that he was entering extremely dangerous ground now, Morgan answered carefully, "No, that isn't quite what I mean. The note is yours; the Château is free of debt *and* the dowry is yours too."

Contemplatively, Leonie stared up at him, her head cocked a little to one side. Inside her breast was a raging conflict, part of her overjoyed and delighted that the Château had been saved, but another part of her confused and perhaps just a little angry at his high-handed actions. She hadn't expected him to shoulder her debts; all she had ever wanted was what had been owed to her, and she wasn't quite certain how she felt about his generous action. Her pride would allow no hint of charity, though, and stiffly she said, "With the debt paid I shall not need the dowry . . . except what little would have remained."

"Nonsense!" Morgan snapped testily, his mouth thinning slightly. "I *owe* you the Château, as well as the dowry, you little fool!" he said sharply. "If Ash—If *I* hadn't taken the dowry when I did, there would have been no debt in the first place. And you should be entitled to some sort of interest on money I've had the use of for these past years."

Leonie wasn't so positive she liked being called a little fool and her sea-green eyes sparkled with growing anger. Proudly, she returned, "There was never any discussion of interest between us in the beginning. I see no reason why you should bring it up now."

"Well, I damn well am!" Morgan shot back angrily, his temper rising as quickly as hers. Controlling himself with an effort, he said in a calmer tone of voice, "I'm probably handling this delicate situation with ham-fisted finesse, sweetheart, but I don't mean to. As your husband I want to pay off the Château and I want you to have the dowry—can't you understand that?" Dryly, he added, "Accept it as a sign of my reformed character—take it as proof that I am not the scoundrel you thought."

Her indecision was plain. She wanted to take his words at face value, to take this overwhelmingly unexpected action as a sign that he cared for her, but suspicion and pride died hard. Suspicion she could deal with, firmly quashing any ugly thoughts, but her pride was something else. It wasn't proper, she decided stubbornly, for him to take on her debts. And while she appreciated his efforts in her behalf, she could not accept such lavish generosity. Her heart was warmed by his extravagant gift though, and she was aware of an intense feeling of pleasure at the thought of his gracious activity on her behalf.

A regretful little smile curving her mouth, she said gently, "Monsieur, I do not want to appear boorish, but I cannot accept such a generous present from you." Her eyes pleading with his, she added, "Please understand . . . it wouldn't be fitting."

Morgan regarded her thoughtfully, wanting furiously to shake her until her teeth rattled and force her to give in, and yet, he was oddly touched and moved at her reluctance to do so. Finally he shrugged his shoulders, and said mildly, "Very well, my dear, if you don't want it, you don't have to have it. But it really is a shame, you know."

Wary now, the uncertainty obvious in the sea-green eyes, she asked, "Why?"

Morgan sighed heavily, dramatically. "Well, you see . . . I had rather hoped that we could form a . . . partnership. It so happens that I am buying all of the land that originally went with the Château Saint-André." Glancing at her, he added with deceptive indifference, "It would have been an excellent situation—the combining of the entire estate into one ownership again. Ah well, I guess it isn't to be."

Leonie stared at him openmouthed, and swallowed convulsively. A look of dawning wonderment, of fierce joy sweeping across her face, she suddenly clutched his jacket lapels and almost squeaked, "All of it? You bought all of it?"

A little smile lifting the corner of his mouth, a gently mocking light in the blue eyes, he nodded his head. "All of it," he said calmly.

For endless moments Leonie looked at him, her thoughts chaotic, a dozen different suggestions rioting through her brain. She was literally—and perhaps for the first time in her life—speechless. It had been her secret dream, a dearly cherished fantasy that some day, all of the land might be reclaimed. She had known it was only a wild dream, but she had clung to it as fiercely as she had the desire to regain her home. Suddenly, unexpectedly to have it within her reach was stunning, breathtaking.

She swallowed again with difficulty and then to her utter horror she felt her eyes film over and she burst into tears. Something inside of her had snapped, and her entire body shook with the force of the sobs that racked her slender form.

Almost as horrified as she was, Morgan stared at her helplessly for a second, and then enfolded her in his embrace, his strong arms cradling her trembling body. "Sweetheart, don't cry," he begged into her tawny curls. "Please, don't cry. I thought you'd be happy. I thought it would please you . . . once you got over the idea of my paying off the note."

"I *am* happy!" Leonie stated gruffly, as she hastily scrubbed away a betraying tear. "It is just that I—I never expected such—such a wonderful thing to happen."

"A lot of wonderful things are going to happen for us, cateyes," Morgan muttered huskily, his gaze compulsively fastening on her soft mouth. Unable to help himself, he bent his head and his lips captured hers in a long, searching kiss.

It was a sweetly fierce kiss, full of barely leashed passion and yet, there was an odd gentleness about it. They stayed locked tightly together, each one assuaging a sudden, urgent hunger, each almost unbearably aware of the other until at last, reluctantly, the embrace was broken. Slowly, unwillingly, Morgan raised his mouth from hers and said in a shaken voice, "If I continue to kiss you, and if you are so sweetly obliging, I shall not be responsible for my actions."

Shyly, Leonie met his gaze and said with sudden bravery, "But should you be? I am your wife."

A curiously shuttered look fell across his face, and abruptly he turned away, saying flatly, "I think it is time that we headed back for the inn. It is getting late and we still have several hours of traveling ahead of us."

In a queerly tense atmosphere they walked towards the Château and eventually came to the horses and the curricle. Silently Morgan helped her into the curricle and a few minutes later, they were driving swiftly away from the plantation.

Morgan wasn't displeased with the afternoon's work—

although, he could have done without her innocent reminder of the true state of affairs. When she had called herself his wife, his heart had contracted painfully and he had wished passionately that it had been true. But even if he could not yet bring himself to explain about Ashley, at least, he told himself consolingly, she knew the Château was safe now, and he had confessed his purchase of the remainder of the Saint-André lands. He smiled faintly, remembering the expression on her face. Then he sighed —that she would argue further about his payment of the note in greater detail he fully expected.

And he was right. After several minutes had passed, and Leonie had regained her composure, she brought up the subject again. But while Morgan allowed her to trot out her heart-felt objections to his generosity, he remained infuriatingly steadfast in his blunt refusal to let her use the dowry to repay him.

She argued heatedly during most of the four-hour journey, and it was only when they were approximately a mile from their destination, that she came to the angry conclusion that he was the most enraging, unreasonable creature she had ever met. With impotent rage she glared at his handsome profile longing to smack his face. *Beast!* she thought furiously. But then a tender smile curved her mouth; he *was* impossible, arrogant, overbearing, and completely outrageous, but she wouldn't have changed one hair on his dark head for an emperor's ransom!

It had been a long day for Leonie. A long, exciting, disturbing, emotional day, and by the time the inn came into sight, she was aware of a sudden feeling of exhaustion. The hour wasn't late, it was just after ten o'clock in the evening, but she longed for nothing more than her bed, for peace and quiet in which to review the events of the day. Time in which to dream of a future that was growing more exciting, more enchanting and wonderful with every passing moment.

Consequently, when Morgan made the suggestion that she retire for the night, she had no argument, and even the fact that he did no more than drop another of those chaste kisses on her mouth didn't disturb the dreamlike state she had entered. And not fifteen minutes after he had bidden her good night, she was curled up in her bed, sound asleep, her head full of her infuriating husband and the incredibly happy life they were sure to share . . . as soon as he stopped being so exasperatingly stubborn about certain things!

For Morgan there were no such rosy thoughts of the future, and not liking the idea of facing his lonely room with Ashley's specter rising up to taunt him, he turned away from his door and went downstairs and out into the night. Standing on the gallery of the house, he absently lit a cheroot and smoked it in silence, wondering at the cruel tricks that fate could play.

Thinking of Ashley, and of his own intolerable position, Morgan suddenly found that the cheroot tasted vile and with a furious motion, he tossed it into the darkness. He didn't like his own duplicity—the lies he was telling or the role that he was playing. And yet, he couldn't bring himself to tell Leonie the truth, unwilling at the moment to face the hostility and disbelief she was certain to experience. *In time,* he thought moodily, *in time, I can tell her . . . when she has learned to trust me. If she ever does.*

Finding no solace from the night, he eventually made his way to his room. Entering his bedchamber, he sensed the presence of another person almost immediately.

Halting instantly just inside the doorway of the darkened room, his eyes pierced the blackness, searching for the cause of the curious prickle along his spine—a feeling he hadn't experienced since he'd left France and the attendant dangers of spying behind. Cursing himself for going about unarmed, he stood there indecisively for perhaps a second, a dozen improbable thoughts careening through his brain, as he desperately tried to pinpoint the source of his uneasiness.

From the corner of the room there was a sudden brief flash of flame, and then a well-remembered, affectionate voice drawled, "Do come in, Morgan! And if you're armed, for God's sake, don't shoot! I have no desire at all to be shot down in cold blood by one of my dearest friends."

A snort of exasperated laughter broke from Morgan, and crossing the room swiftly he quickly lit the lamp on a table near his bed. Swinging around, he shone the light on the man who lounged with indifferent elegance on the chair in the corner.

"Brett Dangermond!" he said half-amusedly, half-angrily. "You're just damned lucky I *wasn't* armed! And by all that's holy, what the hell are you doing here?"

"Looking for adventure," came the laconic reply, as Brett carelessly continued to light a thin black cheroot. Shooting Morgan a mocking glance from deceptively lazy green eyes, he added, "What other reason could there be?"

Morgan snorted again. "With you, one never knows," he replied.

Brett only shrugged his powerful shoulders, and his lean, sardonic face filled with amusement, he murmured teasingly, "I can see that marriage hasn't sweetened your disposition."

Morgan threw him a look. "You know about that, do you?"

"Mmm, yes. Couldn't help but know with the entire Natchez district buzzing with it . . . and before I came to New Orleans, I paid a visit to Bonheur. Missed you the night of the ball for Burr and had planned to visit you at home, but Dominic explained your sudden departure."

"And did he also explain about the marriage?"

Brett appeared thoughtful. "Enough," he finally said, "to make me wonder if you've lost your wits."

Morgan smiled faintly. He and Brett had grown up together and there wasn't much about the one the other didn't know. They had shared for a number of years the same bitter attitude about women, and though Leonie's entrance into his life had changed Morgan, Brett was still a confirmed misogynist. And remembering certain unpleasant things in his friend's past, Morgan couldn't say that he blamed him. But still he made an attempt to explain the current situation. Glancing across at Brett, he said lightly, "Leonie isn't the jade I assumed—Ashley impersonated me and married her under my name. I've written Dominic, but he wouldn't have yet received my letter when he spoke to you."

There was a low whistle of surprise from Brett and for the next hour or so, over several glasses of brandy, the two men brought each other up to date on their affairs.

The marriage dominated the conversation, and watching the pain that crossed Morgan's face when he talked of Ashley and the fact that Leonie was legally his cousin's wife, Brett suddenly asked with misleading indifference, "Shall I find him for you . . . and kill him?"

Morgan stiffened, knowing that there was nothing casual about Brett's question. It was a solution, but one he found distasteful, and shaking his head he met Brett's eyes and said firmly, "No. And I mean it, Brett."

Brett shrugged carelessly. "Very well, if you insist. But," he added in a deadly tone, "my friend, if I do happen to cross Ashley's path, don't expect me to ignore him."

Morgan looked at him a long time. "I don't want you to do it, Brett."

"But if positions were reversed . . . ?"

Morgan grimaced, knowing Brett had him there. "Just don't go looking for him."

"Agreed," Brett said cheerfully.

The subject of Ashley and the marriage was dropped, and taking another sip of his brandy Morgan asked, "Besides just sheer wanderlust, why are you here? You never did say."

"Little Burr," Brett said easily. "The man fascinates me. I'd like to know what he's up to. And so . . ."

Morgan cocked an eyebrow at him. "Just Burr?"

Brett threw him a mocking glance from between his thick black lashes. "Burr *and* Wilkinson," he conceded amiably. "That's an unholy alliance if there ever was one, and it has aroused my curiosity." A frown suddenly creasing his forehead, he asked Morgan, "You were in New Orleans when Governor Gayoso died, weren't you?"

Surprised and showing it, Morgan nodded his head.

"And Wilkinson was there too, wasn't he?" Brett said musingly. "You know, over the years I've heard some curious stories about the night Gayoso died . . . that and some wild theories about *how* Gayoso really died."

Despite Brett's air of idle speculation, Morgan wasn't fooled. Almost resignedly, he demanded, "And you want to know if I noticed anything?"

One finely shaped eyebrow rising with mock astonishment, Brett replied dulcetly, "Whatever gave you that idea?"

Ignoring Brett's rhetorical question, Morgan told him what he remembered of that night. He ended his recital with, "I'll admit that I was surprised when Wilkinson showed up, and I thought at the time that there might be more to his being at Gayoso's than chance, but I never heard or saw anything that strengthened that view." Shooting his friend a considering look, he asked, "What have you heard?"

Brett made a steeple of his long fingers. "Not a great deal and at the moment, it is pure speculation on my part. But one or two of the governor's servants have whispered that it wasn't a fever that Gayoso died of. I know for a fact from a few of the Spanish officers I've happened to have conversation with over the years, that Gayoso was upset with Wilkinson about something; no one will come out with it, but I gather they have their suspicions that the governor did *not* die a natural death."

"Rubbish!" Morgan said firmly. "Gayoso's death was sudden, but surely you don't suspect Wilkinson of murder?"

"Why not?" Brett returned cooly. "Especially if Gayoso was displeased with Wilkinson? Don't make the mistake of underestimating our esteemed general, Morgan. He may bluster and appear an incompetent fool, but he has the instincts of a cornered rattlesnake and you should remember it."

Morgan bit his lip, recalling that he'd had just the same thought at one time. Reflectively, he said, "No one has ever proved that Wilkinson was working for the Spanish . . . but if he were . . ."

"And if Gayoso had found him out in playing a double game . . . ?" Brett supplied smoothly.

Morgan frowned blackly. "What the hell does all this have to do with Burr?"

Brett shrugged. "Perhaps nothing. But I've also heard tales of the existence of a map—a map supposedly drawn by Philip Nolan, a map that could guide an armed expedition into Spanish Territory." His green eyes meeting Morgan's, Brett said softly, "Wilkinson was Nolan's patron and there have always been whispers that Wilkinson has a more than polite relationship with Spain . . . but it wouldn't be out of character for him to betray them without a backward glance. Add Aaron Burr, a fallen angel in search of a kingdom, a man far more influential than Wilkinson, and all sorts of possibilities exist. Especially since Little Burr has come here to New Orleans, where intrigues are as common as the rising sun."

"You really think Wilkinson murdered Gayoso? That he has a map presumably of Nolan's, and that he and Burr plan to invade Spanish Territory?" Morgan finally asked, not really believing it, and yet aware that it wasn't impossible.

They talked for some time longer, and then finally Brett set down his brandy glass, and rose to his feet in one lithe movement. "I think it's time I found my own bed, but I'll see you again before I leave; perhaps at that time, I'll have more than just idle speculation to share with you." A sardonic expression on his face, he added dryly, "And mayhap by then you will have resolved your difficulties with your ladylove."

Ruefully Morgan conceded, "Perhaps. But I wouldn't count on it, my friend."

29

After Brett departed, Morgan lay sleepless in his lonely bed, longing to have Leonie in his arms. Knowing that was not possible, he mulled over the conversation with Brett. Had Wilkinson murdered Gayoso? Was Burr connected to Wilkinson's penchant for intrigue? Finding no answers he pushed the thoughts away, feeling that if anyone could solve the puzzle it would be Brett. Let Brett worry about Burr and Wilkinson, he decided—he had enough to worry about with Leonie!

As a consequence of Brett's visit, the next morning Morgan procured a pistol that was easily concealed beneath his clothing. He also acquired a wicked looking knife that fit into his boot—he hadn't liked his feeling of defenselessness when he had opened the door and sensed that someone else was there. There would not be a second time.

The next two weeks flew by for Morgan. Each day was a bittersweet glimpse of heaven for him. All his doubts and suspicions about Leonie had been put to rest. He fell even deeper under her spell, but he was always painfully, gallingly aware that she was Ashley's wife. During the pleasurable days that followed their trip to the Château Saint-André, a dozen different times he brought himself to the point of telling her the truth, but something invariably postponed the announcement. Sometimes it was simply his own inability to destroy the happiness and growing trust that he saw in those eyes. On other occasions it had been bad timing; someone or thing always interrupted them just as he was about to begin his disagreeable explanation. He viewed the interruptions with a combination of fury and relief.

But even with Ashley's shadow hanging over his head,

there was a great deal of pleasure in his time with her. Cautiously they began to learn of one another, and he discovered a hundred things about her that made him love her more completely, and though his body hungered for hers and his arms ached to hold her next to him, he forced himself to sleep away from her. It wasn't the fact that she was married to Ashley that kept him from seeking her bed, but the bitter knowledge that until *she* knew the truth, he would be taking advantage of her belief that he was her husband.

Fortunately, the days were busy and Morgan didn't have time to brood over the situation. With the debt against the Château taken care of, and his purchase of the additional acreage completed, there was nothing to stop their restoration of the old plantation. There was a short, heated argument about the use of his money from Leonie, but Morgan had taken her by the shoulders and shaken her soundly. His temper fraying, the blue eyes hard and cold, he had snapped, "I am growing weary of this constant battle between us about my money! God damn it, Leonie, do we have to live in poverty because *you* don't have the money to pay for the things that are needed to make the Château livable? I am, may God forgive me, a rich man! Must I resign myself to moldy walls, a rutted driveway and mouse-eaten mattresses, because *you* cannot afford to have them taken care of? For heaven's sake, *I* have the bloody money!"

It was blunt, but it was effective. Leonie had stared at him as if she hated him, and had said stiffly, "Very well, monsieur, if that is the way you feel about it. I shall not argue with you further."

An exasperated sigh had broken from Morgan when he had looked at the proud, miserable expression on her face. Gently he had tipped up her small face. "Must we argue over money, sweetheart? It is for both of us! Does it really matter who pays the piper, as long as he gets paid?"

Leonie couldn't resist the coaxing note in his voice and gruffly she had replied, "No, monsieur, it doesn't. And—and I am sorry to have been so silly."

Morgan had smiled then and, sweeping her into his

arms, he had kissed her and muttered, "Not silly, darling
. . . adorable!"

That particular obstacle out of the way, things had
moved at an astonishing pace. Morgan hired an army of
workmen to start putting the old plantation in order. The
driveway was the first thing to show signs of improvement, the ruts and ditches now a thing of the past. The
shaggy, unkempt shrubbery and grasses were also already
showing the attention of several gardeners, the lawn in
front of the house neatly scythed and trimmed; the various
bushes, the scarlet camellias and white azeleas, the rioting bougainvillea and honeysuckle vines had been pruned
into some semblance of order. The sagging fences now
stood proudly upright, the new posts and rails obvious by
their unpainted state. Soon, though, the entire fence line
would be a glistening, pristine white.

Only minor work had been done to the house itself—the
hanging shutters straightened; the missing balustrades
restored, and the broken steps of the horseshoe-shaped
staircase replaced. But there was a new air of vitality
about the house, almost as if the building sensed that its
time was coming, that soon the real restoration of it would
start.

Leonie and Morgan had continued to stay at Madame
Brosse's for some days after their initial survey of the
house. It was, as Morgan had pointed out, far more practical until certain things were decided upon. At first Leonie
hadn't known what he meant, but she soon found out—
there were numerous trips to the cabinetmakers and the
upholstery shops; there was the necessity of selecting not
only individual pieces of furniture, but the styles and type
of wood as well as the fabrics. Floor coverings and carpets
had to be decided upon, window hangings and curtains obtained, and Leonie's head was pleasurably spinning as she
viewed all the lovely materials and goods that were so def-
erentially displayed for her—the fact that Monsieur Slade
was a wealthy man had not gone unnoticed by the various
merchants, nor the fact that he wanted only the finest mer-
chandise for his home.

Once the main selections had been made and the interior of some of the rooms in the house had been put to

rights until such time as the *real* work on them began, Morgan and Leonie had moved to the Château.

For Leonie everything had taken on a delightful dream-like quality. Each day brought some enchanting new surprise for her to revel in, and the only blots on her horizon were Justin's absence and the peculiar state of affairs between herself and her husband.

Justin's absence would soon be taken care of—he and the others were expected soon, but the situation with Morgan . . . It was hard for her to identify what was wrong. He was spending money on the plantation lavishly. He had, as he had promised, paid back the dowry. And while he was as polite and considerate as any woman could wish, Leonie sensed a barrier between them. There was an aloofness about him that puzzled her, as did the fact that there was only the mildest intimacy between them. It wasn't that he didn't desire her; she admitted wistfully, too often in the past days she had caught his gaze upon her, and the expression in those blue eyes had been unmistakable. But if he wanted her, then why, she wondered bewilderedly, didn't he seek her out?

Blushing in spite of herself, she knew that if Morgan came to her that she would deny him nothing, that her body longed for his desperately. The sleepless nights she had lain awake, her passionate young body yearning for his touch, were ample proof that her desire for him was far stronger than she would have cared to admit.

Though love had never been spoken aloud between them, Leonie wanted with an almost painful intensity to believe that he had begun to love her. No man could be so unfailingly generous, so attentive, so flatteringly considerate and kind and *not* be in love, she told herself repeatedly, uncertain whether she was stating a fact, or convincing herself that it was so. Of her own feelings there was no doubt—his actions in recent days put to rest at last whatever suspicions she might have harbored. She loved him! . . . But did he love her?

Morgan was helplessly besotted, but his hands were cruelly chained by the knowledge of Ashley's impersonation. He might be able to keep a respectable distance from Leonie, but his eyes betrayed him every time he looked at her.

Loving her, wanting her, needing the warmth and sweetness she represented, he knew that he could not delay the moment of truth much longer. She had a right to know and he was grimly aware that he lied to himself every time he found a logical reason to postponing the telling of the distasteful tale.

The twelfth of July saw the arrival of Justin, Dominic, Robert, Yvette, and the rest of the Saint-André servants who had traveled to Natchez with Leonie. Watching the apparently endless cavalcade of wagons and vehicles Morgan had wondered sourly if his entire family were about to descend upon him.

An hour later, after an exuberant greeting by Justin, and the usual exchange of greetings between the others, Morgan had collared Dominic and asked him dryly, "Correct me if I'm wrong, but I did request that you travel light, didn't I?"

Dominic grinned sheepishly. "I tried Morgan, but you know the family. . . ."

Morgan grimaced. "Of course. How could I have forgotten maman's fondness for adding a bit of this and that. Do tell me, for God's sake, what is in all of those damned wagons?"

"Mmm, let's see. I think maman mentioned something about the rest of Leonie's wardrobe. And naturally there were things of Justin's . . . And, oh yes—china and linens."

Torn between amusement and vexation, Morgan said dryly, "I'm to be well and truly inundated with the trappings of a family man, it seems."

Dominic had smiled in commiseration and then a serious expression crossing his face, he had asked abruptly, "Have you learned anything new? I kept my mouth shut as you requested, but it was damned hard, I can tell you! By God, *how* could we have forgotten that Ashley was in New Orleans that summer?" He shook his head in disgust. "It would have explained *everything!*" Throwing Morgan a quizzical look, he inquired, "Have you told Leonie yet?"

"No," Morgan replied curtly. "I've never considered myself a coward before, Dom, but I'd rather face a horde of Comanche warriors unarmed, than try to explain this to

405

her." He sighed deeply. "But it has to be done . . . and *soon.*"

Dominic sympathetically concurred, but for the time being they put the unpleasant subject behind them while Morgan gave him a quick tour of the estate. The subject of Ashley could only be avoided for so long though, and that night as he prepared for bed, Morgan knew that he could no longer delay telling Leonie the truth. Not, he admitted bitterly, *if I want to retain any self-respect.*

Now that the family had arrived, it was even more difficult to find a private moment with her, he decided irritably the next morning. The house was not large, and the arrival of his two brothers and the others had filled it to overflowing. Servants were everywhere, and the added workmen made the entire place a hive of activity. Finding a moment alone *and* uninterrupted was going to take a miracle, he thought as he made his way downstairs.

Speaking with Leonie that morning proved fruitless. It was only in the late afternoon that Morgan saw his chance. Whisking her away on the pretext that he wanted her opinion about a further improvement to the road leading to the house, he managed at last to secure some privacy.

They walked in silence for several minutes, Leonie conscious that Morgan was looking unusually grim, his jaw clenched in a way that boded ill. She peeped up at him, a growing sense of unease creeping over her at the black frown that now marred his forehead. Correctly feeling that there was something dreadfully amiss, and unable to stand the suspense, she blurted out, "There is something wrong, isn't there? You don't want to talk about the road at all, do you?"

Morgan's mouth tightened. "No, I didn't want to talk about the road," he admitted tautly. "That was only an excuse to speak to you alone."

Leonie stopped walking and stared up at him searchingly. "What is it, then?"

His left hand formed a fist, a muscle in his lean cheek jerked, and for a moment she thought he wasn't going to answer. Releasing his breath in a sharp sigh, he motioned her off the road and slowly they walked across the grass to

406

the faded white fence that encircled the Saint-André family graveyard.

Leonie watched him uneasily, as he rested one booted foot on the bottom rail and casually leaned against the wooden fence. The feeling that something was grievously wrong crystallized in her mind and all hope for the future began to crumble. Hoping her tone was light, she inquired, "What do you want to talk about?"

Lost in his own hell, Morgan stared blindly out over the small graveyard, almost unaware of Leonie's presence. At the sound of her voice he looked at her, his heart contracting painfully.

Unconsciously straightening his broad shoulders, the blue eyes locked on hers, he said broodingly, "I have something to tell you that I should have told you the afternoon we visited Père Antoine." His mouth twisted and he added bitterly, "Like a base coward, I have put off the moment for as long as I could."

Leonie felt very cold as she tried desperately to guess what awful thing had brought about the obvious end to their increasing rapport. For Morgan to call himself a base coward seemed to portend something very ominous indeed. She said carefully, "I can't ever imagine your doing something cowardly." Her face was a little rueful as she added, "Arrogant, yes, *that* I can definitely believe! But cowardly, never!"

Morgan's dark mood lifted slightly and a faint derisive smile twitched at the corner of his full mouth. "Thank you, madame, for those kind words." But almost instantly his smile vanished, the ugliness of the situation bearing down upon him. He gave a low, frustrated groan and shifting his position a little, he reached out and pulled her into his arms.

His gaze was intent upon her upturned face. "Leonie, I . . ." His voice trailed off, the words sticking like quills in his throat and softly he cursed the loss of his usually facile tongue. *Love,* he thought viciously, *has much to answer for!*

Furious with himself, despising this weakness, he pulled her tighter to him, and rested his chin against her bright curls. "I suppose it would be easier, if I started by explaining about my family—my father's side, the English branch. That and the fact that most members of the Slade family bear a remarkable resemblance to one another. In some cases," he continued with a harsh note in his voice, "the resemblance is almost uncanny—one would think that certain individuals were actually twins."

Her cheek resting against the fine material of his jacket, Leonie nodded her head, saying quietly, "I know what you mean—without being introduced, one would know instantly that Dominic and Robert were your brothers. Alexandre and Cassandre also are unmistakably Slades."

It was so lovely standing here in his strong arms, the warmth of his big body seeping into hers that Leonie forgot the air of impending tragedy that surrounded him. The cloth of his jacket felt smooth and comforting beneath her cheek and her slender form was suddenly shaken by a swift, violent surge of love for him. Unaware that she did it, her own arms tightened around his hard waist and she pressed herself closer to him.

It was a romantic picture that they unknowingly formed as they stood there together. Morgan's head rested on Leonie's tawny curls, his long, loose-limbed body seemed to be offering protection as her slim body curved into his, her jonquil yellow dress flowing gracefully about their feet. The small graveyard in the background added a poignant touch, the pink and coral roses that climbed the fence filled the air with a sweet, haunting fragrance, and the towering, moss-draped oaks created a secluded bower around the two still figures.

It was a tender scene, but the tall man who rode slowly in their direction didn't find it romantic in the least. Instead, the sight of Morgan with his arms about Leonie sent a curious blend of fury and fear through his veins, and with unnecessary violence, he yanked his horse to a standstill, his twisted brain assimilating this unpleasant turn of events.

Neither Leonie or Morgan was aware of his presence; they were both too absorbed in their own private world to pay attention to anything but each other. The rider silently edged his mount closer, until he was close enough to hear their conversation. As he listened, an ugly smile came over his face.

Having started his explanation, Morgan forced himself to continue. His voice hardening, he said, "Yes, it's true that all of us do look very much alike—but I have an English cousin, Ashley, who bears a striking resemblance to me. In fact," he added flatly, "we have been mistaken for each other several times . . . usually by people who don't know either one of us very well."

Lifting his head, Morgan stepped slightly away from her, and tipping her chin upwards with a light, almost caressing motion, he explained sardonically, "Ashley, is without a doubt, the most thoroughgoing scoundrel one could ever meet—and I speak without malice. Mention his name to any member of the family and they will, in varying degrees, confirm my statement. He also," Morgan said slowly, "has upon occasion impersonated me, invariably to the detriment of my character."

Leonie's forehead puckered in a tiny frown, her eyes fixed earnestly on his, she asked cautiously, "And he has done something that will affect us?"

Morgan smiled mirthlessly. "Oh, yes, I think you could safely say that his actions will most definitely affect us!" he admitted dryly. Steeling himself, his body braced for a blow, Morgan said tautly, "Leonie, when you first appeared in Natchez and I denied ever having seen you before, I wasn't lying. I *hadn't* ever laid eyes on you before —you were a complete and utter stranger to me!"

Leonie's breath caught painfully in her throat, and her eyes widening with dismay and disbelief, she stared up at him. Was this a trick on his part? And why now, after he had paid the dowry? Or, and her heart seemed to freeze, was he telling the truth? Had he never seen her before? Had his cousin, Ashley . . . Her brain could not complete the thought, and she swallowed with difficulty, before saying in a small voice, "Would you please explain exactly what you mean?"

The watcher entered the scene just then, his ugly laughter shattering their intimacy. Moving his horse a few steps closer, Ashley said nastily, "Well, if this isn't a pretty picture! I arrive this morning from France for the express purpose of finding my bride and what do I discover? My estimable cousin busy defaming my character to her! Not to

409

mention taking reprehensible and unpardonable liberties with her person!"

There was a curious stillness about Morgan, and almost indolently he turned to look at his cousin. His voice cool and unmoved, he said casually, "Hello, Ash. Somehow I suspected you would show up." A dangerous overtone shading his words, he added, "A jackel usually returns to scavenge what it can."

Ashley's face darkened. Sneeringly, he returned, "Aren't the positions somewhat reversed? I never thought to see you nosing around my leavings."

Morgan regarded him thoughtfully for several long, unnerving minutes, and something in the dark blue eyes caused Ashley to move his horse back a short distance. Morgan smiled derisively at his actions, and with deceptive calm, he murmured, "That was a wise move, Ash. After all, you don't want me to kill you here and now, do you?"

Leonie, who had been staring at Ashley's face with numbing understanding and growing revulsion, unconsciously shivered at Morgan's words. But his presence didn't really intrude into the terrifying nightmare that she was having. Dazed, her eyes and attention remained painfully riveted on the man who so resembled Morgan. She understood everything now, the truth of what must have happened six years ago erupting agonizingly through her body the moment she heard Ashley's hateful, drawling voice.

How could I have mistaken one for the other? she thought dully, as she stared from Morgan to Ashley. And all the tiny inconsistencies that had puzzled her, the many differences she had unknowingly noticed were now glaringly apparent. Her heart frozen in her chest, she was oblivious to the deadly currents that swirled through the air between the two men. Slowly, almost blindly she moved away from Morgan, walking towards Ashley.

Standing next to his horse, she looked up at him, seeing clearly the weakness of his chin, the cruel thinness of his mouth, that were such direct opposites of Morgan's strong, powerful features. Huskily, her voice hardly above a whisper she got out difficultly, "I remember you. You were the

410

one I met. You were the one who said he was Morgan Slade."

Ashley smiled wolfishly. "Not quite, my dear. I never *said* I was my cousin—you and your grandfather assumed I was. And I was the one who *did* marry you . . . you are *my* wife."

Leonie took a deep, painful breath and glanced back beseechingly at Morgan. Unaware of the note of pleading in her voice, she asked, "But if he married me under your name, if we thought he was you . . . would the marriage be valid?"

Ashley answered her. "I don't know if Morgan has checked out that little technicality, but before I left France, I did, and while it *is* a bit awkward, the marriage is valid. I am your husband, and as such I am in control of your person and fortune."

Leonie shrank back from him in revulsion. The sea-green eyes flashing with contempt, she spat, "Never! You are a foul beast, not even worthy enough to call yourself a man. And Morgan maligns the jackel when he compares it to you!"

Forgetting Morgan for the moment, Ashley glared at her and said furiously, "Why you little bitch! We'll just see how brave you are once I have you in France!"

"France?" Leonie shot back swiftly. "What makes you think I would go to France with you?"

Ashley's eyes suddenly glistened with greed. "I think for a fortune, you would. How does the title *comtesse* sound to you? It will be yours in France, along with all the great estates that belonged to your family. *That* is why you will come with me and why I have come to this godforsaken place in search of you!"

Morgan had begun to walk forward, but Ashley's remarks halted him in his tracks. A countess? Leonie?

As for Leonie, she looked up openmouthed at Ashley, unable to believe that he seriously thought she would go willingly anywhere with him.

Unfortunately, Ashley mistook her reaction and smiling arrogantly he said, "Yes, you may well stare! A fortune, my dear! And it is all ours, once we return to France."

Leonie took in a deep, furious breath, and her eyes

nearly gold with molten rage, she snarled, "You contemptible blackguard! You trick my grandfather out of a fortune, you lie and deceive me, and you expect me to help you gain a fortune?" She snapped her fingers disdainfully almost under his nose. "Bah! That for your fortune! My home is here and what lies in France holds no appeal for me."

Ashley couldn't believe what he was hearing, and seeing the incredulous expression on his face, Morgan could have laughed out loud. His step forward had been an instinctive, protective movement, but listening to Leonie's spirited replies, he relaxed slightly.

Unable to believe what she had said, Ashley scowled at her. Stupid bitch! Whistle down a fortune, would she? Not if he could help it! And with that thought in mind, he suddenly spurred his horse forward and reached out cruelly for Leonie's arm.

His deliberately brutal clasp brusing her soft flesh, the dark-blue eyes narrowed and mean beneath his heavy black brows, Ashley growled, "We'll just see about that! You're coming with me! No one is going to stop me from claiming that fortune!"

The instant Ashley's horse had moved, Morgan too was in motion, and with a lightning swift action, his hand found the small pistol in his vest and in a low, implacable voice, he said, "Loose her, Ash. Loose her *now*, or you're a dead man!"

Ashley's jaw tightened and for a brief second he hesitated, flashing a malevolent glance from Leonie to Morgan, and back again to Leonie. It was obvious he was weighing his chances.

Morgan took a few steps nearer, saying in a mild voice, "I wouldn't try it, if I were you . . . or have you forgotten what a particularly excellent marksman I am. And at this distance, I could kill you easily." The blue eyes very hard and icy, he added with dangerous calm, "I'd like to kill you, Ash. It would solve so many problems . . . I might give into temptation."

Ashley released Leonie's arm. His mouth thin with frustration and his eyes full with something ugly and deadly,

412

he muttered, "You win this time, Morgan . . . but I'll be back. Remember she's *my* wife and the law is on my side."

"We'll just see about that, won't we?" Morgan returned cooly. "I wouldn't go to the law if I were you—there are the questions of fraud and impersonation to be settled. I'm afraid you might find the officials here in New Orleans inclined to look askance at anything you might want to do concerning your rights as Leonie's husband."

Ashley's chest swelled with rage, and viciously jerking his horse around, he snarled, "Think you've brought me to a standstill, do you? Well, think again, *cuz!* I'll best you yet!" And with that he spurred his horse and raced pell-mell down the road in the direction from which he had come.

30

Most of what Ashley had snarled to Morgan had been sheer bravado, but by the time he made the long journey back to New Orleans, he had begun to think he *would* best his cousin. He was, after all, married to the bitch, even if there was a question of fraud or impersonation. She *was* his wife and that should give him some sort of edge against his cousin.

Reaching the seedy waterfront tavern, where he had secured a room, he carelessly threw the reins of his rented horse to a surly servant. As he sat in his shabby room, he reviewed his situation. It had never occurred to him that the promise of a fortune would not bring Leonie to his side. He had also not thought that Morgan would be anywhere on the scene.

Morgan's presence had been a definite shock, but one that Ashley promptly recovered from—Morgan was an obstacle, yes, but it was the woman who interested him, not his cousin. And if Morgan proved to be too much of a problem—well, then, he would kill him.

Drinking what the tavern keeper had claimed was "good" whiskey, Ashley contemplated his next move. Obviously it wasn't going to be quite as simple as he had first thought to convince Leonie to come to France with him.

But Ashley was not easily deterred, and despite his ignoble defeat, after a few more glasses of whiskey, he had convinced himself that while Morgan may have won the first skirmish, *he* would win the war!

The key to the entire situation was Leonie. He had handled her badly, he realized belatedly. He shouldn't have been quite so forward. No, that wasn't the way with his dear little wife. An apology should have come first, he decided finally. He should have apologized for taking advantage of her and for his fraudulent impersonation. Softened her up a bit, acted ashamed for his behavior, aroused her sympathy with a heartrending tale. Then he could have brought into play his easy charm and skillfully wooed her into compliance.

Ashley had mixed emotions about Morgan's presence on the scene. One part of him would have been happier if his cousin wasn't around—it would have made things so much simpler. But on the other hand, the opportunity to avenge himself on Morgan for destroying the profitable agreement he'd had with the French had presented itself. Ashley's lips curved in a cruel smile.

With an effort he wrenched his thoughts away from revenge and concentrated on Leonie. And as the hour grew late, Ashley became positive that the sheer size of the fortune waiting in France would give him a much needed advantage. *No one,* he thought incredulously, would let an inheritance of that magnitude go begging.

By the time he went to bed, he had come to the conclusion that it was imperative that he see Leonie again . . . and alone. Once she understood just how much money was at stake, he was certain that, with the aid of his calculated flattery, she would see reason. And if she didn't . . . His handsome face was suddenly ugly. If she didn't come willingly, she'd come as his captive.

His decision about Leonie made, Ashley's thoughts once again turned towards his cousin . . . and revenge. And remembering this afternoon's scene between Morgan and Leonie a malicious smile lit his face. By God, but it had been amusing to see his usually unshakable cousin struggling to tell the chit the truth! Damnation! He'd had given a pretty penny to have been around when Leonie first presented herself to Morgan's notice. His smile faded just a little. It would have better for his plans, naturally, if they hadn't met, and at first he dismissed Morgan's interest in Leonie as negligible. But then his eyes narrowed slightly as he remembered the expression on Morgan's face above the deadly pistol, and the air of tenderness that had surrounded the pair of them as they had stood near the little graveyard. Could it be, he wondered with spiteful astonishment, that his proper cousin had fallen in love? And with *his* wife? Ashley laughed out loud. What a jest, what a royal jest! And what a perfect revenge to snatch her out of Morgan's arms! Obviously, Morgan had been on the point of explaining the truth to her, and just as obviously from the impression of intimacy between them he had taken advantage of his supposed position as her husband and bedded the wench. The bitch will claw his eyes out, Ashley thought with satisfaction. I'd wager my life on it!

Ashley would have lost his wager, although the urge to do exactly that had been Leonie's first inclination. She had stood like a small, frozen statue for a second, watching Ashley's diminishing figure, but the dust from his horse's hooves hadn't even settled before she had rounded furiously on Morgan, her sea-green eyes spitting golden fire. "Have you enjoyed yourself?" she demanded fiercely, the pain of betrayal knifing through her body. The fact that the despicable creature who had just ridden away was her real husband was agonizing enough to accept, but to know that Morgan had kept that knowledge from her, hurt even more. But she was also badly frightened. To know that she was legally married to Ashley Slade was devastating, as much because of his depraved character as the yawning, black chasm that opened without warning between her and Morgan. And because she was frightened and hurt, she lashed out at the nearest person, the one person she had been learning to trust but who had betrayed her. Wanting to wound him as deeply, as painfully as she had been, she shouted at him, "Answer me, damn you! Or are you a craven coward like your cousin?" Taking a few steps nearer to him, she exclaimed with self-derision, "How you must have laughed at me when I appeared demanding my dowry from you! Did you and your family snicker behind my back? And when the jest wore thin, when you had taken your fill of me, did you arrange for my"—The words froze in her throat, but with an effort she spat out—"my *husband* to arrive to take me away?"

Morgan appeared unmoved by her outburst, his face

416

impassive as he put the pistol away. His blue eyes wandered over her flushed, expressive features, silently noting the fury, the fright, and the pain that she couldn't conceal. His jaw tightened slightly, but he asked calmly enough, "Do you really believe that, Leonie? Do you honestly think that I and my family would laugh at you? That we are the type of people to do such a thing? That we knew of his actions and not only condoned them, but took advantage of it?"

Her face working with emotion, she furiously dashed away a tear and said angrily, "I don't know what to believe! Everything is suddenly—" Her voice broke and she turned away from him, her slender shoulders shaking.

Her distress was more than he could bear and with a swift stride he was next to her, spinning her around and pulling her into his arms. "Sweetheart, listen to me," he began passionately. "I would have given my life to spare you this! I was trying to tell you of Ashley when he arrived. I certainly had no idea that he was coming here, and if I had, I would have seen to it that you were forewarned. My God, do you truly believe that I would, under any circumstances, allow him to lay a hand on you? Allow him to take you away from me?"

Hating the stupid tears that slid down her cheeks, furious at her own lack of control, almost resentfully she asked, "Why shouldn't you? I've caused you and your family prodigious embarrassment and scandal, so why should you care what happens to me?"

His face softened, his eyes full of tenderness, he demanded huskily, "Not care about what happens to my life? Not care about the bewitching little creature who exploded into my world and captured my heart?"

Leonie's breath caught in her throat, the tears instantly drying, and with wide, incredulous eyes she stared up at his dark, intent features. There was no sign of guile on that lean, beloved face, no malice in those dark blue eyes that stared so piercingly into hers, no weakness in the curve of that full, sensuous mouth so near her own. Yet unable to comprehend what was so clearly revealed by his expression, desperately needing his emotions more plainly stated, she stammered, "W-wha-what do y-you mean?"

417

For a long moment their eyes were locked on each other and Morgan's pulse leaped within his veins at what he hoped he saw reflected in her own face. With a low groan, he pulled her urgently to him and muttered thickly into her silky hair, "I love you, Leonie! I have practically since the first second I laid eyes on you at the Marshall ball. Why else," he demanded roughly, "do you think that believing the worst of you, certain you were a conniving, lying bitch, that I suggested we live together at Le Petit?"

Ashley instantly forgotten, the entire world forgotten except for Morgan and this wonderous dream she was experiencing, Leonie burrowed herself closer to his tall, powerful length. A delicious warmth was seeping into her veins, driving away the deadly cold; her very bones felt as if they had turned to hot, sweet honey as the moments passed and Morgan's hands moved caressingly over her shoulders and back. It was heavenly to be here in his arms, to know at last that he did love her, but an imp of devilment compelled her to say gruffly, "You didn't suggest—you ordered me to live at Le Petit!"

With a determined hand he tipped up her chin. Bright laughter gleaming in the blue eyes, he mocked, "But you will forgive me, won't you?" Mesmerized, Leonie nodded her head, knowing she would forgive him anything. "And you will now," he breathed tantalizingly against her mouth, "tell me what I most want to hear from you . . . that my feelings are very definitely reciprocated. You will confess to loving me, won't you, cat-eyes?"

But he couldn't wait for her reply, the tempting mouth was too near his own, and smothering her answer, his lips trapped hers in a fierce, sweet kiss. With a tender urgency his mouth moved slowly, intoxicatingly against her soft lips, compelling, demanding, and yet oddly questing, seeking the answer he wanted from her generous, eager response. Leonie responded wildly to his embrace, her slender arms clutching him frantically, as if she feared he would escape her, her body melting joyously against his hard shape. For a timeless moment, the universe faded, and they were lost in the wonder of their own new, bright, magnificent creation . . . love.

418

When Morgan finally lifted his dark head, he was breathless, and Leonie's eyes were shining with golden stars. His hand shaking just a little, he gently pushed away a lock of tawny hair from her temple. The blue eyes very intent, he demanded softly, "You do love me? I wasn't just imagining things?"

Her hands clung to his broad shoulders, and vehemently she shook her head, breathing fervently, "Ah, no, Morgan, you were not imagining. I *do* love you! And I have been so miserable these past weeks not understanding how I could love you, when you appeared to be such a blackguard. My mind told me you were a villain, but my heart"—her mouth curved with a soft, reminiscent smile—"my heart knew. My heart was not deceived."

Caressingly his fingers slowly traced the outline of her mouth. A rueful smile on his own lips, he confessed, "Mine too, I'm afraid. I tried to tell myself that you were everything despicable in a woman, but I couldn't stop myself from wanting you . . . from loving you."

It was an extraordinary moment for them, a moment when all the past misunderstandings were swept away, a moment when they could speak freely their hearts' desire; a lovely, lasting moment that surrounded them in warmth, protecting them from the icy reality that awaited them. They had moved as they spoke beneath one of the many great oak trees that grew nearby. Morgan sat with his back comfortably propped against a massive trunk, his long legs stretched out in front of him. Leonie's head was cradled on his shoulder, her body curled gently next to his, her fingers idly toying with the buttons on his vest as they talked, the rise and fall of their voices only stopping when their lips met. Cocooned and insulated by the warmth of their love, they exchanged all the sweet vows that countless lovers before them had, certain that no one could ever love as deeply, as passionately, as completely as they did . . . as they always would.

But all too soon, reality intruded, destroying their secure little world. It was Morgan who did it a short while later. His lips against her smooth forehead, he said painfully, "Under normal circumstances, right now I'd be demanding that you promise to marry me, but as it is . . ."

He stopped, and shifting their positions so that she lay back against the lush summer grass, he loomed over her and muttered, "You *will* marry me, though—once we have this damnable situation with Ashley settled?"

Her happiness faded, the stars in her eyes blurring just a little as, insidiously, the seeming insurmountable problem they faced suddenly towered before her. She tried to hide the worry, the fear she felt, and bravely she forced a smile on her mouth, and asked softly, wonderingly, "Need you ask? I am yours, Morgan . . . I will be forever, no matter what your wicked cousin may try to do."

Morgan smiled grimly. "Hopefully we can stop him from doing anything, especially now that you and I know the truth. Together we will escape this tangle."

They discussed the ugly matter at length, Morgan explaining quietly what he and the lawyer Monsieur Ramey had decided upon.

"You were so sure of me?" Leonie asked uncomfortably.

He shot her a look that made her entire body tingle. "No, I can't say that I was," he admitted carefully. "The only thing I was sure of was that *no* woman would willingly want to remain married to a man who had defrauded and deceived her."

Leonie's gaze dropped from his, and in an embarrassed whisper she asked, "Do very many people know what really happened? Your family, do they know the truth?"

Morgan shook his head, glad to have something he could reassure her about. "No. I've tried to keep as few people as I could from knowing. Not five people besides ourselves and Ashley know the truth and none of them would ever speak of it. Dominic is the only one in the family who knows, and you need not fear he will mention it." Throwing her an oddly uncertain glance, he said huskily, "Once this is behind us, I had planned that we would marry secretly and allow the world to believe that we did marry six years ago."

The knowledge that he had never been offered a choice concerning marriage with her in the first place knifed through her, and suddenly assailed by an agonizing wave of shame, when she thought of everything he had done for her these past weeks, she turned her head away from him, saying in a small voice. "You don't have to, Morgan. Ashley's actions d-d-don't b-b-bind you to anything."

Urgently Morgan swung her face back towards him. His eyes darkening with emotion, he muttered half-savagely, half-tenderly, "But my heart binds me. I love you, Leonie, can't you understand that? It doesn't matter what went on before, all that matters now is that we have found each other! I won't let you go!" And fiercely his mouth came down on hers, his hard kiss burning away everything but the love they shared.

Dusk was only an hour away, when they finally arrived, arm in arm, back at the house. Both of them were subdued, each one busy with thoughts in which Ashley figured prominently, if not pleasantly.

Morgan went in search of Dominic almost immediately and tersely he informed him of Ashley's presence in Louisiana. "We'll have to keep a close watch on Leonie and Justin these next few days," he ended grimly. "I wouldn't put it past Ashley to attempt to kidnap either one of them."

Not unnaturally Leonie was quiet during dinner, and afterward, wanting time alone to think, she slipped away to the old barn, where she had frequently gone as a child. After climbing up a new ladder to the hayloft, sighing unhappily, she settled herself in the sweet-smelling hay. Below she could hear Morgan's thoroughbreds moving restively in their temporary stalls, but staring blindly out the half-patched hole that still remained in the roof, that faint sound faded away as Ashley's sneering features rose up before her and she plunged headlong into the black abyss he had created six years ago.

Having seen Ashley in Morgan's presence, she could understand how she and her grandfather had been fooled. The resemblance was startling and to someone who was barely acquainted with either of them, it would be difficult to tell them apart . . . at first. With a shudder she remembered the look in Ashley's eyes before he had ridden away. Thieving, lying blackguard! She would never be his wife, she vowed furiously.

All the differences she had noticed, all the bewilderment

Morgan's actions had caused were now perfectly understood and she wondered impatiently how she could ever
have mistaken Morgan for Ashley. I should have known
that morning when he first saw Justin, she thought disgustedly. Ashley wouldn't have reacted the way Morgan
had—that was for damn sure! But it didn't really matter
now, she reminded herself forlornly. The truth was out and
she must make the best of it.

The knowledge of Morgan's love warmed her heart and
beat back some of the demons that threatened to tear her
apart, but even his love couldn't comfort her entirely. She
was Ashley's wife, and despite Morgan's assurances that
an annulment could be obtained, she was aware that the
future could be extremely unpleasant. And of course, there
was her prickly pride to contend with.

Thinking of all that Morgan had done for them, of his
many kindnesses and generosity, she writhed with shame.
He hadn't owed them a solitary thing—not his time, his
name, his interest, or his money, and yet he had given
freely, abundantly of all. Her eyes filled with tears of hu-
miliation. It was one thing to accept the unstinting bounty
of a husband, another to take from a man who was more
sinned against than sinning. Tortured by her thoughts, a
small half-miserable, half-angry sob broke from her throat
and she twisted over on her stomach, pressing her face into
the fresh hay.

In the stable below Morgan heard the faint heart-
wrenching sound and he walked to the ladder and silently
climbed up into the loft. His eyes adjusting to the gloom,
he spotted her crumpled form in the hay, and moved
swiftly to her side. Sinking down next to her, his hand
gently touching her shoulder, he said softly, "Sweetheart,
don't cry so! You'll break my heart."

Leonie had been so lost in her own misery that she
hadn't heard his light-footed approach and the sound of his
voice and touch of his hand startled her. She jumped and
turned over to face him. Hastily fighting down a sob, she
asked almost gruffly, "What are you doing here? How did
you find me?"

Not put off by her unenthusiastic greeting, Morgan
sprawled lazily in the hay beside her, one elbow propping

him up as he stared down into her face. "I followed you," he admitted easily. Aware of the probable cause of her tears and seeking, momentarily at least, to distract her, he added provocatively, "You slunk off so quickly after dinner that I—"

"I did not slink off!" she interrupted indignantly, the tears drying.

He smiled and murmured thoughtfully, "Well, perhaps not. Marched, might be a better description."

Uncertainly she regarded him. "Are you teasing me?"

He reached out and ran a caressing finger down her cheek. "Is that not permitted? I'm afraid I assumed with this afternoon's events behind us, that I could upon occasion dare to tease you. A husband-to-be *does* have certain rights, I'm told."

She sent him a misty smile, her own hand traveling the small distance between them to lay against his chest. "Monsieur, you have all the rights you could ever want where I am concerned."

Morgan's breath caught sharply in his diaphragm, any thoughts of rational conversation disappearing instantly. An intent, hungry blaze in his blue eyes, he bent nearer to her and asked huskily, *"All* rights? Even the right to touch you like this?" and his hand lightly, knowingly, cupped one breast. His mouth coming closer to hers, he added thickly, "And the right to kiss you like this?"

Blindly Leonie met his descending mouth, her lips opening eagerly under the half-brutal, half-tender assault of his kiss. Her one hand curved urgently around his neck, pulling his dark head nearer, her body arching uncontrollably up next to his. He was her man, her lover, and she wanted to deny him nothing . . . wanted his passionate lovemaking to drive away the devils, wanted the fires of desire that flared so powerfully between them to burn away all thought of Ashley, leaving behind, glowing bright and strong, only their love.

For the first time, doubt and suspicion did not lay beside them as tenderly, urgently their hands and bodies touched and caressed the other. There was only love and a bittersweet joy between them, each one seeking to pleasure the other, unconsciously seeking passion to destroy Ashley's malevolent spectre.

To have Morgan near her like this, to know he loved her, to have his hands stroking and sliding sensuously over her body was paradise, and Leonie made no effort to escape the hot tide of desire that engulfed her. With impatient hands she tugged at the clothes that separated them, needing Morgan's naked flesh next to hers, needing desperately to show him with her body how very much she loved him.

Leonie's ardent response to his caresses unleashed all the passion Morgan had controlled these past weeks, and with a low groan, he slowly undid the fastenings of her gown, his warm hand gliding softly over her silken skin. He was trembling from the force of the emotions that thundered through his big body, and with hurried, swift movements he shifted her pliant form and jerked the clothes from her body.

A soft sigh of satisfaction came from him, when at last she lay naked on the hay before him. Her tawny hair tumbled wildly around her face and shoulders, and the soft golden skin gleamed faintly from the light of the waning moon that shone in through the hole in the roof. There was a slumberous expression in the sea-green eyes and her lips were slightly parted as she looked back at him, and Morgan couldn't stop himself from leaning over and kissing her deeply on that inviting full mouth, his own clothes forgotten for the moment.

Freed from the trappings of her gown and undergarments, Leonie's entire body was his to explore and he did so with undeniable pleasure, his hands and fingers sliding lovingly over her breasts, hips, and thighs. But his clothes proved a barrier neither of them would tolerate and with a muttered curse a few seconds later, he sat up and began to strip off the offending garments with swift, decisive movements.

Made brazen by the overpowering emotions that ruled her body, Leonie could not even bear for him to be gone from her for that short time and like a small, seducing siren when he turned from her to tug off his boots, she knelt behind him and pressed herself closer to his muscled back, moving her hips sensuously against him, until he said in a shaken voice, "If you don't stop that, little witch, I'll take you as I am, and boots and breeches, be damned!"

Love gave her boldness and sinking back on her haunches she murmured mockingly, "Perhaps monsieur does not want me?" Morgan shot her a smoldering look that dispelled that notion in an instant and with one violent jerk the last of his clothes were shed. Swinging around to face her, he felt his blood leap with an odd mingling of possession and white-hot passion at the blatantly sensual picture she made.

She was half-sitting on her haunches, the tawny hair curling wildly about her shoulders, the taut, coral-tipped breasts peeking impudently through the silken strands of hair. With her eyes drowsy with ill-concealed desire, the faint moonlight caressing her naked belly and thighs, and her mouth curved in a provocative smile, she was irresistible.

He reached for her hungrily, jerking her to him with barely suppressed violence. But there was nothing violent about his touch, it was as tender, as sweetly caressing as any woman could ever want. Gently his mouth moved over hers, his tongue ravenously tasting the warm wine he found between her lips. His fingers slowly, tantalizingly teased her nipples until they were hard, throbbing points of fire and then and only then, did his hand slide lower, searching for the soft tangle of curls between her legs. He found it, and Leonie's body jumped with pleasure as he tenderly stroked and fondled her, his fingers insidiously exploring where they would.

Unable to remain passive, her entire body tingling and aching with desire, she kissed him back lovingly, her hands beginning an exploration of their own as they slid down his back, over his taut buttocks to his muscled thighs. His skin was smooth and hard beneath her questing fingertips and she reveled in the feel of the powerful sinews that lay just under the warm flesh. She arched her body up closer to him, delighting in the soft cushion of hair that crushed against her breasts, and lingeringly, savoringly, her mouth traveled down his neck to his shoulders.

Her nipples were like two tips of flame against his chest, and when she reached for him, her small hand closing around the swollen length of him, Morgan shuddered with pleasure. Compulsively his mouth sought hers, his tongue filling her mouth and his hands beginning to caress her with a fervent intensity, wanting to give her the same sweet ecstasy she was giving him.

Despite the passion that ran deep and strong between them, there was an odd air of feverish urgency about their lovemaking, as if they both feared this might be the last time they could ever touch one another this way, ever share such exquisite lovemaking. With a tender fierceness Morgan lavished his caresses over her body, his lips and hands sliding warmly over her breasts and stomach, arousing Leonie to a delirious state of blind, hungry yearning. Even when his head dipped lower, and his tongue flicked like fire over the most intimate part of her body, she didn't deny him. Almost with a will of their own her legs parted, letting him explore and caress as he wished.

Nearly mindless with the pleasure he was giving her, she moaned and writhed beneath his searching caress, her hands reaching for him, wanting to touch him, wanting to share this shamelessly erotic experience. But he wouldn't let her, never ceasing the gentle probings of his tongue, his hands closed around her breasts holding her prisoner, pushing her back down into the hay.

Helplessly her hands sought for some way to caress him, her fingers traveling over his powerful shoulders before they found the dark hair on his head. And when the first sharp spasm of ecstasy washed over her, her body tightened like a bowstring, her fingers gripped the thick black hair with frenzied pleasure and she sobbed aloud her gratification. Again and again her body arched with ecstasy so great she thought she would go mad with it, but then gradually it lessened to a sweet ache of satisfaction. It was only when she was lying limp and satiated, that Morgan raised his head, and a glazed intent look in his eyes, he stared at her. His voice thick and slurred, he muttered, "I told you the next time we would do it my way . . . are you sorry?"

Imperceptibly Leonie shook her head, too replete, too completely shaken by what she had experienced to do more. Morgan watched her a second longer, and then slowly his body slid up hers, his lips scorching a fiery trail as they traveled up her flat stomach to her breasts, where he lingered awhile until her nipples were once again hard and throbbing before he finally sought her mouth.

Leonie's body had leaped with renewed hunger the moment his lips had touched her breasts and when his mouth found hers, she was already aflame for his possession. Unable to hold himself back any longer, Morgan swiftly moved between her thighs, and with a low groan of excitement he thrust himself urgently into the warm softness he knew awaited him. Their mouths were locked together in mutual hunger, his hard flesh pleasuring them both as he drove endlessly into her. He prolonged the sweet joining as long as he could, but then he felt Leonie's body beneath his, trembling from the force of her pleasure. He lost control of himself and shuddering with ecstasy, he gave himself up to bliss.

That night when they retired to bed there was no question of separate rooms and throughout the long night, again and again their ardent bodies pledged their love, each time seeming more precious and sweet than the time before. And between the almost frantic lovemaking, they would lie in each other's arms murmuring their love, vowing that nothing would ever part them.

Ashley's name remained unspoken until just before dawn and it was then that Morgan asked quietly, "Leonie, about the fortune he mentioned—if it really does exist, and I suspect it does, considering his presence here, do you want to claim it?"

Her head resting comfortably against his shoulder, her body relaxed and exhausted from his lovemaking, she thought about it for a few minutes. Finally she said softly, "No. France and everything connected with it is so far removed from what is important to me. When my great-grandfather came to this country, he turned his back on his homeland, and this became his home. It is the only home I have known. I was born here and I have no desire to

427

lay claim to whatever fortune might await me in France."
Propping herself up on one elbow she stared down into his
dark face. Lightly tracing the outline of his full masculine
mouth, she murmured, "Everything I want is here: my
home, my son . . . and you."

With a groan, Morgan pulled her down next to him and
proceeded to show her just how very much he loved her.

31

Ashley was awake before dawn, and within an hour, he was on his way to Château Saint-André. He reached the road that led to the plantation by eleven o'clock, but instead of riding directly to the plantation, he veered his horse off the road into the underbrush. It was difficult going, but eventually he found himself near the house. He dismounted and tied his horse's reins to the lower branch of a young oak tree and then crept nearer to the house.

Positioning himself where he had a good view of the house, he settled down to watch the comings and goings of the inhabitants. A definite plan hadn't formed in his mind yet, but he was determined to see Leonie and *make* her understand about the fortune.

Besides Leonie, there was only one other person whose movements interested him, and when he saw Morgan ride away from the house about one o'clock, his spirits rose. Now was his chance, he thought exultantly. Morgan was out of the way and before he returned Leonie must be made to see reason.

He waited a few minutes longer, just to make certain his cousin wasn't returning, and then he rode boldly up to the house. Just as brazenly he walked up the horseshoe staircase and gained entrance to the house.

There were servants and people everywhere, but Ashley assumed correctly that they would mistake him for Morgan, especially if he didn't linger and watched himself carefully.

Composing a pleasant expression on his face, he wandered casually through the house, finding Leonie, to his great delight, alone in a small room at the rear of the house. She was looking at various swatches of material and when he entered she looked up, a lovely smile breaking over her face.

Unaware, at first, that it was Ashley before her, she asked lightly, "Shall we have a rose watered silk for the walls in the dining room or would you prefer moss green? I can't make up my mind."

Carefully shutting the door behind him, Ashley turned to look at her. The hard blue eyes taking in the demure picture she presented as she sat on a shabby sofa, her gown of apricot muslin falling gracefully around her ankles, he said casually, "Quite the domesticated little woman, aren't you, my dear?"

Leonie went rigid, immediately recognizing that sneering voice. Rising to her feet, the swatches scattering wildly, she spat angrily, *"You!* What are you doing here? Morgan will kill you if he finds you here!"

"But he won't, will he?" Ashley returned confidently. "I took the precaution of waiting until I saw him riding away before entering the house. And believe me, I will be gone long before he returns."

Not frightened of him, too angry to be frightened and aware that there were others only a call away, Leonie watched him warily. She was conscious of a scalding core of fury against him burning deep within her, and making no attempt to hide her scorn and contempt, she demanded hostilely, "What do you want? There is nothing here for you!"

Too pleased with himself to tread carefully, Ashley smiled, almost enjoying the situation. "Ah, but there is. My *wife* is here, after all."

When Leonie's hand balled into a fist and her eyes flashed dangerously at his words, Ashley said hastily, "Now, now, my dear; don't take umbrage so quickly. I know that we have started off badly, but circumstances were such that I had no choice but to act as I did." Keeping a pleasant expression on his face, he approached a little closer to her, but Leonie retreated instantly. His smile slipped a little, but persevering, he said, "I'll admit freely that I haven't been the most exemplary husband in the world, but if you'll just give me a chance, I'm certain you'll

430

see that I intend to make amends for the cavalier way I was forced to treat you in the past."

Not the least bit mollified by his speech, and deciding that two could play this false game, she said sweetly, "Oh? Does that mean you've come to repay my dowry?"

Ashley frowned. Clearing his throat, he said testily, "Not exactly." Shooting her an uncertain glance, he added, "Your dowry, my dear, is a paltry amount compared to what I can assure you in France." His face filling with apparent tenderness, he said softly, "Come to France with me—I shall show you a wondrous world of wealth and power."

Unable to prevent herself, she shot back tartly, *"You* can assure me? I thought it was *my* fortune."

His eyes narrowing with dislike, the facile charm beginning to fray around the edges, he retorted sharply, "It is your fortune, but you need me to get it. I know people in power . . . I am a close adviser to Napoleon, and once we are in France, it will be a simple matter for him to order the return of the Saint-André lands and monies to their rightful owner."

"I see," Leonie murmured thoughtfully. "And of course without me, you can't lay your hands on it, can you?" A mocking smile on her mouth, she added, "I begin to understand why you have suddenly decided it would be advantageous to find your wife after all these years."

All pretense of politeness vanishing, he snapped, "Don't toy with me, my dear! I want that money and you are going to come to France with me to secure it! It is your duty as my wife."

Leonie laughed out loud at that. Her eyes dancing with derision, she said softly, "My duty? What about yours? You deserted me, remember? I'll concede that we had agreed to make no demands on one another, but that was an agreement I had with *Morgan* Slade, not you! You are a fraud, an impostor of the blackest kind! I won't lift one finger to help you gain anything!"

"I don't think you understand the full situation." he said maliciously. And when Leonie's brow flew up quizzically, he went on, "I am not so easily deterred from what I want, my dear. And while I may have defrauded you, that doesn't change the fact that you are my wife, that you are committing flagrant adultery with my cousin." A sneer marring the handsome features, his voice dripping with slyness, he added, "I wonder what the good and proper people of New Orleans would think of that? Morgan is well-connected in the city, I know, because his mother comes from a prominent Creole family here. The gossip such knowledge would cause! Naturally Morgan would be forgiven . . . the man always is, but you?" He smiled nastily. "You my dear, would become a pariah, a woman without character."

Ashley's words hit with painful accuracy; Leonie was very aware of the ostracism she would face if the truth became known. But she didn't dare let Ashley see her doubts. Her jaw set in a stubborn line, she gritted out, "Go ahead—spread the gossip, but it won't gain you the Saint-André fortune!"

Ashley appeared to consider that aspect for a long moment. "No, that's true . . . but there is no reason for it to be this way." Putting on his most sincere expression, he said coaxingly, "Come to France with me, regain your fortune, and then I shall divorce you there. No one need ever know. Let me have the monies in France and you can go free."

Leonie looked at him with revulsion. "You're mad!" she breathed disgustedly. "Mad and a fool, if you think I would believe *anything* you would say!"

Ashley's face suffused with rage and with a snarl he lunged forward to grab her. And at that precise moment, Justin came bounding into the room.

Ashley heard the door opening and pulled himself up instantly. Leonie who had been intent upon avoiding his touch went limp with relief . . . until she saw that it was her son who was coming into the room.

Completely oblivious to the tension that swirled thickly in the air between the two adults, Justin ran up to Leonie and throwing his arms around her legs, he said happily, "Ah, maman, here you are! I have looked everywhere for you! You must come and see the new saddle that papa has bought me. It is red and very beautiful! Come!"

Her hand shaking slightly, Leonie reached down to ca-

432

ress his tousled curls. "Not now, Justin. In a short while, *mon coeur.*"

Ashley stood staring thunderstruck at the child. And when Justin turned his head and he saw the same sea-green eyes as Leonie's, he sucked his breath in sharply. He opened his mouth to speak, but Justin spoke first. Smiling at the man who so resembled Morgan, he started toward him, saying excitedly, "Papa! How did you get here ahead of me?"

"Papa?" Ashley burst out explosively. His face harsh and furious, he glared at Leonie and said jeeringly, "I understand now why your grandfather was in such a hurry to marry you off!" A shout of ugly laughter escaped him. "By God, to think I was duped into marrying you for the oldest reason in the world!" he spat viciously.

Justin had stopped in confusion, and his small face bewildered, he stared hard at Ashley and then took an uncertain step backward. "You're not my papa!" he said accusingly. "You look like him, but you are not my papa! Who are you?"

Ashley looked at him with dislike. "None of your business, brat!" And glancing at Leonie, he sneered, "You dare to call me an impostor? What about you, my dear? Presenting one's husband with a bastard isn't the most honorable thing to do! You slut! You and your grandfather must have danced with glee when I stumbled into the trap meant for Morgan!"

Justin had moved nearer his mother with every word Ashley spoke, and his big eyes wide and frightened, he clutched at Leonie's skirts. "Go away!" he said fiercely. "You are a *bad* man!"

Blinded by scarlet rage, her breath coming in angry gasps and yet conscious of the child clinging to her gown, Leonie snarled softly, "Ashley, I will ask you only once to leave here. And I will tell you only *once* to leave your filthy tongue off my son!"

"You'll not tell me a damn thing! Not with what I know about you!" Ashley retorted spitefully. "I'll keep my mouth shut about the little bastard . . . provided you come to France with me."

"Never!" she uttered furiously. "And get out of my house before I do you violence!"

His lips curving in a sneer, Ashley arrogantly walked up to the pair of them. Defiantly Leonie and Justin faced him. Ashley looked them up and down, an unpleasant expression on his face. "Who is his father?" he demanded suddenly. And when Leonie glared at him contemptuously and remained rebelliously mute, he was enraged. Not only was the bitch being infuriatingly stubborn about falling in with his plans, but she and that damned old grandfather of hers had tricked him! Furious with the entire situation, he vented his spleen the only way he knew how—with all his strength behind it, he slapped Leonie viciously across the cheek. *"Whore!"* he thundered.

His action was a mistake because Justin and Leonie reacted violently. Justin moved instinctively, his sharp young teeth biting deeply into the detestable creature's thigh, even as Leonie's fingers clawed down the side of Ashley's face. With a howl of rage and pain, Ashley danced away from the pair of them, shaking off Justin as he did so. But Ashley's greatest mistake had been thinking that Morgan had ridden away . . . that and his timing.

It had been Dominic that Ashley had seen leaving, and Morgan, returning to the house from the stables a few minutes after Justin, had come in search of Leonie. He had just opened the door when Ashley had demanded to know of Justin's parentage, and he was already in motion, already springing across the room when Ashley's hand connected with Leonie's cheek. Ashley didn't even have a second for recovery, because in the next instant, he felt a powerful hand whip him around and had a startling brief look at Morgan's dangerous features, before Morgan's fist smashed into his face.

The force of the blow spun Ashley around, knocking him to the floor. For a moment he lay there groaning, shaking his head trying to clear it. Then he turned over on his back and gingerly touched the spot where Morgan's fist had connected so effectively. Wiping away the trickle of blood that oozed from the broken skin, he looked up at Morgan's cool, deadly visage.

Everything had happened so swiftly that Leonie had

434

barely time to comprehend Morgan's presence before he said quietly, "Leonie, you and Justin had better leave. I have a few items to discuss with my cousin."

Leonie wasted not a minute, sweeping Justin with her as she ran out of the room in search of Robert or Dominic.

Morgan's eyes had never left Ashley lying supine on the floor, and Leonie and Justin had hardly disappeared before he was across the room, next to Ashley. Kneeling in one lithe movement beside his cousin, he had the knife drawn from its hiding place in his riding boot and held painfully against Ashley's throat before Ashley realized what he was about.

A dangerous glitter in the blue eyes, Morgan drawled softly, "Don't move, Ash. Don't even breath heavily."

Ashley lay very still, his eyes wary and cornered as he stared up into Morgan's face. But Ashley knew Morgan well, and despite everything Ashley was no coward; evenly he said, "You're not going to kill me. At least not in cold blood, cuz. So shall we discuss this like gentlemen?"

Morgan smiled mirthlessly, relaxing back on his haunches. "You tempt me, Ash, you really do," he murmured. Idly he ran the knife down Ashley's throat, leaving a thin, bright line of blood behind the blade. Looking into his cousin's eyes, Morgan said conversationally, "Did you know I spent a few years with the Comanches? No? Well, I did, Ash, and they taught me many things to do with a knife. I could skin you whole and still leave you alive, if I wished. But I won't . . . and not because you think you know me so well, but because I would dislike your blood staining the floor in what will be my study."

Ashley held his breath, fear entering the blue eyes for the first time. Morgan saw it and smiled grimly. Pressing the knife a little harder, he remarked coolly, "I should slit your throat on principle. If you touch Leonie again, I will, I promise you, Ash."

There was such deadly assurance in the quiet tones that Ashley shivered. Morgan watched him narrowly for a long moment and then rising to his feet with easy grace, he commanded, "Get up!"

Hastily, although he kept a wary eye on the knife, Ashley did so. Straightening his clothes with short, jerky movements he snapped, "This doesn't change anything—she's still my wife!"

"Yes, that's so." Morgan agreed amiably. "But you're going to allow the annulment to go through without any further problems. You're also going to leave here now and go back to New Orleans." Casually putting the knife back into his boot, he lit a thin, black cheroot, and over the blue smoke that drifted from its glowing tip, he regarded his cousin. "You're not a fool, Ash," Morgan said calmly, "and so you're going to arrange passage on the first ship leaving from New Orleans." His voice hardening, he added, "I don't care where it's going, you are to be on it. Name any bank in England and I'll arrange for a sizable sum to be deposited there in your name. Have I made myself clear?"

"And if I don't?" Ashley inquired icily.

"Then I'll kill you," Morgan replied indifferently.

Ashley blanched, and his fists clenching impotently, he glared at Morgan. He didn't say a word, though. His face contorted by rage, he spun on his heels and stalked out of the room, brushing furiously past Robert and Leonie, who were just opening the door.

Robert's face was full of astonishment as he stared after Ashley's departing figure and dumbly he said, "Wasn't that . . . ? What was *he* doing here?" An arrested look springing to his eyes, he muttered softly under his breath, "So *that's* what happened!"

Resignedly, Morgan said, "Yes, Rob, that's what happened. Now kindly come in and shut the door."

Morgan hadn't wanted Robert to know, but there was no help for it and he didn't fear that Robert would be any more loose-tongued than Dominic. When Dominic returned, the entire incident had been thoroughly discussed, although Morgan had waited until he was alone with his brothers to explain precisely *what* inducements he had used to make Ashley agree to his demands. And while he felt fairly certain that Dominic, Robert, and himself would provide adequate protection for Leonie and Justin, he wanted something more. He had hesitated about informing the servants of Ashley's presence, but taking no chances and wanting no repeat of today's potentially dangerous intrusion, he called them all together and carefully

436

explained that for the next several days that they should be on their guard against an impostor . . . an impostor who might attempt to harm Leonie and Justin. He gave as Ashley's motive revenge against himself.

Dealing with Justin was a delicate task. Morgan didn't want to frighten the child, yet Justin definitely needed to be prepared in case he came face to face with Ashley again. Consequently Morgan and Leonie had as gently as possible warned Justin to have nothing to do with the "bad man" who had struck maman this morning.

In a way, Morgan was satisfied with the day's work. He had taken precautions to protect his family, and he and Ashley had laid their cards on the table. Hopefully Ashley was wise enough to know when he was beaten. Ashley was greedy, but he disliked risking his precious skin, and the threat of death was a definite incentive to leave New Orleans. Ashley had always beat a hasty retreat once his perfidies had been discovered, and Morgan hoped he would act no differently this time.

Ashley did book passage back to France the next morning, making arrangements to sail on a ship that was leaving at the end of the week. As Morgan had said, he wasn't a fool, and Morgan's attitude had been daunting to say the least, even to someone like Ashley.

Ashley brooded most of that day in his room, trying desperately to think of a way to turn the tables on Morgan. The thought of being bested one more time by his cousin and of returning to France empty-handed was extremely distasteful. Even the idea of the money Morgan would give him didn't cheer his black spirits, especially when compared to what could be his if he could have gotten Leonie to come to France with him. Bitch! If he could only get her alone . . . she was too smart, too quick to be caught by his wiles, he conceded peevishly. But what if he had some way of forcing her?

He suddenly sat up in his chair. *The child!* Of course, why hadn't he considered that sooner? The child would bring her running, assure her complete compliance with whatever he planned. Grinning, he poured himself a generous drink of whiskey. His passage was already arranged.

437

The addition of the boy would make little difference. A note to be delivered to his mother, *after* the ship had sailed, would explain just what was expected of her, *if* she wanted to see her bastard again.

The timing would have to be precise, he decided slowly. There was no use snatching the bratling until the very last moment, no use giving Morgan time to find them. His dear cousin would never think of coming directly to the docks, never think that he would take the child to France with him.

The ship was due to sail in three days, on Thursday with the evening tide. So the kidnapping had to be done Thursday afternoon, leaving just enough time to arrive back in New Orleans.

Tuesday found Ashley surveying the activities at Saint-André from a place of concealment in the encroaching wilderness that surrounded the house. He was bored most of the time; only one thing interested him, Justin. He had planned well though, bringing food, water and bedding with him, which allowed him to remain hidden and yet able to keep an eye on everyone at all times. By Thursday morning he was poised and ready to strike.

He had observed that Justin usually spent the afternoons playing in a small clearing a short distance away from the house, and Ashley had positioned himself in the underbrush, not far from that spot. His horse was tethered nearby in readiness for a swift escape and as the noonday sun rose higher in the sky, and still no sign of Justin, Ashley moved restlessly in his hiding place.

Once again he reviewed his plan, confident it had no flaws. He didn't like the fact that one of the Slade brothers, as well as a young black woman, had been with Justin the past two days, but contemptuously Ashley dismissed them. The servant would prove no obstacle—they never did—and as for the Slade, a sharp blow to the head, a lunge for the child, and away he would be. Then onto France and a fortune! *Who knows,* he thought kindly, *I might even let the bitch and her whelp live, provided of course, they give me no trouble.* And if they did . . . well, he wouldn't mind being a wealthy widower.

The sound of Justin's happy laughter broke into his musings and like a snake preparing to strike he froze, his eyes riveted on the scampering figure not ten feet away. The *lone* scampering figure . . .

Justin had awakened early from his nap, and never stopping to think of letting anyone know he was up and around, he had dragged on his clothes and rushed outside eager to play in the warm sun. Normally a servant watched over him while he slept, but she had just slipped away for a moment to get a drink of water, never suspecting that Justin would wake during the short time she was gone.

Ashley glanced around. Good. There was no one else in sight. He knew for a fact that at least two of the Slade brothers were gone from the plantation—he'd seen one of them leaving, obviously on his way to do some hunting. And not half an hour ago, to his intense satisfaction, he'd watched Morgan ride away toward the river, which left only one Slade, the women, and the servants at the house. His wolfish grin widened and he slowly rose to his feet, lightly dusting away the twigs and moss that clung to his breeches.

Infused with a brazen confidence, he mounted his horse and rode boldly into the clearing where Justin was busily poking sticks into an abandoned rabbit burrow that had caught his attention. Hearing the rider approaching through the woods, Justin stood up and looked curiously in that direction. And for the first few seconds he made the mistake of thinking it was Morgan who sat astride the big, black gelding.

But only for seconds, and then as he remembered the cruel smile, his stick went flying and he turned to run. "The bad man!" he cried, his legs moving as fast as they could.

The servant, Julie, appeared just then from around the corner of the house. She didn't see Ashley, her eyes fixed with relief on Justin. Scolding softly under her breath she ran quickly towards him, intending to take him back into the house.

Ashley viciously spurred his horse into motion, intent upon his quarry. He caught Justin before the child had run more than a few feet, his powerful arm swooping down and effortlessly plucking up the little figure. Roughly flinging his squirming, kicking prey across the front of the saddle he wheeled the horse around and as they raced past the openmouthed, stunned servant, Ashley deliberately lashed out with his foot, his heel connecting solidly with the woman's head. She sank to the ground with a small whimper. Horse, rider, and captive plunged into the forest out of sight.

Julie was only stunned, and after a second, she shook her head slightly, and with uneven, jerky movements lurched to her feet. Her dark eyes wide and frightened, she began to stumble towards the house screaming loudly.

People came running from several directions around the house and by the time Leonie and Robert came flying down the stairs, there was a small, agitated crowed gathered around the sobbing girl. Her face full of confusion, Julie said bewilderedly, "It was the bad Master! He kicked me and then steal our little boy."

Robert stiffened and Leonie's face went white and her heart seemed to stop beating within her breast. *Mon Dieu! Julie's words could only mean one thing—Ashley has kidnapped Justin!*

Galvanized into action, Leonie whirled around to one of the stable hands and ordered sharply, "Get me a horse, immediately!" And then looking at Saul, she said tautly, "Go find Morgan—he's at the docks. Tell him Ashley has taken Justin and that I have gone after them!"

Glancing back at the weeping Julie, she said in a voice that only shook slightly, "Julie, tell me again what happened. What direction did this man take Justin?"

Between frightened gulps, Julie repeated her tale, ending with, "And then he ride away through the woods to the swamp."

Against Robert's protestations, Leonie had just swung up onto the back of a sleek, gray mare when Morgan, on Tempête, came thundering to a halt in front of her. Taking in the air of tragedy that hung over the group, and Leonie's tense, frightened expression, he demanded urgently, "What's happened? Saul met me on my way back to the

440

house with some garbled tale of a madman! Was it Ashley?"

The horse dancing impatiently under her light weight, Leonie cried out with angry despair, "He's taken Justin!"

A terrible shaft of fear pierced his heart, but ignoring the horror that snaked through his big body, his face suddenly grim and deadly, Morgan snarled, "Which direction did he go?"

"Julie says towards the swamps."

Silently cursing himself for not realizing just how tenacious Ashley was, Morgan wheeled Tempête around and commanded Robert tightly, "Have Dominic found as soon as possible! He went squirrel hunting near Black Bayou. The two of you come after me—you'll be able to follow the trail I'll leave for you."

"I'm going with you!" Leonie stated fiercely, her face set and determined.

He threw her a furious, harassed glance, but he didn't dare waste the time arguing with her. "Very well," he said curtly and dug his heels into Tempête's silken hide. With a snort the blood-bay stallion bounded forward, Leonie's mare hot behind him.

They found the trail with little effort, the mad dash of Ashley's horse through the tangled forest evident from the snapped and broken limbs and the wild disturbance of the matted forest floor. There were few words between Leonie and Morgan as they rode swiftly deeper into the nearly tropical undergrowth, each one too busy struggling against their own particular demons.

A sort of numb disbelief had fallen over Leonie, her brain unwilling to let the terror that lurked just under the surface of her thoughts come exploding through. She knew Ashley had her son, knew they must find him soon, but beyond that there was nothing but a blessed, emotionless void.

Leonie had a mother's instinctive fear for her child's survival, but Morgan had to face not only the horror of what Ashley might do to a child he had come to love as his own, but the terrible memory of Phillippe's death. It was his most terrifying nightmare come true, an icy, dreadful feeling of déjà vu riding with him every step of the way. Every

441

twist, every curve in the winding, zigzagging trail brought
back that awful memory of his desperate, futile chase after
Phillippe, and somewhere along this frightening ride Justin and Phillippe merged into one being.

The forest seemed to close in on them, the tangled, verdant growth nearly suffocating with its presence. As they
rode deeper into the wilderness, the forest gradually gave
way to a swampy, marshy area. Creepers and vines hung
snakelike through the branches of the cypress and tupelo
trees and ferns and palmettos created a smothering corridor through which they traveled. The farther they rode,
the more swamplike the area became, and finally, Morgan
pulled up his horse and glanced around with a frown.

"Ashley must be lost," he said flatly. "The trail is too erratic."

Her face damp with perspiration, her green eyes huge
with apprehension, Leonie asked, "Will we catch him?"

Morgan smiled mirthlessly. "Oh, yes, we'll catch him! If
he keeps traveling in this direction, he's going to end up at
the edge of the big swamp and there's no way he's going to
get his horse through that." He reached up and bent a
small branch. Tying a strip of material torn from his once
elegant cravat around the branch, he muttered, "That
should keep Robert and Dominic on our trail."

He glanced back at Leonie, taking in the now ripped and
stained green gown that she wore, noting her rigid control.
Turning his head to stare blankly ahead at the luxuriant
jungle that greeted his gaze, he hesitated.

There was no way of knowing what was going to happen
when he finally faced Ashley, but he knew that they had
gone beyond those differences that could be settled ratio-
nally. He was too aware of the fury and hatred that now
coiled and clawed up through his body, needing, demanding release, to act logically. He knew also that Ashley,
himself, had passed over the threshold of civilized behavior and that when they met there would be bloodshed.

Not looking at Leonie, he said evenly, "I want you to
wait here for Robert and Dominic."

"Non!" Leonie spat, her eyes gleaming yellow-green like
a cat's. "He has my *son,* Morgan!"

An implacable set to his features, he sent her a cold

442

glance. Seeing the determination in her face, he swore virulently under his breath. "God damn it, Leonie! Ashley is going to be dangerous and, and—" He couldn't tell her bluntly that her son might already be dead—or that he might die before their eyes. Even thinking it made his body tremble with denial, but the horror of his nightmare wouldn't go away this time; this time there was no thankful awakening.

Leonie sensed what he was thinking, and moving her horse up beside his, she reached out and touched his arm gently. Her own fear was evident and her voice shook as she said, "I know what you are trying to spare me. But wouldn't it be better if we faced it together?" Tears shining in her eyes, she murmured huskily, "You once said we could overcome anything together. Please, let us confront whatever may lie at the end of this trail together . . . whatever it may be."

32

They found Ashley's wind-broken, lamed horse not twenty minutes later. And just a few hundred yards beyond his abandoned mount they found Ashley and Justin standing uncertainly on a narrow spit of land formed by the merging of two bayous.

Ashley had been lost from the moment his horse raced away from the Château Saint-André. Completely unfamiliar with the terrain, used to the open, gentle landscape of England and France, he had been positive as time passed and his horse had continued to plunge ahead, that at any moment they would break free of the endless jungle. But they hadn't, and as minutes went by and nothing but more and more tangled undergrowth met his gaze, he grew frustrated and a little uneasy.

Justin hadn't helped his state of mind either. His incessant wiggling, the small fists flying out indiscriminately, and his wild kicking had made him nearly impossible to control. He was also very vocal. "You put me down! You're a *bad* man! I hate you! *Put me down!*" he had shouted furiously.

Ashley's temper thoroughly exacerbated by such antics, he had considered slitting the brat's throat. But as finding their way out of this wretched wilderness was his first priority, he had contented himself with giving Justin a brutal shaking and a vicious blow across his small face. "Shut up!" he had snarled. "Open your mouth again, and I'll beat you until you're half-dead."

That silenced Justin for a while, but soon enough, he was back at it, muttering dire threats under his breath and squirming rebelliously in Ashley's grip. Ashley shook him again and again during their twisting course through the woods, but it didn't do much good.

Lost, saddled with an imp of Satan, Ashley was growing desperate, and when the horse went lame, he cursed long and venomously. Justin had regarded him cheerfully, saying with relish, "My papa will find us now! You'll see, he won't let you keep me."

Smothering the urge to strangle him, Ashley had started off on foot, jerking Justin along behind him. "We'll just see about that, you little demon!"

They didn't walk long before they came to the spot where Morgan and Leonie found them. Ashley had been staring with mingled fury and bafflement at the swampy expanse before him, when Justin had cried joyfully, "Maman, papa! I told him you would come for me!"

Stiffening, his handsome face contorted by rage, Ashley spun around to face them as they rode slowly out of the forest.

It was an eerie place where Ashley had finally come to bay. Half swamp, half marshland spread out behind him, and before him the thick, tangled wilderness loomed up menacingly. In the watery distance, bald cypress and water locust grew rampant, their limbs draped with gray-green, ghostlike moss, the gnarled, knobby knees of the cypress jutting mysteriously into the dark, murky waters. Reeds pressed close to the banks of the sluggish moving bayous and the air was dank and heavy.

Very little light permeated the tattered curtains of moss, but on a half-submerged log, a snapping turtle dozed in an errant shaft of sunlight. Nearby, at the far edge of the bayou, looking much like a log himself, lay a large alligator. Easily twenty feet long, his cold eyes were fixed on the two figures across the water from him.

The sound of Justin's voice was pure heaven to Leonie and the sight of his small, sturdy body standing next to Ashley was the dearest thing in the world to her at the moment. Her face radiant, she would have spurred her horse forward if Morgan hadn't put out a restraining hand.

"Wait," he said quietly. "Ashley may be armed."

"How clever of you to guess!" Ashley retorted harshly,

445

for the first time revealing a small pistol, much like the one Morgan carried. Holding the weapon to Justin's head, a smug curve to his full mouth, he said with satisfaction, "I believe this time the advantage is mine, cuz. Now if you and your slut will carefully dismount and just as carefully hand me your reins, I'll be on my way."

Morgan remained motionless, his brain considering and discarding various options. The fact that Justin was still alive and apparently unharmed had left him almost weak with relief, but he knew that the most dangerous moments of all lay just ahead. Once Ashley was no longer afoot, once they had acceded to his demands, all the cards would be in his hand. Taking Justin with him, he could abandon them here in the swamps and make his escape. Or, Morgan thought calmly, Ashley could kill him and take both Leonie and Justin as his captives. No matter what happened, whether he lived or died, Justin was lost to them—*unless . . . unless I can get that pistol away from him,* he decided cooly.

"Didn't you hear me?" Ashley demanded impatiently, when Morgan made no move to obey his orders. "I said dismount and give me your reins! Do it quickly, or I'll shoot the boy!"

The nightmares of the past and present fused into one grotesque, horrifying vision, and Morgan was aware of an icy perspiration trickling down his spine, of a thunderous shriek of anguish rising uncontrollably from his deepest, innermost being. He had lost his own son to murder; he could not bear to lose Justin the same way, and his hands tightened on Tempête's reins, causing the stallion to paw the ground nervously and toss his head impatiently.

Leonie was already sliding from her horse, her eyes fastened painfully on Justin, and Morgan knew he had to act within seconds. There was only one choice, he realized bleakly, and that choice involved a most horrifying gamble with Justin's life. Forcing down the fear and terror that howled and stabbed in his brain, reminding himself savagely that Justin was as good as dead if Ashley managed to escape with him, Morgan's heels suddenly, viciously jabbed into Tempête's sides. The stallion gave a

446

furious scream of rage, and rearing up, his hooves raking the air before him, he lunged forward.

Caught totally by surprise, confronted by two thousand pounds of hooved death bearing down on him, Ashley instantly released the child and oblivious to Justin's swift dart away from him, he swung the pistol in Tempête's direction and fired—just as Morgan had prayed he would. The shot missed the stallion, but the bullet tore a long, deep gash across Morgan's temple. It didn't stop or slow him down though; the blue eyes blazing with fury, he dove off Tempête, his hands outstretched for Ashley's throat.

The two men fell together onto the damp ground, their bodies locked in a deadly embrace. Having no chance to reload, the pistol was useless to Ashley and with a muffled grunt he flung it away from him and concentrated on breaking the stranglehold Morgan had on his throat.

The blood from his wound nearly blinded Morgan, but he was too intent upon wreaking vengence against this man who had dared to play with Justin's life to be deterred. He was losing blood, though, at an alarming rate, and as he and Ashley fought on the muddy ground, he could feel himself weakening.

Ashley knew it too, and he managed to work his arms between their bodies, finally positioning the palms of his hands up under Morgan's chin. With a powerful shove, he broke Morgan's grasp from around his throat. Gulping in sweet air to his lungs, his fist connected with Morgan's cheek, violently snapping Morgan's head back from the force of the blow.

A short distance away, her hand clasped around a stout branch she had picked up, Justin's face buried in her skirts, Leonie watched the ugly battle with angry helplessness. The two men were moving too fast, the struggle too furious for her to be able to get a clear strike at Ashley. Her hand tightened around the branch, but if the moment came . . .

It was a particularly vicious fight; they were literally beating one another to death. Ashley had the slight advantage of being unwounded when they started, but Morgan had the electrifying knowledge that if he lost, Leonie and

Justin would be left to Ashley's tender mercies. That brutal knowlege alone kept him striking out, kept him pounding away when he might have faltered.

Rolling and twisting, their breathing ugly and labored in the muggy air, they fought across the ground to the edge of the bayou, and gathering up his failing strength, Morgan struck Ashley a mighty blow that knocked him out into the dark, murky waters. Unnoticed by any of them, roused by their splashing, the large alligator lazily drifted nearer.

The dunk in the bayou revived Ashley slightly, and standing in chest-deep water, he eyed Morgan, who stood swaying unsteadily, the water gently rippling around his knees. His cousin, as far as he could tell, didn't have much strength left. If he could lure him further into the bayou it should be an easy enough task to drown him. Shaking a strand of wet, black hair from his forehead, Ashley taunted, "You'll never beat me standing there, cuz! Delay too long and you're going to pass out from loss of blood, so come and get me!"

Exhausted, the blood loss from his wound draining his strength second by second, his body aching from the savage battle, Morgan stumbled a few steps further into the bayou. Ashley was right, he told himself numbly, he had to finish the fight now. His fingers were bruised and bloody but painfully, he clenched his hands into fists, and blearily he sought out Ashley's position in the bayou.

Ashley had moved a little deeper into the water, the dark, opaque waters nearly reaching his shoulders now, and he jeered, "Come on, don't let it be said you were a coward, cuz!"

Morgan stared at him with fury and it was then, out of the corner of his eye that he saw the wide snout, the deadly, sinuous shape barely two feet behind Ashley. Before even a word of warning could be offered, the reptile lunged. With a sudden, lethal burst of speed the huge alligator was upon Ashley, the powerful jaws snapping shut around his upper arm, near his shoulder. Morgan had one look at Ashley's disbelieving, terrified face, heard his fearful shriek, and then in that peculiar twisting, churning motion of the species, the creature flipped him over and over again, violently, viciously, before carrying him down beneath the unfathomable waters of the bayou. It all happened in an instant,—one second the waters of the bayou were violently agitated and the next just the faintest ripple marred their smooth surface; there wasn't even a trace of blood to mark the passage of prey and hunter.

Shuddering, his gaze fixed with stunned horror at the spot where his cousin had disappeared, Morgan stumbled backward to the shore. *Not even Ashley would I have condemned to such a fate,* he thought dully, just before he sank unconscious to the ground near Leonie's feet.

When Robert and Dominic arrived an hour and a half later he was still unconscious and to everyone's growing anxiety, he remained so all during the slow journey back to the plantation. But by the time he had been bathed gently, his wounds seen to, and laid comfortably in his own bed, his eyelids flickered and then a moment later his eyes flew wide open, a terrified glitter in their blue depths.

He looked wildly around until he saw Leonie sitting quietly on the edge of the bed, and then he gave a great sigh, his big body relaxing. Softly he muttered, "I was afraid . . . afraid you wouldn't be here . . . afraid that perhaps I'd dreamed myself a happy ending."

Love shining out of her eyes, she slowly shook her head. "I'm no dream, Morgan, and we will have a happy ending."

Of Ashley's death they did not speak. It had been frightful and while Morgan could regret the manner of it, he found it hard to mourn his cousin's passing. He would have preferred to free Leonie from her fraudulent marriage through less violent channels, but with Ashley's death every barrier to their own marriage was removed.

They were married less than ten days later, on what should have been their sixth wedding anniversary. It was a very quiet wedding and to the curious, they gave out the news that they merely wished to repledge their troth.

Lying in bed that night, her body sated from Morgan's lovemaking, Leonie asked curiously, "I wonder what would

449

have happened if *grand-père* had made his offer to you instead of Ashley."

His lips quirking into a smile, Morgan pulled her closer to him and murmured, "Why, exactly what did happen . . . except we would have had six years together instead of less than two months."

Leonie frowned in the darkness, her hand gently tracing the contours of his muscled chest. "Are you saying that if he had suggested a marriage *you* would have agreed?"

Shifting her slightly, he dropped a kiss on her forehead. "That's exactly what I'm saying. I might have come to New Orleans with marriage the *last* thing on my mind, but I know myself well enough to be aware that if he had made the offer, curiosity alone would have driven me at least to meet you. And once I'd seen you . . ." His voice thickened, and pushing her down into the pillows of the bed, he leaned over her, his eyes caressing her features. "Once I'd seen you, I would have agreed to anything to make you mine. I'd have married you, with or without that damned dowry, and it wouldn't have mattered a hell of a lot to me that you weren't interested in marriage. I would have been!"

Wrapping her arms tightly around him, pressing her slim body ardently next to his, she said fiercely, "Ah, *mon coeur,* how I wish it had been you he saw! We have lost so many years of loving!"

Passion flaming in the dark blue eyes, his mouth came down hungrily on hers and they were swept up once again in the sweet fire of love.

Life was being very good to him, Morgan thought some days later. Leonie was his wife; Justin was as fine a son as any man could wish for and everything seemed at the moment to be taking shape just as he wanted.

There was still a great deal of work to be done on the plantation, but all in all, Morgan wasn't displeased with the progress. He was presently reviewing some plans for the construction of two long wings at either side of the house, and glancing at his watch he saw that it was nearing lunch time. The small golden crucifix that dangled from its chain caught his eye and for a second he stared at it, a rueful smile tugging at the corners of the mobile mouth. *What an insolent swine I was in those days!* he mused derisively. *And how very blessed I am now that Leonie and Justin are part of my life . . . are my life!* Knowing he no longer wanted any reminders of the cold cynicism that had been his for so long, he gently unfastened the cricifix from his watchchain, and dropped it carelessly into his vest pocket. Perhaps one of the servants would like it, he thought to himself. And whistling under his breath, overwhelmingly happy with his life, he went in search of Leonie.

He found her downstairs in the storage rooms, sorting through the various articles that had been amassed over the years. She had a smudge on her nose, the tawny curls were tumbling untidily about her slim shoulders, and there were dust stains around the hem of the rose linen gown, but Morgan thought she had never looked lovelier.

Kissing her lightly on the mouth, he asked, "Is there very much that you want to save?"

She gave a sigh. "No. There isn't even that much *worth* saving. The damp has gotten to the few things that might have been salvagable. Unfortunately, after *grand-père* died, there wasn't anything left that had any value. I sold everything I could to pay off the debts."

Morgan's lips thinned. Damn Ashley! Without his interference, none of this would have been necessary. Turning away abruptly to hide the rage he could still feel against Ashley, he wandered over to where several chairs were piled haphazardly in the corner. Glancing at the tangle they made, he noticed what looked like a few portrait canvases stacked precariously on the top of the heap. Reaching up to pull one of the canvases down, he asked over his shoulder, "What are these?" A teasing glint in the blue eyes, he murmured, "The illustrious ancestors?"

Leonie wrinkled her nose at him, and coming to stand at his side, she said delightedly, "Oh, it is! That's my ma-man!"

Curious about the woman who had given birth to his wife, Morgan glanced at the portrait, and recognizing the tawny hair and mysterious sea-green eyes that stared so

451

serenely back from the oil painting, he knew where Leonie had gotten her coloring. An indulgent grin on his lips, he asked, "Shall I have them all refurbished and reframed? We can hang them in one of the new wings."

A sad little smile curving her mouth, she gently touched the canvas. "I would like that very much. I never knew her, but I would like some momento of hers near me." Almost reverently, her hand slid to the small, intricate crucifix that lay on her mother's breast. "My father had it especially commissioned for her to commemorate my birth. It was the only thing of hers that I had."

Idly Morgan's gaze dropped to the object in question, and feeling as if he had suddenly been hit viciously in the stomach by a barge pole, he stared incredulously at the delicate cross depicted in the painting. It was very familiar to him—he looked at it not ten minutes ago. In a strangled voice he asked, "Had? What happened to it? Did you lose it?"

Her eyes clouded and turning away from the portrait, she said somberly, "Yes, as a matter of fact I did. But I don't brood over it anymore. It was lost a long time ago."

Morgan's hand closed with a viselike grip on her arm, spinning her around. With painful intentness, his gaze traveled over her features, trying desperately to remember a night over six years ago, a night a virgin whore had come to his rooms at the governor's mansion.

Leonie stared up at him in astonishment. "What is it, *mon coeur?*" she asked with concern.

Morgan swallowed with difficulty, the most inconceivable certainty taking hold in his mind. "When and where did you lose it?" he demanded tautly.

Puzzled by his actions, she searched his face. That he was laboring under some great stress was obvious and slowly, hesitantly, she admitted, "I lost it at the governor's mansion, the night Governor Gayoso died."

Morgan sucked in his breath sharply. "How?" he prompted almost savagely.

Shooting him a defiant glance, she stated bluntly, "I had to get my hands on the vowels that I knew *grand-père* would sign that night, and so I planned to steal them. I

452

waited until everyone had left and then I crept into the mansion and stole them!" Almost resentfully she continued, "I got lost inside and trying to find a way out, I stumbled into a room." The memory of what had happened in that room cutting through her like a knife, she cried out in distress, "I don't want to talk about it anymore! I told you once I was someplace I shouldn't have been the night I was raped. Why do you insist that I speak of it again? It is in the past, dead and forgotten! It has *nothing* to do with us!"

His voice incredibly gentle, he said softly, "But you see, I didn't know we were talking about the same night . . . the night you lost your virginity and Justin was conceived."

Angrily, she shrugged off his slackened hold. "Bah! It doesn't matter anymore!"

The sound of Justin's laughter drifted in from outside, and Morgan thought it was one of the sweetest sounds he had ever heard . . . his son's voice. His throat tight, the blue eyes nearly black with emotion, he declared raggedly, "I, too, was at the governor's mansion the night Gayoso died. Did you know that?"

Leonie watched him with a wary, uncertain expression. "No, I didn't."

His hand trembling slightly he reached out and touched her hair and lips. Almost in a whisper, he muttered, "Gayoso had promised to send me a woman, and when a woman finally arrived, I assumed it was the one he had mentioned."

Leonie stiffened, her eyes widening with disbelief. She started to speak, but Morgan laid a silencing finger against her soft mouth. Huskily he confessed, "I remember that she had bright hair and that she was young. It was only after she had run out of my room that I discovered she had also been a virgin." Their eyes riveted with painful, unswerving attention on each other, he said with a rough sort of tenderness, "She also threw my money in my face."

Leonie was white, her lips quivering, tears of exquisite, nearly unbearable happiness brimming in her eyes. "It was *you!*" she exclaimed half accusingly, half joyously.

Not answering her, he reached inside his vest pocket, and with a hand that shook noticeably, he extended his

453

palm to her, a small, golden crucifix lying in its center. "I believe," he said thickly, "this is yours."

A ray of afternoon sunlight streamed into the room, intensifying the gold of the crucifix, causing it to blaze with an almost blinding light—a light as gold and as warm and bright as their future together would be.

GOLDEN ROSES by Patricia Hagan

With her father dead, Amber Forrest was alone in a foreign land, at the mercy of a cruel stepbrother who vowed he would make her his bride.

But Amber was a prize all men wanted. Mexico's most dashing matador promised his life to save her—yet her heart was drawn to the handsome American who demanded her love.

Forced to fight for her destiny, Amber was torn between the storm of two men's passions—her vicious stepbrother whose pleasure was her pain ... and the rugged American whose tender violence was love.

A GENTLE FEUDING by Johanna Lindsey

He would never let her go—and she would never sacrifice her innocence to shame ...

In trembling fear, she dared to refuse him, though her gentle beauty was the prize of his sword. And he, in his violent, aching need, could have taken her by force ...had she not made him want so much more.

Between them were the hatreds of their warring Scottish clans. Yet she struggled in vain to escape her desire for this enemy lord. For beneath his roughness was a fierce, ardent tenderness that held her more strongly than the walls of his far Highland castle.

Honor's pride told her she must hate him. Yet her woman's heart, awakening to the ecstasy of his touch, yearned desperately to yield ... to surrender, and possess him completely ... to be joined with him forever in love.

WHILE PASSION SLEEPS by Shirley Busbee

Beth Ridgeway was a violet-eyed platinum beauty—the kind of woman who made men burn with desire. Yet her husband didn't want her . . .

Rafael Santana was the handsome, arrogant son of a wealthy Texas family. As a child he had been kidnapped and raised by the Comanches. Even now, all his gentleman's breeding couldn't conceal the savage strength beneath his aristocratic bearing.

Beth thought he was cruel and insensitive, a man who used women only for his selfish pleasure and then tossed them away. Rafael thought she was a common wench—flirtatious and unfaithful—who took pride in breaking men's hearts.

Yet something had happened when their eyes first met at a dazzling New Orleans ball. Something their hearts could not deny, something neither the years nor the violent misunderstandings could diminish. Because, for the first time, both Beth and Rafael were awakening/to the magnificent passions of love.

Coming soon from Corgi/Avon

COME LOVE A STRANGER by Kathleen Woodiwiss

In the commanding desire of Ashton's embrace, she was Lieren, the enchanting bride he had carried home to his family's plantation.

But to another man, she was Lenore, the bride he dragged through a nightmare of dark passions and murder.

Confused and afraid, her memories of young happiness destroyed by tragedy and violence, she now remembered nothing. Not who she was, not the horrors she had suffered—nor the two men who now fought to claim her.

But her heart had not forgotten. She knew she belonged to one man, to the stranger who adored her—and made her remember what her love could never forget.

Other titles available from Corgi/Avon

: 12520 2	DECEIVE NOT MY HEART	*Shirley Busbee*	£2.50
: 12362 5	WHILE PASSION SLEEPS	*Shirley Busbee*	£1.95
: 12398 6	NO GREATER LOVE	*Patricia Gallagher*	£1.95
: 12391 9	CASTLES IN THE AIR	*Patricia Gallagher*	£2.50
: 12517 2	GOLDEN ROSES	*Patricia Hagan*	£1.95
: 12519 9	A GENTLE FEUDING	*Johanna Lindsey*	£1.95
: 12305 0	SO SPEAKS THE HEART	*Johanna Lindsey*	£1.95
: 12516 4	HEART OF THUNDER	*Johanna Lindsey*	£1.95
: 12415 X	WILD BELLS TO THE WILD SKY	*Laurie McBain*	£2.50
: 12306 4	PALACES	*Neal Travis*	£1.95
: 12634 9	ROMANCING THE STONE	*Joan Wilder*	£1.75
: 12304 8	A ROSE IN WINTER	*Kathleen Woodiwiss*	£2.50
: 99123 6	COME LOVE A STRANGER	*Kathleen Woodiwiss*	£2.50